THE RAGGED TROUSERED PHILANTHROPISTS

THE RAGGED TROUSERED PHILANTHROPISTS

BY

ROBERT TRESSALL

First Published in 1914
Indian Reprint in 2017

Published by

Kalpaz Publications
C-30, Satyawati Nagar,
Delhi – 110052
E-mail: kalpaz@hotmail.com
Website: kalpazpublications.com
Ph.: +91-9212142040

Cataloging in Publication Data—DK
Courtesy: D.K. Agencies (P) Ltd. <docinfo@dkagencies.com>

Tressell, Robert, 1870-1911, **author.**
The ragged trousered philanthropists / by Robert Tressall.
pages cm
Novel.
"First published in 1914"—Title page verso.
ISBN 9789351283997 (HB)

1. Socialists—Fiction. 2. Capitalism—Fiction. 3. Working class—Fiction. 4. Social classes—Fiction. 5. Labor movement—Fiction. 6. Social conflict—Fiction. 7. Working class families—Fiction. 8. England—Fiction. 9. Political fiction, English. 10. English fiction—Irish authors. I. Title.

LCC PR5671.T85R34 2017 | DDC 823.8 23

CONTENTS

PREFACE

A few months ago a friend asked me to look at the manuscript of a novel, 'The Ragged Trousered Philanthropists,' the work of a socialistic house-painter, who wrote his book and died. I consented without enthusiasm, expecting to be neither interested nor amused—and found I had chanced upon a remarkable human document.

With grim humour and pitiless realism the working man has revealed the lives and hearts of his mates, their opinion of their betters, their political views, their attitude towards Socialism. Through the busy din of the hammer and the scraping knife, the clang of the pail, the swish of the whitewash, the yell of the foreman, comes the talk of the men, their jokes and curses, their hopes and terrors, the whimpering of their old people, the cry of their children.

In reducing a large mass of manuscript to the limitations of book form, it has been my task to cut away superfluous matter and repetition only. The rest remains as it came from the pen of Robert Tressall, house-painter and sign-writer, who recorded his criticism of the present scheme of things, until, weary of the struggle, he slipped out of it.

JESSIE POPE.

CHAPTER I

An Imperial Banquet

The house was named 'The Cave.' It was a large old-fashioned three-storied building, standing in about an acre of ground, a mile outside the town of Mugsborough. It had been unoccupied for many years, and was now being altered and renovated for its new owner by the firm of Rushton and Company, Builders and Decorators.

Altogether, about twenty-five men were working there—carpenters, plumbers, plasterers, bricklayers and painters besides several unskilled labourers. They were putting new floors where the old ones were decayed, and making two rooms into one by demolishing the parting wall and substituting an iron girder. They were replacing window frames and sashes, re-plastering cracked ceilings and walls, cutting openings and fitting doors where no doors had ever been before. They were taking down broken chimney pots and fixing new ones in their places. They were washing the old whitewash off the ceilings, and scraping the old paper off the walls. The air was full of the sounds of hammering and sawing, the ringing of trowels, the rattle of pails, the splashing of water brushes and the scraping of the stripping knives. It was also heavily laden with dust and disease germs, powdered mortar, lime, plaster, and the dirt that had been accumulating within the old house for years. In brief, those employed there might be said to be living in a Tariff Reform Paradise—they had Plenty of Work.

At twelve o'clock Bob Crass, the painter's foreman, blew a prolonged blast upon a whistle and all hands assembled in the kitchen, where Bert the apprentice had already prepared the tea in the large galvanised iron pail placed in the middle of the floor. By the side of the pail were a number of old jam jars, mugs, dilapidated tea-cups and one or two empty condensed milk tins. Each man on the 'job' paid Bert threepence a week for the tea and sugar—they did not have milk—and although they had tea at breakfast time as well as at dinner the lad was generally considered to be making a fortune.

Two pairs of steps laid sideways in front of the fire at a distance of about eight feet with a plank placed across, several upturned pails, and the drawers belonging to the dresser, formed the seating accommodation. The floor was covered with all manner of débris, dust, dirt, fragments of old mortar and plaster.

A sack of cement was leaning against one of the walls, and a bucket containing some stale whitewash stood in one corner.

As each man came in he filled his cup, jam jar, or condensed milk tin with tea from the steaming pail, before sitting down. Most of them brought their food in little wicker baskets, which they held on their laps, or placed on the floor beside them.

At first there was no attempt at conversation and nothing was heard but the sounds of eating and drinking and the frizzling of the bloater which Easton, one of the painters, was toasting on the end of a pointed stick at the fire.

'I don't think much of this bloody tea,' suddenly remarked Sawkins, one of the labourers.

'Well, it oughter be all right,' retorted Bert; 'it's bin bilin' ever since 'arf past eleven.'

Bert White was a frail-looking, weedy, pale-faced boy, fifteen years of age and about four feet nine inches in height. His trousers were part of a suit that he had once worn for best, but that was so long ago that they had become too small for him, fitting rather tightly and scarcely reaching the top of his patched and broken hobnailed boots. The knees had been patched with square pieces of cloth, several shades darker than the original fabric, and these patches were now all in rags. His coat was several sizes too large for him and hung about him like a dirty ragged sack. He was a pitiable spectacle of neglect and wretchedness as he sat there on an upturned pail, eating his bread and cheese with fingers that, like his clothing, were grimed with paint and dirt.

'Well then, you can't have put enough tea in, or else you've bin' usin' up wot was left yesterday,' continued Sawkins.

'Why the bloody 'ell don't you leave the boy alone?' said Harlow, another painter; 'if you don't like the tea you needn't drink it. I'm sick of listening to you about it every dam day.'

'It's all very well for you to say I needn't drink it,' answered Sawkins, 'but I've paid my share an' I've got a right to express an opinion. It's my belief that 'arf the money we give 'im is spent in penny 'orribles; 'e's always got one in 'is hand; an' to make wot tea 'e does buy last, 'e collects all the slops wot's left and biles it up day after day.'

'No I don't!' says Bert, who was on the verge of tears. 'It's not me wot buys the things at all. I gives all the money I gets to Crass, and 'e buys them 'imself, so there!'

At this revelation some of the men furtively exchanged significant glances, and Crass, the foreman, became very red.

'You'd better keep your bloody thruppence and make your own tea after this week,' he said, addressing Sawkins, 'and then p'raps we'll 'ave a little peace at meal times.'

'An' you needn't ask me to cook no bloaters or bacon for you no more,' added Bert, tearfully, ''cos I won't do it.'

Sawkins was not popular with any of the others. When, about twelve months previously, he first came to work for Rushton and Company, he was a simple labourer, but since then he had 'picked up' a slight knowledge of the trade, and having armed himself with a putty knife and put on a white jacket, regarded himself as a fully qualified painter. The others perhaps did not object to him trying to better his condition, but his wages—fivepence an hour—were twopence an hour less than the standard rate, and the result was that in slack turns a better workman was often 'stood off' when Sawkins was kept on. Moreover he was generally regarded as a sneak who carried tales to the foreman and the 'Bloke.' Every new hand was usually warned by his mates 'not to let that swine Sawkins see anything.'

The unpleasant silence which now ensued was at length broken by one of the men, who told a dirty story, and in the laughter and applause that followed, the incident of the tea was forgotten.

'How did you get on yesterday?' asked Crass, addressing Bundy, the plasterer, who was intently studying the sporting columns of the 'Daily Obscurer.'

'No luck,' replied Bundy gloomily. 'I had a bob each way on Stockwell, in the first race, but it was scratched before the start.'

This gave rise to a conversation between Crass, Bundy, and one or two others concerning the chances of different horses in the morrow's races. It was Friday, and no one had much money, so at the suggestion of Bundy a syndicate was formed, each member contributing threepence, for the purpose of backing 'a dead certainty' given by the renowned Captain Kiddem of the 'Obscurer.' One of those who did not join the syndicate was Frank Owen, who as usual seemed absorbed in a newspaper. He was generally regarded as a bit of a crank, for it was felt that there must be something wrong about a man who took no interest in racing or football, and was always talking a lot of rot about religion and politics. If it had not been for the fact that he was generally admitted to be an exceptionally good workman, they would have had but little hesitation in thinking him mad. Owen was about thirty-two years of age, and of medium height, but so slightly built that he appeared taller. His clean shaven face showed a suggestion of refinement, his complexion was ominously clear, and an unnatural colour flushed the thin cheeks.

There was a certain amount of justification for the attitude of his fellow-workmen, for Owen held the most unusual and unorthodox opinions, and it was because he was in the habit of discussing them openly, that his fellow-workmen came to the conclusion that there was probably something wrong with his mind.

When all the members of the syndicate had handed over their contributions, Bundy went out to arrange matters with the bookie, and during his absence Easton annexed the copy of 'The Obscurer' that Bundy had thrown away and proceeded to work laboriously through some carefully cooked statistics relating to Free Trade and Protection. Bert, his eyes starting out of his head and his mouth wide open, was devouring the contents of a paper called 'The Chronicles of Crime.' Ned Dawson—a poor devil who was paid fourpence an hour for acting as mate or labourer to Bundy, or the brick-layers, or anyone else who wanted him—lay down on the dirty floor in a corner of the room, and with his coat rolled up as a pillow, went to sleep. Sawkins with the same intention, stretched himself at full length on the dresser.

Most of the men lit their pipes and a desultory conversation ensued.

'Is the gent what's bought this 'ouse any relation to Sweater the Draper?' asked Payne, the carpenter's foreman.

'It's the same bloke,' replied Crass.

'Didn't he used to be on the Town Council or something?'

''E's bin on the Council for years,' returned Crass. ''E's on it now. 'E's mayor this year. 'E's bin mayor several times before.'

'Let's see,' said Payne, reflectively. ''E married old Grinder's sister, didn't 'e? You know who I mean, Grinder the greengrocer.'

'Yes, I believe 'e did,' said Crass.

'It wasn't Grinder's sister,' chimed in old Jack Linden, 'It was 'is niece. I know, because I remember working in their 'ouse just after they were married, about ten years ago.'

'Oh yes, I remember now,' said Payne, 'she used to manage one of Grinder's branch shops.'

'Yes,' replied Linden. 'I remember it very well because there was a lot of talk about it at the time. No one never thought as ole Sweater'd ever git married at all, although there was always several young women about what would have been glad enough to 'ave him.'

This important matter being disposed of, there followed a brief silence, which was presently broken by Harlow.

'Funny name to call a 'ouse, ain't it?' he said. '" The Cave." I wonder what made 'em give it a name like that?'

'They calls 'em all sorts of outlandish names nowadays,' said old Jack Linden.

'There's generally some sort of meaning to it though,' observed Payne; 'for instance, if a bloke backed a winner and made a pile 'e might call 'is 'ouse "Epsom Lodge" or "New-market Villa."'

'Or sometimes there's a hoak tree or a cherry tree in the garding,' said another man, 'then they calls it "Hoak Lodge" or "Cherry Cottage."'

'Well, there's a cave up at the end of this garden,' said Harlow with a grin, 'you know, the cesspool, what the drains of the 'ouse runs into; praps they called it after that.'

'Talking about the drains,' said old Jack Linden, when the laughter produced by this elegant joke had ceased; 'talking about the drains, I wonder what they're going to do about them.'

'There's going to be a new set of drains altogether,' replied Crass, 'carried right out to the road and connected with the main.'

Crass really knew no more about what was going to be done in this matter than did Linden, but he felt certain that this course would be adopted. He never missed an opportunity of enhancing his own prestige with the men by insinuating that he was in the confidence of the firm.

'That's goin' to cost a good bit,' said Linden.

'Yes, I suppose it will,' replied Crass, 'but money ain't no object to old Sweater. 'E's got tons of it; you know 'e's got a large wholesale business in London and shops all over the bloody country, besides the one 'e's got 'ere.'

Easton was still reading the 'Obscurer.' He was not able to understand exactly what the compiler of the figures was driving—at probably the latter never intended that anyone should understand—but he was conscious of a growing feeling of indignation and hatred against foreigners of every description, who were ruining this country, and he began to think that it was about time we did something to protect ourselves. Still, it was a very difficult question; to tell the truth he himself could not make head or tale of it. At length he said aloud, addressing himself to Crass:

'Wot do you think of this 'ere fissical policy, Bob?'

'Ain't thought much about it,' replied Crass.' I don't never worry my 'ed about politics.'

'Much better left alone,' chimed in old Jack Linden, sagely, 'argyfying about politics generally ends up with a bloody row an' does no good to nobody.'

At this there was a murmur of approval from several of the others. Most of them were averse from arguing or disputing about politics. If two or three men of similar opinions happened to be together they might discuss such things in a friendly and superficial way, but in a mixed company it was better left alone. The 'Fissical Policy' emanated from the Tory Party. That was the reason why some of them were strongly in favour of it, and for the same reason others were opposed to it. Some of them were under the delusion that they were Conservatives; others imagined themselves to be Liberals; as a matter of fact most of them were nothing. They knew as much about the public affairs of their own country as they did of the condition of affairs in the planet Jupiter.

Easton began to regret that he had broached so objectionable a subject, when, looking up from his paper, Owen said:

'Does the fact that you never trouble your heads about politics prevent you from voting at election times?'

No one answered, and there ensued a brief silence, Easton, however, in spite of the snub he had received, could not refrain from talking.

'Well, I don't go in for politics much, either, but if what's in this 'ere paper is true, it seems to me as we oughter take some interest in it, when the country is being ruined by foreigners.'

'If you're goin' to believe all that's in that bloody rag you'll want some salt,' said Harlow.

The 'Obscurer' was a Tory paper and Harlow was a member of the local Liberal club.

Harlow's remark roused Crass.

'Wots the use of talkin' like that?' he said. 'You know very well that the country *is* being ruined by foreigners. Just go to a shop to buy something; look round the place an' you'll see that more than 'arf the dam stuff comes from abroad. They're able to sell their goods 'ere because they don't 'ave to pay no dooty, but they takes care to put 'eavy dooties on our goods to keep 'em out of their countries; and I say it's about time it was stopped.'

''Ear, 'ear!' said Linden, who always agreed with Crass, because the latter, being in charge of the job, had it in his power to put in a good—or bad—word for a man to the boss. ''Ear, 'ear! Now that's wot I call common sense.'

Several other men, for the same reason as Linden, echoed Grass's sentiments, but Owen laughed contemptuously.

'Yes, it's quite true that we gets a lot of stuff from foreign countries, 'said Harlow, 'but they buys more from us than we do from them.'

'Now you think you know a 'ell of a lot,' said Crass; ''ow much more did they buy from us last year than we did from them?'

Harlow looked foolish; as a matter of fact his knowledge of the subject was not much wider than Grass's. He mumbled something about having no 'ed for figures, and offered to bring full particulars next day.

'You're wot I call a bloody windbag,' continued Crass; 'you've got a 'ell of a lot to say, but wen it comes to the point you don't know nothin'.'

'Why even 'ere in Mugsborough,' chimed in Sawkins—who though still lying on the dresser had been awakened by the shouting—'we're overrun with 'em! Nearly all the waiters and the cook at the Grand Hotel, where we was working last month, is foreigners.'

'Yes,' said old Joe Philpot, tragically, 'and then there's all them Hitalian horgan grinders, an' the blokes wot sells chestnuts; an' wen I wos goin' 'ome last night I see a lot of them Frenchies sellin' hunions, an' a little wile afterwards I met two more of 'em comin' up the street with a bear.'

Notwithstanding the disquieting nature of this intelligence, Owen again laughed, much to the indignation of the others, who thought it was a very serious state of affairs and said it was a dam shame that these people were allowed to take the bread out of English people's mouths: they ought to be driven into the bloody sea.

And so the talk continued, principally carried on by Crass and those who agreed with him. None of them really understood the subject; not one of them had ever devoted fifteen consecutive minutes to the earnest investigation of it. The papers they read were filled with vague and alarming accounts of the quantities of foreign merchandise imported into this country, the enormous number of aliens constantly arriving, their destitute condition, how they lived, the crimes they committed, and the injury they did to British trade. These were the seeds which, cunningly sown in their minds, caused a bitter undiscriminating hatred of foreigners to grow up within them. To them the mysterious thing which they called either the 'Friscal Policy,' the 'Fistical Policy,' or the 'Fissical Question,' was a great Anti-Foreign Crusade. The country was in a hell of a state; poverty, hunger, and misery in a hundred forms had already invaded thousands of homes and stood upon the threshold of thousands more. How came these things to be? It was the bloody foreigner! Therefore, down with the foreigners and all their works. Out with them. Drive them into the bloody sea! The country would be ruined if not protected in some way. This Friscal, Fistical, Fissical or whatever the hell policy it was called, *was* Protection, therefore no one but a bloody fool could hesitate to support it. It was all quite plain—quite simple. One did not need to think twice about it. It was scarcely necessary to think about it at all.

This was the conclusion reached by Crass and such of his mates who thought they were Conservatives—the majority of them could not have read a dozen sentences aloud without stumbling—it was not necessary to think or study or investigate anything. It was all as clear as daylight. The foreigner was the enemy, and the cause of poverty and bad trade.

When the storm had in some degree subsided, Owen said sneeringly:

'Some of you seem to think that it was a great mistake on God's part to make so many foreigners. You ought to hold a mass meeting about it and pass a resolution something like this: "This meeting of British Christians hereby indignantly protests against the action of the Supreme Being in having created so many foreigners, and calls upon Him to rain down fire, brimstone, and mighty rocks forthwith upon the heads of all those Philistines, so that they may be utterly exterminated from the face of the earth, which rightly belongs to the British people".'

Crass looked very indignant, but could think of nothing to say in answer to Owen, who continued:

'A little while ago you made the remark that you never trouble yourself about what you call politics, and some of the rest agreed with you that to do so is not worth while. Well, since you never "worry" yourself about these things, it follows that you know nothing about them; yet you do not hesitate to express the most decided opinions concerning matters of which you admittedly know nothing. Presently, when there is an election, you will go and vote in favour of a policy of which you know nothing. I say that since you never take the trouble to find out which side is right or wrong you have no right to express any opinion. You are not fit to vote. You should not be allowed to vote.'

Crass was by this time very angry.

'I pays my rates and taxes,' he shouted, 'an' I've got as much right to express an opinion as you 'ave. I votes for who the bloody 'ell I likes. I shan't arst your leave nor nobody else's! Wot the 'ell's it got to do with you who I votes for?'

'It has a great deal to do with me. If you vote for protection you will be helping to bring it about, and if you succeed, and if Protection is the evil that some people say it is, I shall be one of those who will suffer. I say you have no right to vote for a policy which may bring suffering upon other people, without taking the trouble to find out whether you are helping to make things better or worse.'

Owen had risen from his seat and was walking up and down the room emphasizing his words with excited gestures.

'As for not trying to find out wot side is right,' said Crass, somewhat overawed by Owen's manner, and by what he thought was the glare of madness in his eyes, 'I reads the "Ananias" every week, and I generally takes the "Daily Chloroform" or the "Hobscurer", so I ought to know summat about it.'

'Just listen to this,' interrupted Easton, wishing to create a diversion and beginning to read from the copy of the 'Obscurer' which he still held in his hand:

"GREAT DISTRESS IN MUGSBOROUGH
HUNDREDS OUT OF EMPLOYMENT
WORK OF THE CHARITY SOCIETY
789 CASES ON THE BOOKS

'"Great as was the distress among the working classes last year, unfortunately there seems every prospect that before the winter which has just commenced is over the distress will be even more acute.

'"Already the Charity Society and kindred associations are relieving more cases than they did at the corresponding time last year. Applications to the Board of Guardians have also been much more numerous, and the Soup Kitchen has had to open its doors on 7th Nov., a fortnight earlier than usual. The number of men, women and children provided with meals is three or four times greater than last year."'

Easton stopped; reading was hard work to him.

'There's a lot more,' he said, 'about starting relief works: two shillings a day for marriedmen, and one shilling for single, and something about there's been 1572 quarts of soup given to poor families wot was not even able to pay a penny, and a lot more. And 'ere's another thing, an advertisement:

"THE SUFFERING POOR

Sir—Distress among the Poor is so acute that I earnestly ask you for aid for The Salvation Army's great Social Work on their behalf. Some 6,000 are being sheltered nightly. Hundreds are found work daily. Soup and bread are distributed in the midnight hours to homeless wanderers in London. Additional workshops for the unemployed have been established. Our Social Work for men, women, and children, for the characterless and the outcast, is the largest and oldest organised effort of its kind in the country, and greatly needs help. 10,000 is required before Christmas day. Gifts may be made to any specific section or home, if desired. Can you please send us something to keep the work going? Please address cheques, crossed 'Bank of England' (Law Courts Branch), to me at 101, Queen Victoria Street, E.C. Balance Sheets and Reports upon application.

BRAMWELL BOOTH."

'Oh, that's part of the great 'appiness an' prosperity wot Owen makes out Free Trade brings,' said Crass, with a jecring laugh.

'I never said Free Trade brought happiness or prosperity,' said Owen.

'Well, praps you didn't say exactly them words, but that's wot it amounts to.'

'I never said anything of the kind. We've had Free Trade for the last fifty years and to-day most people are living in a condition of more or less abject poverty, and thousands are literally starving. When we had Protection things were worse still. Other countries have Protection and yet many of their people are glad to come here and work for starvation wages. The only difference between Free Trade and Protection is that under certain circumstances one might be a little worse than the other, but as remedies for poverty neither of them are of any real use whatever, for the simple reason that they do not deal with the real causes of poverty.'

'The greatest cause of poverty is hover-population,' remarked Harlow.

'Yes,' said old Joe Philpot, 'if a boss wants two men, twenty goes after the job; there's too many people and not enough work.'

'Over-population,' cried Owen, 'when there's thousands of acres of uncultivated land in England without a house or human being to be seen! Is over-population the cause of poverty in France? Is over-population the cause of poverty in Ireland? Within the last fifty years the population of Ireland has been reduced by more than half. Four millions of people have been exterminated by famine or got rid of by emigration, but they haven't got rid of the poverty. Pr'aps you think that half the people in this country ought to be exterminated as well. That's the sort of opinion that Philanthropists like you, who spend your lives in slavery for other people, might be expected to hold.'

Here Owen was seized with a violent fit of coughing, and resumed his seat. When the cough had ceased he sat wiping his mouth with his handkerchief and listening to the talk that ensued.

'Drink is the cause of most of the poverty,' said Slyme.

This young man had been through some strange process which he called 'conversion'. He had had a 'change of 'art' and looked down with pious pity upon those he called 'worldly' people. He was not 'worldly', he did not smoke or drink and never went to the theatre. He had an extraordinary notion that total abstinence was one of the fundamental principles of the Christian religion.

It never occurred to what he called his mind, that this doctrine is an insult to the Founder of Christianity.

'Yes,' said Crass, agreeing with Slyme, 'an' there's plenty of 'em wot's too lazy to work when they can get it. Some of the swine who go about pleading poverty 'ave never done a fair day's work in all their bloody lives. Then there's all this new fangled machinery,' continued Crass, 'that's wot's ruinin' everything. Even in our trade there's them machines for trimmin' wall paper, an' now they've brought out a paintin' machine. There's a pump an' a 'ose pipe, an' they reckon two men can do as much with this 'ere machine as twenty could without it.'

'Another thing is women,' said Harlow, 'there's thousands of 'em nowadays doin' work wot oughter be done by men.'

'In my opinion there's too much of this 'ere eddication, nowadays,' remarked old Linden, 'wot the 'ell's the good of eddication to the likes of us?'

'None whatever,' said Crass, 'it just puts foolish ideas into people's 'eds and makes 'em too lazy to work.'

Owen was listening to this pitiable farrago with feelings of contempt and wonder. Were they all hopelessly stupid? Had their intelligence never developed beyond the stage of childhood? Or was he mad himself?

'Early marriages is another thing,' said Slyme, 'no man oughtn't to be allowed to get married unless he's in a position to keep a family.'

'How can marriage be a cause of poverty?' said Owen, contemptuously. 'A man who is not married is living an unnatural life. Why don't you continue your argument a little further and say that the practice of eating and drinking is the cause of poverty, or that if people were to go barefoot and naked there would be no poverty? The man who is so poor that he cannot marry is in a condition of poverty already.'

'Wot I mean,' said Slyme, 'is that no man oughtn't to marry till he's saved up enough so as to 'ave some money in the bank; an' another thing, I reckon a man oughtn't to get married till 'e's got a 'ouse of 'is own. It's easy enough to buy one in a building society if you're in reg'lar work.'

At this there was a general laugh.

'Why, you bloody fool,' said Harlow, scornfully, 'most of us is walkin' about 'arf our time. It's all very well for you to talk; you've got almost a constant job on this firm. If they're doin' anything at all you're one of the few wot gets a show in. And another thing,' he added with a sneer, 'we don't all go to the same chapel as old Misery.'

'Old Misery' was Rushton and Company's manager or walking foreman. 'Misery' was only one of the nick-names bestowed upon him by the hands: he was also known as 'Nimrod' and 'Pontius Pilate.'

'And wot about drink?' demanded old Joe Philpot suddenly.

''Ear, 'ear,' cried Harlow. 'That's the bleedin' talk. I wouldn't mind 'avin 'arf a pint now, if somebody else will pay for it.'

Joe Philpot—or as he was usually called, 'old Joe'—was in the habit of indulging rather freely in the cup that inebriates. He was not very old, being only a little over fifty, but he looked much older. He had lost his wife some five years ago and was now alone in the world, for his three children had died in their infancy. Slyme's reference to drink had roused Philpot's indignation; he felt that it was directed against himself. The muddled condition of his brain did not permit him to take up the cudgels in his own behalf, but he knew that although Owen was a teetotaller himself, he disliked Slyme.

'There's no need for us to talk about drink or laziness,' returned Owen, impatiently, 'because they have nothing to do with the matter. The question is, what is the cause of the lifelong poverty of the majority of those who are not drunkards and who *do* work? Why, if by some miracle, all the drunkards and won't-works and unskilled or inefficient workers could be transformed into sober, industrious and skilled workers tomorrow, it would, under the present conditions, be so much the worse for us, because there isn't enough work for all *now*, and those people by increasing the competition for what work there is, would inevitably cause a reduction of wages and a greater scarcity of employment. The theories that drunkenness, laziness or inefficiency are the causes of poverty are so many devices invented and fostered by those who are selfishly interested in maintaining the present state of affairs, for the purpose of preventing us from discovering the real causes of our present condition.'

'Well, if we're all wrong,' said Crass with a sneer, 'praps you can tell us what the real cause is?'

'An' praps you think you know how it's to be altered,' remarked Harlow, winking at the others.

'Yes, I do think I know the cause,' declared Owen, 'and I do think I know how it could be altered——'

'It can't never be haltered,' interrupted old Linden. 'I don't see no sense in all this 'ere talk. There's always been rich and poor in the world, and there always will be.'

'Wot I always say is this 'ere,' remarked Philpot, whose principal characteristic—apart from thirst—was a desire to see everyone comfortable, and who hated rows of any kind, 'there aint no use in the likes of us trubblin' our 'eds or quarrelling about politics. It don't make a dam bit of difference who you votes for or who gets in. They're hall the same: workin' the horicle for their own benefit. You can talk till you're black in the face, but you won't never be able to alter it. It's no use worrying. The sensible thing is to try and make the best of things as we find 'em: enjoy ourselves, and do the best we can for each other. Life's too short to quarrel and we'll hall soon be dead!'

At the end of this lengthy speech, the philosophic Philpot abstractedly grasped a jam jar and raised it to his lips; but suddenly remembering that it contained stewed tea and not beer, set it down again without drinking.

'Let us begin at the beginning,' continued Owen, taking no notice of these interruptions. ' First of all, what do you mean by Poverty?'

'Why if you've got no money, of course,' said Crass impatiently.

The others laughed disdainfully. It seemed to them such a foolish question.

'Well, that's true enough as far as it goes,' returned Owen, 'that is, as things are arranged in the world at present. But money in itself is not wealth; it's of no use whatever.'

At this there was another outburst of jeering laughter.

'Supposing for example that you and Harlow were ship-wrecked on a desolate island, and *you* had saved nothing from the wreck but a bag containing a thousand sovereigns, and he had a tin of biscuits and a bottle of water.'

'Make it beer!' cried Harlow appealingly.

'Who would be the richer man, you or Harlow?'

'But then you see we aint ship-wrecked on no dissolute island at all,' sneered Crass. 'That's the worst of your arguments. You can't never get very far without supposing some bloody ridiclus thing or other. Never mind about supposing things wot aint true; let's 'ave facts and common sense.'

''Ear, 'ear,' said old Linden, 'that's wot we want—a little common sense.'

'What do *you* mean by poverty, then?' asked Easton.

'What I call poverty is when people are not able to secure for themselves all the benefits of civilisation—the necessaries, comforts, pleasures and refinements of life: leisure, books, theatres, pictures, music, holidays, travel, good and beautiful homes, good clothes, good and pleasant food.'

Everybody laughed. It was so ridiculous. The idea of the likes of *them* wanting or having such things! Any doubts that any of them had entertained as to Owen's sanity disappeared. The man was as mad as a March hare.

'If a man is only able to provide himself and his family with the bare necessaries of existence, that man's family is living in poverty. Since he cannot enjoy the advantages of civilisation he might just as well be a savage; better, in fact, for a savage does not know what he is deprived of. What we call civilisation—the accumulation of knowledge which has come down to us from our forefathers—is the fruit of thousands of years of human thought and toil. It is not the result of the labour of the ancestors of any separate class of people who exist to-day, and therefore it is by right the common heritage of all. Every little child that is born into the world, no matter whether he is clever or dull, whether he is physically perfect or lame, or blind, no matter how much he may excel or fall short of his fellows in other respects, in one thing at least he is their equal—he is one of the heirs of all the ages that have gone before.'

Some of them began to wonder whether Owen was not sane after all. He certainly must be a clever sort of chap to be able to talk like this. It sounded almost like something out of a book, and most of them could not understand one half of it.

'Why is it,' continued Owen, 'that we are not only deprived of our inheritance—we are not only deprived of nearly all the benefits of civilisation, but we and our children are also often unable to obtain even the bare necessaries of existence?'

No one answered.

'All these things,' Owen proceeded, 'are produced by those who work. We do our full share of the work, therefore we should have a full share of the things that are made by work.'

The others continued silent. Harlow thought of the overpopulation theory, but decided not to mention it. Crass, who could not have given an intelligent answer to save his life, for once had sufficient sense to remain silent. He did think of calling out the patent paint pumping machine and bringing the hose pipe to bear on the subject, but abandoned the idea; after all, he thought, what was the use of arguing with such a fool as Owen?

Sawkins pretended to be asleep.

Philpot, however, had suddenly grown very serious.

'As things are now,' went on Owen, 'instead of enjoying the advantages of civilisation we are really worse off than slaves, for if we were slaves our owners, in their own interest, would see to it that we always had food and—'

'Oh, I don't see that,' roughly interrupted old Linden, who had been listening with evident anger and impatience, 'you can speak for yourself, but I can tell yer I don't put *myself* down as a slave.'

'Nor me neither,' said Crass, sturdily, 'let them call theirselves slaves as wants to.'

At this moment a footstep was heard in the passage leading to the kitchen.

Old Misery, or perhaps the Bloke himself!

Crass hurriedly pulled out his watch.

'Jesus Christ! 'he gasped,' it's four minutes past one!'

Linden frantically seized hold of a pair of steps and began wandering about the room with them.

Sawkins scrambled hastily to his feet and snatching a piece of sandpaper from the pocket of his apron started furiously rubbing down the scullery door.

Easton threw down the copy of the 'Obscurer' and scrambled hastily to his feet.

The boy crammed the 'Chronicles of Crime' into his trousers pocket.

Crass rushed over to the bucket and began stirring up the stale white-wash it contained, although the stench which it gave forth was simply appalling.

Consternation reigned.

They looked like a gang of malefactors suddenly interrupted in the commission of a crime.

The door opened. It was only Bundy returning from his mission to the Bookie.

CHAPTER II

Nimrod: A Mighty Hunter Before the Lord

Mr Hunter, as he was called to his face and as he was known to his brethren at the Shining Light Chapel, or 'Misery' or 'Nimrod,' as he was named behind his back by the workmen over whom he tyrannised, was the general or walking-foreman or 'manager' of the firm, whose card is herewith presented to the reader:

Rushton & Co.
MUGSBOROUGH

Builders, Decorators, and General Contractors
Funerals Furnished
Estimates given for General Repairs to House Property
First-class Work only at Moderate Charges

There were a number of sub-foremen or 'coddies,' but Hunter was *the* foreman.

He was a tall thin man, whose clothes hung loosely on the angles of his round-shouldered, bony form. His long thin legs, about which the baggy trousers draped in ungraceful folds, were slightly knock-kneed and terminated in large flat feet. His arms were very long even for such a tall man, and the hugh bony hands were gnarled and knotted. When he removed his bowler hat, as he frequently did to wipe away with a red handkerchief the sweat occasioned by furious bicycle riding, it was seen that his forehead was high, flat and narrow. His nose was a large, fleshy, hawk-like beak, and from the side of each nostril a deep indentation extended downwards until it disappeared in the drooping moustache that concealed his mouth, the vast extent of which was perceived only when he opened it to bellow exhortations at the workmen to greater exertions. His chin was large and extraordinarily long. His eyes were pale blue, very small and close together, surmounted by spare, light coloured, almost invisible eyebrows, with a deep vertical cleft between them over the nose. His head, covered with thick coarse brown hair, was very large at the back, the ears were small and laid close to the head. If one were to make a full face drawing of his cadaverous visage it would be found that the outline resembled the lid of a coffin.

This man had been with Rushton for fifteen years, in fact almost from the time when the latter commenced business. Rushton had at that period realised the necessity of having a deputy who could be used to do all the drudgery and running about so that he himself might be free to attend to more pleasant and profitable matters. Hunter was then a journeyman, but was on the point of starting on his own account, when Rushton offered him a constant job as foreman, two pounds a week, and two and a half per cent of the profits of all work done. On the face of it this appeared a generous offer. Hunter closed with it, gave up the idea of starting for himself, and threw himself heart and mind into the business. When an estimate was to be prepared, it was Hunter who measured up the work and laboriously figured out the probable cost. When their tenders were accepted it was he who superintended the work and schemed how to scamp it, where possible, using mud where mortar was specified, mortar where there ought to have been cement, sheet zinc where they were supposed to put sheet lead, boiled oil instead of varnish, and three coats of paint where five were paid for. In fact, scamping the work was with this man a kind of mania. It grieved him to see anything done properly. Even when it was more economical to do a thing well, he insisted from force of habit on having it scamped. Then he was almost happy, because he felt that he was doing someone down. If there were an architect superintending the work Misery would square him or bluff him. If it were not possible to do either, at least he had a try; and in the intervals of watching, driving and bullying the hands, his vulture eye was ever on the look out for fresh jobs. His long red nose was thrust into every estate agent's office in the town in the endeavour to smell out what properties had recently changed hands or been let, in order that he might interview the new owners and secure the order for whatever alterations or repairs might be required. He it was who entered into unholy compacts with numerous charwomen and nurses of the sick, who, in return for a small commission, would let him know when some poor sufferer was passing away, and would recommend Rushton and Company to the bereaved and distracted relatives. By these means often—after first carefully inquiring into the financial position of the stricken family—Misery would contrive to wriggle his unsavoury carcase into the house of sorrow, seeking, even in the chamber of death, to further the interests of Rushton and Company, and to earn his miserable two and a half per cent.

It was to make the attainment of this object possible that Misery slaved and drove and schemed and cheated. It was for this that the workers' wages were cut down to the lowest possible point, and their offspring went ill clad, ill shod, and ill fed, and were driven forth to labour while they were yet children, because their fathers were unable to earn enough to support their homes.

Fifteen years!

Hunter realised now that Rushton had had considerably the best of the bargain. In the first place it will be seen that the latter had bought over one who might have proved a dangerous competitor, and now, after fifteen years, the business that had been so laboriously built up, mainly by Hunter's energy, industry and unscrupulous cunning, belonged to Rushton and Company. Hunter was but an employee, liable to be dismissed like any other workman, the only difference being that he was entitled to a week's instead of an hour's notice, and was but little better off financially than when he started for the firm.

Fifteen years!

Hunter knew now that he had been used, but he also knew that it was too late to turn back. He had not saved enough to make a successful start on his own account even if he had felt mentally and physically capable of beginning all over again, and if Rushton were to discharge him now he was too old to get a job as a journeyman. Further in his zeal for Rushton and Company, and his anxiety to earn his commission, he had often done things that had roused the animosity of rival firms to such an extent that it was highly improbable that any of them would employ him, and even if they would, Misery's heart failed him at the thought of having to meet on an equal footing those workmen whom he had tyrannised over and oppressed. It was for these reasons that Hunter was as terrified of Rushton as the hands were of himself.

Over the men stood Misery, ever threatening them with dismissal and their wives and children with hunger. Behind Misery was Rushton, ever bulging and goading him on to greater excesses and efforts for the furtherance of the good cause—which was—to enable the head of the firm to accumulate money.

Mr Hunter, at the moment when the reader first makes his acquaintance on the afternoon of the day when the incidents recorded in the first chapter took place, was executing a kind of strategical movement in the direction of the house where Crass and his mates were working. He kept to one side of the road because by so doing he could not be perceived by those within the house until the instant of his arrival. When he was within about a hundred yards of the gate he dismounted from his bicycle, there being a sharp rise in the road just there, and as he toiled up, pushing the bicycle in front, his breath showing in the frosty air, he observed a number of men hanging about. Some of them he knew; they had worked for him at various times, but were now out of a job. There were five altogether, three were standing in a group, the other two stood each by himself, being strangers to the rest. The three men who stood together were nearest to Hunter and as the latter approached, one of them advanced to meet him.

'Good morning, sir.'

Hunter replied by an inarticulate grunt, without stopping. The man followed.

'Any chance of a job, sir?'

'Full up,' replied Hunter, still without stopping. The man still followed, like a beggar soliciting charity.

'Be any use calling round in a day or so, sir? '

'Don't think so,' Hunter replied; 'can if you like; but we're full up.'

'Thank you, sir,' said the man, and turned back to his friends.

By this time Hunter was within a few yards of one of the other two men, who also came to speak to him. This man felt there was no hope of getting a job; still there was no harm in asking. Besides, he was getting desperate. It was over a month now since he had finished up for his last employer. It had been a very slow summer altogether. Sometimes a fortnight for one firm, then perhaps a week doing nothing, then three weeks or a month for another firm, then out again, and so on. And now it was November. Last winter they had got into debt. That was nothing unusual, but owing to the bad summer they had not been able, as in other years, to pay off the debts accumulated in winter. It was doubtful, too, whether they would be able to get credit again this winter. In fact, this morning, when his wife sent their little girl for some butter the grocer had refused to let the child have it without the money. So although he felt it to be hopeless he accosted Hunter.

This time Hunter stopped; he was winded by his climb up the hill.

'Good morning, sir.'

Hunter did not return the salutation; he had not the breath to spare. But the man was not hurt, being used to such treatment.

'Any chance of a job, sir?'

Hunter did not reply at once; he was short of breath, and he was thinking of a plan that was ever recurring to his mind, and which he had lately been hankering to put into execution. It seemed to him that the long waited for opportunity had come. Just now Rushton and Company were almost the only firm in Mugsborough who had any work. There were dozens of good workmen out. Yes, this was the time. If this man agreed he would give him a start. Hunter knew the man was a good workman, he had worked for Rushton and Company before. To make room for him old Linden, or some other full price man, could be got rid of; it would not be difficult to find some excuse.

'Well,' Hunter said at last in a doubtful, hesitating kind of way, 'I'm afraid not, Newman. We're about full up.'

He ceased speaking and remained waiting for the other to say something more. He did not look at the man, but stooped down, fidgetting with the mechanism of the bicycle as if adjusting it.

'Things have been so bad this summer,' Newman went on, 'I've had rather a rough time of it. I would be very glad of a job even if it was only for a week or so.'

There was a pause. After a while Hunter raised his eyes to the other's face, but immediately let them fall again.

'Well,' said he, 'I might—perhaps—be able to let you have a day or two. You can come here to this job,' and he nodded his head in the direction of the house where the men were working, 'to-morrow at seven. Of course you know the figure?' he added, as Newman was about to thank him. 'Six and a half.'

Hunter spoke as if the reduction were already an accomplished fact. The man was more likely to agree, if he thought that others were already working at the reduced rate.

Newman was taken by surprise, and hesitated. He had never worked under price, indeed he had sometimes gone hungry rather than do so; but now it seemed that others were doing it. And then he was so awfully hard up. If he refused this job he was not likely to get another in a hurry. He thought of his home and his family. Already they owed five weeks' rent, and last Monday the collector had hinted pretty plainly that the landlord would not wait much longer. Not only that, but if he did not get a job how were they to live? This morning he himself had had no breakfast to speak of, only a cup of tea and some dry bread. These thoughts crowded up on each other in his mind, but still he hesitated.

Hunter began to move off.

'Well,' he said, 'if you like to start you can come here at seven in the morning.' Then as Newman still hesitated he added impatiently, 'Are you coming or not?'

'Yes, sir,' said Newman.

'All right,' said Hunter, affably, 'I'll tell Crass to have a kit ready for you.'

He nodded in a friendly way to the man, who went off feeling like a criminal.

As Hunter resumed his march, well satisfied with himself, the fifth man, who had been waiting all this time, came to meet him. As he approached. Hunter recognised him as one who had started work for Rushton and Company early in the summer but who had left suddenly of his own accord, having taken offence at some bullying remark of Hunter's.

Hunter was glad to see this man. He guessed that the fellow must be very hard pressed to come again and ask for work after what had happened.

'Any chance of a job, sir?'

Hunter appeared to reflect.

'I believe I have room for one,' he said at length. 'But you're such an uncertain kind of chap. You don't seem to care much whether you work or not. You're too independent you know; one can't say two words to you but you must needs clear off.'

The man made no answer.

'We can't tolerate that kind of thing, you know,' Hunter added, 'if we were to encourage men of your stamp we should never know where we are.'

So saying, Hunter moved away and again proceeded on his journey.

When he arrived within about three yards of the gate he noiselessly laid his machine against the garden fence. The high evergreens that grew inside still concealed him from the observation of anyone who might be looking out of the windows of the house. Then he carefully crept along till he came to the gate post, and bending down he peeped cautiously round to see if he could detect anyone idling, or talking, or smoking. There was no one in sight except old Jack Linden, who was rubbing down the lobby doors with pumice stone and water. Hunter noiselessly opened the gate and crept quietly along the grass border of the garden path. His idea was to reach the front door without being seen, so that Linden could not give notice of his approach to those within. In this he succeeded and passed silently into the house. He did not speak to Linden; to do so would have proclaimed his presence to the rest. He crawled stealthily over the house but was disappointed in his quest, for everyone he saw was hard at work. Upstairs he noticed that the door of one of the rooms was closed.

Old Joe Philpot had been working in this room all day, washing off the old whitewash from the ceiling and removing the old papers from the walls with a broad-bladed square-topped knife called a stripper. Although it was only a small room Joe had had to tear into the work pretty hard all the time, for the ceiling seemed to have had two or three coats of whitewash which had never been washed off, and there were several thicknesses of paper on the walls. The difficulty of removing these papers was increased by the fact that the dado had been varnished. In order to get this off it had been necessary to soak it several times with strong soda water, and although Joe was as careful as possible he had not been able to avoid getting some of this stuff on his fingers. The result was that his nails were all burnt and discoloured and the flesh round them cracked and bleeding. However, he had got it all off at last, and he was not sorry, for his right arm and shoulder were aching from the prolonged strain, and in the palm of the right hand there was a blister as large as a shilling, caused by the handle of the stripping knife.

All the old paper being off, Joe washed down the walls with water, and having swept the paper into a heap in the middle of the floor, he mixed some cement and proceeded to stop up the cracks and holes in the walls and ceiling. After a while, feeling very tired, it occurred to him that he deserved a spell and a smoke for five minutes. He closed the door and placed a pair of steps against it. There were two windows in the room almost opposite each other; these he opened wide in order that the smoke and smell of his pipe might be carried away. Having taken these precautions against surprise he ascended to the top of the step ladder that he had laid against the door and sat down at ease. Within easy reach was the top of a cupboard where he had concealed a pint of beer in a bottle. To this he now applied himself. Having taken a long pull at the bottle he tenderly replaced it on the top of the cupboard and proceeded to 'hinjoy' a quiet smoke, remarking to himself:

'This is where we get some of our own back.'

He held, however, his trowel in one hand, ready for immediate action in case of interruption.

Philpot wore no white jacket, only an old patched apron; his trousers were old, very soiled with paint and ragged where they fell over the much patched, broken and down-at-heel boots. The part of his waistcoat not protected by his apron was covered with spots of dried paint. He wore a coloured shirt and a 'dickey,' also soiled and splashed with paint, one side of which was projecting from the opening of the waistcoat. His head was covered with an old cap heavy and shining with paint. He was very thin and stooped slightly. Although he was really only fifty-five, he looked much older, for he was prematurely aged.

He had not been getting his own back for more than five minutes when Hunter softly turned the handle of the lock. Philpot immediately put out his pipe, and descending from his perch opened the door. When Hunter entered, Philpot closed it again and mounting the steps went on stopping the wall just above. Nimrod looked at him suspiciously wondering why the door had been closed. He looked all round the room but could see nothing to complain of. He snuffed the air to try if he could detect the odour of tobacco, and if he had not been suffering from a cold in the head there is no doubt that he would have perceived it. However, as it was he could smell nothing, but all the same he was not quite satisfied, although he remembered that Crass always gave Philpot a good character.

'I don't like to have men working on a job like this with the door shut,' he said at length. 'It always gives me the idear that the man's 'avin' a mike. You can do what you're doin' just as well with the door open.'

Philpot, muttering something about it being all the same to him—shut or open—got down from the steps and opened the door. Hunter went out again without making any further remark and once more began crawling over the house.

Owen was working by himself in a room on the same floor as Philpot. He was at the window, burning off with a paraffin torch-lamp those parts of the old paintwork that were blistered or cracked.

In this work the flame of the lamp is directed against the old paint, which becomes soft and is removed with a chisel knife, or a scraper called a shavehook. The door was ajar and he had opened the top sash of the window for the purpose of letting in some fresh air, because the atmosphere of the room was foul with the fumes of the lamp and the burning paint, besides being heavy with moisture. The ceiling had only just been water-washed and the walls stripped, and the old paper, saturated with water, was piled up in a heap in the middle of the floor.

Presently, as he was working, he began to feel conscious of some other presence in the room. He looked round. The door was open about six inches and in the opening appeared a long pale face with a huge chin, surmounted by a bowler hat and ornamented with a large red nose, a drooping moustache, and two small glittering eyes set very close together. For some seconds this apparition regarded Owen intently, then it was silently withdrawn, and he was again alone. He had been so surprised and startled that he had nearly dropped the lamp, and now that the ghastly countenance was gone, Owen felt the blood surge into his own cheeks. He trembled with suppressed fury, and longed to be able to go out there on the landing and hurl the lamp into Hunter's face.

Meanwhile, on the landing outside Owen's door, Hunter stood thinking. Someone must be got rid of to make room for the cheap man to-morrow. He had hoped to catch one of the men doing something that would have served as an excuse for instant dismissal, but there was now no hope of that happening. What was to be done? He would like to get rid of Linden, who was now really too old to be of much use, but as the old man had worked for Rushton on and off for many years, Hunter felt that he could scarcely sack him ofthand without some reasonable pretext. Still the fellow was really not worth the money he was getting. Sevenpence an hour was an absurdly large wage for an old man like him. It was preposterous: he would have to go, excuse or no excuse.

Hunter crawled downstairs again.

Jack Linden was about sixty-seven years old, but, like Philpot and as is usual with working men, he appeared older, because he had had to work very hard all his life, frequently without proper food and clothing. His life had been passed in the midst of a civilisation, the benefits of which he had never been permitted to enjoy. But of course he knew nothing about all this. He had never expected or wished to be allowed to enjoy such things; he had always been of opinion that they were never intended for the likes of him. He called himself a Conservative and was very patriotic. At the time when the Boer war commenced, Linden was an enthusiastic jingo: his enthusiasm had been somewhat damped when his youngest son, a reservist, had been called to the front, where he had died of fever and exposure. When this soldier son went away, he left his wife and two children, aged respectively four and five years, in his father's care. After he died they stayed on with the old people. The young woman earned a little occasionally by doing needlework, but was really dependent on her father-in-law. Notwithstanding his poverty he was glad to have them in the house, because of late years his wife had been getting very feeble, and, since the shock occasioned by the news of the death of her son, needed someone constantly with her.

Linden was still working at the vestibule doors when the foreman came downstairs. Misery stood watching him for some minutes without speaking. At last he said loudly:

'How much longer are you going to be messing about those doors? Why don't you get them under colour? You were fooling about there when I was here this morning. Do you think it'll pay to have you playing about there hour after hour with a bit of pumice stone? Get the work done! Or if you don't want to, I'll very soon find someone else who does! I've been noticing your style of doing things for some time past and I want you to understand that you can't play the fool with me. There's plenty of better men than you walking about. If you can't do more than you've been doing lately you can clear out; we can do without *you* even when we're busy.'

Old Jack trembled. He tried to answer, but was unable to speak. If he had been a slave and had failed to satisfy his master the latter might have tied him up somewhere and thrashed him. Hunter could not do that; he could only take his food away. Old Jack was frightened—it was not only his food that might be taken away. At last, with a great effort, for the words seemed to stick in his throat, he said:

'I must clean the work down, sir, before I go on painting.'

'I'm not talking about what you're doing, but the time it takes you to do it!' shouted Hunter. 'And I don't want any back answers or argument about it. You just move yourself a bit quicker or leave it alone altogether.'

Linden did not answer: he went on with his work, his hand trembling to such an extent that he was scarcely able to hold the pumice stone.

Hunter shouted so loud that his voice filled all the house. Everyone heard and was afraid. Who would be the next, they thought.

Finding that Linden made no further answer, Misery again began walking about the house.

As he looked at them the men did their work in a nervous, clumsy, hasty sort of way. They made all sorts of mistakes and messes. Payne, the foreman carpenter, who was putting some new boards in a part of the drawing-room floor, was in such a state of panic that, while driving a nail, he accidentally struck the thumb of his left hand a severe blow with his hammer. Bundy was also working in the drawing-room, putting some white glazed tiles in the fireplace. Whilst cutting one of these in half in order to fit it into its place, he inflicted a deep gash on one of his fingers. He was afraid to leave off to bind it up while Hunter was there, and consequently, as he worked, the white tiles became all smeared and spattered with blood. Easton, who was working with Harlow on a plank, washing off the old distemper from the hall ceiling, was so upset that he was scarcely able to stand on the plank, and presently the brush fell from his trembling hand with a crash upon the floor.

Everyone was afraid. They knew that it was almost impossible to get a job for any other firm. They knew that this man had the power to deprive them of the means of earning a living—that he possessed the power to deprive their children of bread.

Owen, listening to Hunter over the banisters upstairs, felt that he would like to take him by the throat with one hand and smash his face in with the other.

And then?

Why then he would be sent to gaol, or at the best he would lose his employment: he and his family would be deprived of food. That was why he only ground his teeth and cursed and beat the wall with his clenched fist. So! and So! and So!

If it were not for his wife and child!

Owen's imagination ran riot.

First he would seize him by the collar with his left hand, dig his knuckles into his throat, force him up against the wall, and then, with his right fist, smash! smash! smash! until Hunter's face was all cut and covered with blood.

But then, what about those at home? Was it not braver and more manly to endure in silence?

Owen leaned against the wall, white faced, panting and exhausted.

Downstairs, Misery was still going to and fro in the house and walking up and down in it. Presently he stopped to look at Sawkins's work. This man was painting the woodwork of the back staircase. Although the old paintwork here was very dirty and greasy, Misery had given orders that it was not to be cleaned before being painted.

'Just dust it down and slobber the colour on,' he had said. Consequently, when Crass made the paint, he had put into it an extra large quantity of driers, which to a certain extent destroyed the 'body' of the colour, so that it did not cover well, and would require two coats. When Hunter perceived this he was furious. He was sure it could be made to do with one coat with a little care; he believed Sawkins was doing like this on purpose. Really, these men seemed to have no conscience.

Two coats—and he had estimated for only three!

'Crass!'

'Yes, sir.'

'Come here!'

'Yes, sir.'

Crass came hurrying along.

'What's the meaning of this? Didn't I tell you to make this do with one coat? Look at it!'

'It's like this, sir,' said Crass. 'If it had been washed down—'

'Washed down be damned!' shouted Hunter. 'The reason is that the colour ain't thick enough. Take the paint and put a little more body in it and we'll soon see whether it can be done or not. I can make it cover if you can't.'

Crass took the paint, and, superintended by Hunter, made it thicker. Misery then seized the brush and prepared to demonstrate the possibility of finishing the work with one coat. Crass and Sawkins looked on in silence.

Just as Misery was about to commence, he fancied he heard someone whispering somewhere. He laid down the brush and crawled stealthily upstairs to see who it was. Directly his back was turned, Crass seized a bottle of oil that was standing near and, tipping about half a pint of it into the paint, stirred it up quickly. Misery returned almost immediately: he had not caught anyone; it must have been fancy. He took up the brush and began to paint. The result was worse than Sawkins's.

He messed and fooled about for some time but could not make it come right. At last he gave it up.

'I suppose it'll have to have two coats after all,' he said, mournfully; 'but it's a thousand pities.'

He almost wept.

The firm would be ruined it things went on like this.

'You'd better go on with it,' he said as he laid down the brush.

He began to walk about the house again. He wanted to go away now, but he did not want them to know that he was gone, so he sneaked out of the back door, crept round the house and out of the gate, mounted his bicycle and rode away.

No one saw him go.

For some time the only sounds that broke the silence were the noises made by the hands as they worked: the musical ringing of Bundy's trowel, the noise of the carpenters' hammers and saws, and the occasional moving of a pair of steps.

No one dared to speak.

At last Philpot could stand it no longer. He was very thirsty.

He had kept the door of his room open since Hunter arrived.

He listened intently. He felt certain that Hunter must be gone: he looked across the landing and could see Owen working in the front room. Philpot made a little ball of paper and threw it at him to attract his attention. Owen looked round, and Philpot began to make signals: he pointed downwards with one hand and jerked the thumb of the other over his shoulder in the direction of the town, winking grotesquely the while. This Owen interpreted to be an inquiry as to whether Hunter had departed. He shook his head and shrugged his shoulders to intimate that he did not know.

Philpot cautiously crossed the landing and peeped furtively over the banisters, listening breathlessly. 'Was it gorn or not?' he wondered.

He crept along on tiptoe towards Owen's room, glancing left and right, the trowel in his hand, and looking like a stage murderer. 'Do you think it's gorn?' he asked in a hoarse whisper when he reached Owen's door.

'I don't know,' replied Owen in a low tone.

Philpot pondered. He *must* have a drink, but it would never do for Hunter to see him with the bottle: he must find out somehow whether he was gone or not.

At last an idea came. He would go downstairs to get some more cement. Having confided this plan to Owen, he crept quietly back to the room in which he had been working, then he walked noisily across the landing again.

'Got a bit of stopping to spare, Frank?' he asked in a loud voice.

'No,' replied Owen, 'I'm not using it.'

'Then I suppose I'll have to go down and get some. Is there anything I can bring up for you?'

'No, thanks,' replied Owen.

Philpot marched boldly down to the scullery, which Crass had utilised as a paint shop. Crass was there, mixing some colour.

'I want a bit of stopping,' Philpot said as he helped himself to some.

'Is the swine gorn?' whispered Crass.

'I don't know,' replied Philpot. 'Where's his bike?'

''E always leaves it outside the gate, so's we can't see it,' replied Crass.

'Tell you what,' whispered Philpot, after a pause. 'Give the boy a hempty bottle and let 'im go to the gate and look if the bike's there. If Misery sees him 'e can pretend to be goin' to the shop for some hoil.'

This was done. Bert went to the gate and returned immediately: the bike was gone.

As the good news spread through the house a chorus of thanksgiving burst forth.

'Thank Gord!' said one.

'Hope he falls orf and breaks 'is bloody neck,' said another.

'These Bible thumpers are all the same; no one ever knew one to be any good yet,' cried a third.

Directly, they knew for certain that he was gone, nearly everyone left off work for a few minutes to curse him. Then they again went on working, and now that they were relieved of the embarrassment that Misery's presence inspired, they made better progress. A few of them lit their pipes and smoked as they worked.

One of these was old Jack Linden. He was upset by the bullying he had received, and when he noticed some of the others smoking he thought he would have a pipe: it might steady his nerves. As a rule he did not smoke when working; it was contrary to orders.

As Philpot was returning to work again, he paused for a moment to whisper to Linden, with the result that the latter accompanied him upstairs.

On reaching Philpot's room the latter placed the step-ladder near the cupboard, and taking down the bottle of beer handed it to Linden with the remark, 'Get some of that acrost yer, matey, it'll put yer right.'

While Linden was taking a hasty drink, Joe kept watch on the landing outside, in case Hunter should suddenly and unexpectedly reappear.

When Linden was gone downstairs again, Philpot, having finished what remained of the beer and hidden the bottle up the chimney, resumed the work of stopping up the holes and cracks in the ceiling and walls. He must make a bit of a show to-night or there would be a hell of a row when Misery came in the morning.

Owen worked on in a disheartened, sullen way. He felt like a beaten dog.

He was more indignant on poor old Linden's account than on his own, and was oppressed by a sense of impotence and shameful degradation.

All his life it had been the same: incessant work under similar more or less humiliating conditions, and with no more result than being just able to avoid starvation.

And the future, as far as he could see, was as hopeless as the past; darker, in fact, for there would surely come a time, if he lived long enough, when he would be unable to work any more.

He thought of his child. Was he to be a slave and a drudge all his life also? It would be better for the boy to die now.

As Owen thought of his child's future, there sprung up within him a feeling of hatred and fury against the majority of his fellow workmen.

They were the enemy—those ragged trousered philanthropists who not only quietly submitted like so many cattle to their miserable slavery for the benefit of others, but defended it, and opposed and ridiculed any suggestion of reform.

They were the real oppressors—the men who spoke of themselves as 'the likes of us,' who, having lived in poverty and degradation all their lives, considered that what had been good enough for them was good enough for the children they had been the means of bringing into existence.

He hated and despised them, because they calmly saw their children condemned to hard labour and poverty for life, and deliberately refused to make any effort to secure better conditions for them than they had for themselves.

It was because they were indifferent to the fate of *their* children that he would be unable to secure a natural and human life for *his*. It was their apathy or active opposition that made it impossible to establish a better system of society, under which those who did their fair share of the world's work would be honoured and rewarded. Instead of helping to do this, they abased themselves and grovelled before their oppressors, and compelled and taught their children to do the same. *They*were the people who were really responsible for the continuance of the present system.

Owen laughed bitterly to himself. What a very comical system it was.

Those who worked were looked upon with contempt and subjected to every possible indignity. Nearly everything they produced was taken away from them and enjoyed by the people who did nothing. And then the workers bowed down and grovelled before those who had robbed them of the fruits of their labour, and were childishly grateful to them for leaving anything at all.

No wonder the rich despised them and looked upon them as dirt. They *were* despicable. They *were* dirt.

And they admitted it and gloried in it.

While these thoughts were seething in Owen's mind, his fellow workmen still patiently toiled on downstairs. Most of them had by this time dismissed Hunter from their thoughts. They did not take things as seriously as Owen. They flattered themselves that they had too much sense. It could not be altered.

Grin and bear it. After all, it was only for life! Make the best of things, and get your own back whenever you get a chance.

Presently Harlow began to sing. He had a good voice and it was a good song, but his mates just then did not appreciate either one or the other. His singing was the signal for an outburst of exclamations and catcalls.

'Shut it, for Christ's sake!'

'That's enough of that bloody row!'

And so on.

Harlow stopped.

'How's the enemy?' asked Easton, presently, addressing no one in particular.

'Don't know,' replied Bundy. 'It must be about half past four. Ask Slyme, he's got a watch.'

It was a quarter past four.

'It gets dark very early now,' said Easton.

'Yes,' replied Bundy, 'it's been very dull all day. I think it's goin' to rain. Listen to the wind.'

'I 'ope not,' replied Easton. 'That means a wet shirt goin' 'ome.'

He called out to old Jack Linden, who was still working at the front doors:

'Is it raining, Jack?'

Old Jack, his pipe still in his mouth, turned to look at the weather. It was raining, but Linden did not see the large drops which splashed heavily upon the ground. He saw only Hunter, who was standing at the gate watching him. For a few seconds the two men looked at each other in silence. Linden was paralysed with fear. Recovering himself, he hastily removed his pipe, but it was too late.

Misery strode up.

'I don't pay you for smoking,' he said, loudly. 'Make out your time sheet, take it to the office and get your money. I've had enough of you!'

Jack made no attempt to defend himself: he knew it was of no use. He silently put aside the things he had been using, went into the room where he had left his tool-bag and coat, removed his apron and white jacket, folded them up and put them into his tool-bag along with his tools—a chisel knife and a shavehook—put on his coat, and, with the tool-bag slung over his shoulder, went away from the house.

Without speaking to anyone else, Hunter hastily walked over the place, noting what progress had been made by each man during his absence. He then rode away, as he wanted to get to the office in time to give Linden his money.

It was now very cold and dark within the house, and as the gas was not yet laid on, Crass distributed a number of candles to the men, who worked silently, each occupied with his own gloomy thoughts. Who would be next?

Outside, sombre masses of lead-coloured clouds gathered ominously in the sky. The gale roared round the old-fashioned house, and the windows rattled discordantly. Rain fell in torrents.

They said it meant getting wet through going home, but, all the same, Thank God it was nearly five o'clock.

CHAPTER III

The Financiers

That night as Easton walked home through the rain he felt very depressed. It had been a bad summer for most people, and he had fared no better than the rest.

He was a man of medium height, about twenty-three years old, with fair hair and moustache and blue eyes. He wore a stand-up collar with a coloured tie, and his clothes, though shabby, were clean and neat.

He was married. His wife was a young woman whose acquaintance he had made when he happened to be employed with others painting the outside of the house where she was a general servant. They had 'walked out' for about fifteen months. Easton had been in no hurry to marry, for he knew that, taking good times with bad, his wages did not average a pound a week. At the end of that time, however, he found that he could not honourably delay longer, so they were married.

That was twelve months ago.

As a single man he had never troubled much if he happened to be out of work; he always had enough to live on, and pocket money besides, but now that he was married it was different: the fear of being 'out' haunted him.

He had started for Rushton and Company on the previous Monday, after having been idle for three weeks, and as 'The Cave' had to be done right through, he had congratulated himself on having secured a job that would last till Christmas. But he now began to fear that what had befallen Jack Linden might also happen to himself at any time. He would have to be very careful not to offend Crass in any way, for he knew that Crass could get him the sack at any time, and would not scruple to do so if he wanted to make room for some crony of his own. Although Crass was the 'coddy' or foreman of the job, he had no very unusual abilities, and was if anything inferior to the majority of his fellow-workmen. But he pretented to know everything, and his vague references to 'tones' and 'shades' and 'harmony' had impressed Hunter, who entertained a high opinion of his capacity. It was by pushing himself forward in this way, and by judicious toadying, that Crass managed to get himself put in charge of the job.

But though he did as little work as possible himself, he took care that the others worked hard. Any man who failed to satisfy him in this respect he reported to Hunter as being 'no good' or 'too slow for a funeral.' The result was that that man was dispensed with at the end of the week.

As he walked along, Easton realised that it was not possible to foresee what a day or even an hour might bring forth.

By this time he had arrived at his home—a small house, one of a long row, and containing four rooms.

The front door opened into a narrow passage, covered with oilcloth. At the end of this passage was a flight of stairs leading to the upper part of the house. The first door on the left led into the front sitting-room, an apartment about nine feet square, with a bay window. This room was very rarely used and was always very tidy and clean.

The mantelpiece was of wood, painted black and ornamented with jagged streaks of red and yellow, which were supposed to give it the appearance of marble. The wall paper was a pale terra cotta with a pattern of large white roses and chocolate-coloured leaves and stalks.

There was a small iron fender with fire-irons to match, and on the mantel-shelf stood a clock in a polished wood case, a pair of blue glass vases, and some photographs in frames. The floor was covered with oilcloth of a tile pattern in yellow and red. On the walls were two or three framed coloured prints such as are presented with Christmas numbers of illustrated papers. There was also a photograph of a group of Sunday school girls with their teachers, with the church for the background. In the centre of the room was a round deal table about three feet six inches across, the legs stained red to look like mahogany. Against one wall was an old couch covered with faded cretonne, four chairs to match standing with their backs to the wall in different parts of the room. The table was covered with a red cloth with a yellow crewel-work design in the centre. And on the table were a lamp and a number of brightly-bound books.

Some of these things, the couch and the chairs, Easton had bought second-hand and had done up himself. The table, oilcloth, fender, hearthrug, etc., had been obtained on the hire system and were not yet paid for. The windows were draped with white lace curtains, and in the bay was a small bamboo table on which reposed a large Holy Bible, cheaply but showily bound.

If anyone had ever opened this book they would have found that its pages were as clean as the other things in the room, and on the fly-leaf might have been read the following inscription: 'To dear Ruth, from her loving friend Mrs Starvem, with the prayer that God's Word may be her guide and that Jesus may be her very own Saviour. Oct. 12, 19—.' Mrs Starvem was Ruth's former mistress, and this had been her parting gift when Ruth left to get married. It was supposed to be a keepsake, but Ruth never opened the book and never willingly allowed her thoughts to dwell upon the scenes of which it reminded her.

For the memory of the time she spent in the house of 'her loving friend' was the reverse of pleasant. It comprised a series of recollections of petty tyrannies, insults and indignities. Six years of cruelly excessive work, beginning every morning two or three hours before the rest of the household were awake, and ceasing only when she went exhausted to bed late at night.

She had been what is called a 'slavey,' but if she had been really a slave her owner would have had some regard for her health and welfare; her 'loving friend' had had none. Mrs Starvem's only thought had been to get the greatest possible amount of labour out of Ruth and to give her as little as possible in return.

When Ruth looked back upon that dreadful time she saw it, as one might say, surrounded by a halo of religion. She never passed by a chapel, or heard the name of God or the singing of a hymn, without thinking of her former mistress. To have looked into this Bible would have reminded her of Mrs Starvem; that was one of the reasons why the book reposed unopened and unread, a mere ornament on the table in the bay window.

The second door in the passage, near the foot of the stairs, led into the kitchen or living room; from here another door led into the scullery, and upstairs were two bedrooms.

As Easton entered the house his wife met him in the passage and asked him not to make a noise as the child had just gone to sleep. They kissed each other and she helped him to remove his wet overcoat. Then they both went softly into the kitchen.

This room was about the same size as the sitting-room. At one end was a small range with an oven and a boiler, a high mantelpiece painted black. On the mantel-shelf was a round alarm clock and some brightly-polished tin canisters. At the other end of the room, facing the fireplace, was a small dresser, on the shelves of which were neatly arranged a number of plates and dishes. The walls were papered with oak paper. On one wall, between two coloured almanacks, hung a tin lamp with a reflector behind the light. In the middle of the room was an oblong deal table with a white tablecloth, upon which the tea things were set ready. There were four kitchen chairs, two of which were placed close to the table. Overhead, about eighteen inches from the ceiling, were stretched several cords upon which were drying a number of linen or calico undergarments, a coloured shirt, and Easton's white apron and jacket. On the back of a chair at one side of the fire more clothes were drying. At the other side, on the floor, was a wicker cradle in which a baby was sleeping. Near by stood a chair with a towel hung on the back, arranged so as to shade the infant's face from the light of the lamp. An air of homely comfort pervaded the room; the atmosphere was warm, and the fire blazed cheerfully over the whitened hearth.

They walked softly to the cradle and stood looking at the child, who kept turning uneasily in its sleep. Its face was very flushed and its eyes were moving under the half-closed lids. Every now and again its lips were drawn back slightly, showing part of the gums; presently it began to whimper, drawing up its knees as if in pain.

'He seems to have something wrong with him,' said Easton.

'I think it's his teeth,' replied the mother. 'He's been very restless all day and he was awake nearly all last night.'

'P'raps he's hungry.'

'No, it can't be that. He had the best part of an egg this morning, and I've nursed him several times to-day. And then at dinner-time he had a whole saucer full of fried potato with little bits of bacon in it.'

Again the infant whimpered and twisted in its sleep, its lips drawn back, showing the gums; its knees pressed closely to its body, the little fists clenched, and face flushed. Then after a few seconds it became placid, the mouth resumed its usual shape, the limbs relaxed, and the child slumbered peacefully.

'Don't you think he's getting thin?' asked Easton. 'It may be fancy, but he don't seem to me to be as big now as he was three months ago.'

'No, he's not quite so fat,' admitted Ruth. 'It's his teeth what's wearing him out; he don't hardly get no rest at all with them.'

They continued looking at him a little longer. Ruth thought he was a very beautiful child; he would be eight months old on Sunday. They were sorry they could do nothing to ease his pain, but consoled themselves with the reflection that he would be all right once those teeth were through.

'Well, let's have some tea,' said Easton at last.

Whilst he placed his wet boots and socks in front of the fire, and put on dry socks and a pair of slippers in their stead, Ruth half filled a tin basin with hot water from the boiler and gave it to him, and he then went into the scullery, added some cold water and began to wash the paint off his hands. This done, he returned to the kitchen and sat down at the table.

'I couldn't think what to give you to eat to-night,' said Ruth, as she poured out the tea. 'I hadn't got no money left and there wasn't nothing in the house except bread and butter and that piece of cheese. So I cut some bread and butter and put some thin slices of cheese on it and toasted it on a plate in front of the fire. I hope you'll like it: it was the best I could do.'

'That's all right; it smells very nice, anyway, and I'm very hungry.'

As they were taking their tea, Easton told his wife about Linden's affair and his apprehensions as to what might befall himself. They were both very indignant, and sorry for poor old Linden, but their sympathy for him was soon almost forgotten in their fears for their own immediate future.

They remained at the table in silence for some time, then:

'How much rent do we owe now?' asked Easton.

'Four weeks, and I promised the collector the last time he called that we'd pay two weeks next Monday. He was quite nasty about it.'

'Well, I suppose you'll have to pay it, that's all,' said Easton.

'How much money will you have to-morrow?' asked Ruth.

He began to reckon up his time: he had started on Monday and to-day was Friday; five days from seven to five, less half an hour for breakfast, and an hour for dinner, eight and a half hours a day—forty-two hours and a half. At sevenpence an hour that came to one pound four and ninepence halfpenny.

'You know I only started on Monday,' he said, 'so there's no back day to come. To-morrow goes into next week.'

'Yes, I know,' replied Ruth.

'If we pay the two weeks' rent, that'll leave us twelve shillings to live on.'

'But we won't be able to keep all that,' said Ruth, 'because there's other things to pay.'

'What other things?'

'We owe the baker eight shillings for the bread he let us have while you were not working, and there's about twelve shillings owing for groceries. We'll have to pay them something on account. Then we want some more coal; there's only about a shovelful left, and—'

'Wait a minit,' said Easton. 'The best way is to write out a list of everything we owe; then we shall know exactly where we are. You get me a piece of paper and tell me what to write. Then we'll see what it all comes to.'

'Do you mean everything we owe, or everything we must pay to-morrow.'

'I think we'd better make a list of all we owe, first.'

While they were talking the baby was sleeping restlessly, occasionally uttering plaintive little cries. The mother now went and knelt at the side of the cradle, which she gently rocked with one hand, patting the infant with the other.

'Except the furniture people, the biggest thing we owe is the rent,' she said when Easton was ready to begin.

'It seems to me,' said he, as—after having cleared a space on the table, and arranged the paper—he began to sharpen his pencil with a table-knife, 'that you don't manage things as well as you might. If you was to make out a list of just the things you *must* have before you went out of a Saturday, you'd find the money would go much farther. Instead of doing that you just take the money in your hand, without knowing exactly what you're going to do with it, and when you come back it's all gone and next to nothing to show for it.'

His wife made no reply: her head was bent down over the child.

'Now, let's see,' went on her husband. 'First of all there's the rent. How much did you say we owe?'

'Four weeks. That's the three weeks you was out and this week.'

'Four sixes is twenty-four; that's one pound four,' said Easton, as he wrote it down. 'Next?'

'Grocer, twelve shillings.'

Easton looked up in astonishment.

'Twelve shillings. Why, didn't you tell me only the other day that you'd paid up all we owed for groceries?'

'Don't you remember we owed thirty-five shillings last spring? Well, I've been paying that bit by bit all the summer. I paid the last of it the week you finished your last job. Then you was out three weeks—up till last Saturday—and as we had nothing in hand I had to get what we wanted without paying for it.'

'But do you mean to say it costs us three shillings a week for tea and sugar and butter?'

'It's not only them. There's been bacon and eggs and cheese and other things.'

The man was beginning to become impatient.

'Well,' he said, 'what else?'

'We owe the baker eight shillings. We did owe nearly a pound, but I've been paying it off a little at a time.'

This was added to the list.

'Then there's the milkman. I've not paid him for four weeks. He hasn't sent a bill yet, but you can reckon it up; we have two penn'orth every day.'

'That's four and eight,' said Easton, writing it down. 'Anything else?'

'One and seven to the greengrocer for potatoes, cabbage, and paraffin oil.'

'Anything else?'

'We owe the butcher two and sevenpence.'

'Why, we haven't had any meat for a long time,' said Easton. 'When was it?'

'Three weeks ago; don't you remember? A small leg of mutton.'

'Oh, yes,' and he added the item.

'Then there's the instalments for the furniture and oilcloth—twelve shillings. A letter came from them to-day. And there's something else.'

She took three letters from the pocket of her dress and handed them to him.

'They all came to-day. I didn't show them to you before, as I didn't want to upset you before you had your tea.'

Easton drew the first letter from its envelope.

CORPORATION OF MUGSBOROUGH

General District and Special Rates

FINAL NOTICE

MR W. EASTON,

I have to remind you that the amount due from you as under, in respect of the above Rates, has not been paid, and to request that you will forward the same within Fourteen Days from this date.

You are hereby informed that after this notice no further call will be made, or intimation given, before legal proceedings are taken to enforce payment.

By order of the Council.

JAMES LEAH,

Collector, No. 2. District.

District Rate… … …13		11	
Special Rate … … …10		2	
	1	4	1

The second communication was dated from the office of the Assistant Overseer of the Poor. It was also a Final Notice, and was worded in almost exactly the same way as the other, the principal difference being that it was 'By order of the Overseers,' instead of 'The Council.' It demanded the sum of 1 1 5½ for Poor Rate within fourteen days, and threatened legal proceedings in default.

Easton laid this down and began to read the third letter:—

J. DIDLUM & CO., LTD.,

Complete House Furnishers,

QUALITY STREET, MUGSBOROUGH.

Mr W. EASTON,

SIR,

We have to remind you that three monthly payments of four shillings each (12s. in all) became due on the first of this month, and we must request you to let us have this amount *by return of post.*

Under the terms of your agreement you guaranteed that the money should be paid on Saturday of every fourth week. To prevent unpleasantness, we must request you for the future to forward the full amount punctually upon that day.

Yours truly,

J. DIDLUM & CO., LTD.

He read these communications several times in silence, and finally with an oath threw them down on the table.

'How much do we still owe for the oilcloth and the furniture?' he asked.

'I don't know exactly. It was seven pound odd, and we've had the things about six months. We paid one pound down and three or four instalments. I'll get you the card if you like.'

'No, never mind. Say we've paid one pound twelve; so we still owe about six pound.'

He added this amount to the list.

'I think it's a great pity we ever had the things at all,' he said, peevishly. 'It would have been much better to have gone without until we could pay cash for them; but you would have your way, of course. Now we'll have this bloody debt dragging on us for years, and before the dam stuff is paid for it'll be worn out.'

The woman did not reply at once. She was bending down over the cradle arranging the coverings which the restless movements of the child had disordered. She was crying silently, unnoticed by her husband.

For months past—in fact ever since the child was born—she had been existing without sufficient food. If Easton was unemployed they had to stint themselves so as to avoid getting further into debt than was absolutely necessary. When he was working they had to go short in order to pay what they owed; but of what there was Easton himself, without knowing it, always had the greater share. If he was at work she would pack into his dinner basket over-night the best there was in the house. When he was out of work she often pretended, as she gave him his meals, that she had had hers while he was out. And all this time the baby was draining her life away, and her work was never done.

She felt very weak and weary as she crouched over there, crying furtively and trying not to let him see.

At last she said, without looking round:

'You know quite well that you was just as much in favour of getting them as I was. If we hadn't got the oilcloth there would have been illness in the house because of the way the wind used to come up between the floorboards. Even now of a windy day the oilcloth moves up and down.'

'Well, I'm sure I don't know,' said Easton, as he looked alternately at the list of debts and the three letters, 'I give you nearly every farthing I earn and I never interfere about anything, because I think it's your part to attend to the house, but it seems to me you don't manage things properly.'

The woman suddenly burst into a passion of weeping, laying her head on the seat of the chair that was standing near the cradle.

Easton started up in surprise.

'Why, what's the matter?' he said.

Then as he looked down upon the quivering form of the sobbing woman he was ashamed. He knelt down by her, embracing her and apologising, protesting that he had not meant to hurt her like that.

'I always do the best I can with the money,' Ruth sobbed. 'I never spend a farthing on myself, but you don't seem to understand how hard it is. I don't care nothing about having to go without things myself, but I can't bear it when you speak to me like you do lately. You seem to blame me for everything. You usen't to speak to me like that before I—before—. Oh, I am so tired—I am so tired, I wish I could lie down somewhere and sleep and never wake up any more.'

She turned away from him, half kneeling, half sitting on the floor, her arms folded on the seat of the chair, and her head resting upon them. She was crying in a heartbroken, helpless way.

'I'm sorry I spoke to you like that,' said Easton, awkwardly, 'I didn't mean what I said. It's all my fault. I leave things too much to you, and it's more that you can be expected to manage. I'll help you to think things out in future, only forgive me, I'm very sorry. I know you try your best.'

She suffered him to draw her to him, laying her head on his shoulder as he kissed and fondled her, protesting that he would rather be poor and hungry with her than share riches with anyone else.

The child in the cradle—who had been twisting and turning restlessly all this time—now began to cry loudly. The mother took it up and began to hush and soothe it, walking about the room and rocking it in her arms. The child, however, continued to scream, so she sat down to nurse it. For a little while the infant refused to take anything, struggling and kicking in its mother's arms, then for a few minutes it was quiet, feeding in a half-hearted, fretful way. Then it again began to scream and twist and struggle.

They both looked at it in a helpless manner. Whatever could be the matter with it? It must be those teeth.

Suddenly as they were soothing and patting him, the child vomited a mass of undigested food all over its own and its mother's clothing. Mingled with the curdled milk were fragments of egg, little bits of bacon, bread, and particles of potato.

Having rid his stomach of this unnatural burden, the unfortunate baby began to cry afresh, his face very pale, his lips colourless, and his eyes red-rimmed and running with water.

Easton walked about with him while Ruth cleaned up the mess and got ready some fresh clothing. They both agreed that it was the coming teeth that had upset the poor child's digestion. It would be a good job when they were through.

This work finished, Easton, who was still convinced in his own mind that with the aid of a little common sense and judicious management their affairs might be arranged more satisfactorily, said:

'We may as well make a list of all the things we must pay and buy to-morrow. The great thing is to think out exactly what you are going to do before you spend anything; that saves you from getting things you don't really need and prevents you forgetting the things you *must* have. Now, first of all, the rent; two weeks, twelve shillings.'

He took a fresh piece of paper and wrote this item down.

'What else is there that we must pay or buy to-morrow?'

'Well, you know I promised the baker and the grocer that I would begin to pay them directly you got a job, and if I don't keep my word they won't let us have anything another time, so you'd better put down two shillings each for them.'

'I've got that,' said Easton.

'Two-and-seven for the butcher. We must pay that. I'm ashamed to pass the shop, because when I got the meat I promised to pay him the next week and it's nearly three weeks ago now.'

'I've put that down. What else?'

'A hundred of coal, one-and-six.'

'Next?'

'The instalment for the furniture and floorcloth, twelve shillings.'

'Next?'

'We owe the milkman four weeks; we'd better pay one week on account; that's one-and-two.'

'Next?'

'The greengrocer, one shilling on account.'

'Anything else?'

'We shall want a piece of meat of some kind, we've had none for nearly three weeks. You'd better say one-and-six for that.'

'That's down.'

'One-and-nine for bread; that's one loaf a day.'

'But I've got two shillings down for bread already,' said Easton.

'Yes, I know, dear, but that's to go towards paying off what we owe, and what you have down for the grocer and milkman's the same.'

'Well, go on, for Christ's sake, and let's get it done,' said Easton irritably.

'We can't say less than three shillings for groceries.'

Easton looked carefully at his list. This time he felt sure that the item was already down; but finding he was mistaken he said nothing and added the amount.

'Well, I've got that. What else?'

'Milk, one-and-two.'

'Next?'

'Vegetables, eightpence.'

'Yes.'

'Paraffin oil and firewood, sixpence.'

Again the financier scrutinised the list. He was positive that it was down already. However, he could not find it, so the sixpence was added to the column of figures.

'Then there's your boots; you can't go about with them old things in this weather much longer, and they won't stand mending again. You remember the man said they wasn't worth it when you had that patch put on a few weeks ago.'

'Yes. I was thinking of buying a new pair to-morrow. My socks was wet through to-night. If it's raining some morning when I'm going out and I have to work all day with wet feet I shall be laid up.'

'At that second-hand shop down in High Street I saw a very good pair when I was out this afternoon, just your size, for two shillings.'

Easton did not reply at once. He did not much fancy wearing the cast-off boots of some stranger, who for all he knew, might have suffered from some disease, but then remembering that his old ones were literally falling off his feet he realised that he had practically no choice.

'If you're quite sure they'll fit you'd better get them. It's better to do that than for me to catch cold and be laid up for God knows how long.'

So the two shillings were added to the list.

'Is there anything else?'

'How much does it come to now?' asked Ruth.

Easton added it all up. When he had finished he remained staring at the figures in consternation for a long time without speaking.

'Jesus Christ!' he ejaculated at last.

'What's it come to?' asked Ruth.

'Forty-four-and-tenpence.'

'I knew we wouldn't have enough,' said Ruth, wearily. 'Now if you think I manage so badly, p'raps you can tell me which of those things we ought to leave out.'

'We'd be all right if it wasn't for the debts,' said Easton, doggedly.

'When you're not working we must either get into debt or starve.'

Easton made no answer.

'What'll we do about the rates?' asked Ruth.

'I'm sure I don't know; there's nothing left to pawn except my black coat and vest. You might get something on that.'

'It'll have to be paid somehow,' said Ruth, 'or you'll be taken off to jail for a month, the same as Mrs Newman's husband was last winter.'

'Well, you'd better take the coat and vest and see what you can get on 'em to morrow.'

'Yes,' said Ruth, 'and there's that brown silk dress of mine—you know the one I wore when we was married—I might get something on that, because we won't get enough on the coat and vest. I don't like parting with the dress, although I never wear it; but we'll be sure to be able to get it out again, won't we?'

'Of course,' said Easton.

They remained silent for some time, Easton staring at the list of debts and the letters. She was wondering if he still thought she managed badly, and what he would do about it. She knew she had always done her best.

At last she said, wistfully, trying hard to speak plainly, for there seemed to be a lump in her throat:

'And what about to-morrow? Would you like to spend the money yourself, or shall I manage as I've done before, or will you tell me what to do?'

'I don't know, dear,' said Easton sheepishly. 'I think you'd better do as you think best.'

'Oh, I'll manage all right, dear, you'll see,' replied Ruth, who seemed to think it a sort of honour to be allowed to starve herself and to wear shabby clothes.

The baby, who had been for some time quietly sitting up on his mother's lap, looking wonderingly at the fire—his teeth appeared to trouble him less since he got rid of the eggs and bacon and potatoes—now began to nod and dose, which Easton perceiving, suggested that the infant should not be allowed to go to sleep with an empty stomach, because it would probably wake up hungry in the middle of the night. He therefore woke him up as much as possible and mashed a little of the bread and toasted cheese with a little warm milk. Then taking the baby from Ruth he began to try to induce it to eat. As soon, however, as the child understood his object, it began to scream at the top of its voice, closing its lips firmly and turning its head rapidly from side to side, every time the spoon approached its mouth. It made such a dreadful noise that Easton at last gave in. He began to walk about the room with it, and presently the child sobbed itself to sleep.

After putting the baby into its cradle Ruth set about preparing Easton's breakfast and packing it into his basket. This did not take very long, there being only bread and butter—or to be more correct, margarine.

Then she poured what tea was left in the tea-pot into a small saucepan and placed it on the top of the oven, but away from the fire; cut two more slices of bread and spread on them all the margarine that was left; then put them on a plate on the table, covering them with a saucer to prevent them getting hard and dry during the night. Near the plate she placed a clean cup and saucer and the milk and sugar.

In the morning Easton would light the fire and warm up the tea in the saucepan so as to have a cup of tea before going out. If Ruth was awake and he was not too pressed for time he generally took a cup of tea to her in bed.

Nothing now remained to be done but to put some coal and wood ready in the fender so that there would be no unnecessary delay in the morning.

The baby was still sleeping and Ruth did not like to wake him up yet to dress him for the night. Easton was sitting by the fire smoking, so everything being done, Ruth sat down at the table and began sewing. Presently she spoke:

'I wish you'd let me try to let that back room upstairs; the woman next door has got hers let unfurnished to an elderly woman and her husband for two shillings a week. If we could get someone like that it would be better than having an empty room in the house.'

'And we'd always have them messing about down here, cooking and washing and one thing and another,' objected Easton. 'They'd be more trouble than they was worth.'

'Well, we might try and furnish it. There's Mrs Crass across the road has got two lodgers in one room. They pay her twelve shillings a week each; board, lodging, and washing. That's one pound four she has coming in reg'lar every week. If we could do the same we'd very soon be out of debt.'

'What's the good of talking? You'd never be able to do the work even if we had the furniture.'

'Oh, the work's nothing,' replied Ruth, 'and as for the furniture, we've got plenty of spare bed-clothes, and we could easily manage without a washstand in our room for a bit, so the only thing we really want is a small bedstead and mattress; we could get them very cheap second-hand.'

'There ought to be a chest of drawers,' said Easton doubtfully.

'I don't think so,' replied Ruth. 'There's a cupboard in the room, and whoever took it would be sure to have a box.'

'Well, if you think you can do the work I've no objection,' said Easton. 'It'll be a nuisance having a stranger in the way all the time, but I suppose we must do something of the sort or else we'll have to give up the house and take a couple of rooms somewhere. That would be worse than having lodgers ourselves.'

'Let's go and have a look at the room,' he added, getting up and taking the lamp from the wall.

They had to go up two flights of stairs before arriving at the top landing, where there were two doors, one leading into the front room—their bedroom—and the other into the empty back room. These two doors were at right angles to each other. The wallpaper in the back room was damaged and soiled in several places.

'There's nearly a whole roll of this paper on the top of the cupboard,' said Ruth, 'you could easily mend all those places. We could hang up a few almanacks on the walls; our wash-stand could go there by the window; a chair just there, and the bed along that wall behind the door. It's only a small window, so I can easily manage to make a curtain out of something. I'm sure I could make the room look quite nice without spending hardly anything.'

Easton reached down the roll of paper. It was the same pattern as that on the wall. The latter was a good deal faded, of course, but it would not matter much if the patches showed a little.

They returned to the kitchen.

'Do you think you know anyone who would take it? ' asked Ruth.

Easton smoked thoughtfully.

'No,' he said at length. 'But I'll mention it to one or two of the chaps on the job; they might know of someone.'

'And I'll get Mrs Crass to ask her lodgers; p'raps they might have a friend what would like to live near them.'

So it was settled; and as the fire was nearly out and it was getting late, they prepared to retire for the night. The baby was still sleeping, so Easton lifted it, cradle and all, and carried it up the narrow staircase into the front bedroom, Ruth leading the way, carrying the lamp and some clothes for the child. So that the infant might be within easy reach of its mother during the night, two chairs were arranged close to her side of the bed and the cradle placed on them.

'Now we've forgot the clock,' said Easton, pausing. He was half undressed, and had already removed his slippers.

'I'll slip down and get it,' said Ruth.

'Never mind, I'll go,' said Easton, beginning to put his slippers on again.

'No, you get into bed. I've not started undressing yet; I'll get it,' replied Ruth, who was already on her way down.

'I don't know as it was worth the trouble of going down,' said Ruth, when she returned with the clock. 'It stopped three or four times to-day.'

'Well, I hope it don't stop in the night,' Easton said. 'It would be a bit of all right not knowing what time it was in the morning. I suppose the next thing will be that we'll have to buy a new clock.'

He woke several times during the night and struck a match to see if it was yet time to get up. At half past two the clock was still going and he again fell asleep. The next time he woke up the ticking had ceased. He wondered what time it was. It was still very dark, but that was nothing to go by because it was always dark at six now. He was wide awake; it must be nearly time to get up. It would never do to be late; he might get the sack.

He got up and dressed himself. Ruth was asleep, so he crept quietly downstairs, lit the fire, and heated the tea. When it was ready he went softly upstairs again. Ruth was still sleeping, so he decided not to disturb her. Returning to the kitchen he poured out and drank a cup of tea, put on his boots, overcoat and hat, and taking his basket went out of the house.

The rain was still falling, and it was very cold and dark. There was no one else in the street.

Easton shivered as he walked along wondering what time it could be. He remembered there was a clock over the front of a jeweller's shop a little way down the main road. When he arrived at this place he found that the clock being so high up he could not see the figures on the face distinctly, because it was still very dark. He stood staring for a few minutes vainly trying to see what time it was, when suddenly the light of a bull's-eye lantern was flashed into his eyes.

'You're about very early,' said a voice, the owner of which Easton could not see. The light blinded him.

'What time is it?' said Easton, 'I've got to get to work at seven and our clock stopped during the night.'

'Where are you working?'

'At "The Cave," in Elmore Road. You know, near the old toll gate.'

'What are you doing here, and who are you working for?' the policeman demanded.

Easton explained.

'Well,' said the constable, 'it's very strange that you should be wandering about at this hour. It's only about three quarters of an hour's walk from here to Elmore Road. You say you've got to get there at seven, and it's only a quarter to four now. Where do you live? What's your name?'

Easton gave his name and address and began repeating the story about the clock having stopped. 'What you say may be all right, or it may not,' interrupted the policeman. 'I'm not sure but that I ought to take you to the station. All I know about you is that I find you loitering outside this shop. What have you got in that basket?'

'Only my breakfast,' Easton said, opening the basket and displaying its contents.

'I'm inclined to believe what you say,' said the policeman, after a pause. 'But to make quite sure I'll go home with you. It's on my beat, and I don't want to run you in if you're what you say you are, but I should advise you to buy a decent clock, or you'll be getting yourself into trouble.'

When they arrived at the house Easton opened the door, and after making some entries in his note-book the officer went away, much to the relief of Easton, who went upstairs, set the hands of the clock right and started it going again. He then removed his overcoat and lay down on the bed in his clothes, covering himself with the quilt. After a while he fell asleep, and when he awoke the clock was still ticking. The time was exactly seven o'clock.

CHAPTER IV

The Placard

Frank Owen was the son of a journeyman carpenter who had died of consumption when the boy was only five years old. His mother earned a scanty living as a needle-woman, and when Frank was thirteen he went to work for a master decorator who was a man of a type that has now almost disappeared, being not merely an employer but a craftsman of a high order.

Though at one time he had had a good business in the town, of late years the number of his customers had dwindled considerably, for there had arisen a new generation which cared nothing about craftsmanship or art, and everything for cheapness and profit. From this man and by laborious study and practice in his spare time, aided by a certain measure of natural ability, Frank acquired a knowledge of decorative painting and design, and graining and signwriting.

His mother died when he was twenty-four, and a year afterwards he married the daughter of a fellow-workman.

In those days trade was fairly good, and although there was not much demand for the more artistic kinds of work, still the fact that he was capable of doing them, if required, made it comparatively easy for him to obtain employment. They had one child—a boy—and were very happy, and for some years all went well. But gradually this state of things altered. Broadly speaking, the change came slowly and imperceptibly, although there were occasional sudden fluctuations.

Even in summer Owen could not always find work, and in winter it was almost impossible to get a job of any sort. At last, about twelve months previously, he had determined to leave his wife and child at home and go to try his fortune in London, intending to send for them when he got employment.

It was a vain hope. He found London, if anything, worse than his native town. Wherever he went he was confronted with the legend: 'No hands wanted'. He walked the streets day after day; pawned or sold all his clothes save those he stood in, and stayed in London for six months, sometimes starving and only occasionally obtaining a few days or weeks' work.

At the end of that time he was forced to give in. The privations he had endured, the strain on his mind and the foul atmosphere of the city combined to defeat him. Symptoms of the disease that had killed his father began to manifest themselves, and yielding to the repeated entreaties of his wife he returned to his native town, the shadow of his former self.

That was six months ago, and since then he had worked for Rushton and Company, though occasionally when they had no work in hand he was 'stood off' until something came in.

Ever since his return from London Owen had been gradually abandoning himself to hopelessness. Every day he felt that the disease he suffered from was obtaining a stronger grip on him. The doctor told him to 'take plenty of nourishing food,' and prescribed costly medicines which Owen had not the money to buy.

Then there was his wife. Naturally delicate, she needed many things that he was unable to procure for her. And the boy—what hope was there for him? Often as Owen moodily thought of their circumstances and prospects he told himself that it would be far better if they could all three die now, together.

He was tired of suffering himself, tired of impotently watching the sufferings of his wife, and appalled at the thought of what was in store for the child.

Of this nature were his reflections as he walked homewards on the evening of the day when old Linden was dismissed.

There was no reason to believe or hope that the existing state of things would be altered for a long time to come.

Thousands of people like himself dragged out a wretched existence on the very verge of starvation, and for the greater number of people life was one long struggle against poverty. Yet practically none of these people knew or even troubled themselves to enquire why they were in that condition; and for anyone else to try to explain to them was a ridiculous waste of time, for they did not want to know.

The remedy was so simple, the evil so great and so glaringly evident, that the only possible explanation of its continued existence was that the majority of his fellow-workers were devoid of the power of reasoning. If they had not been they would have swept this silly system away long ago.

Why, even those who were successful or wealthy could not be sure that they would not eventually die of want.

No matter how prosperous a man might be he could not be certain that his children would never want for bread.

As Owen strode rapidly along, his mind filled with these thoughts, he was almost unconscious of the fact that he was wet through to the skin. He was without an overcoat: it had been pawned in London, and he had not yet been able to redeem it. His boots were leaky and sodden with mud and rain.

He was nearly home now. At the corner of the street in which he lived there was a newsagent's shop, and on a board outside the door was displayed a placard:

TERRIBLE DOMESTIC TRAGEDY

DOUBLE MURDER AND SUICIDE

He went in to buy a copy of the paper. He was a frequent customer here, and as he entered the shopkeeper greeted him by name.

'Dreadful weather,' he remarked, as he handed Owen the paper. 'It makes things pretty bad in your line, I suppose?'

'Yes,' responded Owen, 'there's a lot of men idle, but fortunately I happen to be working inside.'

'You're one of the lucky ones, then,' said the other. 'You know, there'll be a job here for some of 'em as soon as the weather gets a little better. All the outside of this block is going to be done up. That's a pretty big job, isn't it?'

'Yes,' returned Owen; 'who's going to do it?'

'Makehaste and Sloggit. You know, they've got a place over at Windley.'

'Yes, I know the firm,' said Owen, grimly. He had worked for them once or twice himself.

'The foreman was in here to-day,' the shopkeeper went on; 'he said they're going to make a start Monday morning if it's fine.'

'Well, I hope it will be,' said Owen, 'because things are very quiet just now.'

Wishing the other good-night Owen again proceeded homewards.

Halfway down the street he paused irresolutely: he was thinking of the news he had just heard and of old Jack Linden.

As soon as it became generally known that this work was about to be started there was sure to be a rush after it, and it would be a case of first come first served. If he saw Jack to-night the old man might be in time to secure a job.

Owen hesitated: he was wet through: it was a long way to Linden's place, nearly twenty minutes' walk. Still, he would like to let him know, because unless he was one of the first to apply Linden would not stand such a good chance as a younger man.

Owen said to himself that if he walked very fast there was not much risk of catching cold. Standing about in wet clothes might be dangerous, but so long as one kept moving it was all right.

He turned back and set off in the direction of Linden's house; although he was but a few yards from his own home he decided not to go in because his wife would be sure to try to persuade him not to go out again.

As he hurried along he presently noticed a small dark object on the doorstep of an untenanted house. He stopped to examine it more closely and perceived that it was a black kitten. The tiny creature came towards him and began walking about his feet, looking into his face and crying piteously.

He stooped down and stroked it, shuddering as his hands came in contact with its emaciated body. Its fur was saturated with rain, and every joint of its backbone was distinctly perceptible to the touch. As he caressed it, the starving creature mewed pathetically.

Owen decided to take it home to the boy, and as he picked it up and put it inside his coat the little outcast began to purr.

This incident served to turn his thoughts into another channel. If, as so many people pretended to believe, there was an infinitely loving God, how was it that this helpless creature that He had made was condemned to suffer? It had never done any harm, and was in no sense responsible for the fact that it existed. Was God unaware of the miseries of His creatures? If so, then he was not all-knowing. Was God aware of their sufferings, but unable to help them? Then He was not all powerful. Had He the power but not the will to make His creatures happy? Then He was not good. No; it was impossible to believe in the existence of an individual, infinite God. In fact, no one did so believe; and least of all those who pretended, for various reasons, to be the disciples and followers of Christ. The anti-Christs were those who went about singing hymns, making long prayers and crying Lord, Lord, but never doing the things which He said. It was not necessary to call in the evidence of science, or to refer to the supposed inconsistencies, impossibilities, contradictions and absurdities contained in the Bible, in order to prove that there was no truth in the so-called Christian religion. All that was necessary was to look at the conduct of the individuals who were its votaries.

Jack Linden lived in a small cottage in Windley. He had occupied this house ever since his marriage, over thirty years ago.

His home and garden were his hobby; he was always doing something, painting, white-washing, papering and so forth. The result was that although the house itself was not of much account he had managed to get it into very good order, and as a result it was very clean and comfortable.

Another result of his industry was that—seeing the improved appearance of the place—Mr Sweater, the landlord, had on two occasions raised the rent. When Linden first took the house the rent was six shillings a week. Five years after it was raised to seven shillings, and after the lapse of another five years it had been increased to eight shillings.

During the thirty years of his tenancy he had paid altogether nearly six hundred pounds in rent, more than double the amount of the present value of the house. Jack did not complain of this—in fact he was very well satisfied. He often said that Mr Sweater was a very good landlord, because on several occasions when, being out of work, he had been a few weeks behind with his rent, the agent acting for the benevolent Sweater had allowed Linden to pay off the arrears by instalments. As old Jack was in the habit of remarking, many a landlord would have sold up their furniture and turned them into the street.

Linden's household consisted of his wife, his two grand-children and his daughter-in-law, the widow and children of his youngest son, the reservist, who had been a plasterer, working for Rushton and Company before the war.

They had just finished their tea when Owen knocked at their front door. The young woman went to see who was there.

'Is Mr Linden in?'

'Yes: who is it?'

'My name's Owen.'

Old Jack, however, had already recognised Owen's voice, and came to the door, wondering what he wanted.

'As I was going home I heard that Makehaste and Sloggit are going to start a large job on Monday, so I thought I'd run over and let you know.'

'Are they?' said Linden, 'I'll go and see them in the morning. But I'm afraid I won't stand much chance, because a lot of their regular hands are waiting for a job; but I'll go and see 'em all the same.'

'Well, you know, it's a big job. All the outside of that block at the corner of Kerk Street and Lord Street. They're almost sure to want a few extra hands.'

'Yes, there's something in that,' said Linden. 'Anyhow, I'm much obliged to you for letting me know. But come in out of the rain. You must be wet through.'

'No, I won't stay,' responded Owen; 'I don't want to stand about any longer than I can help in these wet clothes.'

'But it won't take you a minit to drink a cup of tea,' Linden insisted. 'I won't ask you to stop longer than that.'

Owen entered, and the old man closed the door and led the way into the kitchen.

At one side of the fire, Linden's wife, a frail-looking old lady with white hair, was seated in a large arm-chair, knitting. Linden sat down in a similar chair on the other side. The two grandchildren, a boy and girl about seven and eight years of age respectively, were still seated at the table.

A treadle sewing machine stood at one end of the room, and on the dresser was a pile of sewing—ladies' blouses in process of making. This was another instance of the goodness of Mr Sweater, from whom Linden's daughter-in-law obtained the work. It was not much, because she was only able to do it in her spare time, but then, as she often remarked, every little helped.

The floor was covered with linoleum, there were several framed pictures on the walls, and on the high mantel-shelf a number of brightly polished tins and copper utensils. The room had that indescribable homelike, cosy air that is found only in those houses in which the inhabitants have dwelt for a very long time.

The younger woman was already pouring out a cup of tea.

Old Mrs Linden, who had never seen Owen before, although she had heard of him, belonged to the Church of England and was intensely religious. She looked curiously at the Atheist as he entered the room. He had taken off his hat and she was surprised to find that he was not repulsive to look at, rather the contrary in fact. But then she remembered that Satan often appears as an angel of light. Appearances are deceitful. She wished that her husband had not asked him into the house and hoped that no evil consequences would follow.

Then as she looked at Owen, she was horrified to perceive a small black head with a pair of glistening green eyes peeping out of the breast of his coat, and immediately afterwards the kitten, catching sight of the cups and saucers on the table, began to mew frantically and scrambled suddenly out of its shelter, inflicting a severe scratch on Owen's restraining hands as it jumped to the floor.

It clambered up the tablecloth and began rushing all over the table, darting madly from one plate to another, seeking something to eat.

The children screamed with delight. Their grandmother was filled with a feeling of superstitious alarm. Linden and the young woman stood staring with astonishment at the unexpected visitor.

Before the kitten had time to do any damage Owen caught hold of it and despite its struggles lifted it off the table.

'I found it in the street as I was coming along,' he said; 'it seems to be starving.'

'Poor little thing. I'll give it something,' exclaimed the young woman.

She put some milk and bread into a saucer and the kitten ate ravenously, almost upsetting the saucer in its eagerness, much to the amusement of the two children, who stood by watching it with admiration.

Their mother now handed Owen a cup of tea. Linden insisted on his sitting down and then began to talk about Hunter.

'You know I *had* to spend some time on them doors to make 'em look anything at all. But it wasn't the time I took, or even the smoking what made 'im go on like that. He knows very well the time it takes. The real reason is that he thinks I was gettin' too much money. Work is done so rough nowadays that chaps like Sawkins is good enough for most of it. Hunter shoved me off just because I was getting the top money; and you'll see I won't be the only one.'

'I'm afraid you're right,' returned Owen. 'Did you see Rushton when you went for your money?'

'Yes,' replied Linden. 'I hurried up as fast as I could, but Hunter was there first. He passed me on his bike before I got half way, so I suppose he told his tale before I came. Anyway, when I started to speak to Mr Rushton he wouldn't listen, said he couldn't interfere between Mr Hunter and the men.'

'Ah! they're a bad lot, them two,' said the old woman shaking her head sagely, 'but it'll all come 'ome to 'em, you'll see. They'll never prosper. The Lord will punish them.'

Owen did not feel very confident of this. Most of the people he knew who had prospered were very similar in character to the two worthies in question. However, he did not want to argue with this poor old woman.

'When Tom was called up to go to the war,' said the young woman, bitterly, 'Mr Rushton shook hands with him and promised to give him a job when he came back. But now that poor Tom's gone and they know that me and the children's got no one to look to but father, they do *this*.'

Although at the mention of her dead son's name old Mrs Linden was evidently distressed, she was still mindful of the Atheist's presence, and hastened to rebuke her daughter-in-law.

'You shouldn't say we've got no one to look to, Mary,' she said; 'we're not as them who are without God and without hope in the world. The Lord is our shepherd. He careth for the widow and the fatherless.'

Owen was very doubtful about this also. He had seen so many badly cared for children about the streets lately, and what he remembered of his own sorrowful childhood was all evidence to the contarry.

An awkward silence succeeded. Owen did not wish to continue this conversation: he was afraid that he might say something that would hurt the old woman. Besides, he was anxious to get away; he began to feel cold in his wet clothes.

As he put his empty cup on the table he said:

'Well, I must be going. They'll be thinking I'm lost at home.'

The kitten had finished all the bread and milk and was gravely washing its face with one of its fore paws, to the great delight of the two children, who were sitting on the floor beside it. It was an artful looking kitten, all black, with a very large head and a very small body. It reminded Owen of a tadpole.

'Do you like cats?' he asked, addressing the children.

'Yes,' said the boy; 'give it to us, will you, mister?'

'Oh, do leave it 'ere, mister,' exclaimed the little girl; 'I'll look after it.'

'So will I,' said the boy.

'But haven't you one of your own?' asked Owen.

'Yes, we've got a big one.'

'Well, if you have one already and I give you this, then you'd have two cats, and I'd have none. That wouldn't be fair, would it?'

'Well, you can 'ave a lend of our cat for a little while if you give us this kitten,' said the boy, after a moment's thought.

'Why would you rather have the kitten?'

'Because it would play; our cat don't want to play, it's too old.'

'Perhaps you're too rough with it,' returned Owen.

'No, it aint that; it's just because it's old.'

'You know cats is just the same as people,' explained the little girl, wisely; 'when they're grown up I suppose they've got their troubles to think about.'

Owen wondered how long it would be before her troubles commenced. As he gazed at these two little orphans he thought of his own child, and of the rough and thorny way they would all three have to travel if they were so unfortunate as to outlive their childhood.

'Can we 'ave it, mister?' repeated the boy.

Owen would have liked to grant the children's request, but he wanted the kitten himself. Therefore he was relieved when their grandmother exclaimed:

'We don't want no more cats 'ere. We've got one already; that's quite enough.'

She was not yet quite satisfied in her mind that the creature was not an incarnation of the devil; but whether it was or not she did not want it, or anything else of Owen's, in the house. She wished he would go, and take his kitten or his familiar or whatever it was with him. No good could come of his being there. Was it not written in the Word: 'If any man love not the Lord Jesus Christ, let him be Anathema Maran-atha.'? She did not know exactly what Anathema Maranatha meant, but there could be no doubt that it was something very unpleasant. It was a terrible thing that this blasphemer who—as she had heard—did not believe there was a hell and said that the Bible was not the word of God, should be here in the house sitting on one of their chairs, drinking from one of their cups, and talking to their children.

The children stood by wistfully when Owen put the kitten under his coat and rose to go away.

As Linden prepared to accompany him to the front door, Owen, happening to notice a timepiece standing on a small table in the recess at one side of the fireplace, exclaimed:

'That's a very nice clock.'

'Yes, it's all right, ain't it?' said old Jack, with a touch of pride. 'Poor Tom made that—not the clock itself, but just the case.'

It was the case that had attracted Owen's attention. It stood about two feet high and was made of fretwork in the form of an Indian mosque, with a pointed dome and pinnacles. It was a very beautiful thing, and must have cost many hours of patient labour.

'Yes,' said the old woman, in a trembling, broken voice, and looking at Owen with a pathetic expression. 'Months and months he worked at it, and no one ever guessed who it were for. And then, when my birthday came round, the very first thing I saw when I woke up in the morning were the clock standing on a chair by the bed with a card:

"To dear mother, from her loving son, Tom.
Wishing her many happy birthdays."

But he never had another birthday himself, because just five months afterwards he were sent out to Africa, and he'd only been there five weeks when he died, five years ago come the fifteenth of next month.'

Owen, inwardly regretting that he had unintentionally broached so painful a subject, tried to think of some suitable reply, but had to content himself with murmuring some words of admiration of the work.

As he wished her good-night, the old woman, looking at him, could not help observing that he appeared very frail and ill: his face was thin and pale, and his eyes were unnaturally bright.

Possibly the Lord in His infinite loving kindness and mercy was chastening this unhappy castaway in order that He might bring him to Himself. After all, he was not altogether bad: it was certainly very thoughtful of him to come all this way to let her husband know about that job. She observed that he had no overcoat, and the storm was still raging fiercely outside, furious gusts of wind frequently striking the house and shaking it to its very foundations.

The natural kindliness of her character asserted itself; her better feelings were aroused, triumphing momentarily over the bigotry of her religious opinions.

'Why, you ain't got no overcoat!' she exclaimed. 'You'll be soaked goin' 'ome in this rain.' Then turning to her husband she continued: 'There's that old one of yours; you might lend him that; it would be better than nothing.'

But Owen would not hear of this. He thought, as he became very conscious of the clamminess of his saturated clothing, that he could not get much wetter than he already was. Linden accompanied him as far as the front door, and Owen once more set out on his way homeward through the storm that howled around like a wild beast hungry for its prey.

CHAPTER V

Owen at Home

Owen's wife and little son were waiting for him, in the living room of their small top-floor flat. Although the low ceiling showed the formation of the roof, the place was clean and comfortable, the tea was laid, and an old suit and some underclothing of Owen's hung by the fire to replace his wet garments on his return.

The woman was half sitting, half lying, on a couch by the other side of the fire. She was very thin, and her pale face bore the traces of much physical and mental suffering. She was sewing, a task which her reclining position rendered somewhat difficult. Although she was really only twenty-eight years of age, she appeared older.

The boy, who was sitting on the hearthrug playing with some toys, bore a strong resemblance to his mother. He also appeared very fragile, and in his childish face was reproduced much of the delicate prettiness which she had once possessed. His feminine appearance was increased by the fact that his yellow hair hung in long curls on his shoulders. The pride with which his mother regarded this long hair was by no means shared by Frankie, who was always entreating her to cut it off.

Presently the boy stood up and, walking gravely over to the window, looked down into the street, scanning the pavement for as far as he could see.

'I wonder wherever he's got to,' he said, as he returned to the fire.

'I'm sure I don't know,' returned his mother. 'Perhaps he's had to work overtime.'

'You know, I've been thinking lately,' observed Frankie, after a pause, 'that it's a great mistake for Dad to go out working at all. I believe that's the very reason why we're so poor.'

'Nearly everyone who works is more or less poor, dear, but if Dad didn't go out to work we'd be even poorer than we are now. We should have nothing to eat.'

'But Dad says that the people who do nothing get lots of everything.'

'Yes, and it's quite true that most of the people who never do any work get lots of everything; but where do they get it from, and how do they get it?'

'I'm sure I don't know,' replied Frankie, shaking his head in a puzzled fashion.

'Supposing Dad didn't go to work, or that he had no work to go to, or that he was ill and not able to do any work, then we'd have no money to buy anything. How should we get on then?'

'I'm sure I don't know,' repeated Frankie, looking round the room in a thoughtful manner. 'The chairs that's left aren't good enough to sell, and we can't sell the beds, or your sofa, but you might pawn my velvet suit.'

'But even if all the things were good enough to sell, the money we'd get for them wouldn't last very long, and what should we do then?'

'Well, I suppose we'd have to go without, that's all, the same as we did when Dad was in London. But *how* do the people who never do any work manage to get lots of money, then?' added Frankie.

'Oh, there's lots of different ways. For instance, you remember when Dad was in London, and we had no food in the house, I had to sell the easy chair.'

Frankie nodded. 'Yes,' he said; 'I remember you wrote a note and I took it to the shop, and afterwards old Didlum came up here and bought it, and then his cart came and a man took it away.'

'And do you remember how much he gave us for it?'

'Five shillings,' replied Frankie, promptly. He was well acquainted with the details of the transaction, having often heard his father and mother discuss it.

'And when we saw it in his shop window a little while afterwards, what price was marked on it?'

'Fifteen shillings.'

'Well, that's one way of getting money without working.'

Frankie played with his toys in silence for some minutes. At last he said:

'What other ways?'

'Some people who have some money already get more in this way: they find some people who have no money and say to them: "Come and work for us." Then the people who have no money go and work for the people that have the money. The people who have the money pay the workers just enough wages to keep them alive whilst they are at work. Then, when the things that the working people have been making are finished, the workers are sent away, and as they still have no money, they are soon starving. In the meantime the people who had the money take all the things that the workers have made and sell them for a great deal more money than they gave to the workers for making them. That's another way the idlers have of getting lots of money without doing any useful work.'

'When I'm grown up into a man,' said Frankie, with a flushed face, 'I'm going to be one of the workers, and when we've made a lot of things I shall stand up and tell the others what to do. If any of the idlers come to take our things away they'll get something they won't like.'

In a state of suppressed excitement and scarcely conscious of what he was doing, the boy began gathering up the toys and throwing them violently one by one into the box.

'I'll teach 'em to come taking our things away,' he exclaimed, relapsing momentarily into his street style of speaking. 'First of all we'll all stand quietly on one side. Then when the idlers come in and start touching our things, we'll go up to 'em and say: "'Ere, watcher doin' of? Just you put it down, will yer?" and if they don't put it down at once it'll be the worse for 'em, I can tell you.'

All the toys being collected, Frankie picked up the box and placed it noisily in its accustomed corner of the room.

'I should think the workers will be jolly glad when they see me coming to tell them what to do, shouldn't you, Mum?'

'I don't know, dear; you see so many people have tried to tell them, but they won't listen, they don't want to hear. They think it's quite right that they should work very hard all their lives, and quite right that most of the things they help to make should be taken away from them by the people who do nothing. The workers think that their children are not as good as the children of the idlers, and they teach their children that as soon as ever they are old enough they must be satisfied to work very hard and to have only very bad food and clothes and homes.'

'Then I should think the workers ought to be jolly well ashamed of themselves, Mum, don't you?'

'Well, in one sense they ought, but you must remember that that's what they've always been taught. But you have been taught differently. Do you remember what you told me the other day, when you came home from school, about the scripture lesson?'

'About St Thomas?'

'Yes. What did the teacher say St Thomas was?'

'She said he was a bad example; and she said I was worse than him because I asked too many foolish questions. She always gets in a wax if I talk too much.'

'Well, why did she call St Thomas a bad example?'

'Because he wouldn't believe what he was told.'

'Exactly. Well, when you told Dad about it what did he say?'

'Dad told me that really St Thomas was the only sensible man in the whole crowd of apostles. That is,' added Frankie, correcting himself, 'if there ever was such a man at all.'

'But did Dad say that there never was such a man?'

'No; he said *he* didn't believe there ever was, but he told me to just listen to what the teacher said about such things, and then to think about it in my own mind, and wait till I'm grown up and then I can use my own judgment.'

'Well now, that's what *you* were told, but all the other children's mothers and fathers tell them to believe, without thinking, whatever the teacher says. So it will be no wonder if those children are not able to think for themselves when they're grown up, will it?'

'Don't you think it will be any use, then, for me to tell them what to do to the idlers?' asked Frankie, dejectedly.

'Hark!' said his mother, holding up her finger.

'Dad!' cried Frankie, rushing to the door and flinging it open.

He ran along the passage and opened the staircase door before Owen reached the top of the last flight of stairs.

'Why ever do you come up at such a rate?' exclaimed Owen's wife reproachfully, as he came into the room exhausted from the climb upstairs and sank panting into the nearest chair.

'I al—ways—for—get,' he replied, when he had in some degree recovered.

As he lay back in the chair, his face haggard and of a ghastly whiteness, and with the water dripping from his saturated clothing, Owen presented a terrible appearance.

Frankie noticed with childish terror the extreme alarm with which his mother looked at his father.

'You're always doing it,' he said with a whimper. 'How many more times will Mother have to tell you about it before you take any notice?'

'It's all right, old chap,' said Owen, drawing the child nearer to him and kissing the curly head. 'Listen, and see if you can guess what I've got for you under my coat.'

In the silence the purring of the kitten was distinctly audible.

'A kitten!' cried the boy, taking it out of its hiding place. 'All black, and I believe it's half a Persian. Just the very thing I wanted.'

While Frankie amused himself playing with the kitten, which had been provided with another saucer of bread and milk, Owen went into the bedroom to put on the dry clothes, and as they were taking tea, he explained the reason of his late home coming.

'I'm afraid he won't find it very easy to get another job,' he remarked, referring to Linden; 'even in the summer nobody will be inclined to take him on. He's too old.'

'It's a dreadful prospect for the two children,' answered his wife,

'Yes,' replied Owen, bitterly, 'It's the children who will suffer most. As for Linden and his wife, although of course one can't help feeling sorry for them, at the same time there's no getting away from the fact that they deserve to suffer. All their lives they've been working like brutes and living in poverty. Although they have done more than their fair share of the work, they have never enjoyed anything like a fair share of the things they have helped to produce. And yet, all their lives they have supported and defended the system that robbed them, and have resisted and ridiculed every proposal to alter it. It's wrong to feel sorry for such people; they deserve to suffer.'

After tea, as he watched his wife clearing away the tea things and re-arranging the drying clothing by the fire, Owen for the first time noticed that she looked unusually ill.

'You don't look well to-night, Nora,' he said, crossing over to her and putting his arm around her.

'I don't feel well,' she replied, resting her head wearily against his shoulder. 'I've been very bad all day and I had to lie down nearly all the afternoon. I don't know how I should have managed to get the tea ready if it had not been for Frankie.'

'I set the table for you, didn't I, Mum?' said Frankie, with pride; 'and I tidied up the room as well,'

'Yes, darling, you helped me a lot,' she answered, and Frankie went over to her and kissed her hand.

'Well, you'd better go to bed at once,' said Owen. 'I can put Frankie to bed presently and do whatever else is necessary.'

'But there are so many things to attend to. I want to see that your clothes are properly dry and to put something ready for you to take in the morning before you go out, and then there's your breakfast to pack up—'

'I can manage all that.'

'1 didn't want to give way to it like this,' the woman said, 'because I know you must be tired out yourself, but I really do feel quite done up now.'

'Oh, I'm all right,' replied Owen, who was really so fatigued that he was scarcely able to stand. 'I'll go and draw the blinds down, and light the other lamp; so say good-night to Frankie and come at once.'

'I won't say good-night properly now, Mum,' remarked the boy, 'because Dad can carry me into your room before he puts me into bed.'

A little later, as Owen was undressing Frankie, the latter remarked, as he looked affectionately at the kitten, which was sitting on the hearthrug watching the child's every movement under the impression that it was part of some game:

'What name do you think we ought to call it, Dad?'

'You may give him any name you like,' replied Owen absently.

'I know a dog that lives down the road,' said the boy; 'his name is Major. How would that do? Or we might call him Sergeant.'

The kitten, observing that he was the subject of their conversation, purred loudly and winked as if to intimate that he did not care what rank was conferred upon him so long as the commissariat department was properly attended to.

'I don't know, though,' continued Frankie, thoughtfully. 'They're all right names for dogs, but I think they're too big for a kitten, don't you, Dad?'

'Yes, p'raps they are,' said Owen.

'Most cats are called Tom or Kitty, but I don't want a *common* name for him.'

'Well, can't you call him after someone you know?'

'I know! I'll call him after a little girl that comes to our school; a fine name—Maud! That'll be a good one, won't it, Dad?'

'Yes,' said Owen.

'I say, Dad,' said Frankie, suddenly realising the awful fact that he was being put to bed; 'you're forgetting all about my story, and you promised that you'd have a game of trains with me to-night.'

'I hadn't forgotten, but I was hoping that you had, because I'm very tired and it's very late, long past your usual bed-time, you know. You can take the kitten to bed with you to-night and I'll tell you two stories to-morrow and have the game as well. I shall have plenty of time to-morrow because it's Saturday.'

'All right, then,' said the boy, contentedly.

After the child was in bed, Owen sat alone by the table in the draughty sitting-room, thinking.

Although there was a bright fire the room was very cold, being so close to the roof. The wind roared loudly round the gables, shaking the house in a way that threatened every moment to hurl it to the ground.

The lamp on the table had a green glass reservoir which was half full of oil. Owen watched this with unconscious fascination. Every time a gust of wind struck the house the oil in the lamp was agitated, and rippled against the glass like the waves of a miniature sea.

Staring abstractedly at the lamp, he thought of the future.

A few years ago the future had seemed a region of wonderful and mysterious possibilities of good, but to-night the thought brought no such illusions, for he knew that the story of the future was to be much the same as the story of the past.

The story of the past would continue to repeat itself for a few years longer. He would continue to work and they would all three have to go without most of the necessaries of life.

When there was no work they would starve.

For himself he did not care much because he knew that at the best—or worst—it would only be a very few years. Even if he were able to have proper food and clothing and take reasonable care of himself, he could not live much longer; but when that time came, what was to become of *them*?

There would be some hope for the boy if he were more robust and if his character were less gentle and more selfish.

In order to succeed in the world it was necessary to be brutal, selfish and unfeeling: to push others aside and to take advantage of their misfortunes.

That was the ideal character.

Owen knew that Frankie's character did not come up to this lofty ideal.

Then there was Nora, how would she fare?

Owen stood up and began walking about the room, oppressed with a kind of terror. Presently he returned to the fire and began re-arranging his clothes that were drying. He found that the boots, having been placed too near the fire, had dried too quickly, and consequently the sole of one of them had begun to split away from the upper. He remedied this as well as he was able, and while turning the wetter parts of the clothing to the fire, he noticed the newspaper in the coat pocket. He drew it out with an exclamation of pleasure. Here was something to distract his thoughts. But as soon as he opened the paper his attention was rivetted by the staring headlines of one of the principal columns:

TERRIBLE DOMESTIC TRAGEDY.

WIFE AND TWO CHILDREN KILLED.

SUICIDE OF THE MURDERER.

It was one of the ordinary crimes of poverty. The man had been without employment for many weeks and they had pawned or sold their furniture and other possessions. But even this resource must have failed at last, and one day the neighbours noticed that the blinds remained down and that there was a strange silence about the house. When the police entered they found, in one of the upper rooms, the dead bodies of the woman and the two children, with their throats cut, laid out side by side upon the bed, which was saturated with their blood.

There was no bedstead, and no furniture in the room except the straw mattress and the ragged clothes and blankets upon the floor.

The man's body was found in the kitchen, lying with outstretched arms face downwards on the floor, surrounded by the blood from the terrible wound in his throat, which had evidently been inflicted by the razor that was grasped in his right hand.

No particle of food was found, but attached to a nail in the kitchen wall was a piece of blood-smeared paper on which was written in pencil:

'This is not *my* crime, but Society's.'

The report went on to explain that the deed must have been perpetrated during a fit of temporary insanity, brought on by the sufferings the man had endured.

'Insanity!' muttered Owen, as he read this glib theory, 'Insanity! It seems to me that he would have been insane if he had *not* killed them.'

Surely it was wiser and better and kinder to send them all to sleep, than to let them continue to suffer.

At the same time it seemed strange that the man should have chosen to do it in that way, when there were so many other cleaner, easier and less painful ways of accomplishing his object.

One could take poison. Of course, there was a certain amount of difficulty in procuring it, and one would have to be very careful not to select one that would cause a lot of pain.

Owen went over to his bookshelf and took down 'The Cyclopaedia of Practical Medicine,' an old, rather out-of-date book, which he thought might contain the required information. He was astonished to find what a number of poisons there were within easy reach of whoever wished to make use of them: poisons which could be relied upon to do their work certainly, quickly and without pain. Why, it was not even necessary to buy them; one could gather them from the hedges by the roadside and in the fields.

The more he thought of it the stranger it seemed that such a clumsy method as a razor should be so popular. Strangulation or even hanging would be better than that, though the latter method could scarcely be adopted in their flat, because there were no beams or rafters or anything from which it would be possible to suspend a cord. Still, he could drive some large nails or hooks into one of the walls. For that matter, there were already some clothes hooks on some of the doors. He began to think that this would be a more excellent way than poison: he could easily pretend to Frankie that he was going to show him some new kind of play. The boy would offer no resistance, and in a few minutes it would all be over.

He threw down the book and pressed his hands over his ears. He fancied he could hear the boy's hands and feet beating against the panels of the door as he struggled in his death agony.

Then, as his arms fell nervelessly by his side again, he thought he heard Frankie's voice calling:

'Dad! Dad!'

Owen hastily opened the door.

'Are you calling, Frankie?'

'Yes. I've been calling you quite a long time.'

'What do you want?'

'I want you to come here. I want to tell you something.'

'Well, what is it, dear? I thought you were asleep a long time ago,' said Owen, as he came into the room.

'That's just what I want to speak to you about. The kitten's gone to sleep all right, but I can't go. I've tried all different ways, counting and all, but it's no use, so I thought I'd ask you if you'd mind coming and staying with me, and letting me hold your hand for a little while, and then p'raps I could go.'

The boy twined his arms round Owen's neck and hugged him very tightly.

'Oh, Dad, I love you so much!' he said, 'I love you so much, I could squeeze you to death.'

'I'm afraid you will, if you squeeze me so tightly as that.'

The boy laughed softly as he relaxed his hold.

'That *would* be a funny way of showing you how much I loved you, wouldn't it, Dad? Squeezing you to death!'

'Yes, I suppose it would,' replied Owen, huskily, as he tucked the bedclothes round the child's shoulders. 'But don't talk any more, dear, just hold my hand and try to sleep.'

Lying there very quietly, holding his father's hand and occasionally kissing it, the child presently fell asleep.

Then Owen got up very gently and went into the bedroom. Nora was still awake.

'Are you feeling any better, dear?' he said.

'Yes; I'm ever so much better since I've been in bed, but I can't help worrying about your clothes. I'm afraid they'll never be dry enough for you to put on the first thing in the morning. Couldn't you stay at home till after breakfast, just for once?'

'No, I mustn't do that. If I did, Hunter would probably tell me to stay away altogether. I believe he would be glad of an excuse to get rid of another full price man just now.'

'But if it's raining like this in the morning, you'll be wet through before you get there.'

'It's no good worrying about that, dear; besides, I can wear this old coat that I have on now, over the other.'

'And if you wrap your old shoes in some paper, and take them with you, you can take off your wet boots as soon as you get to the place.'

'Yes, all right,' responded Owen. 'Besides,' he added, reassuringly, 'even if I do get a little wet, we always have a fire there, you know.'

'Well, I hope the weather will be a little better than this in the morning,' said Nora. 'Isn't it a dreadful night! I keep feeling afraid that the house is going to be blown down.'

Long after Nora was asleep, Owen lay listening to the howling of the wind and the noise of the rain as it poured heavily on the roof. But it was not the storm only that kept him awake. Through the dark hours of the night his thoughts were still haunted by the words on that piece of blood-stained paper on a kitchen wall: 'This is not my crime but Society's.'

CHAPTER VI

The Exterminating Machines

'Come on, Saturday!' shouted Philpot, just after seven o'clock, one Monday morning as they were getting ready for work.

It was still dark outside, but the scullery was dimly illuminated by the flickering light of two candles which Crass had lighted and stuck on the shelf over the fire-place in order to serve out the different lots of paint and brushes to the men.

'Yes, it do seem a 'ell of a long week, don't it?' remarked Harlow as he hung his overcoat on a nail and proceeded to put on his apron and blouse. 'I've 'ad bloody near enough of it already.'

'Wish to Christ it was breakfast time,' growled the more easily satisfied Easton.

Extraordinary though it may appear, none of them took any pride in their work: they did not 'love' it. They had no conception of that lofty ideal of 'Work for work's sake,' which is so popular with the people who do nothing. On the contrary, when the workers arrived in the morning they wished it was breakfast time. When they started work after breakfast they wished it was dinner time. After dinner they wished it was one o'clock on Saturday.

So they went on, day after day, year after year, wishing their time was over and, without realising it, really wishing that they were dead.

Crass poured several lots of colour into separate pots.

'Harlow,' he said, 'you and Sawkins, when he comes, can go up and do the top bedrooms out with this colour. You'll find a couple of candles up there. It's only goin' to 'ave one coat, so see that you make it cover all right, and just look after Sawkins a bit so as 'e doesn't make a bloody mess of it. You do the doors and windows and let 'im do the cupboards and skirtings.'

'That's a bit of all right, I must say,' Harlow said, addressing the company generally, 'We've got to teach 'im so as 'e can do us out of a job presently by working under price.'

'Well, I can't 'elp it,' growled Crass, 'you know 'ow it is: 'Unter sends 'im 'ere to do paintin', and I've got to put 'im on it. There aint nothin' else for 'im to do.'

Further discussion on this subject was prevented by Sawkins' arrival, nearly a quarter of an hour late.

'Oh, you 'ave come then,' sneered Crass, 'thought praps you'd gorn for a 'oliday.'

Sawkins muttered something about oversleeping himself, and having hastily put on his apron, he went upstairs with Harlow.

'Now let's see,' Crass said, addressing Philpot, 'you and Newman 'ad better go and make a start on the second floor: this is the colour, and 'ere's a couple of candles. You'd better not both go in one room or 'Unter will growl about it. You take one of the front and let Newman take one of the back rooms. Take a bit of stoppin' with you: they're goin' to 'ave two coats, but you'd better putty up the 'oles as well as you can, this time.'

'Only two coats!' said Philpot, 'Them rooms will never look nothing with two coats—a light colour like this.'

'It's only goin' to get two, anyway,' returned Crass, testily, ''Unter said so, so you'll 'ave to do the best you can with 'em, and get 'em smeared over middlin' sudden, too.'

Crass did not think it necessary to mention that according to the copy of the specification of the work which he had in his pocket the rooms in question were supposed to have four coats.

Crass now turned to Owen.

'There's that drorin' room,' he said. 'I don't know what's goin' to be done with that yet. I don't think they've decided about it. Whatever's to be done to it will be an extra, because all that's said about it in the contract is to face it up with putty and give it one coat of white. So you and Easton 'ad better get on with it.'

Slyme was busy softening some putty by rubbing and squeezing it between his hands.

'I suppose I'd better finish the room I started on on Saturday?' he asked.

'All right,' replied Crass, 'Have you got enough colour?'

'Yes,' said Slyme.

As he passed through the kitchen on the way to his work Slyme accosted Bert, the boy, who was engaged in lighting a fire to boil the water to make the tea for breakfast at eight o'clock.

'There's a bloater I want's cooked,' he said.

'All right,' replied Bert, 'Put it over there on the dresser along of Philpot's and mine.'

Slyme took the bloater from his food basket, but as he was about to put it in the place indicated, he observed that his was rather a larger one than either of the other two. This was an important matter. After they were cooked it would not be easy to say which was which; he might possibly be given one of the smaller ones instead of his own. He took out his pocket-knife and cut off the tail of the large bloater.

''Ere it is, then,' he said to Bert, 'I've cut off the tail of mine so as you'll know which it is.'

It was now about twenty minutes past seven and having started all the other men at work, Crass washed his hands under the tap. Then he went into the kitchen and rigged up a seat by taking two of the drawers out of the dresser and placing them on the floor about six feet apart and laying a plank across. This done he sat down in front of the fire which was now burning brightly, and lit his pipe. The boy went into the scullery and began washing up the cups and jars for the men to drink out of.

Bert was a lean undersized boy about fifteen years of age and about four feet nine inches in height. He had light brown hair and hazel eyes, and his clothes were of many colours, being thickly encrusted with paint, the result of the unskilful manner in which he did his work, for he had only been at the trade about a year. Some of the men had nicknamed him 'the walking paint shop,' a title which he accepted good humouredly.

This boy was an orphan. His father had been a railway porter, who had worked very laboriously for twelve or fourteen hours every day for many years, with the usual result: namely, that he and his family lived in a condition of perpetual poverty. Bert, who was their only child and not very robust, had early shown a talent for drawing, so when his father died, a little over a year ago, his mother readily assented when the boy said that he wished to become a decorator. It was a nice light trade, and she thought that a really good painter, such as she was sure he would become, was at least always able to earn a good living. Resolving to give the boy the best chance, she decided if possible to place him at Rushton's, that being one of the leading firms in the town. At first Mr Rushton demanded ten pounds as a premium, the boy to be bound for five years, no wages the first year, two shillings a week the second, and a rise of one shilling every year for the remainder of the term. Afterwards as a special favour—a matter of charity in fact as she was a very poor woman—he agreed to accept five pounds.

This sum represented the thrifty savings of years, but the poor woman parted with it willingly in order that the boy should become a skilled workman. So Bert was apprenticed—bound for five years to Rushton and Company.

For the first few months his life had been spent in the paint-shop at the yard, a place that was something between a cellar and a stable. There, surrounded by the poisonous pigments and materials of the trade, the youthful artizan worked, generally alone, cleaning the dirty paintpots brought in by the workmen from finished 'jobs' outside, and occasionally mixing paint according to the instructions of Mr Hunter or one of the sub-foremen.

Sometimes he was sent out to carry materials to the places where the men were working—heavy loads of paint or white lead; sometimes pails of whitewash that his slender arms were too feeble to carry more than a few yards at a time.

Often his fragile, childish figure was seen staggering manfully along, bending beneath the weight of a pair of steps or a heavy plank.

He could manage a good many parcels at once, some in each hand, and some tied together with string and slung over his shoulders. Occasionally however, when they were more than he could carry, they were put into a handcart which he pushed or dragged after him to the distant jobs.

But in all this he had seen no hardship. With the unconsciousness of boyhood, he worked hard and cheerfully. As time went on, the goal of his childish ambition was reached: he was sent out to work with the men! And he carried the same spirit with him, always doing his best to oblige those with whom he was working.

He tried hard to learn, and to be a good boy, and he succeeded fairly well.

He soon became a favourite with Owen, for whom he conceived a great respect and affection, noticing that whenever there was any special work of any kind to be done it was Owen who did it. On such occasions Bert, in his artful boyish way, would scheme to be sent to assist Owen, and the latter whenever possible would ask that the boy might be allowed to work with him.

Bert's regard for Owen was equalled in intensity by his dislike of Crass, who was in the habit of jeering at the boy's aspirations. 'There'll be plenty of time for you to think about doin' fancy work arter you've learnt to do plain painting,' he would say.

This morning, when he had finished washing up the cups and mugs, Bert returned with them to the kitchen.

'Now let's see,' said Crass thoughtfully, 'you've put the tea in the pail, I s'pose.'

'Yes.'

'And now you want a job, don't yer?'

'Yes,' replied the boy.

'Well, get a bucket of water and that old brush and a swab, and go and wash the old whitewash and colouring orf the pantry ceiling and walls.'

'All right,' said Bert. When he got as far as the door leading into the scullery he looked round and said:

'I've got to git them three bloaters cooked by breakfast time.'

'Never mind about that,' said Crass, 'I'll do them.'

Bert got the pail and the brush, drew some water from the tap, got a pair of steps and a short plank, one end of which he rested on the bottom shelf of the pantry and the other on the steps, and proceeded to carry out Grass's instructions.

It was very cold and damp and miserable in the pantry, and the candle only made it seem more so. Bert shivered; he would like to have put on his jacket but that was out of the question at a job like this. He lifted the bucket of water to one of the shelves and climbing on to the plank took the brush from the water and soaked about a square yard of the ceiling; then he began to scrub it with the brush.

He was not very skilful yet, and as he scrubbed the water ran over the stock of the brush, down his hand and uplifted arm, wetting the turned-up sleeves of his shirt. When he had scrubbed it sufficiently he rinsed it off as well as he could with the brush, and then, to finish with, he thrust his hand into the pail of water and taking out the swab wrung the water out of it and wiped the part of the ceiling that he had washed, dropping the swab back into the pail. Then, shaking his numbed fingers to restore the circulation, he peeped into the kitchen where Crass was still seated by the fire, smoking, and toasting one of the bloaters at the end of a pointed stick. Bert wished he would go upstairs, or anywhere, so that he himself might go and have a warm at the fire.

''E might just as well 'ave let me do them bloaters,' he muttered to himself, regarding Crass malignantly through the crack of the door. 'This is a fine job to give anybody—a cold mornin' like this.'

He shifted the pail of water a little further along the shelf and went on with the work.

A little later, Crass, still sitting by the fire, heard footsteps approaching along the passage. He started up guiltily and thrusting the hand holding his pipe into his apron pocket, retreated hastily into the scullery. He thought it might be Hunter, who was in the habit of turning up at all sorts of unlikely times, but it was only Easton.

'I've got a bit of bacon I want the young 'un to toast for me,' he said as Crass came back.

'You can do it yourself if you like,' replied Crass, affably, looking at his watch; 'it's about ten to eight.'

Easton had been working for Rushton and Company for a fortnight, and had been wise enough to stand Crass a drink on several occasions; he was consequently in that gentleman's good books for the time being.

'How are you getting on in there?' Crass asked, alluding to the work Easton and Owen were doing in the drawing-room. 'You ain't fell out with your mate yet, I s'pose?'

'No; 'e ain't got much to say this morning; 'is cough's pretty bad. I can generally manage to get on all right with anybody, you know,' Easton added.

'Well, so can I as a rule, but I get a bit sick listening to that fool. Accordin' to 'im, everything's wrong! One day it's religion, another it's politics, and the next it's something else.'

'Yes, it is a bit thick too much of it,' agreed Easton, 'but I don't take no notice of 'im; that's the best way.'

'Of course, we know that things is a bit bad just now,' Crass went on, 'but if the likes of 'im could 'ave their own way, they'd make 'em a bloody sight worse.'

'That's just what I say,' replied Easton.

'I've got a pill ready for 'im, though, next time 'e starts yappin',' Crass continued, as he drew a small piece of printed paper from his waistcoat pocket. 'Just read that; it's out of the "Obscurer."'

Easton took the newspaper cutting and read it: 'Very good,' he remarked as he handed it back.

'Yes, I think that'll about shut 'im up. Did yer notice the other day when we was talking about poverty, and men bein' cut of work, 'ow 'e dodged out of answerin' wot I said about machinery bein' the cause of it? 'E never answered me, started talkin' about something else!'

'Yes, I remember 'e never answered it,' said Easton, who had really no recollection of the incident at all.

'I mean to tackle 'im about it at breakfast time. I don't see why 'e should be allowed to get out of it like that. There was a bloke down at the "Cricketers" the other night talkin' about the same thing—a chap as takes a interest in politics and the like—and 'e said the very same as me. Why, the number of men what's been throwed out of work by all this 'ere newfangled machinery is something chronic!'

'Of course,' agreed Easton. 'Everyone knows it.'

'You ought to give us a look in at the "Cricketers" some night. There's a decent lot of chaps comes there.'

'Yes, I think I will.'

'What 'ouse do you usually use?' asked Crass after a pause.

Easton laughed. 'Well, to tell you the truth I've not used anywheres lately. Been 'avin too many 'ollerdays.'

'That do make a bit of difference, don't it?' said Crass. 'But you'll be all right 'ere till this job's done. Just watch yerself a bit, and don't get comin' late in the mornins. Ole Nimrod's dead nuts on that.'

'I'll see to that all right," replied Easton; 'I don't believe in losing time when there *is* work to do. It's bad enough when you can't get it.'

'You know,' Crass went on, confidentially, 'between me an' you an' the gatepost, as the sayin' is, I don't think Mr bloody Owen will be 'ere much longer. Nimrod 'ates the sight of 'im!'

Easton had it in his mind to say that Nimrod seemed to hate the sight of all of them, but he made no remark and Crass continued:

''E's 'eard all about the way Owen goes on about politics and religion, an' one thing an' another, an' about the firm scampin' the work. You know that sort of talk don't do, does it?'

'Of course it don't.'

''Unter would 'ave got rid of 'im long ago, but it wasn't 'im as took 'im on in the first place. It was Rushton 'imself as giv 'im a start. It seems Owen took a lot of samples of 'is work an' showed 'em to the Bloke.'

'Is them the things wot's 'angin' up in the shop winder?'

'Yes,' said Crass, contemptuously; 'but 'e's no good on plain work. Of course e' does a bit of grainin' an' writin'—after a fashion—when there's any to do, and that ain't often; but on plain work, why Sawkins is as good as 'im for most of it any day!'

'Yes, I suppose 'e is,' replied Easton, feeling rather ashamed of himself for the part he was taking in this conversation.

Although he had for the moment forgotten the existence of Bert, Crass had instinctively lowered his voice; but the boy—who had left off working to warm his hands by putting them into his trousers pockets—managed, by listening attentively, to hear every word.

'You know there's plenty of people wouldn't give the firm no more work if they knowed about it,' Crass continued; 'just fancy sendin' a swine like that to work in a lady's or gentleman's 'ouse—a bloody Atheist!'

'Yes, it is a bit orf, when you look at it like that.'

'I know my missis—for one—wouldn't 'ave a feller like that in our place. We 'ad a lodger once and she found out that 'e was a freethinker or something and she cleared 'im out bloody quick, I can tell yer!'

'Oh, by the way,' said Easton, glad of an opportunity to change the subject, 'you don't happen to know of anyone as wants a room, do you? We've got one more than we want, so the wife thought that we might as well let it.'

Crass thought for a moment. 'Can't say as I do,' he answered, doubtfully, 'Slyme was talking last week about leaving the place 'e's lodging at, but I don't know whether 'e's got another place to go to. You might ask him. I don't know of anyone else.'

'I'll speak to 'im,' replied Easton. 'What's the time? It must be nearly on it.'

'So it is: just on eight,' exclaimed Crass, and drawing his whistle he blew a shrill blast upon it to apprise the others of the fact.

'Has anyone seen old Jack Linden since 'e got the push?' enquired Harlow, during breakfast.

'I seen 'im Saturday,' said Slyme.

'Is 'e doin' anything?'

'I don't know: I didn't 'ave time to speak to 'im.'

'No, 'e aint got nothing,' remarked Philpot. 'I seen 'im Saturday night, an' 'e told me 'e's been walkin' about ever since.'

Philpot did not add that he had 'lent' Linden a shilling, which he never expected to see again.

''E won't be able to get a job again in a 'urry,' remarked Easton, ''e's too old.'

'You know, after all, you can't blame Misery for sackin' 'im,' said Crass after a pause. ''E was too slow for a funeral.'

'I wonder how much *you'll* be able to do when you're as old as he is?' said Owen.

'Praps I won't want to do nothing,' replied Crass, with a feeble laugh. 'I'm goin' to live on me means.'

'I should say the best thing old Jack could do would be to go in the Union,' said Harlow.

'Yes: I reckon that's what'll be the end of it,' said Easton, in a matter-of-fact tone.

'It's a grand finish, isn't it?' observed Owen. 'After working hard all one's life to be treated like a criminal at the end.'

'I don't know what you call bein' treated like criminals,' exclaimed Crass; 'I reckon they 'as a bloody fine time of it, an' we've got to find the money.'

'Oh, for Gord's sake don't start no more arguments,' cried Harlow, addressing Owen. 'We 'ad enough of that last week. You can't expect a boss to employ a man when 'e's too old to work.'

'Of course not,' said Crass.

Old Joe Philpot said—nothing.

'I don't see no sense in always grumblin',' Crass proceeded; 'these things can't be altered. You can't expect there can be plenty of work for everyone with all this 'ere labour savin' machinery what's been invented.

'Of course,' said Harlow, 'the people what used to be employed on the work what's now done by machinery, has to find something else to do. Some of 'em goes to our trade, for instance. The result is there's too many at it, and there aint enough work to keep 'em all goin'.'

'Yes,' cried Crass, eagerly, 'that's just what I say. Machinery is the real cause of all the poverty. That's what I said the other day.'

'Machinery is undoubtedly the cause of unemployment,' replied Owen, 'but it's not the cause of poverty: that's another matter altogether.'

The others laughed derisively.

'Well, it seems to me to amount to the same thing,' said Harlow, and nearly everyone agreed.

'It doesn't seem to me to amount to the same thing,' Owen replied. 'In my opinion we are all in a state of poverty even when we have employment. The condition we are reduced to when we're out of work is more properly described as destitution.'

'Poverty,' continued Owen, after a short silence, 'consists in a shortage of the necessaries of life. When those things are so scarce or so dear that people are unable to obtain sufficient of them to satisfy all their needs, they are in a condition of poverty. If you think that the machinery which makes it possible to produce all the necessaries of life in abundance is the cause of the shortage, it seems to me that there must be something the matter with your minds.'

'Oh, of course we're all bloody fools except you,' snarled Crass. 'When they was servin' out the sense they give you such a 'ell of a lot there wasn't none left for nobody else.'

'If there wasn't something wrong with your minds,' continued Owen, 'you would be able to see that we might have "Plenty of Work" and yet be in a state of destitution. The miserable wretches who toil sixteen or eighteen hours a day—father, mother, and even the little children—making match-boxes, or shirts or blouses, have "Plenty of Work," but I for one don't envy them. Perhaps you think that if there was no machinery and we all had to work thirteen or fourteen hours a day in order to obtain a bare living we should not be in a condition of poverty? Talk about there being something the matter with your minds—if there were not you wouldn't talk one day about Tariff Reform as a remedy for unemployment and then the next day admit that machinery is the cause of it! Tariff Reform won't do away with machinery, will it?'

'Tariff Reform is the remedy for bad trade,' returned Crass.

'In that case Tariff Reform is the remedy for a disease that does not exist. If you would only take the trouble to investigate for yourself you would find out that trade was never so good as it is at present: the output—the quantity of commodities of every kind—produced in and exported from this country is greater than it has ever been before. The fortunes amassed in business are larger than ever. But at the same time, owing, as you have just admitted, to the continued introduction and extended use of wages-saving machinery, the number of human beings employed is steadily decreasing. I have here,' continued Owen, taking out his pocket book, 'some figures which I copied from the "Daily Mail Year Book" for 1907, page 33:

"It is a very noticeable fact that although the number of factories and their value have vastly increased in the United Kingdom, there is an absolute decrease in the number of men and women employed in those factories between 1895 and 1901. This is doubtless due to the displacement of hand labour by machinery."

'Will Tariff Reform deal with that? Are the good, kind capitalists going to abandon the use of wages-saving machinery if we tax all foreign made goods? Does what you call "Free Trade" help us here, or do you think that abolishing the House of Lords, or disestablishing the Church, will enable the workers who are displaced to obtain employment? Since it *is* true—as you admit—that machinery is the principal cause of unemployment, what are you going to do about it? What's your remedy?'

No one answered, because none of them knew of any remedy; and Crass began to feel sorry that he had re-introduced the subject at all.

'In the near future,' continued Owen, 'it is probable that horses will be almost entirely superseded by motor cars and electric trams. As the services of horses will no longer be required, all but a few will die out; they will no longer be bred to the same extent as formerly. We can't blame the horses for allowing themselves to be exterminated. They have not sufficient intelligence to understand what's being done. Therefore they will submit tamely to the extinction of the greater number of their kind.

'As we have seen, a great deal of the work which was formerly done by human beings is now being done by machinery. This machinery belongs to a few people; it is being worked for the benefit of those few, just the same as were the human beings it displaced.

'These few have no longer any need of the services of so many human workers, so they propose to exterminate them! The unnecessary human beings are to be allowed to starve to death! And they are also to be taught that it is wrong to marry and breed children because the Sacred Few do not require so many people to work for them as before!'

'Yes, and you'll never be able to prevent it, mate!' shouted Crass.

'Why can't we?'

'Because it can't be done!' cried Crass, fiercely. 'It's impossible!'

'You're always sayin' that everything's all wrong,' complained Harlow, 'but why the 'ell don't you tell us 'ow they're goin' to be put right?'

'It doesn't seem to me as if any of you really wish to know, I believe that even if it were proved that it could be done, most of you would be sorry and would do all you could to prevent it.'

''E don't know 'isself,' sneered Crass. 'Accordin' to 'im, Tariff Reform ain't no bloody good, Free Trade ain't no bloody good, and everybody else is wrong! But when you arst 'im what ought to be done, 'e's flummuxed!'

Crass did not feel very satisfied with the result of this machinery argument, but he consoled himself with the reflection that he would be able to flatten out his opponent on another subject. The cutting from the 'Obscurer' which he had in his pocket would take a bit of answering! When you have a thing in print—in black and white—why there it is, and you can't get away from it! If it wasn't all right a paper like that would never have printed it. However, as it was now nearly half past eight he resolved to defer this triumph till another occasion. It was too good a thing to be disposed of in a hurry.

CHAPTER VII

The Cap on the Stairs

After breakfast, when they were working together in the drawing-room, Easton, desiring to do Owen a good turn, thought he would put him on his guard, and repeated to him in a whisper the substance of the conversation he had held with Crass concerning him.

'Of course, you needn't mention that I told you, Frank,' he said, 'but I thought I ought to let you know. You can take it from me, Crass ain't no friend of yours.'

'I've known that for a long time, mate,' replied Owen. 'Thanks for telling me, all the same.'

'The bloody rotter's no friend of mine either, or anyone else's, for that matter,' Easton continued, 'but of course it doesn't do to fall out with 'im, because you never know what he'd go and say to old 'Unter.'

'Of course we all know what's the matter with 'im as far as *you're* concerned,' Easton went on; 'he don't like 'avin' anyone on the firm wot knows more about the work than 'e does 'imself—thinks 'e might get worked out of 'is job.'

Owen laughed bitterly.

'He needn't be afraid of *me* on *that* account. I wouldn't have his job if it were offered to me.'

'But '*e* don't think so,' replied Easton, 'and that's why 'e's got 'is knife into you.'

'I believe that what he said about Hunter is true enough,' said Owen. 'Every time he comes here he tries to goad me into doing or saying something that would give him an excuse to tell me to clear out. I might have done it before now if I had not guessed what he was after, and been on my guard.'

Meantime, Crass, in the kitchen, had resumed his seat by the fire with the purpose of finishing his pipe of tobacco. Presently he took out his pocket book and began to write in it with a piece of blacklead pencil, and, having torn out the leaf, went into the pantry, where Bert was still struggling with the old whitewash.

'Ain't yer nearly finished? I don't want yer to stop in 'ere all day, yer know.'

'I ain't got much more to do now,' said the boy; 'just this bit under the bottom shelf and then I'm done.'

'Yes, and a bloody fine mess you've made, what I can see of it!' growled Crass. 'Look at all this water on the floor!'

Bert looked guiltily at the floor and turned very red.

'I'll clean it all up,' he stammered; 'as soon as I've got this bit of wall done, I'll wipe all the mess up with a swab.'

Crass now took a pot of paint and some brushes and having put some more fuel on the fire, began in a leisurely way to paint some of the woodwork in the kitchen.

Presently Bert came in.

'I've finished out there,' he said.

'About time, too. You'll 'ave to look a bit livelier than you do, you know, or me and you will fall out.'

Bert did not answer.

'Now I've got another job for yer. You're fond of drorin, ain't yer?' continued Crass in a jeering tone.

'Yes, a little,' replied the boy, shamefacedly.

'Well,' said Crass, giving him the leaf he had torn out of the pocketbook, 'you can go to the yard and git them things and put 'em on a truck and dror it up 'ere, and git back as soon as you can. Just look at the paper and see if you understand it before you go. I don't want you to make no mistakes.'

Bert took the paper and with some difficulty read as follows:—

1 pare steppes 8 foot
½ galoon Plaster off perish
1 pale off witewash
12 lbs wite led
½ galoon Linsede Hoil
Do. Do. turps.

'I can make it out all right.'

'You'd better bring the big truck,' said Crass, 'because I want you to take the venetian blinds with you on it when you take it back to-night. They've got to be painted at the shop.'

'All right.'

When the boy had departed Crass took a stroll through the house to see how the others were getting on. Then he returned to the kitchen and proceeded with his work.

Crass was about thirty-eight years of age, rather above middle height and rather stout. He had a considerable quantity of curly black hair and wore a short beard of the same colour. His head was rather large, but low, and flat on the top. When among his cronies he was in the habit of referring to his obesity as the result of good nature and a contented mind. Behind his back other people attributed it to beer, some even going so far as to nickname him the 'tank.'

There was no work of a noisy kind being done this morning, both the carpenters and the bricklayers having gone away, temporarily, to another 'job.' At the same time there was not absolute silence; occasionally Crass could hear the voices of the other workmen as they spoke to each other, sometimes shouting from one room to another. Now and then Harlow's voice rang through the house as he sang snatches of music hall songs or a verse of a Moody and Sankey hymn, and occasionally some of the others joined in the chorus or interrupted the singer with squeals and catcalls. Once or twice Crass was on the point of telling them to make less row: there would be a fine to do if Nimrod came and heard them. Just as he had made up his mind to tell them to stop the noise, it ceased of itself and he heard loud whispers.

'Look out! Someone's comin'.'

The house became very quiet. Crass put out his pipe and opened the window and the back door to get rid of the smell of the tobacco smoke. Then he shifted the pair of steps noisily, and proceeded to work more quickly than before. Most likely it was old Misery.

He worked on for some time in silence, but no one came to the kitchen; whoever it was must have gone upstairs. Crass listened attentively. Who could it be? He would have liked to go to see but at the same time, if it were Nimrod, Crass wished to be discovered at work. He therefore waited a little longer and presently he heard the sound of voices upstairs but was unable to recognise them. He was just about to go out into the passage to listen, when the intruder began to descend the stairs. Crass at once resumed his work. The footsteps came along the passage leading to the kitchen, slow, heavy, ponderous footsteps, but yet the sound was not such as would be made by a man heavily shod. It was not Misery, evidently.

As the footsteps entered the kitchen, Crass looked round and beheld Mr Sweater, the owner of 'The Cave,' a very tall, obese figure, with a large, coarse featured, clean-shaven face, and a great double chin, the complexion being of the colour and appearance of the fat of uncooked bacon. His nose was large and fleshy, and his weak-looking, pale blue eyes had slightly inflamed lids and were almost destitute of eyelashes. His large fat feet were cased in soft calf-skin boots, with drab-coloured spats. His overcoat, heavily trimmed with sealskin, reached just below the knees; and although the trousers were very wide they were filled by the fat legs within, the shape of the calves being distinctly perceptible. He was so large that his figure completely filled up the doorway, and as he came in he stooped slightly to avoid damaging the glistening silk hat on his head. One gloved hand was thrust into the pocket of the overcoat and in the other he carried a small gladstone bag.

When Crass beheld this being, he touched his cap respectfully.

'Good morning, sir.'

'Good morning. They told me upstairs that I should find the foreman here. Are you the foreman?'

'Yes, sir.'

'I see you're getting on with the work here.'

'Ho yes, sir, we're beginning to make a bit hov a show, now, sir,' replied Crass, speaking as if he had a hot potato in his mouth.

'Mr Rushton isn't here yet, I suppose?'

'No sir; 'e don't horfun come hon the job hin the mornin' sir; 'e generally comes hafternoons, sir, but Mr 'Unter's halmost sure to be 'ere presently, sir.'

'It's Mr Rushton I want to see. I arranged to meet him here at ten o'clock, but'—looking at his watch—'I'm rather before my time.'

'He'll be here presently, I suppose,' added Mr Sweater, 'I'll just take a look round till he comes.'

'Yes, sir,' responded Crass, walking behind him obsequiously as he went out of the room.

Hoping that the gentleman might give him a shilling, Crass followed him into the front hall and began explaining what progress had so far been made with the work, but as Mr Sweater answered only by monosyllables and grunts, Crass presently concluded that his conversation was not appreciated and returned to the kitchen.

Meantime, upstairs, Philpot had gone into Newman's room and was discussing with him the possibility of extracting from Mr Sweater the price of a little light refreshment.

'I think,' he remarked, 'that we oughter see-ise this 'ere tuneropperty to touch 'im for an allowance.'

'We won't git nothin' out of '*im*, mate,' returned Newman. ''E's a red 'ot teetotaller.'

'That don't matter. 'Ow's 'e to know that we buys beer with it? We might 'ave tea, or ginger ale, or lime juice and glycerine for all 'e knows!'

Mr Sweater now began ponderously re-ascending the stairs and presently came into the room where Philpot was at work. The latter greeted him with respectful cordiality.

'Good morning, sir.'

'Good morning. You've begun painting up here then.'

'Yes, sir, we've made a start on it,' replied Philpot, affably.

'Is this door wet?'—asked Sweater, glancing apprehensively at the sleeve of his coat.

'Yes, sir,' answered Philpot, and added, as he looked meaningly at the great man, 'the *paint* is wet, sir, but the *painters* is dry.'

'Confound it!' exclaimed Sweater, ignoring, or not hearing the latter part of Philpot's reply. 'I've got some of the beastly stuff on my coat sleeve.'

'Oh, that's nothing, sir,' cried Philpot, secretly delighted; 'I'll get that orf for yer in no time. You wait just 'arf a mo!'

He had a piece of clean rag in his tool bag, and moistening it slightly with turpentine he carefully removed the paint from Sweater's sleeve.

'It's all orf now, sir,' he remarked as he rubbed the place with a dry part of the rag;' the smell of the turps will go away in about a hour's time.'

'Thanks,' said Sweater.

Philpot looked at him wistfully, but Sweater evidently did not understand, and began looking about the room.

'I see they've put a new piece of skirting here,' he observed.

'Yes, sir,' said Newman, who came into the room just then to get the turps, 'the old piece was all to bits with dry rot.'

'I feel as if I 'ad a touch of the dry rot meself, don't you?' said Philpot to Newman, who smiled feebly and cast a side-long glance at Sweater, who did not appear to notice the significance of the remark, but walked out of the room and began climbing up to the next floor, where Harlow and Sawkins were working.

'Well, there's a bleeder for yer!' said Philpot, with indignation. 'After all the trouble I took to clean 'is coat! Not a bloody stiver! Well, it takes the cake, don't it?'

'I told you 'ow it would be, didn't I?' replied Newman.

'P'raps I didn't make it plain enough,' said Philpot thoughtfully. 'We must try to get some of our own back somehow, you know.'

Going out on the landing he called softly upstairs:

'I say, Harlow.'

'Hallo,' said that individual, looking over the banisters.

''Ow are yer getting on up there?'

'Oh, all right, you know.'

'Pretty dry job, ain't it?' Philpot continued, raising his voice a little and winking at Harlow.

'Yes, it is, rather,' replied Harlow with a grin.

'I think this would be a very good time to take up the collection, don't you?'

'Yes; it wouldn't be a bad idear.'

'Well, I'll put me cap on the stairs,' said Philpot, suiting the action to the word; 'you never knows yer luck. Things is gettin a bit serious on this floor, you know; my mate's fainted away once already!'

Philpot now went back to his room to await developments; but as Sweater made no sign, he returned to the landing and again hailed Harlow.

'I always reckon a man can work all the better after 'e's 'ad a drink; you can seem to get over more of it, like.'

'Oh, that's true enough,' responded Harlow; 'I've often noticed it meself.'

Sweater came out of the front bedroom and passed into one of the back rooms without any notice of either of the men.

'I'm afraid it's a frost, mate,' Harlow whispered, and Philpot, shaking his head sadly, returned to work; but in a little while he came out again and once more accosted Harlow.

'I knowed a case once,' he said in a melancholy tone, 'where a chap died—of thirst—on a job just like this; and at the inquest the doctor said as 'arf a pint would 'a saved 'im!'

'It must 'ave been a norrible death,' remarked Harlow.

''Orrible ain't the word for it, mate,' replied Philpot mournfully; 'it was something chronic!'

After this final heartrending appeal to Sweater's humanity they returned to work, satisfied that, whatever the result of their efforts, they had done their best, and the issue now rested with him.

But it was all in vain. Sweater either did not or would not understand, and when he came downstairs he took no notice whatever of the cap which Philpot had placed so conspicuously in the centre of the landing floor, and reached the hall at the same moment as Rushton entered by the front door. They greeted each other in a friendly way, and after a few remarks concerning the work, went into the drawing-room where Owen and Easton were busy.

'What about this room?' remarked Rushton. 'Have you made up your mind what you're going to have done to it?'

'Yes,' replied Sweater, 'but I'll tell you about that afterwards. What I'm anxious about is the drains. Have you brought the plans?'

'Yes.'

'What's it going to cost?'

'Just wait a minute,' said Rushton, with a slight gesture calling Sweater's attention to the presence of the two workmen. Sweater understood.

'You might leave that for a few minutes, will you?' Rushton continued, addressing Owen and Easton. 'Go and get on with something helse for a little while.'

When they were alone Rushton closed the door and remarked: 'It's always as well not to let these 'ere fellows know more than is necessary.'

Sweater agreed.

'Now this 'ere drain work is really two separate jobs,' said Rushton. 'First, the drains of the house: that is, the part of the work that's actually on your ground. When that's done, there will 'ave to be a pipe carried right along under this private road to the main road to connect the drains of the house with the town main. You follow me?'

'Perfectly. What's it going to cost for the lot?'

'For the drains of the house £25, and for the connecting pipe £30—£55 for the lot.'

''Um: that's the lowest you can do it for, eh?'

'That's the lowest. I've figured it out most carefully, the time and material, and that's practically all I'm charging you.'

The truth of this matter was that Rushton had had nothing whatever to do with estimating the cost of this work; he had not the necessary knowledge. Hunter had drawn the plans, calculated the cost and prepared the estimate.

'I've been thinking over this business lately,' said Sweater, looking at Rushton with a cunning leer. 'I don't see why I should have to pay for the connecting pipe. The Corporation ought to pay for that. What do you say?'

Rushton laughed. 'I don't see why not,' he replied.

'I think we could arrange it all right, don't you?' Sweater went on. 'Anyhow, the work will have to be done, so you'd better let 'em get on with it. £55 covers both jobs, you say?'

'Yes.'

'Oh, all right, you get on with it and we'll see what can be done with the Corporation later on.'

'I don't suppose we'll find 'em very difficult to deal with,' said Rushton with a grin, and Sweater smiled agreement.

As they were passing through the hall they met Hunter, who had just arrived. He was rather surprised to see them, as he knew nothing of their appointment. He wished them 'Good morning' in an awkward, hesitating undertone as if he were doubtful how his greeting would be received. Sweater nodded slightly, but Rushton ignored him altogether, and Nimrod passed on looking and feeling like a disreputable cur that had just been kicked.

As Sweater and Rushton walked together about the house, Hunter hovered about them at a respectful distance, hoping that presently some notice might be taken of him. His dismal countenance became even longer than usual when he observed that they were about to leave the house without appearing to know that he was there. However, just as they were going out, Rushton paused on the threshold and called him:

'Mr Hunter!'

'Yes, sir.'

Nimrod ran to him like a dog taken notice of by his master. If he had possessed a tail it is probable that he would have wagged it. Rushton gave him the plans with an intimation that the work was to be proceeded with.

For some time after they were gone Hunter crawled silently about the house, in and out of the rooms, up and down the corridors and the staircases. After a while he went into the room where Newman was and stood quietly watching him for about ten minutes as he worked. The man was painting the skirting, and just then he came to a part that was split in several places, so he took his knife and began to fill the cracks with putty. He was so nervous under Hunter's scrutiny that his hand trembled to such an extent that it took him about twice as long as it should have done, and Hunter told him so with brutal directness.

'Never mind about puttying up such little cracks as them!' he shouted. 'Fill 'em up with the paint. We can't afford to pay you for messing about like that!'

Newman made no reply.

Misery found no excuse for bullying anyone else, because they were all tearing into it for all they were worth. He sneaked into the drawing-room and after standing with a malignant expression, silently watching Owen and Easton, he came out again without having uttered a word.

Although he frequently acted in this manner, yet somehow to-day the circumstance worried Owen considerably. He wondered uneasily what it meant, and began to feel vaguely apprehensive. Hunter's silence seemed more menacing than his speech.

CHAPTER VIII

THE LONG HILL

BERT arrived at the shop, and with as little delay as possible loaded up the handcart with the things he had been sent for and started on the return journey. He got on all right in the town, because the roads were level and smooth, being paved with wood blocks. If it had only been like that all the way it would have been easy enough, although he was a very small boy for such a large heavily loaded truck. While the wood road lasted the principal trouble was in keeping a lookout ahead, the hand-cart being too high for him to see over, especially with the pair of steps on the top of the other things. However, by taking great care he managed to get through the town safely, although he narrowly escaped colliding with several vehicles, including two or three motor cars and an electric tram, besides nearly knocking over an old woman who was carrying a large bundle of washing. From time to time he saw other small boys of his acquaintance, some of them carrying heavy loads of groceries in baskets, and others with wooden trays full of joints of meat.

Unfortunately the wood paving ceased at the very place where the ground began to rise. Bert now found himself at the beginning of a long stretch of macadamised road which rose slightly but persistently all the way. Having pushed a cart up this road many times before the boy knew the best method of tackling it, and as experience had taught him that a frontal attack on this hill was liable to failure, he now followed his usual plan of making diagonal movements, crossing the road repeatedly from right to left and left to right, after the fashion of a sailing ship tacking against the wind, and halting about every twenty yards to rest and take breath. The various tacks were regulated, not so much by his powers of endurance as by the various wayside objects, particularly lamp-posts. During each rest he would look ahead and select a certain lamp-post or street corner as the next stopping place, and when he started again the goal ahead stimulated his strenuous and desperate efforts.

Very often the object he selected was too far away, for he usually overestimated his strength, and whenever he was forced to give in he ran the truck against the kerb, and stood there panting for breath and feeling profoundly disappointed at his failure.

During one of these rests, it flashed upon him that he was being a very long time; he would have to buck up or he would get into a row; he was not even half way up the road yet!

Selecting a distant lamp-post, he determined to reach it before resting again.

The cart had a single shaft with a cross piece at the end, forming the handle. He gripped this fiercely with both hands and placing his chest against it, with a mighty effort he pushed it along before him.

It seemed to get heavier and heavier every foot of the way. His whole body, but especially the thighs and the calves of his legs, ached terribly, but still he strained and struggled and said to himself that he would not give in until he reached the lamp-post.

Finding that the handle hurt his chest he lowered it to his waist, but as that was even more painful he raised it again to his chest, and struggled savagely on, panting for breath and with his heart beating wildly.

The cart became heavier and heavier. After a while it seemed to the boy as if there were someone at the front of it trying to push him back down the hill. This was such a funny idea that for a moment he felt inclined to laugh, but the inclination went almost as soon as it came and was replaced by the dread that he would not be able to hold out long enough to reach the lamp-post after all. Clenching his teeth he made a tremendous effort and staggered forward two or three more steps and then—the cart stopped. He struggled with it despairingly for a few seconds but all the strength had suddenly gone out of him: his legs felt so weak that he nearly collapsed to the ground, and the cart began to move backwards down the hill. He was just able to stick to it and guide it so that it ran into and rested against the kerb, and then he stood holding it in a half dazed way, pale, trembling, and saturated with sweat, while his legs shook so much that he felt that unless he could sit down for a little, he would *fall*down.

He lowered the handle very carefully so as not to spill the whitewash out of the pail which was hanging from a hook underneath the cart, then sitting down on the kerbstone, he leaned wearily against the wheel.

A little way down the road was a church with a clock in the tower. It was five minutes to ten by this clock. Bert said to himself that when it was ten he would make another start.

Whilst he was resting he thought of many things. Just behind that church was a field with several ponds in it where he used to go with other boys to catch effets. If it were not for the cart he would go across now, to see whether there were any still there. He remembered that he had been very eager to leave school and go to work, but they used to be fine old times after all.

Then he thought of the day when his mother took him to Mr Rushton's office to 'bind' him. He remembered that day very vividly; it was almost a year ago. How nervous he had been! His hand had trembled so that he was scarcely able to hold the pen. And even when it was all over, they had both felt miserable, somehow. His mother had been very nervous in the office also, and when they got home she cried a lot and held him close to her and kissed him and called him her poor little fatherless boy, and said she hoped he would be good and try to learn; and then he cried as well, and promised her that he would do his best. He reflected with pride that he was keeping his promise about being a good boy and trying to learn; in fact he knew a great deal about the trade already—he could paint back doors and railings as well as anybody! Owen had taught him lots of things and had promised to do some patterns of graining for him so that he might practise copying them at home in the evenings. Owen was a fine chap. Bert resolved that he would tell him what Crass had been saying to Easton. Just fancy, the cheek of a rotter like Crass, trying to get Owen the sack! It would be more like it if Crass was to be sacked himself, so that Owen could be the foreman.

One minute to ten.

With a heavy heart Bert watched the clock. His legs were still aching very badly. He could not see the hands of the clock moving, but they were creeping on all the same. Now, the minute hand was over the edge of the number, and he began to deliberate whether he might not rest for another five minutes, but he had been such a long time already on his errand that he dismissed the thought. The minute hand was now upright, and it was time to go on.

Just as he was about to get up a harsh voice behind him said:

'How much longer are you going to sit there?'

Bert started up guiltily and found himself confronted by Mr Rushton, who was regarding him with an angry frown, whilst close by towered the colossal figure of the obese Sweater, the expression on his greasy countenance betokening the pain he experienced at beholding such an appalling example of juvenile indolence.

'What do yer mean by sich conduct?' demanded Rushton, indignantly. 'The idea of sitting there like that, when most likely the men are waiting for them things!'

Crimson with shame and confusion, the boy made no reply.

'You've been there a long time,' continued Rushton, 'I've been watchin' you all the time I've been comin' down the road.'

Bert tried to speak to explain why he had been resting, but his mouth and his tongue had become quite parched from terror and he was unable to articulate a single word.

'You know, that's not the way to get on in life, my boy,' observed Sweater, lifting his forefinger and shaking his fat head reproachfully.

'Get along with you at once!' Rushton said roughly, 'I'm surprised at yer! The idear! Sitting down in my time!'

This was quite true. Rushton was not merely angry, but astonished at the audacity of the boy. That anyone in his employment should dare to have the impertinence to sit down in his time was incredible.

The boy lifted the handle of the cart and once more began to push it up the hill. It seemed heavier now than ever, but he managed to get on somehow. He kept glancing back after Rushton and Sweater, who presently turned a corner and were lost to view; then he ran the cart to the kerb again to have a breath. He couldn't have kept up much further without a spell even if they had still been watching him, but he didn't rest for more than about half a minute this time, because he was afraid they might be peeping round the corner.

After this he gave up the lamp-post system and halted for a minute or so at regular short intervals. In this way he at length reached the top of the hill, and with a sigh of relief congratulated himself that the journey was practically over.

Just before he arrived at the gate of the house he saw Hunter sneak out and mount his bicycle and ride away. Bert wheeled his cart up to the front door and began carrying in the things. Whilst thus engaged he noticed Philpot peeping cautiously over the banisters of the staircase, and called out to him:

'Give us a hand with this bucket of whitewash, will yer, Joe?'

'Certainly, me son, with the greatest of hagony,' replied Philpot as he hurried down the stairs.

As they were carrying it in Philpot winked at Bert and whispered:

'Did yer see Pontius Pilate anywheres outside?'

''E went away on 'is bike just as I come in the gate.'

'Did 'e! Thank Gord for that! I don't wish 'im no 'arm,' said Philpot fervently, 'but I 'opes 'e gets runned over with a motor.'

In this wish Bert entirely concurred, and similar charitable sentiments were expressed by all the others as soon as they heard that Misery was gone.

Just before four o'clock that afternoon Bert began to load up the truck with the Venetian blinds, which had been taken down some days previously.

'I wonder who'll have the job of paintin' 'em?' remarked Philpot to Newman.

'Praps they'll take a couple of us away from 'ere.'

'I shouldn't think so. We're short 'anded 'ere already. Most likely they'll put on a couple of fresh 'ands. There's a 'ell of a lot of work in all them blinds, you know! I reckon they'll 'ave to 'ave three or four coats, the state they're in.'

'Yes, no doubt that's what will be done,' replied Newman, and added with a mirthless laugh:

'I don't suppose they'll have much difficulty in getting a couple of chaps.'

'No, you're right, mate. There's plenty of 'em walkin' about as a week's work would be a gordsend to.'

'Come to think of it,' continued Newman, after a pause, 'I believe the firm used to give all their blind work to old Latham, the Venetian blind maker. Prap's they'll give 'im this lot to do.'

'Very likely,' replied Philpot; 'I should think 'e can do 'em cheaper even than us chaps, and that's all the firm cares about.'

How far their conjectures were fulfilled will appear later.

Shortly after it became so dark that it was necessary to light the candles, and Philpot remarked that although he hated working under such conditions, yet he was always glad when lighting up time came because then knocking off time was not very far behind.

About five minutes to five, just as they were all putting their things away for the night, Nimrod suddenly appeared in the house. He had come hoping to find some of them ready dressed to go home before the proper time. Having failed in this laudable enterprise he stood silently by himself for some seconds in the drawing-room. This was a spacious and lofty apartment with a large semi-circular bay window. Round the ceiling was a deep cornice. In the semi-darkness the room appeared to be of even greater proportions than it really was. After standing thinking in this room for a little while Hunter turned and strode out to the kitchen, where the men were preparing to go home. Owen was taking off his blouse and apron as the other entered. Hunter addressed him with a malevolent snarl:

'You can call at the office to-night as you go home.'

Owen's heart seemed to stop beating. All the petty annoyances he had endured from Hunter rushed into his memory, together with what Easton had told him that morning. He stood, still and speechless, holding his apron in his hand and staring at the manager.

'What for?' he ejaculated at length. 'What's the matter?'

'You'll find out what you're wanted for when you get there,' returned Hunter as he went out of the room and away from the house.

When he was gone a dead silence prevailed. The hands ceased their preparations for departure and looked at each other and at Owen in astonishment. To stand a man off like that—when the job was not half finished—and for no apparent reason; and of a Monday, too. It was unheard of. There was a general chorus of indignation. Harlow and Philpot especially were very wroth.

'If it comes to that,' Harlow shouted, 'they've got no bloody right to do it! We're entitled to an hour's notice.'

'Of course we are!' cried Philpot, his goggle eyes rolling wildly with wrath. 'And I should 'ave it, too, if it was me. You take my tip, Frank: *Charge up to six o'clock* on yer time sheet and get some of your own back.'

Everyone joined in the outburst of indignant protest. Everyone, that is, except Crass and Slyme. But then they were not exactly in the kitchen. They were out in the scullery putting their things away and so it happened that they said nothing, although they exchanged significant looks.

Owen had by this time recovered his self-possession. He collected all his tools and put them with his apron and blouse into his tool bag with the purpose of taking them with him that night, but on reflection he resolved not to do so. After all, it was not absolutely certain that he was going to be 'stood off'; possibly they were going to send him to some other job.

The men kept together—some walking on the pavement and some in the road—until they got down town, and then separated. Crass, Sawkins, Bundy and Philpot adjourned to the 'Cricketers' for a drink, Newman went on by himself, Slyme accompanied Easton, to see the bedroom to let, and Owen went in the direction of Rushton's office.

CHAPTER IX

Hands and Brains

When Easton, accompanied by Slyme, arrived home that evening, Ruth had just been putting the child to sleep, and she stood up as they came in, hastily fastening the bodice of her dress.

'I've brought a gentleman to see you,' said Easton.

Although she knew that he was looking out for someone for the room, Ruth had not expected him to bring anyone home in this sudden manner, and she could not help wishing that he had told her beforehand of his intention. She had been very busy all day and was conscious that she was rather untidy. The coils of her long brown hair had become loosened with her exertions, and she blushed in an embarrassed way as the young man stared at her.

Easton introduced Slyme by name and they shook hands; and then at Ruth's suggestion Easton took a light to show him the room, while Ruth hurriedly tidied her hair and dress.

When they came down again Slyme said he thought the room would suit him very well. What were the terms?

Did he wish to take the room only—just to lodge, enquired Ruth, or would he prefer to board as well?

Slyme intimated that he desired the latter arrangement.

In that case she thought twelve shillings a week would be fair. She believed that was about the usual amount. Of course that would include washing, and if his clothes needed a little mending she would do it for him.

Slyme expressed himself satisfied with these terms, which were—as Ruth had said—about the usual ones. He would take the room, but he was not leaving his present lodgings until Saturday. It was therefore agreed that he was to bring his box on Saturday evening.

When he had gone, Easton and Ruth stood looking at each other in silence. Ever since this plan of letting the room first occurred to them they had been very anxious to accomplish it; and yet, now that it was done, they felt dissatisfied and unhappy, as if they had suddenly experienced some irreparable misfortune. In that moment they remembered nothing of the darker side of their life together. The hard times and the privations seemed insignificant beside the fact that this stranger was for the future to share their home. To Ruth especially it seemed that the happiness of the past twelve months had suddenly come to an end. She shrank with involuntary aversion and apprehension from the picture that rose before her in which this intruder appeared the most prominent figure, interfering with every detail of their home life. Of course they had known all this before, but somehow it had never seemed so objectionable as it did now, and as Easton thought of it he was filled with an unreasonable resentment against Slyme, as if the latter had forced himself upon them against their will.

'Damn him!' he thought. 'I wish I'd never brought him here at all!'

'Well?' he said at last. 'What do you think of him?'

'Oh, he'll be all right, I suppose.'

'For my part, I wish he wasn't coming,' Easton continued.

'That's just what I was thinking,' replied Ruth, dejectedly. 'I don't like him at all. I seemed to turn against him directly he came in the door.'

'I've a good mind to back out of it somehow, to-morrow,' exclaimed Easton, after another silence. 'I could tell him we've unexpectedly got some friends coming to stay with us.'

'Yes,' said Ruth, eagerly, 'it would be easy enough to make some excuse or other.'

As this way of escape presented itself she felt as if a weight had been lifted from her mind, but almost in the same instant, remembering how necessary it was to let the room, she added disconsolately:

'It's foolish for us to go on like this, dear. We must let the room and it might just as well be him as anyone else. We must make the best of it, that's all.'

Easton stood with his back to the fire, staring gloomily at her.

'Yes, I suppose that's the right way to look at it,' he replied at length. 'If we can't stand it, we'll give up the house and take a couple of rooms, or a small flat—if we can get one.'

Ruth agreed, although neither alternative was very inviting.

After all, the unwelcome alteration in their circumstances was not without its compensations, because it had the effect of renewing and intensifying their love for each other. They remembered with acute regret that hitherto they had not always fully appreciated the happiness of that exclusive companionship of which there now remained but one week more. For once the present was esteemed at its proper value, being invested with some of the glamour which almost always envelops the past.

Meanwhile Owen, in consequence of Hunter's order, had made his way straight to the office.

Rushton and Company's premises were situated in one of the principal streets of Mugsborough and consisted of a double fronted shop which extended to a narrow back street. The front part of the shop was stocked with wall hangings, mouldings, stands showing patterns of embossed wall and ceiling decorations, cases of brushes, tins of varnish and enamel, and similar things.

The office, which was at the rear and separated from the shop by a partition, had two doors, one giving access to the front shop, and the other opening on to the back street near a window on which was painted 'Rushton and Company' in black letters on a white ground.

Owen stood outside this window for two or three seconds. There was a bright light in the office. Then he knocked at the door, which was at once opened by Hunter.

Rushton was seated in an armchair at his desk, smoking a cigar and reading one of several letters that were lying before him.

He was a tall, clumsily built man, about thirty-five years of age. His eyes were light grey, and his hair and moustache were fair. He was not corpulent, but appeared to be well fed and 'in good condition.' He wore a grey Norfolk suit, and his clothes were well made and of good quality.

Rushton glanced up carelessly as Owen came in, but took no further notice of him, and Hunter, after conversing with his master in a low tone, put on his hat and went out of the office through the partition door which led into the front shop.

Owen stood waiting for Rushton to speak. He wondered why Hunter had sneaked off, and felt inclined to open the door and call him back. One thing he was determined about. He meant to have some explanation; he would not submit tamely to be dismissed without any just reason.

When Rushton had finished reading the letter, he looked up, and leaning comfortably back in his chair, blew a cloud of smoke from his cigar, and said in an affable, indulgent tone, such as one might use to a child:

'You're a bit of a hartist, aint yer?'

Owen was so surprised at this reception that for the moment he was unable to reply.

'You know what I mean,' continued Rushton; 'decorating work, something like them samples of yours what's hanging up there.'

He noticed the embarrassment of Owen's manner, and was gratified. He thought the man was confused at being spoken to by such a superior person.

'Yes,' replied Owen at last, 'I can do a little of that sort of work, although of course I don't profess to be able to do it as well or as quickly as a man who does nothing else.'

'Oh, no, of course not; but I think you could manage this all right. It's that drawing-room at the "Cave." Mr Sweater's been speaking to me about it. It seems that when he was over in Paris he saw a room as took his fancy. The walls and ceiling was not papered, but painted—sort of panelled out, and decorated with stencils and hand painting. This 'eres a photer of it; it's done in a sort of *Japanese* fashion.'

He handed the photograph to Owen as he spoke. It represented a room, the walls and ceiling of which were decorated in a Moorish style.

'At first Mr Sweater thought of getting a firm from London to do it,' continued Rushton, 'but 'e gave up the idear on account of the expense; but if you can do it so that it doesn't cost too much, I think I can persuade 'im to go in for it. But if it's goin' to cost a lot it won't come off at all. 'E'll just 'ave a frieze put up and 'ave the room papered in the ordinary way.'

This was not true; Rushton said it in case Owen might want to be paid extra wages while doing the work. Sweater was going to have the room decorated in any case, and intended to get a London firm to do it. He had consented rather unwillingly to let Rushton and Company submit him an estimate because he thought they would not be able to do the work satisfactorily.

Owen examined the photograph closely.

'Could you do anything like that in that room?'

'Yes, I think so,' replied Owen.

'Well, you know, I don't want you to start on the job and not be able to finish it. Can you do it or not?'

Rushton felt sure that Owen could do it, and was very desirous that he should undertake it, but he did not want him to know that. He wished to convey the impression that he was almost indifferent whether Owen did the work or not. In fact he wished to seem to be conferring a favour upon him by procuring him such a nice job as this.

'I'll tell you what I *can* do,' Owen replied; 'I can make you a water-colour sketch—a design—and if you think it good enough of course I can reproduce it on the ceiling and the walls, and I can let you know, within a little, how long it will take.'

Rushton appeared to reflect. Owen stood examining the photograph, and began to feel an intense desire to do the work.

Rushton shook his head dubiously.

'If I let you spend a lot of time over the sketches and then Mr Sweater does not approve of your design, where do I come in?'

'Well, suppose we put it like this: I'll draw the design at home, in the evenings—in my own time. If it's accepted I'll charge you for the time I've spent upon it. If it's not suitable I won't charge the time at all.'

Rushton brightened up considerably. 'All right, you can do so,' he said with an affectation of good nature. 'But you mustn't pile it on too thick, in any case, you know, because, as I said before, 'e don't want to spend too much money on it. In fact, if it's goin' to cost a great deal 'e simply won't 'ave it done at all.'

Rushton knew Owen well enough to be sure that no consideration of time or pains would prevent him from putting the very best that was in him into this work. He knew that if the man did the room at all there was no likelihood of his scamping it for the sake of getting it done quickly; and for that matter Rushton did not wish him to hurry over it. But he was anxious to impress upon Owen that he must not *charge too much time*. Any profit that could be made out of the job Rushton meant to secure for himself.

'When do you think you'll have the drawings ready?' enquired Rushton. 'Can you get them done to-night?'

'I'm afraid not,' replied Owen, feeling inclined to laugh at the absurdity of the question. 'It will need a little thinking about.'

'When can you have them ready then? This is Monday—Wednesday morning?'

Owen hesitated.

'We don't want to keep 'im waiting too long, you knows, or 'e may give up the idear altogether.'

'Well, say Friday morning, then,' said Owen, resolving that he would stay up all night if necessary to get it done.

Rushton shook his head.

'Can't you get it done before that? I'm afraid if we keeps 'im waiting all that time we may lose the job altogether.'

'I can't get them done any quicker in my spare time,' returned Owen, flushing; 'if you like to let me stay at home to-morrow and charge the time the same as if I had gone to work at the house, I could go to my ordinary work on Wednesday and let you have the drawings on Thursday morning.'

'Oh, all right,' said Rushton, hastily; 'but all the same, don't pile it on too thick, or we shall 'ave to charge so much for the work that 'e won't 'ave it done at all. Good-night.'

'I suppose I may take this photograph with me?'

'Yes, certainly,' said Rushton, as he returned to the perusal of his letters.

That night, long after his wife and Frankie were asleep, Owen worked in the sitting room, searching old numbers of the 'Decorator's Journal' and through the illustrations in other books of designs for examples of Moorish work, and making rough sketches in pencil.

He did not attempt to finish anything yet, but he roughed out the general plan, and when at last he went to bed he could not sleep for a long time. He almost fancied he was in the drawing room at the 'Cave'. First of all it would be necessary to take down the ugly plaster centre flower with its crevices all filled up with old whitewash. The cornice was all right; it was fortunately a very simple one, with a deep cove and without many enrichments. Then, when the walls and the ceiling had been properly prepared, the ornamentation would be proceeded with: the walls divided into panels and arches containing painted designs and lattice work, the panels of the door decorated in a similar manner; the mouldings of the door and window frames picked out with colours and gold so as to be in character with the other work, the cove of the cornice, a dull yellow with a bold ornament in colour—gold was not advisable in the hollow because of the unequal distribution of the light, but some of the smaller mouldings of the cornice should be gold. On the ceiling there would be one large panel covered with an appropriate design in gold and colours, and surrounded by a wide margin or border. Great care would have to be used when it came to the gilding, because, whilst large masses of gilding are apt to look garish and in bad taste, a lot of fine gold lines are ineffective, especially on a flat surface. Process by process he traced the work, and saw it advancing stage by stage until finally the large apartment was transformed and glorified. And then, in the midst of the pleasure he experienced in the planning of the design, there came the fear that perhaps they would not have it done at all.

The question as to what personal advantage he would gain never once occured to Owen. He simply wanted to do the work; and he was so fully occupied with thinking how it was to be done that the question of profit was crowded out.

On the other hand, this question of profit was the only part of the work that his employer would consider at all, thus illustrating the oft-quoted saying: 'The men work with their hands—the master works with his brains.'

CHAPTER X

The Upper and the Nether Millstones

On Thursday Owen stayed at home until after breakfast to finish the designs which he had promised to have ready that morning.

When he took them to the office at nine o'clock, as he had arranged, he had to wait half an hour before Rushton put in an appearance, for, like many others who 'work with their brains,' he needed a great deal more rest than those who are employed in mere physical labour.

'Oh, you've brought them sketches, I suppose,' he remarked in a surly tone when he came in. 'You know, there was no need for you to wait; you could 'ave left 'em 'ere and gone on to your job.'

He sat down at his desk and looked carelessly at the drawing. It was on a sheet of paper about twenty-four by eighteen inches. The design was drawn with pencil and one half of it was coloured.

'That's for the ceiling,' said Owen, 'I hadn't time to colour all of it.'

With an affectation of indifference Rushton laid the drawing down and took the other which Owen handed to him.

'This is for the large wall. The same design would be adapted for the other walls; and this one shows the door and the panels under the window.'

Rushton expressed no opinion about the merits of the drawings. He examined them carelessly one after the other, and then laying them down he enquired:

'How long would it take you to do this work—if we get the job?'

'About three weeks—say 150 hours. That is for the decorative work only. Of course the walls and ceiling would have to be painted first; they will need three coats of white.'

Rushton scribbled a note on a piece of paper. 'Well,' he said, after a pause, 'you can leave these 'ere and I'll see Mr Sweater about it and tell 'im what it will cost, and if he decides to have it done I'll let you know.'

He put the drawings aside with the air of a man who has other matters to attend to, and began to open one of several letters that were on his desk. He meant this as an intimation that the audience was at an end, and that he desired the 'hand' to retire from the presence. Owen understood, but he did not retire, because it was necessary to mention one or two other things which Rushton would have to allow for when preparing the estimate.

'Of course I should want some help,' he said. 'I should need a man occasionally, and the boy most of the time. Then there's the gold leaf—say fifteen books.'

'Don't you think it would be possible to use gold paint?'

'I'm afraid not.'

'Is there anything else?' enquired Rushton as he finished writing down these items.

'I think that's all, except a few sheets of cartridge paper for stencils and working drawings. The quantity of paint necessary for the decorative work will be very small.'

As soon as Owen was gone Rushton took up the designs and examined them attentively.

'These are all right,' he muttered. 'Good enough for anywhere. If he can paint anything like as well as this on the walls and ceiling of the room, it will stand all the looking at that anyone in the town is likely to give it.'

'Let's see,' he continued, 'He said three weeks, but he's so anxious to do the job that he's most likely under estimated the time. I'd better allow four weeks: that means about two hundred hours. Two hundred hours at eightpence—how much is that? And say he has a painter to help him half the time, one hundred hours at sixpence ha'penny.'

He consulted a ready reckoner that was on the desk.

'Time: £9 7s. 6d. Materials: fifteen books of gold, say a pound. Then there's the cartridge paper and the colours say another pound, at the outside. Boy's time? Well, he gets no wages as yet, so we needn't mention that at all. Then there's the preparing of the room. Three coats of white paint. I wish 'Unter was 'ere to give me an idea what it will cost.'

As if in answer to his wish Nimrod entered the office at that moment, and in reply to Rushton's query said that to give the walls and ceiling three coats of paint would cost about three pounds five, for time and material. Between them the two brainworkers figured that fifteen pounds would cover the entire cost of the work—painting and decorating.

'Well, I reckon we can charge Sweater forty-five pounds for it,' said Rushton. 'It isn't like an ordinary job, you know. If he gets a London firm to do it, it'll cost him double that, if not more.'

Having arrived at this decision Rushton rang up Sweater's Emporium on the telephone, and finding that Mr Sweater was there he rolled up the designs and set out for that gentleman's office.

Hunter had taken on three more painters that morning. Bundy and two labourers were putting in the new drains; the carpenters had returned, and there was also a plumber at work in the house, so there was quite a little crowd in the kitchen at dinner time. Crass had been waiting for a suitable opportunity to produce the newspaper cutting which it will be remembered he showed to Easton on Monday morning, but he had waited in vain, for there had been scarcely any 'political' talk at meal times all the week, and it was now Thursday. As far as Owen was concerned his thoughts were so occupied with the designs for the drawing-room that he had no time for anything else, and most of the others were only too willing to avoid a subject which frequently led to unpleasantness. As a rule Crass himself had no liking for such discussions, but he was so confident of being able to 'flatten out' Owen with the cutting from the 'Obscurer' that he had several times tried to lead the conversation into the desired channel, but so far without success.

During dinner—as they called it—various subjects were discussed. Harlow mentioned that he had found traces of bugs in one of the bedrooms upstairs, and this called forth a number of anecdotes about those insects and of houses infested by them. Philpot remembered working in a house over at Windley where the people were very dirty and had no bedsteads, the beds consisting of dilapidated mattresses and rags on the floor. He declared that these ragged mattresses used to wander about the rooms by themselves. The house was so full of fleas, he said, that if you placed a sheet of newspaper on the floor you could hear and see them jumping on it. In fact, directly anyone went into that house they were covered from head to foot with fleas! During the few days he worked at that place, he continued, he lost several pounds in weight, and of evenings, as he walked homewards, the children and the people in the streets, observing his ravaged countenance, thought he was suffering from some disease and used to get out of his way when they saw him coming.

There were several other of these narratives, four or five men talking at the top of their voices at the same time, each one telling a different story. At first each story-teller addressed himself to the company generally, but after a while, finding it impossible to get a hearing, he would select some particular individual who seemed disposed to listen, and tell him the story. It sometimes happened that in the middle of the tale the listener would remember a somewhat similar adventure of his own which he immediately proceeded to relate without waiting for the other to finish, and both of them were generally so interested in the gruesome details of their own story that they were unconscious of the fact that the other was telling one at all. In a contest of this kind the victory usually went to the man with the loudest voice, but sometimes a man who had a weak voice scored by repeating the same tale several times until some one heard it.

There was one man sitting on an up-ended pail in the far corner of the room, and from the movements of his lips it was evident that he also was relating a story, although nobody knew what it was about or heard a single word of it, for no one took the slightest notice of him. After a time Bundy stood up to help himself to some more tea. The cup he was drinking from had a large piece broken out of one side and did not hold much, so he usually had to have three or four helpings.

'Anyone else want any?' he asked.

Several cups and jars were passed to him. These vessels had been standing on the floor, which was very dirty and covered with dust, so before dipping them into the pail, Bundy—who had been working at the drains all the morning—wiped the bottoms of the jars upon his trousers, on the same place where he was in the habit of wiping his hands when he happened to get some dirt on them. He filled the jars so full that as he held them by the rims and passed them to their owners part of the contents slopped over and trickled through his fingers. By the time he had finished the floor was covered with little pools of tea.

'They say that Gord made everything for some useful purpose,' remarked Harlow, reverting to the original subject, 'but I should like to know what the hell's the use of sich things as bugs and fleas and the like.'

'To teach people to keep theirselves clean, of course,' said Slyme.

'That's a very funny subject, ain't it?' continued Harlow, ignoring Slyme's answer. 'They say as all diseases is caused by little insects. If Gord 'adn't made no cancer germs or consumption microbes there wouldn't be no cancer or consumption.'

'That's one of the proofs that there *isn't* an individual God,' said Owen. 'If we were to believe that the Universe and everything that lives was deliberately designed and created by God, then we must also believe that He made the disease germs you are speaking of for the purpose of torturing His other creatures.'

'You can't tell me a bloody yarn like that,' interposed Crass roughly. 'There's a Ruler over us, mate, and so you're likely to find out.'

'If Gord didn't create the world, 'ow did it come 'ere?' demanded Slyme.

'I know no more about that than you do,' replied Owen. 'That is—I know nothing. The only difference between us is that you *think* you know. You think you know that God made the universe, how long it took Him to do it, why He made it, how long it's been in existence, and how it will finally pass away. You also imagine you know that we shall live after we're dead, where we shall go, and the kind of existence we shall have. In fact, in the excess of your "humility" you think you know all about it. But really you know no more of these things than any other human being does; that is, you know *nothing*.'

'That's only *your* opinion,' said Slyme.

'If we care to take the trouble to learn,' Owen went on, 'we can know a little of how the universe has grown and changed; but of the beginning we know nothing.'

'That's just my opinion, matey,' observed Philpot; 'it's just a bloody mystery, and that's all about it.'

'I don't pretend to 'ave no 'ead knowledge,' said Slyme, 'but 'ead knowledge won't save a man's soul: it's '*eart* knowledge as does that. I knows in my 'eart as my sins is all hunder the Blood, and it's knowin' that wot's given 'appiness and the peace which passes all understanding to me ever since I've been a Christian.'

'Glory, glory, halleujah!' shouted Bundy, and nearly everyone laughed.

'"Christian" is right,' sneered Owen. 'You've got some title to call yourself a "Christian", haven't you? As for the happiness that passes all understanding, it certainly passes *my* understanding how you can be happy when you believe that millions of people are being tortured in hell; and it also passes my understanding why you are not ashamed of yourself for being happy under such circumstances.'

'Ah, well, you'll find it all out when you comes to die, mate,' replied Slyme in a threatening tone. 'You'll think and talk different then!'

'That's just wot gets over *me*,' observed Harlow. 'It don't seem right that after living in misery and poverty all our bloody lives, workin' and slavin' all the hours that Gord a'mighty sends, that we're to be bloody well set fire to and burned in 'ell for all eternity! It don't seem feasible to me, you know.'

'It's my belief,' said Philpot, profoundly, 'that when you're dead, you're done for. That's the end of you.'

'That's what *I say*,' remarked Easton. 'As for all this religious business, it's just a money-making dodge. It's the parson's trade, just the same as painting is ours, only there's no work attached to it, and the pay's a bloody sight better than ours is.'

'It's their livin', and a bloody good livin' too, if you ask me,' said Bundy.

'Yes,' said Harlow, 'they lives on the fat o' the land, and wears the best of everything, and they does nothing for it but talk a lot of twaddle two or three times a week. The rest of the time they spend cadgin' money orf silly old women who thinks it's a sorter fire insurance.'

'It's an old sayin' and a true one,' chimed in the man on the upturned pail, 'parsons and publicans is the worst enemies the workin' man ever 'ad. There may be *some*good 'uns, but they're few and far between.'

'If I could only get a job like the Harchbishop of Canterbury,' said Philpot, solemnly, 'I'd leave this firm.'

'So would I,' said Harlow. 'If I was the Harchbishop o' Canterbury, I'd take my pot and brushes down to the office and shy 'em through the bloody winder, and tell ole Misery to go to 'ell.'

'Religion is a thing that don't trouble *me* much,' remarked Newman, 'and as for what happens to you after death, it's a thing I believes in leavin' till you comes to it—there's no sense in meetin' trouble arf way. All the things they tells us may be true or they may not, but it takes me all my time to look after *this* world. I don't believe I've been to church more than arf a dozen times since I've been married—that's over fifteen years ago now—and then it's been when the kids 'ave been christened. The old woman goes sometimes, and of course, the young 'uns goes; you've got to tell 'em somethin' or other, and they might as well learn what they teaches at the Sunday school as anything else.'

A general murmur of approval greeted this. It seemed to be the almost unanimous opinion that, whether it were true or not, 'religion' was a nice thing to teach children.

'I've not been even once since I was married,' said Harlow, 'and I sometimes wish to Christ I 'adn't gorn then.'

'I don't see as it matters a dam wot a man believes,' said Philpot, 'so long as you don't do no 'arm to nobody. If you see a poor bleeder wot's down on 'is luck, give 'im a 'elpin 'and. Even if you aint got no money you can say a kind word. If a man does 'is work and looks arter 'is 'ome and 'is young 'uns, and does a good turn to a fellow creature when 'e can, I reckon 'e stands as much chance of getting into 'eaven—if there *is* sich a place—as some of these 'ere Bible busters, whether 'e ever goes to church or chapel or not.'

These sentiments were echoed by everyone with the solitary exception of Slyme, who said that Philpot would find out his mistake after he was dead, when he would have to stand before the Great White Throne for Judgment!

'And at the Last Day,' he added, 'when yer sees the moon turned inter blood, you'll be cryin' hout for the mountings and the rocks to fall on yer and 'ide yer from the wrath of the Lamb!'

The others laughed derisively.

'I'm a Bush Baptist meself,' remarked the man on the upturned pail. This individual, Dick Wantley by name, was of what is usually termed a 'rugged' cast of countenance, and strongly resembled an ancient gargoyle.

Most of the hands had by now lit their pipes, but there were a few who preferred chewing their tobacco. As they smoked or chewed they expectorated upon the floor or into the fire. Wantley was one of those who preferred chewing and he had been spitting upon the floor to such an extent that he was by this time partly surrounded by a kind of semicircular moat of dark brown spittle.

'I'm a Bush Baptist,' he shouted across the moat, 'and you all knows wot that is.'

This confession of faith caused a fresh outburst of hilarity, because of course everyone knew what a Bush Baptist was.

'If 'eaven's goin' to be full of sich swines as 'Unter,' observed Easton, 'I think I'd rather go to the other place.'

'If ever ole Misery *does* get into 'eaven.' said Philpot, ''e won't stop there very long. I reckon 'e'll be chucked out of it before 'e's been there a week, because 'e's sure to start pinchin' the jewels out of the other saints' crowns.'

'Well, if they won't 'ave 'im in 'eaven I'm sure I don't know wot's to become of 'im,' said Harlow with assumed concern,' because I don't believe 'e'd be allowed into 'ell, now.'

'Why not?' demanded Bundy. 'I should think it's just the bloody place for sich as 'im.'

'So it used to be at one time o' day, but they've changed all that now.

They've 'ad a revolution down there; deposed the Devil, elected a parson as President, and started puttin' the fire out.'

'From what I hears of it,' continued Harlow when the laughter had ceased, ''ell is a bloody fine place to live in just now. There's underground railways and 'lectric trams, and at the corner of nearly every street there's a sort of pub where you can buy ice cream, lemon squash, four ale, and American cold drinks; and you're allowed to sit in a refrigerator for two hours for a tanner.'

'But puttin' all jokes aside,' said Philpot, 'I can't believe there's sich a place as 'ell. There may be some kind of punishment, but I don't believe it's a real fire.'

'Nor nobody else, what's got any sense,' replied Harlow, contemptuously.

'I believe as *this* world is 'ell,' said Crass, looking around with a philosophic expression. This opinion was echoed by most of the others, although Slyme remained silent and Owen laughed.

'Wot the bloody 'ell are *you* laughin' at?' Crass demanded in an indignant tone.

'I was laughing because you said you think this world is hell.'

'Well, I don't see nothing to laugh at in that,' said Crass.

'So it *is* a 'ell,' said Easton. 'There can't be anywheres much worse than this.'

''Ear, 'ear!' said the man behind the moat.

'What I was laughing at is this,' said Owen; 'the present system of managing the affairs of the world is so bad and has produced such dreadful results that you are of opinion that the earth is a hell, and yet you are a Conservative! You wish to preserve the present system—the system which has made the world into a hell!'

'I thought we shouldn't get through the dinner hour without politics if Owen was 'ere,' growled Bundy. 'Bloody sickenin' I call it.'

'Don't be 'ard on 'im,' said Philpot; 'e's been very quiet fer the last few days.'

'We'll 'ave to go through it to-day, though,' remarked Harlow despairingly. 'I can see it comin'.'

'*I'm* not agoin' through it,' said Bundy, 'I'm orf!' and he accordingly drank the remainder of his tea, closed his empty dinner basket, and having placed it on the mantelshelf, made for the door.

'I'll leave you to it,' he said as he went out. The others laughed.

Crass, remembering the cutting from the 'Obscurer' that he had in his pocket was secretly very pleased at the turn the conversation was taking. He turned roughly on Owen:

'The other day, when we was talkin' about the cause of poverty, you contradicted everybody. Everyone else was wrong! But you yourself couldn't tell us what's the cause of poverty, could yer?'

'I think I could.'

'Oh, of course you think you know,' sneered Crass; 'and of course you think your opinion's right and everybody else's is wrong.'

'Yes,' replied Owen.

Several men expressed their abhorrence of this intolerant attitude of Owen's, but the latter rejoined:

'Of course I think that my opinions are right and that everyone who differs from me is wrong. If I didn't think their opinions were wrong I wouldn't differ from them. If I didn't think my own opinions right I wouldn't hold them.'

'But there's no need to keep on arguin' about it day after day,' said Crass. 'You've got your opinion and I've got mine. Let everyone enjoy his own opinion, I say.' A murmur of approbation from the crowd greeted these sentiments; but Owen rejoined:

'But we can't both be right. If your opinions are right and mine are not, how am I to find out the truth if we never talk about them?'

'Well, wot do you reckon is the cause of poverty, then?' demanded Easton.

'The present system—competition—capitalism.'

'It's all very well to talk like that,' snarled Crass, to whom this statement conveyed no meaning whatever. 'But 'ow do you make it out?'

'Well, I put it like that for the sake of shortness,' replied Owen. 'Suppose some people were living in a house—'

'More supposin'!' sneered Crass.

'And suppose they were always ill, and suppose that the house was badly built, the walls so constructed that they drew and retained moisture, the roof broken and leaky, the drains defective, the doors and windows ill-fitting, and the rooms badly shaped and draughty. If you were asked to name, in a word, the cause of the ill-health of the people who lived there you would say—the house. All the tinkering in the world would not make that house fit to live in, the only thing to do with it would be to pull it down and build another. Well, we're all living in a house called the Money System; and as a result most of us are suffering from a disease called poverty. There's so much the matter with the present system that it's no good tinkering at it. Everything about it is wrong and there's nothing about it that's right. There's only one thing to be done with it and that is to smash it up and have a different system altogether.'

'It seems to me that that's just what you're trying to do,' remarked Harlow, sarcastically, 'you seem to be tryin' to get out of answering the question what Easton asked you.'

'Yes!' cried Crass, fiercely. 'Why don't you answer the bloody question? Wot's the cause of poverty?'

'What the 'ell's the matter with the present system?' demanded Sawkins.

''Ow's it goin' to be altered?' said Newman.

'Wot the bloody 'ell sort of a system do *you* think we ought to 'ave?' shouted the man behind the moat.

'It can't never be altered,' said Philpot; 'human nature's human nature and you can't get away from it.'

'Never mind about human nature,' shouted Crass; 'stick to the point. Wot's the cause of poverty?'

'Oh, damn the cause of poverty!' said one of the new hands. 'I've 'ad enough of this bloody row,' and he stood up and prepared to go out of the room.

This individual had two patches on the seat of his trousers and the bottoms of the legs of that garment were frayed and ragged. He had been out of work for about six weeks previous to this job, and during most of that time he and his family had been existing in a condition of semi-starvation on the earnings of his wife as a charwoman and on the scraps of food she brought home from the houses where she worked. But all the same, the question of what is the cause of poverty had no interest for him.

'There are many causes,' answered Owen, 'but they are all part of and inseparable from the system. In order to do away with poverty we must destroy the causes. To do away with the causes we must destroy the whole system.'

'What are the causes, then?'

'Well, money for one thing.'

This extraordinary assertion was greeted with a roar of merriment, in the midst of which Philpot was heard to say that to listen to Owen was as good as going to a circus. Money the cause of poverty!

'I always thought it was the want of it!' said the man with the patches on the seat of his trousers, as he passed out of the door.

'Other things,' continued Owen, 'are private ownership of land; private ownership of railways, tramways, gasworks, waterworks, factories, and of the other methods of producing the necessaries and comforts of life; competition in business—'

'But 'ow do you make it out?' demanded Crass impatiently.

Owen hesitated. To his mind the thing appeared very clear and simple. The causes of poverty were so glaringly evident that he marvelled that any rational being should fail to perceive them; but at the same time he found it very difficult to define them himself. He could not think of words that would convey his thoughts clearly to these others who were so hostile and unwilling to understand, and who appeared to have made up their minds to oppose and reject whatever he said. They did not know what were the causes of poverty and apparently they did not *want* to know.

'Well, I'll try to show you one of the causes,' he said nervously at last.

He picked up a piece of charred wood that had fallen from the fire and knelt down and began to draw upon the floor. Most of the others regarded him with looks in which an indulgent contemptuous kind of interest mingled with an air of superiority and patronage. There was no doubt, they thought, that Owen was a clever sort of chap: his work proved that; but he was certainly a little bit mad.

By this time Owen had drawn a circle about two feet in diameter. Inside this he had drawn two squares, one much larger than the other. These two squares he filled in solid black with the charcoal.

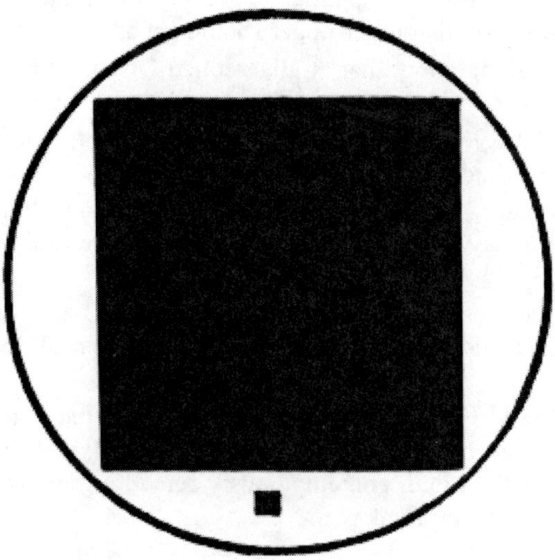

'Wot's it all about?' asked Crass with a sneer.

'Why, can't you see?' said Philpot, with a wink. ''E's goin' to do some conjurin'! In a minit 'e'll make something pass out 'o one 'o them squares into the other and no one won't see 'ow it's done.'

When he had finished drawing, Owen remained for a few minutes awkwardly silent, oppressed by the anticipation of ridicule and a sense of his inability to put his thoughts into plain language. He began to wish that he had not undertaken this task. At last, with an effort, he began to speak in a halting, nervous way:

'This circle—or rather, the space inside the circle—is supposed to represent England.'

'Well, I never knowed it was round before,' jeered Crass. 'I've heerd as the *world* is round—'

'I never said it was the shape—I said it was supposed to *represent* England.'

'Oh, I see. I thought we'd very soon begin supposin'.'

'The two black squares,' continued Owen, 'represent the people who live in the country. The small square represents a few thousand people. The large square stands for the remainder—about forty millions—that is, the majority.'

'We ain't sich bloody fools as to think that the largest number is the minority,' interrupted Crass.

'The greater number of the people represented by the large black square work for their living; and in return for their labour they receive money, some more, some less than others.'

'You don't think they'd be sich bloody fools as to work for nothing, do you?' said Newman.

'I suppose you think they ought all to get the same wages!' cried Harlow. 'Do you think it's right that a scavenger should get as much as a painter?'

'I'm not speaking about that at all, 'replied Owen. 'I'm trying to show you what I think is one of the causes of poverty.'

'Shut up, can't you, Harlow,' remonstrated Philpot, who began to feel interested. 'We can't all talk at once.'

'I know we can't,' replied Harlow in an aggrieved tone, 'but 'e takes sich a 'ell of a time to say wot 'e's got to say. Nobody else can't get a word in hedgeways.'

'In order that these people may live,' continued Owen, pointing to the large black square, 'it is first of all necessary that they shall have a *place* to live in—'

'Well! I should never a' thought it!' exclaimed the man on the pail, pretending to be much impressed. The others laughed, and two or three of them went out of the room, contemptuously remarking to each other in an audible undertone as they went,

'Bloody rot!'

'Wonder wot the bloody 'ell 'e thinks 'e is? A sort of schoolmaster?'

Owen's nervousness increased as he continued:

'Now, they can't live in the air or in the sea. These people are land animals, therefore they must live on the land.'

'Wot do yer mean by animals?' demanded Slyme.

'A human bein' ain't a animal!' said Crass, indignantly.

'Yes we are!' cried Harlow, 'go into any chemist's shop you like and ask the bloke, and 'e'll tell you——'

'Oh, blow that!' interrupted Philpot. 'Let's 'ear wot Owen's sayin'.'

'They must live on the land, and that's the beginning of the trouble, because, under the present system, the majority of the people have really no right to be in the country at all! Under the present system the country belongs to a few—those who are here represented by this small black square. If it would pay them to do so, and if they felt so disposed, these few people have a perfect right, under the present system, to order everyone else to clear out!

'But they don't do that, they allow the majority to remain in the land on one condition; that is: they must pay rent to the few for the privilege of being permitted to live in the land of their birth.

'The amount of rent demanded by those who own this country is so large that, in order to pay it, the greater number of the majority have often to deprive themselves and their children not only of the comforts but even the necessaries of life. In the case of the working classes the rent absorbs, at the lowest possible estimate, about one third of their total earnings, for it must be remembered that the rent is an expense that goes on all the time, whether they are employed or not. If they get into arrears when out of work, they have to pay double when they get employment again.

'The majority work hard and live in poverty in order that the minority may live in luxury without working at all, and as the majority are mostly fools, they not only agree to pass their lives in incessant slavery and want, in order to pay this rent to those who own the country, but they say it is quite right that they should have to do so, and are very grateful to the little minority for allowing them to remain in the country at all.'

Owen paused, and immediately there arose a great clamour from his listeners.

'So it *is* right, ain't it?' shouted Crass, 'If you 'ad a 'ouse and let it to someone, you'd want your rent, wouldn't yer?'

'I suppose,' said Slyme, with resentment, for he had some shares in a local building society, 'after a man's been careful, and scraping and saving and going without things he ought to 'ave 'ad all 'is life, and managed to buy a few 'ouses to support 'im in his old age, they ought all be took away from 'im? Some people,' he added, 'ain't got common honesty.'

Nearly everyone had something to say in reprobation of the views suggested by Owen. Harlow, in a brief but powerful speech, bristling with numerous sanguinary references to the bottomless pit, protested against any interference with the sacred rights of property. Easton listened with a puzzled expression, and Philpot's goggle eyes rolled horribly as he glared silently at the circle and the two squares.

'By far the greater part of the land,' resumed Owen, when the row had ceased, 'is held by people who have absolutely no moral right to it. Possession of much of it was obtained by means of murder and theft perpetrated by the ancestors of the present holders. In other cases, when some king or prince wanted to get rid of a mistress of whom he had grown weary, he presented a tract of our country to some "nobleman" on condition that he would marry her. Vast estates were also bestowed upon the remote ancestors of the present holders in return for real or alleged services. Listen to this,' he continued, as he took a small newspaper cutting from his pocket-book.

Crass looked at the piece of paper dolefully. It reminded him of the one he had in his own pocket, which he was beginning to fear that he would not have an opportunity of producing to-day after all.

"BALLCARTRIDGE RENT DAY."

'"The hundredth anniversary of the battle of Ballcartridge occured yesterday and in accordance with custom the Duke of Ballcartridge handed to the authorities the little flag which he annually presents to the State in virtue of his tenure of the vast tract of this country which was presented to one of his ancestors—the first Duke—in addition to his salary, for his services at the battle of Ballcartridge.

"The flag—which is the only rent the Duke has to pay for the great estate which brings him in several hundred thousands of pounds per annum—is a small tricoloured one with a staff surmounted by an eagle.

"The Duke of Blankmind also presents the State with a little coloured silk flag every year in return for being allowed to retain possession of that part of England which was presented—in addition to his salary—to one of His Grace's very remote ancestors, for his services at the battle of Commissariat—in the Netherlands."

'The Duke of Southward is another instance,' continued Owen 'he "owns" miles of the country we speak of as "ours." Much of his part consists of confiscated monastery lands which were stolen from the owners by King Henry VIII and presented to the ancestors of the present Duke. Whether it was right or wrong that these parts of our country should ever have been given to those people is a question we need not trouble ourselves about now. But, the *present holders* are certainly not deserving people. They do not even take the trouble to pretend that they are. They have done nothing and they do nothing to justify their possession of these "estates," as they call them. And in my opinion no man who is in his right mind can really think it's just that these people should be allowed to prey upon their fellow-men as they are doing now, or that it is right that their children should be allowed to continue to prey upon our children for ever. Just think of the absurdity of it!' continued Owen, pointing to the two squares. 'All those people allowing themselves to be overworked and bullied and starved and robbed by this little crowd here!'

Observing signs of a renewal of the storm of protest, Owen hurriedly concluded:

'Whether it's right or wrong, you can't deny that the fact that this small minority possesses nearly all the land of the country is one of the principal causes of the poverty of the majority.'

'Well, that seems true enough,' said Easton, slowly; 'the rent's the biggest item a workin' man's got to pay. When you're out of work and you can't afford other things you goes without 'em, but the rent 'as to be paid whether you're workin' or not.'

'Yes, that's true enough,' said Harlow impatiently, 'but you gets value for yer money. You can't expect to get a 'ouse for nothing.'

'Suppose we admits as it's wrong, just for the sake of argyment,' said Crass in a jeering tone; 'wot then? Wot about it? 'Ow's it goin' to be altered?'

'Yes!' cried Harlow triumphantly, 'That's the bloody question! 'Ow's it agoin' to be altered? It can't be done!'

There was a general murmur of satisfaction. Nearly everyone seemed very pleased to think that the existing state of things could not possibly be altered.

'Whether it can be altered or not, whether it's right or wrong, Landlordism is one of the causes of poverty,' Owen repeated. 'Poverty is not caused by men and women getting married; it's not caused by machinery; it's not caused by "over-production"; it's not caused by drink or laziness, and it's not caused by "over-population." It's caused by Private Monopoly. That is the present system. They have monopolised everything that it is possible to monopolise. They have got the whole earth, the minerals in the earth and the streams that water the earth. If it had been possible to monopolise the air and compress it into huge gasometers, it would have been done long ago, and we should have been compelled to work in order to get money to buy air to breathe. And if that seemingly impossible thing were accomplished to-morrow, you would see thousands of people dying for want of air—or of the money to buy it—even as now thousands are dying for want of the other necessaries of life. You would see people going about gasping for breath, and telling each other that the likes of them could not expect to have air to breathe unless they had the money to pay for it. Most of you here, for instance, would think so and say so, even as you think that it's right for a few people to own the Earth, the Minerals and the Water, which are all just as necessary as is the air. In exactly the same spirit as you now say: "It's their land," "It's their water," "It's their coal," "It's their iron," so you would say: "It's their air, these are their gasometers, and what right have the likes of us to expect them to allow us to breathe for nothing?"

'I suppose you think the landlords ought to let people live in their 'ouses for nothing?' said Crass, breaking the silence that followed.

'Certainly,' remarked Harlow, pretending to be suddenly converted to Owen's views; 'I reckon the landlord ought to pay the rent to the tenant!'

'Of course, Landlordism is not the only cause,' said Owen, ignoring these remarks. 'The wonderful system fosters a great many others. Employers of labour, for instance, are at great a cause of poverty as landlords are.'

This extraordinary statement was received with astonished silence.

'Do you mean to say that if I'm out of work and a master gives me a job, that 'e's doin' me a injury?' said Crass at length.

'No, of course not,' replied Owen.

'Well, what the bloody 'ell *do* yer mean, then?'

'I mean this. Supposing that the owner of a house wishes to have it repainted, what does he usually do?'

'As a rule 'e goes to three or four master painters and asks 'em to give 'im a price for the job.'

'Yes; and those master painters are so eager to get the work, that they cut the price down to what they think is the lowest possible point,' answered Owen, 'and the lowest usually gets the job. The successful tenderer has cut the price so fine that to make it pay he must scamp the work, pay low wages, and drive and sweat the men whom he employs. He wants them to do two days' work for one day's pay. The result is that a job which, if it were done properly, would employ say twenty men for two months, is rushed and scamped in half that time with half that number of men. This means that—in one such case as this—ten men are deprived of one month's employment; and ten other men are deprived of two months' employment; and all because the employers have been cutting each other's throats to get the work.' Owen paused and there was an uncomfortable silence.

'And we can't 'elp ourselves, you nor me either,' said Harlow. 'Supposing one of us on this job was to make up 'is mind not to tear into it like we do, but just keep on steady and do a fair day's work, wot would 'appin?'

No one answered; but the same thought was in everyone's mind. Such an one would be quickly marked by Hunter, and even if the latter failed to notice him it would not be long before Crass reported his conduct.

'We can't 'elp ourselves,' said Easton, gloomily. 'If one man won't do it there's twenty others ready to take 'is place.'

'We could help ourselves to a certain extent if we would stand by each other; if, for instance, we all belonged to the society,' said Owen.

'I don't believe in the society,' observed Crass. 'I can't see as it's right that a inferior man should 'ave the same wages as me.'

'They're a drunken lot of beer swillers,' remarked Slyme. 'That's why they always 'as their meetings in public 'ouses.'

Harlow made no comment on this question. He had at one time belonged to the union, and he was rather ashamed of having fallen away from it.

'Wot good 'as the society ever done 'ere?' said Easton. 'None that I ever 'eard of.'

'It might be able to do some good if most of us belonged to it; but after all, that's another matter. . . . Whether we could help ourselves or not, the fact remains that we don't. But you must admit that this competition of the employers is one of the causes of unemployment and poverty, because it's not only in our line—exactly the same thing happens in every other trade and industry. Competing employers are the upper and nether millstones which grind the workers between them.'

'I suppose you think there oughtn't to be no employers at all?' sneered Crass. 'Or p'raps you think the masters ought to do all the bloody work theirselves, and give us the money?'

'I don't see 'ow it's goin' to be altered,' remarked Harlow. 'There *must* be masters, and *someone* 'as to take charge of the work and do the thinkin'.'

'Whether it can be altered or not,' said Owen, 'Landlordism and Competing Employers are two of the causes of poverty. But of course they're only a small part of the system which produces luxury, refinement and culture for a few, and condemns the majority to a lifelong struggle with adversity, and many thousands to degradation, hunger and rags. This is the system you all uphold and defend, although you don't mind admitting that it has made the world into a hell.'

Crass slowly drew the 'Obscurer' cutting from his waist-coat pocket, but after a moment's thought he replaced it, deciding to defer its production till a more suitable occasion.

'But you 'aven't told us yet 'ow you makes out that money causes poverty,' cried Harlow, winking at the others; 'that's what *I'm* anxious to 'ear about.'

'So am I,' remarked the man behind the moat. 'I was just wondering whether I 'adn't better tell ole Misery that I don't want no wages this week.'

'I think I'll tell 'im on Saturday to keep *my* money and get 'imself a few drinks with it,' said Philpot. 'It might cheer 'im up a bit and make 'im a little more sociable and friendly like.'

'Money *is* the principal cause of poverty,' said Owen.

''Ow do yer make it out?' cried Sawkins.

But their curiosity had to remain unsatisfied for the time, because at that moment Crass announced that it was 'just on it.'

CHAPTER XI

The Thorough Man

About three o'clock that afternoon Rushton himself suddenly appeared and began walking silently about the house, and listening outside the doors of rooms where the hands were working. He did not succeed in catching anyone idling or smoking or talking. The nearest approach to what the men called 'a capture' that he made was, when he stood outside the door of one of the upper rooms in which Philpot and Harlow were working, and heard them singing one of Sankey's hymns—'Work! for the night is coming.' He listened to two verses and several repetitions of the chorus. Being a 'Christian' he could scarcely object to this, especially as by peeping through the partly open door he could see that they were suiting the action to the word. When he went into the room they glanced round to see who it was, and stopped singing. Rushton did not speak, but stood in the middle of the floor, silently watching them as they worked, for about a quarter of an hour. Then without having uttered a syllable he turned and continued his investigations.

None of the men looked round from their work or spoke. The only sounds heard were the noises made by the saws and hammers of the carpenters who were fixing the frieze rails and dado rails or repairing parts of the woodwork.

Crass placed himself in Rushton's way several times, but beyond curtly acknowledging the foreman's servile 'Good hafternoon, sir,' the master took no notice of him.

After about an hour spent in this manner Rushton went, but as no one saw him go, his departure was not discovered for some considerable time.

Owen was secretly very disappointed. 'I thought he had come to tell me about the drawing-room,' he said to himself, 'but I suppose it's not decided yet.'

Just as the 'hands' were beginning to breathe freely again, Misery arrived, carrying some rolled-up papers in his hand. He also flitted silently from one room to another, peering round corners and listening at doors in the hope of finding an excuse to make an example of someone. Disappointed in this, he presently crawled upstairs to the room where Owen was working and handing to him the roll of papers said:

'Mr Sweater has decided to 'ave this work done, so you can start on it as soon as you like.'

It is impossible to describe without appearing to exaggerate the emotions experienced by Owen as he heard this announcement. For one thing it meant that the work at this house would last longer than it would otherwise have done; and it also meant that he would be paid for the extra time he had spent on the drawings, besides having his wages increased—for he was always paid an extra penny per hour when engaged on special work. But these considerations did not occur to him at the moment at all, for to him it meant much more. Since his first conversation on the subject with Rushton he had thought of little else than this work of decorating the drawing-room.

In a sense he had been *doing* it ever since, repeatedly planning and altering the details and selecting and rejecting the colours for the different parts over and over again. A keen desire to carry it through had grown within him, but he had scarcely allowed himself to hope. His face flushed slightly as he took the drawings from Hunter.

'You can make a start on it to-morrow morning,' continued that gentleman. 'I'll tell Crass to send someone else up 'ere to finish this room.'

'I shan't be able to start to-morrow, because the ceiling and walls will have to be painted first.'

'Yes, I know. You and Easton can do that. One coat tomorrow, another on Friday and the third on Saturday—that is, unless you can make it do with two coats. Even if it has to have the three, you will be able to go on with your decoration on Monday.'

'I won't be able to start it on Monday because I shall have to make some working drawings first.'

'Workin' drorins!' ejaculated Misery with a puzzled expression. 'Wot workin' drorins? You've got *them*, ain't yer?' pointing to the roll of paper.

'Yes; but as the same ornaments are repeated several times, I shall have to make a number of full sized drawings, with perforated outlines, to transfer the design to the walls,' said Owen, and he proceeded to explain laboriously the processes.

Nimrod looked at him suspiciously. 'Is all that really necessary?' he asked. 'Couldn't you just copy it on the wall, freehand?'

'No, that wouldn't do. It would take much longer that way.'

This consideration appealed to Misery.

'Ah, well,' he sighed, 'I s'pose you'll 'ave to do it the way you said; but for Gord's sake don't spend too much time over it, because we've took it very cheap. We only took it on so as you could 'ave a job, not that we expect to make any profit out of it.'

'And I shall have to cut some stencils, so I shall need several sheets of cartridge paper.'

Upon hearing of this additional expense Misery's long visage appeared to become several inches longer; but after a moment's thought he brightened up.

'I'll tell you what!' he exclaimed, with a cunning leer. 'There's lots of odd rolls of old wallpaper down at the shop, couldn't you manage with some of that?'

'I'm afraid it wouldn't do,' replied Owen, doubtfully, 'but I'll have a look at it, and if possible I'll use it.'

'Yes, do!' said Misery, pleased at the thought of saving something. 'Call at the shop on your way home to-night, and we'll see what we can find. 'Ow long do you think it'll take you to make the drorins and the stencils?'

'Well, to-day's Thursday. If you let someone else help Easton prepare the room, I think I can get them done in time to bring them with me on Monday morning.'

'Wot do yer mean: "bring them with you"?' demanded Nimrod.

'I shall have to do them at home, you know.'

'Do 'em at 'ome! Why can't you do 'em 'ere?'

'Well, there's no table, for one thing.'

'Oh, but we can soon fit you out with a table. You can 'ave a pair of paperhanger's trestles and boards, for that matter.'

'I have a lot of sketches and things at home that I couldn't very well bring here,' said Owen.

Misery argued about it for a long time, insisting that the drawings should be made either on the 'job' or at the paint shop down at the yard. How, he asked, was he to know at what hour Owen commenced or left off working, if the latter did them at home?

'I shan't charge any more time than I really work,' replied Owen. 'I can't possibly do them here or at the paint shop. I know I should only make a mess of them under such conditions.'

'Well, I s'pose you'll 'ave to 'ave your own way,' said Misery, dolefully. 'I'll let Harlow help Easton paint the room out so as you can get your stencils and things ready. But for Gord's sake get 'em done as quick as you can. If you could manage to get done by Friday and come down and help Easton on Saturday, it would be so much the better. And when you do get a start on the decoration, I shouldn't take too much care over it, you know, if I was you, because we 'ad to take the job for next to nothing or Mr Sweater would never 'ave 'ad it done at all!'

So saying, Nimrod began to crawl about the house, snarling and grumbling at everyone.

'Now then, you chaps, *Rouse yourselves!*' he bellowed, 'you seem to think this is a 'orspital. If some of you don't make a better show than this, I'll 'ave to 'ave a Alteration! There's plenty of chaps walkin' about who'll be only too glad of a job!'

He went into the scullery where Crass was mixing some colour.

'Look 'ere, Crass!' he said, 'I'm not at all satisfied with the way you're gettin' on with the work. You must push the chaps a bit more than you're doin'. There's not enough being done, by a long way. We shall lose money over this job before we're finished!'

Crass, whose fat face had turned a ghastly green with fright, mumbled something about getting on with it as fast as he could.

'Well, you'll 'ave to make 'em move a bit quicker than this,' Misery howled, 'or there'll 'ave to be a *Alteration*!'

By an 'alteration' Crass understood that he might get the sack, or that someone else might be put in charge of the job, and that would of course reduce him to the ranks and do away with his chance of being kept on longer than the others. He determined to try to ingratiate himself with Hunter and to appease his wrath by sacrificing someone else. He glanced cautiously into the kitchen and up the passage and then, lowering his voice he said:

'They all shapes pretty well, except Newman. I would 'ave told you about 'im before, but I thought I'd give 'im a fair chance. I've spoke to 'im several times myself about not doin' enough, but it don't seem to make no difference.'

'I've 'ad me eye on 'im meself, for some time,' replied Nimrod, in the same tone. 'Anybody would think the work was goin' to be sent to a Exhibition, the way 'e messes about with it, rubbing it with glasspaper and stopping up every little crack! I can't understand where 'e gets all the glasspaper *from*!'

''E brings it 'isself!' said Crass, hoarsely. 'I know for a fact that 'e bought two 'apenny sheets of it, last week, out of 'is own money!'

'Oh, 'e did, did 'e?' snarled Misery. 'I'll give 'im glasspaper! I'll 'ave a Alteration!'

He went into the hall, where he remained alone for a considerable time, brooding. At last, with the manner of one who has resolved on a certain course of action, he turned and entered the room where Philpot and Harlow were working.

'You both get sevenpence an hour, don't you?' he said.

They both replied in the affirmative.

'I've never worked under price yet,' added Harlow.

'Nor me, neither,' observed Philpot.

'Well, of course you can please yourselves,' Hunter continued, 'but after this week we've decided not to pay more than six and a half. Things is cut so fine nowadays, that we can't afford to go on payin' sevenpence any longer. You can work up till to-morrow night on the old terms, but if you're not willin' to accept six and a half you needn't come on Saturday morning. Please yourselves. Take it or leave it.'

Harlow and Philpot were both too much astonished to say anything in reply to this cheerful announcement, and Hunter, with the final remark, 'You can think it over,' left them and went to deliver the same ultimatum to all the other full price men, who took it in the same way as Philpot and Harlow had done. Crass and Owen were the only two whose wages were not reduced.

It will be remembered that Newman was one of those who were already working for the reduced rate. Misery found him alone in one of the upper rooms, to which he was giving the final coat. He was at his old tricks. The woodwork of the cupboard he was doing was in a rather damaged condition, and he was facing up the dents with white lead putty before painting it. He knew quite well that Hunter objected to any but very large holes or cracks being stopped, and yet somehow or other he could not scamp the work to the extent that he was ordered to; and so, almost by stealth, he was in the habit of doing it—not properly—but as well as he dared. He even went to the length of occasionally buying a few sheets of glasspaper with his own money, as Crass had told Hunter. When the latter came into the room he stood with a sneer on his face, watching Newman for about five minutes before he spoke.

'You can make out yer time sheet and come to the office for yer money at five o'clock,' said Nimrod at last, 'we shan't require your valuable services no more after to-night.'

Newman went white.

'Why, what's wrong?' said he. 'What have I done?'

'Oh, it's not wot you've *done*,' replied Misery, 'it's wot you've *not* done. That's wot's wrong! You've not done enough, that's all!' And without further parley, he turned and went out.

Newman stood in the darkening room feeling as if his heart had turned to lead. There rose before his mind the picture of his home and family. He could see them as they were at this very moment, the wife probably just beginning to prepare the evening meal and the children setting the cups and saucers and other things on the kitchen table—a noisy work, enlivened with many a frolic and childish dispute. Even the two year old baby insisted on helping and they had all been so happy lately because they knew that he had work that would last till nearly Christmas, if not longer. And now *this* had happened, to plunge them back into that abyss of wretchedness from which they had so recently escaped. They still owed several weeks' rent, and were already so much in debt to the baker and the grocer that it was hopeless to expect any further credit.

'My God!' said Newman, realising the almost utter hopelessness of the chance of obtaining another 'job,' and unconciously speaking aloud. 'My God! how can I tell them? What *will* become of us?'

When the men realised that Hunter had gone, they began to gather into little groups, and soon nearly all found themselves in the kitchen, discussing the reduction in wages. Sawkins and the other 'lightweights' remained at their work. Some of them got only fourpence half-penny, Sawkins was paid fivepence, so none of these were affected by the change. The other two fresh hands—the journeymen—joined the crowd in the kitchen, being anxious to conceal the fact that they had agreed to accept the reduced rate before being 'taken on.' Owen also was there, having heard the news from Philpot.

There was a lot of furious talk. At first several of them spoke of 'chucking up' at once; but others were more prudent, for they knew that if they left there were dozens of others who would be eager to take their places.

'After all, you know,' said Slyme, who had an idea of presently starting business on his own account, and was only waiting until he had saved enough money. 'After all, there's something in what 'Unter says. It's very 'ard to get a fair price for work now-a-days. Things *is* cut very fine.'

'Yes! We knows all about that!' shouted Harlow. 'And who the bloody 'ell is it cuts 'em? Why, sich swines as 'Unter and Rushton! If this firm 'adn't cut *this* job so fine, some other firm would 'ave 'ad it for more money. Rushton's cuttin' it fine didn't *make* this job, did it? It would 'ave been done just the same if they 'adn't tendered for it at all! The only difference is that we should 'ave been workin' for some other master.'

'I don't believe the bloody job's cut fine at all!' said Philpot. 'Rushton is a pal of Sweater's, and they're both members of the Town Council.'

'That may be,' replied Slyme, 'but all the same I believe Sweater got several other prices besides Rushton's, friend or no friend, and you can't blame 'im—it's only business. But pr'aps Rushton got the preference—Sweater may 'ave told 'im the others' prices.'

'Yes, and a bloody fine lot of prices they was, too, if the truth was known!' said Bundy. 'There was six other firms after this job to my knowledge, and Gord only knows 'ow many more.'

At this moment Newman came into the room. He looked so white and upset that the others involuntarily paused in their conversation.

'Well, what do *you* think of it?' asked Harlow.

'Think of what?' said Newman.

'Why, didn't 'Unter tell you?' cried several voices, whose owners looked suspiciously at him. They thought if Hunter had not spoken to Newman, it must be because he was already working under price. There had been a rumour going about the last few days to that effect. 'Didn't Misery tell you? They're not goin' to pay no more than six and a half after this week.'

'That's not what 'e said to me. 'E just told me to knock off. Said I didn't do enough for 'em.'

'Jesus Christ!' exclaimed Crass, pretending to be overcome with surprise.

Newman's account of what had transpired was listened to in gloomy silence. Those who, a few minutes previously, had been talking loudly of chucking up the job, became filled with apprehension that they might be served in the same manner. Crass was one of the loudest in his expressions of astonishment and indignation, but he rather overdid it and only succeeded in confirming the secret suspicions of the others that he had had something to do with Hunter's action.

The result of the discussion was that they decided to submit to Misery's terms for the time being, until they could see a chance of getting work elsewhere.

As Owen had to go to the office to see the wall-paper which Hunter had mentioned, he accompanied Newman when the latter went to get his wages. Nimrod was waiting for them, and had the money ready in an envelope, which he handed to Newman, who took it without speaking and went away.

Misery had been rummaging amongst the old wall-papers and had got out a great heap of odd rolls, which he now submitted to Owen, but after examining them the latter said that they were unsuitable for the purpose; so after some argument Misery was compelled to sign an order for some proper cartridge paper which Owen obtained at a stationer's on his way home.

CHAPTER XII

Sunday School

Charlie and Elsie Linden had not forgotten the little black kitten, and had called at the Owens' flat more than once to renew their acquaintance with it. On one of these occasions Charlie described the delights of his Sunday School, which was connected with the Shining Light Chapel, with so much enthusiasm that Frankie Owen obtained his mother's permission to accompany his friend the following Sunday. Dressed in his best—a suit made out of one of his mother's dresses—with his long curls carefully brushed, a most unnecessary process from Frankie's point of view, he waited impatiently for Charlie to call for him, and both boys started off in high feather.

The school was not conducted in the chapel itself but in a large lecture hall under it. At one end was a small platform raised about six inches from the floor; on this were a chair and a small table. A number of groups of chairs and benches were arranged at intervals round the sides and in the centre of the room, each group accommodating a separate class. On the walls, which were painted a pale green, were a number of coloured pictures—Moses striking the Rock, the Israelites dancing round the Golden Calf, and so on.

Frankie had never been to a Sunday School of any kind before, and he stood for a moment looking in at the door and half afraid to enter. The lessons had already commenced, but the scholars had hardly settled down to work.

The scene was one of some disorder, some of the children talking, laughing, or playing, and the teachers alternately threatening and coaxing them. The girls' and the very young children's classes were presided over by ladies; the boys' teachers were men, including Mr Rushton and Mr Hunter and Mr Didlum, the furniture dealer. On this occasion, in addition to the teachers and other officials of the Sunday School there were also present a considerable number of prettily dressed ladies and a few gentlemen, who had come in the hope of meeting the Rev. John Starr, the young minister who was acting as temporary pastor in place of Mr Belcher, their regular shepherd, who was going away for a holiday for the benefit of his health. Mr Belcher was not suffering from any particular malady, but was merely 'run down,' and rumour had it that this condition had been brought about by the rigorous asceticism of his life and intense devotion to the arduous labours of his holy calling.

Mr Starr had conducted the service in the Shining Light Chapel that morning, and a great sensation had been produced by his earnest and eloquent address, which was of a very different style from that of their regular minister. Although perhaps they had not quite grasped the real significance of all that he had said, most of them had been favourably impressed by the young pastor's appearance and manner. There were, however, one or two members of the congregation who were not without some misgivings and doubts as to the soundness of his doctrines.

Mr Starr had promised that he would look in some time during the afternoon to say a few words to the Sunday School children, and consequently on this particular afternoon all the grown-ups were looking forward so eagerly to his arrival that not much was done in the way of lessons, and every time a late-comer entered all eyes were directed towards the door.

When Frankie, standing, saw all these people looking at him, he drew back timidly.

'Come on, man,' said Charlie; 'you needn't be afraid; it's not like a week day school; they can't do nothing to us, not even if we don't behave ourselves. There's our class over in that corner, and that's our teacher, Mr Hunter. You can sit next to me. Come on!'

Thus encouraged, Frankie followed Charlie over to the class, and both sat down. The teacher was so kind and spoke so gently to the children that in a few minutes Frankie felt quite at home, though he was too much interested in the pictures on the walls and in looking at the other children to pay much attention to the lesson. He also noticed a very fat man, who was not teaching at all, but drifted aimlessly about the room from one class to another. After a time he came and stood by the class where Frankie was, and, after nodding to Hunter, remained near, listening and smiling patronisingly at the children. He was arrayed in a long garment of costly black cloth, a sort of frock coat, and by the rotundity of his figure be seemed to be one of those accustomed to sit in the chief places at feasts. This was the Rev. Mr Belcher, minister of the Shining Light Chapel. His short thick neck was surrounded by a collar, apparently studless and buttonless, being fastened in some mysterious way known only to himself, and he showed no shirt front. He was exceedingly fat; in fact his figure was almost like a balloon in its rotundity, the large feet, encased in soft calf-skin boots, representing the car.

After exchanging a few words with Hunter, he moved on to another class and presently, with a feeling of awe, Frankie noticed, that the sounds of whispering and giggling that had hitherto pervaded the place were suddenly hushed. The time allotted for lessons had expired, and the teachers were quietly distributing hymn books to the children.

Meantime the balloon had drifted up to the end of the hall and ascended the platform, where it remained stationary by the side of the table, on which were several books and a pile of folded cards. These latter were about six inches by three; there was some printing on the cover, and ruled lines and money columns on the inside.

Presently Mr Belcher reached out a flabby white hand and taking up one of the folded cards he looked around upon the underfed, ill-clad children with a large, sweet, benevolent, fatherly smile, and then in a drawling voice, he said:

'My deah children, this afternoon as I was standing near Brother Hunter's class I heard him telling them of the wanderings of the children of Israel in the wilderness, and of all the wonderful things that were done for them; and I thought how sad it was that they were so ungrateful.

'Now those ungrateful Israelites had received many things, but we have even more cause to be grateful than they, for we have received even more abundantly, and I am sure that none of you would like to be even as those Israelites, ungrateful for all the good things you have received. Oh, how thankful you should be for having been made happy English children. Now, I am sure that you are grateful and that you will all be very glad of an opportunity of showing your gratitude by doing something in return.

'Doubtless some of you have noticed the unseemly condition of the interior of our chapel. The flooring is broken in countless places; the walls are sadly in need of cleansing and distempering, and they also need cementing externally to keep out the draught. The seats and benches and the chairs are also in a most unseemly condition and need varnishing.

'Now, therefore, after much earnest meditation and prayer, it has been decided to open a Subscription List, and although times are very hard just now, we believe we shall succeed in getting enough to have the work done. So I want each of you to take one of these cards and go round to all your friends to see how much you can collect. It doesn't matter how trifling the amounts are, because the smallest donations will be thankfully received.

'Now I hope you will all do your very best. Ask everyone you know; do not refrain from asking people because you think that they are too poor to give a donation, but remind them that if they cannot give their thousands they can give the widow's mite. Ask everyone! First of all ask those who you will feel certain will give; then ask all those who you think may *possibly* give; and, finally, ask all those who you feel certain will *not* give; and you will be surprised to find that many of these last will donate abundantly.

'If your friends are very poor and unable to give a large donation at one time, a good plan would be to arrange to call upon them every Saturday afternoon with your card to collect their donations. And while you are asking others, do not forget to give what you can yourselves. Just a little self denial, and those pennies and halfpennies which you so often spend on sweets and other unnecessary things, might be given—as a donation—to the good cause.

'All those who wish to collect donations will stay behind for a few minutes after school, when Brother Hunter, who has kindly consented to act as secretary to the fund, will issue the cards.

'I would like here to say a few words of thanks to Brother Hunter for the great interest he has displayed in this matter, and for all the trouble he is taking to help us to gather in the donations.'

This tribute was well deserved. Hunter in fact had originated the whole scheme in the hope of securing the job for Rushton and Company, and two and a half per cent. of the profits for himself.

Mr Belcher now replaced the collecting card on the table, and taking up one of the hymn books, gave out the words and afterwards conducted the singing, flourishing one fat hand in the air and holding the book in the other.

As the last strains of the music died away, he closed his eyes and a sweet smile widened his mouth, as he stretched forth his right hand, open, palm down, with the fingers close together, and said:

'Let us pray.'

With much shuffling of feet everyone knelt down. Hunter's lanky form was distributed over a very large area; his body lay along one of the benches, his legs and feet sprawled over the floor, and his huge hands clasped the sides of the seat. His eyes were tightly closed and there was an expression of the most intense misery in his long face.

Mrs Starvem, Ruth Easton's former mistress, was so fat that she knew if she once knelt down she would never be able to get up again, so compromised by sitting on the extreme edge of her chair, resting her elbows on the back of the seat in front of her, and burying her face in her hands. It was a very large face, but her hands were capacious enough to receive it.

In a seat at the back of the hall knelt a pale faced, weary looking little woman about thirty-six years of age, very shabbily dressed, who had come in during the singing. This was Mrs White, the caretaker, Bert White's mother. When her husband died, the Committee of the Chapel, out of charity, gave her this work, for which they paid her six shillings a week. Of course they could not offer her full employment; the idea was that she could get other work as well, charing and things of that kind, and do the Chapel work in between. There wasn't much to do: just the heating furnace to light when necessary; the Chapel, committee rooms, classrooms and Sunday School to sweep and scrub out occasionally; the hymn books to collect, etc. Whenever they had a tea meeting—which was, on an average, about twice a week—there were the trestle tables to fix up, the chairs to arrange, the table to set out, and then, supervised by Miss Didlum or some other lady, the tea to make. There was rather a lot to do on the days following these functions: the washing up; the tables and chairs to put away, the floor to sweep, and so on; but the extra work was supposed to be compensated by the cakes and broken victuals generally left over from the feast, which were much appreciated as a welcome change from the bread and dripping or margarine that constituted Mrs White's and Bert's usual fare.

There were several advantages attached to the position; the caretaker became acquainted with the leading members and their wives, some of whom, out of charity, occasionally gave her a day's work as charwoman, the wages being on about the same generous scale as those she earned at the chapel, occasionally supplemented by a parcel of broken victuals or some cast-off clothing. The possibility that her employers took advantage of her poverty to impose upon her conditions of price and labour which a woman in a more independent position would not have endured, never occurred to Mrs White. On the contrary her heart was filled with gratitude towards her generous benefactors.

During the prayer the door was softly opened and a gentleman in clerical dress entered on tip toe and knelt down next to Mr Didlum. He came in very softly but all the same most of those present heard him and lifted their heads or peeped through their fingers to see who it was, and when they recognised him a sound like a sigh swept through the hall.

At the end of the prayer, amid groans and cries of 'Amen,' the balloon slowly descended from the platform and collapsed into one of the seats, and everyone rose up from the floor. When all were seated and the shuffling, coughing, and blowing of noses had ceased, Mr Didlum stood up and said:

'Before we sing the closin' 'ymn, the gentleman hon my left, the Rev. Mr John Starr, will say a few words.'

An expectant murmur rippled through the hall. The ladies lifted their eyebrows and nodded, smiled and whispered to each other; the gentlemen assumed various attitudes and expressions; and the children were very quiet. Everyone was in a state of suppressed excitement as John Starr rose from his seat and stepping up on to the platform, stood by the side of the table, facing them.

He was about twenty-six years of age, tall and slenderly built. His clean cut, intellectual face, with its lofty forehead and air of refinement and culture, were in striking contrast to the coarse appearance of the other adults in the room.

But it was not merely his air of good breeding and the general comeliness of his exterior that pleased and attracted. There was an indefinable something about him, an atmosphere of gentleness and love that seemed to radiate from his whole being, almost compelling confidence and affection from those with whom he came in contact.

As he stood there facing the others with an inexpressibly winning smile upon his face, it seemed impossible that there could be any fellowship between him and them.

He did not give a very long address this afternoon, only just a few words; but they were very precious, original and illuminating. He told them of certain thoughts that had occured to his mind on the way there that afternoon; and as they listened, Sweater, Rushton, Didlum, Hunter, and the other disciples exchanged significant looks and gestures. Was it not magnificent! Such power! Such reasoning! In fact, as they afterwards modestly admitted to each other, it was so profound that even *they*experienced great difficulty in fathoming the speaker's meaning.

As for the ladies, they were motionless and dumb with admiration. They sat with flushed faces, shining eyes and palpitating hearts, looking hungrily at the dear man as he proceeded:

'Unfortunately our time this afternoon does not permit us to dwell at length upon these Thoughts. Perhaps at some future date we may have the blessed privilege of so doing. But this afternoon I have been asked to say a few words on another subject. The failing health of your dear minister has for some time past engaged the anxious attention of the congregation.'

Sympathetic glances were directed towards the interesting invalid; the ladies murmured 'Poor dear!' and other expressions of anxious concern.

'Although naturally robust,' continued Starr, 'long continued overwork, the loving solicitude for others that often prevented him taking even necessary repose, and a too vigorous devotion to the practice of self denial, have at last brought about the inevitable breakdown, and rendered a period of rest absolutely imperative.'

'With this laudable object,' proceeded Starr, 'a Subscription List was quietly opened about a month ago, and those dear children who had cards and assisted in the good work of collecting donations will be pleased to hear that altogether a goodly sum was gathered, but as it was not quite enough, the committee voted a further amount out of the General Fund, and at a special meeting held last Friday evening, your dear Shepherd was presented with an illuminated address and a purse of gold sufficient to defray the expenses of a month's holiday in the south of France.

'Although, of course, he regrets being separated from you even for such a brief period, he feels that in going he is choosing the lesser of two evils. It is better to go to the south of France for a month than to continue working in spite of the warnings of exhausted nature and to be taken away from you, perhaps altogether—to Heaven.'

'God forbid!' fervently ejaculated several disciples, and a ghastly pallor overspread the features of the object of their prayers.

'Even as it is there is a certain amount of danger. Let us hope and pray for the best, but if the worst *should* happen, and he *is* called upon to Ascend, there will be some satisfaction in knowing that you have done what you could to avert the dreadful calamity.

'He sets out on his pilgrimage to-morrow,' concluded Starr, 'and I am sure he will be followed by the good wishes and prayers of all the members of his flock.'

The reverend gentleman resumed his seat, and almost immediately it became evident from the oscillations of the balloon that Mr Belcher was desirous of rising to say a few words in acknowledgement, but he was restrained by the entreaties of those near him, who besought him not to exhaust himself. He afterwards said that he would not have been able to say much even if they had permitted him to speak, because he felt too full.

'During the absence of our beloved pastor,' said Brother Didlum, who now rose to give out the closing hymn, 'his flock will not be left hentirely without a shepherd, for we 'ave arranged with Mr Starr to come and say a few words to us hevery Sunday.'

When they heard Brother Didlum's announcement a murmur of intense rapture rose from the ladies, and Mr Starr smiled sweetly. Brother Didlum did not mention the details of the 'arrangement'; to have done so at that time would have been most unseemly, but the following extract from the accounts of the chapel will not be out of place here: 'Paid to Rev. John Starr, for service rendered on Sunday, 14th November, £4 4s., per the treasurer.'

After the 'service' was over, most of the children, including Charley and Frankie, remained to get collecting cards. Mr Starr was surrounded by a crowd of admirers, and a little later, when he drove away with Mr Belcher and Mr Sweater in the latter's motor car, the ladies looked hungrily after that conveyance, listening to the melancholy 'pip, pip' of its hooter and trying to console themselves with the reflection that they would see him again in a few hours' time at the evening service.

CHAPTER XIII

The Lodger

In accordance with his arrangement with Hunter, Owen commenced the work in the drawing room on the Monday morning, a fact commented on by Crass when Harlow and Easton, who were distempering some of the ceilings, went down to the scullery to get some more whitewash.

'Well, wot do you think of it?' he said, as he filled their pails.

'Think of what?' asked Easton.

'Why, hour speshul hartist,' replied Crass, with a sneer. 'Do you think 'es goin' to get through with it?'

'Shouldn't like to say,' replied Easton, guardedly.

'You know it's one thing to draw on a bit of paper and colour it with a penny box of paints, and quite another thing to do it on a wall or ceiling,' continued Crass, 'ain't it?'

'Yes, that's true enough,' said Harlow.

'Do you believe they're 'is own designs?' Crass went on.

'Be rather 'ard to tell,' remarked Easton, embarrassed.

Neither Harlow nor Easton shared Grass's sentiments in this matter, but at the same time they could not afford to offend him by sticking up for Owen.

'If you was to ast *me*, quietly,' Crass added, 'I should be more inclined to say as 'e copied it all out of some book.'

'That's just about the size of it, mate,' agreed Harlow.

'It would be a bit of all right if 'e was to make a bloody mess of it, wouldn't it?' Crass continued, with a malignant leer.

'Not arf!' said Harlow.

When the two men regained the upper landing on which they were working they exchanged significant glances and laughed quietly. Hearing these half suppressed sounds of merriment, Philpot, who was working alone in a room close by put his head out of the doorway.

'Wot's the game?' he enquired, in a low voice.

'Ole Crass ain't arf wild about Owen doin' that room,' replied Harlow, and repeated the substance of Grass's remarks.

'It is a bit of a take-down for the bleeder, ain't it, 'avin' to play second fiddle?' said Philpot, with a delighted grin.

''E's 'opin' Owen'll make a mess of it,' Easton whispered.

'Well, 'e'll be disappointed, mate,' answered Philpot. 'I was workin' along of Owen for Pushem and Sloggem about two years ago, and I seen 'im do a job down at the Royal 'Otel—the smokin' room ceilin' it was—and I can tell you it looked a bloody treat!'

'I've heard tell of it,' said Harlow.

'There's no doubt Owen knows 'is work,' remarked Easton. 'Although 'e *is* a bit orf 'is onion about Socialism.'

'I don't know so much about that, mate,' returned Philpot, 'I agree with a lot that 'e ses. I've often thought the same things meself, but I can't talk like 'im 'cause I ain't got no 'ead for it.'

'I agree with some of it, too,' said Harlow, with a laugh, 'but all the same, 'e does say some *bloody* silly things, you must admit. For instance, that cuff about money bein' the cause of poverty.'

'Yes; I can't exactly see that meself,' agreed Philpot.

'We must tackle 'im about that at dinner time,' said Harlow. 'I should rather like to 'ear how 'e makes it out.'

'For Gord's sake don't go startin' no arguments at dinner time,' said Easton. 'Leave 'im alone when 'e *is* quiet.'

'Yes, let's 'ave our dinner in peace, if possible,' said Philpot. 'Sh!!' he added, hoarsely, suddenly holding up his hand warningly.

They listened intently. It was evident from the creaking of the stairs that someone was crawling up them. Philpot instantly disappeared. Harlow lifted up the pail of whitewash and set it down noisily.

'I think we'd better 'ave the steps and the plank over this side, Easton,' he said in a loud voice.

'Yes. I think that'll be the best way,' replied Easton.

While they were arranging their scaffold to do the ceiling, Crass arrived on the landing. He made no remark at first, but walked into the rooms to see how many ceilings they had done.

'You'd better look alive, you chaps,' he said, as he went downstairs again. 'If we don't get these ceilings finished by dinner time, Nimrod's sure to ramp.'

'All right,' said Harlow, gruffly. 'We'll bloody soon slosh 'em over.'

'Slosh' was a very suitable word; very descriptive of the manner in which the work was done. The cornices of the staircase ceilings were enriched with plaster ornaments, the crevices of which were still filled up with old whitewash; and by the time Harlow and Easton had 'sloshed' a lot more whitewash on, they were mere formless unsightly lumps of plaster. The 'hands' who did the 'washing off' were not to blame. They had been hunted away from the work before it was half done.

While Harlow and Easton were distempering these ceilings, Philpot and the other hands were proceeding with the painting in different parts of the inside of the house, and Owen, assisted by Bert, was getting on with the work in the drawing room, striking chalk lines and measuring and setting out the different panels.

There were no 'political' arguments that day at dinner time, to the disappointment of Crass, who was still waiting for an opportunity to produce the 'Obscurer' cutting. After dinner when the others had all gone back to their work, Philpot unobtrusively returned to the kitchen and gathered up the discarded paper wrappers in which some of the men had brought their food. Spreading one of these open he shook the crumbs from the others upon it. In this way and by picking up particles of bread from the floor, he collected a little pile of crumbs and crusts. To these he added some fragments that he had left from his own dinner. He then took the parcel upstairs, and opening one of the windows threw the crumbs on to the roof of the portico. He had scarcely closed the window when two starlings fluttered down and began to eat, while Philpot stood watching with furtive satisfaction from behind the shutter.

The afternoon passed uneventfully. From one till five seemed a very long time to most of the hands, but to Owen and his mate, who were doing something in which they were able to feel some interest and pleasure, the time passed so rapidly that they both regretted the approach of evening.

'Other days,' remarked Bert, 'I always keeps on wishin' it was time to go 'ome; but to-day seems to 'ave gorn like lightnin'!'

After leaving off that night all the men kept together till they arrived down town, and then separated. Owen went by himself; Easton, Philpot, Crass and Bundy adjourned to the Cricketers Arms to have a drink together, and Slyme, who was a teetotaller, returned to the Eastons' house alone.

'Don't wait for me,' said Easton, as he went off with Crass and the others. 'I shall most likely catch you up before you get there.'

This evening Slyme, instead of taking the direct road, turned into the main street, and pausing before the window of a toy shop examined the articles displayed therein attentively. After some minutes he appeared to have come to a decision, and entering the shop he purchased a baby's rattle for fourpence half-penny. It was a pretty toy made of white bone and coloured wool, with a number of little bells hanging upon it, and a ring of white bone at the end of the handle.

He then set out for home, walking rapidly, and found Ruth sitting by the fire with the baby on her lap. She looked up with an expression of disappointment as she perceived that he was alone.

'Where's Will got to again?' she asked.

'He's gone to 'ave a drink with some of the chaps. He said he wouldn't be long,' replied Slyme as he put his food basket on the dresser and went upstairs to his room to wash and to change his clothes.

When he came down again, Easton had not yet arrived.

'Everything's ready, except just to make the tea,' said Ruth, who was evidently annoyed at the continued absence of Easton, 'so you may as well have yours now.'

'I'm in no hurry. I'll wait a little and see if he comes. He's sure to be here soon.'

'If you're sure you don't mind I shall be glad if you will wait,' said Ruth, 'because it will save me making two lots of tea.'

They waited for about half-an-hour, talking at intervals in a constrained, awkward way about trivial subjects. Then as Easton did not come, Ruth decided to serve Slyme without waiting any longer. With this intention she laid the baby in its cot, but the child resented this arrangement and began to cry, so she had to hold him under her left arm while she made the tea. Seeing her in this predicament, Slyme exclaimed, holding out his hands:

'Here, let me hold him while you do that.'

'Will you?' said Ruth, who in spite of her instinctive dislike of the man, could not help feeling gratified with this attention. 'Well, mind you don't let him fall.'

But the instant Slyme took hold of the child it began to cry even louder than it did when it was put into the cradle.

'He's always like that with strangers,' apologised Ruth as she took him back again.

'Wait a minute,' said Slyme. 'I've got something upstairs in my pocket that will keep him quiet. I'd forgotten all about it.'

He went up to his room and presently returned with the rattle. When the baby saw the bright colours and heard the tinkling of the bells he crowed with delight, and clutching at it eagerly allowed Slyme to take him without a murmur of protest. Before Ruth had finished making and serving the tea, the man and the child were on the very best of terms with each other, so much so indeed that when his mother was ready to take him again, the baby seemed reluctant to part from Slyme, who had been dancing him in the air and tickling him in the most delightful way.

Ruth, too, began to have a better opinion of their lodger, and felt inclined to reproach herself for having taken such an unreasonable dislike to him at first. He was evidently a very good sort of fellow after all.

The baby had by this time discovered the use of the bone ring at the end of the handle of the toy and was biting it energetically.

'It's a very beautiful rattle,' said Ruth. 'Thank you very much for it, it's just the very thing he wanted.'

'I heard you say the other day that he wanted something of the kind to bite on to help his teeth through,' answered Slyme, 'and when I happened to notice that in the shop I remembered what you said and thought I'd bring it home.'

The baby took the ring out of its mouth and shaking the rattle frantically in the air laughed and crowed merrily, looking at Slyme.

'Dad! dad! dad!' he cried, holding out his arms.

Slyme and Ruth burst out laughing.

'That's not your dad, you silly boy,' she said, kissing the child as she spoke; 'your dad ought to be ashamed of himself for staying out like this. We'll give him dad, dad, dad, when he does come home, won't we?'

But the baby only shook the rattle and rang the bells and laughed and crowed and laughed again, louder than ever.

CHAPTER XIV

The Cricketers' Arms

Viewed from outside, 'The Cricketers' Arms' was a pretentious-looking building with plate glass windows and a profusion of gilding. The pilasters were painted in imitation of different marbles and the doors grained to represent costly woods. There were panels containing painted advertisements of wines and spirits and beer, written in gold, and ornamented with gaudy colours. On the lintel over the principal entrance was inscribed in small white letters: 'A. Harpy. Licensed to sell wines, spirits and malt liquors by retail to be consumed either on or off the premises.'

The bar was arranged in the usual way, being divided into several compartments. First there was the 'Saloon Bar,' on the glass door of which was fixed a printed bill: 'No four ale served in this bar.' Next was the jug and bottle department, much appreciated by ladies who wished to indulge in a drop of gin on the quiet. There were also two small 'private' bars, only capable of holding two or three persons, where nothing less than four pennyworth of spirits or glasses of ale at threepence were served. Finally, there was the public bar, the largest compartment of all.

Wooden forms provided seating accommodation for the customers, and a large automatic musical instrument—a 'penny in the slot' polyphone, resembling a grandfather's clock in shape—stood close to the counter, so that those behind the bar could reach to wind it up. Hanging on the partition near the polyphone was a board about fifteen inches square, over the surface of which were distributed a number of small hooks, numbered. At the bottom of the board was a net made of fine twine, in which several india rubber rings about three inches in diameter were lying. There was no table in the place but jutting out from the partition which divided the public bar from the others was a hinged flap about three feet long by twenty inches wide, which could be folded down when not in use. This was the 'Shove-ha'penny' board. The coins—old French pennies—used in playing this game were kept behind the bar and might be borrowed on application. On the partition, just above the shove-ha'penny board was a neatly printed notice, framed and glazed:—

NOTICE

GENTLEMEN USING THIS HOUSE ARE REQUESTED
TO REFRAIN FROM USING OBSCENE LANGUAGE.

Alongside this notice were a number of gaudily coloured bills advertising the local theatre and the music hall, and another of a travelling circus and menagerie then visiting the town and encamped on a piece of waste ground about half way on the road to Windley.

The fittings behind the bar, and the counter, were of polished mahogany, with silvered plate glass at the back of the shelves. On these shelves were rows of bottles and cut glass decanters, gin, whiskey, brandy, and wines and liqueurs of different kinds.

When Crass, Philpot, Easton and Bundy entered, the landlord, a well-fed, prosperous looking individual in white shirt sleeves, a bright maroon fancy waistcoat, a massive gold watch chain and a diamond ring, was conversing in an affable, friendly way with one of his regular customers, sitting close to the counter. He was a shabbily dressed, bleary-eyed, degraded, beer-sodden, trembling wretch, about thirty years of age, who spent most of his time and all his money at 'The Cricketers.' He had once been a carpenter, but some years previously had married a woman considerably his senior, the landlady of a third rate lodging house, whose business was sufficiently prosperous to enable him to exist without working and in a condition of perpetual semi-intoxication. He came to the 'Cricketers' every morning, and sometimes earned a pint of beer by assisting the barman in sweeping up the sawdust or cleaning the windows, and usually remained until closing time every night.

The only other occupant of the public bar—previous to the entrance of Crass and his mates—was a semi-drunken house painter, who was sitting on the form near the shove ha'penny board. This individual wore a battered bowler hat; he had a very thin, pale face, with a large, high-bridged nose, and bore a striking resemblance to the portraits of the first Duke of Wellington. He was not a regular customer but, having dropped in casually about two o'clock, was beginning to show the effects of the drink he had taken.

As Crass and the others entered they were hailed with enthusiasm by the landlord and the Besotted Wretch, while the semi-drunk house painter regarded them with fishy eyes and stupid curiosity.

'Wot cheer, Bob!' said the landlord, affably, addressing Crass, and nodding familiarly to the others. ''Ow goes it?'

'All reet, me ole dear!' replied Crass, jovially. ''Ow's yerself?'

'AI.,' replied the 'old dear,' getting up from his chair in readiness to execute their orders.

'Well, wot's it to be?' enquired Philpot of the others.

'Mine's a pint o' beer,' said Crass.

'Half for me,' said Bundy.

'Half o' beer for me, too,' replied Easton.

'That's one pint, two 'arves, and a pint o' porter for meself,' said Philpot, turning and addressing the Old Dear.

While the landlord was serving these drinks the Besotted Wretch finished his beer and set the empty glass down on the counter, and Philpot observing this, said to him:

''Ave one along o' me?'

'I don't mind if I do,' replied the other.

When the drinks were served, Philpot, instead of paying for them, winked significantly at the landlord, who nodding silently and unobstrusively made an entry in an account book that was lying on one of the shelves. Although it was only Monday and he had been at work all the previous week, Philpot was already stoney broke. This was accounted for by the fact that on the Saturday he had paid his landlady something on account of the arrears of board and lodging money which had accumulated while he was out of work; and he had also paid the Old Dear four shillings for drinks obtained on tick during the last week.

'Well, 'ere's the skin orf yer nose,' said Crass, nodding to Philpot, and taking a long pull at the pint glass which the latter had handed to him.

Similar appropriate and friendly sentiments were expressed by the others and suitably acknowledged by Philpot, the founder of the feast.

The Old Dear now put a penny in the slot of the polyphone, and started it playing. It was some unfamiliar tune, but when the semi-drunk painter heard it he rose unsteadily to his feet and began shuffling and dancing about, singing:

Oh, we'll inwite you to the wed—ding,
And we'll 'ave a glorious time!
Where the boys an' the girls is a-dancing,
An' we'll all get drunk on wine!'

''Ere! that's quite enough 'o that!' cried the landlord, roughly. 'We don't want that row 'ere.'

The Semi-Drunk stopped, and looking stupidly at the Old Dear, sank abashed on to the seat again.

'Well, we may as well sit as stand—for a few minutes,' remarked Crass, suiting the action to the word. The others followed his example.

At frequent intervals the bar was entered by fresh customers, most of them working men on their way home, who ordered and drank their pint or half pint of ale or porter and left at once. Bundy began reading the advertisement of the circus and menagerie, and a conversation ensued concerning the wonderful performances of the trained animals. The Old Dear said that some of them had as much sense as human beings, and the manner with which he made this statement implied that he thought it was a testimonial to the sagacity of the brutes. He further said that he had heard a rumour that one of the wild animals, a bear or something, had broken loose and was at present at large. For his own part he didn't believe it, and his hearers agreed that it was highly improbable. Nobody ever knew how these silly yarns got about.

Presently the Besotted Wretch got up, and taking the india rubber rings out of the net with a trembling hand, began throwing them one at a time at the hooks on the board. The rest of the company watched him with much interest, laughing when he made a very bad shot and applauding when he scored.

''E's a bit 'orf to-night,' remarked Philpot aside to Easton, 'but as a rule 'e's a fair knock out at it. Throws a splendid ring!'

The Semi-Drunk regarded the proceedings of the Besotted Wretch with an expression of profound contempt.

'You can't play for nuts,' he said, scornfully.

'Can't I? I can play *you*, anyway.'

'Right you are! I'll play you for drinks round!' cried the Semi-Drunk.

For a moment the Besotted Wretch hesitated. He had not money enough to pay for drinks round. However, feeling confident of winning, he replied:

'Come on then: what's it to be? Fifty up?'

'Anything you like! Fifty or a 'undred or a bloody million!'

'Better make it fifty for a start.'

'All right!'

'You play first if you like.'

'All right,' agreed the Semi-Drunk, anxious to distinguish himself.

Holding the six rings in his left hand the man stood in the middle of the floor at a distance of about three yards from the board, with his right foot advanced. Taking one of the rings between the forefinger and thumb of his right hand, and closing his left eye, he carefully 'sighted' the centre hook, No. 13; then he slowly extended his arm to its full length in the direction of the board; then bending his elbow, he brought his hand back again until it nearly touched his chin, and slowly extended his arm again. He repeated these movements several times, whilst the others watched with bated breath. Getting it right at last he suddenly shot the ring at the board, but it did not go on No. 13; it went over the partition into the private bar.

This feat was greeted with a roar of laughter. The player stared at the board in a dazed way, wondering what had become of the ring, but when someone in the next bar threw it over the partition again, he realised what had happened, and turning to the company with a sickly smile, remarked:

'I ain't got properly used to this board yet: that's the reason of it.'

He now began throwing the other rings at the board rather wildly, without troubling to take aim. One struck the partition to the right of the board, one to the left, one underneath, one went over the counter, one on the floor, the other—the last—hit the board, and amid a shout of applause, caught on the centre hook, No. 13, the highest number possible to score with a single throw.

'I shall be all right now that I've got the range,' observed the Semi-Drunk, as he made way for his opponent.

'You'll see something now,' whispered Philpot to Easton. 'This bloke is a dandy!'

The Besotted Wretch took up his position and with an affectation of carelessness, began throwing the rings. It was really a remarkable exhibition, for notwithstanding the fact that his hand trembled like an aspen leaf, he succeeded in striking the board almost in the centre every time; but somehow or other most of them failed to catch on the hooks, and fell into the net. When he finished his innings he had scored only four, two of the rings having caught on the No. 2 hook.

''Ard lines,' remarked Bundy as he finished his beer and put the glass down on the counter.

'Drink up and 'ave another,' said Easton, as he drained his own glass.

'I don't mind if I do,' replied Crass, pouring what remained of the pint down his throat.

Philpot's glass had been empty for some time.

'Same again,' said Easton, addressing the Old Dear, and putting six pennies on the counter.

By this time the Semi-Drunk had again opened fire on the board, but he seemed to have lost the range this time, for none of the rings scored. They flew all over the place, and he finished his innings without increasing his total.

The Besotted Wretch now sailed in and speedily piled up 37. Then the Semi-Drunk had another go, and succeeded in getting eight. His case appeared hopeless, but his opponent in his next innings seemed to go all to pieces. Twice he missed the board altogether, and when he did hit it he failed to score until the very last throw, when he made one. Then the Semi-Drunk went in again, and got ten.

The scores were now:—

Besotted Wretch. 42

Semi-Drunk. 31

So far it was impossible to foresee the end. It wasanybody's game. Crass became so excited that he absentmindedly opened his mouth and shot his second pint down into his stomach with a single gulp, and Bundy also drained his glass and called upon Philpot and Easton to drink up and have another, which they accordingly did.

While the Semi-Drunk was having his next innings the Besotted Wretch placed a penny on the counter and called for half a pint, which he drank in the hope of steadying his nerves for a great effort. His opponent meanwhile threw the rings at the board and missed it every time, but all the same he scored, for one ring, after striking the partition about a foot above the board, fell down and caught on the hook.

The other man now began his innings, playing very carefully, and nearly every ring scored. As he played, the others uttered explanations of admiration and called out the result of every throw.

'One!'

'One again!'

'Miss!—No! got'im! two!'

'Miss!'

'Miss!'

'Four!'

The Semi-Drunk accepted his defeat with a good grace, and after explaining that he was a bit out of practice, placed a shilling on the counter and invited the company to give their orders. Everyone asked for 'the same again,' but the landlord served Easton, Bundy and the Besotted Wretch with pints instead of half-pints as before, so there was no change out of the shilling.

'You know, there's a great deal in not bein' used to the board,' said the Semi-Drunk.

'There's no disgrace in bein' beat by a man like 'im, mate,' said Philpot, ''e's a champion!'

'Yes, there's no mistake about it. 'E throws a splendid ring!' said Bundy.

This was the general verdict. The Semi-Drunk, though beaten, was not disgraced, and he was so affected by the good feeling manifested by the company that he presently produced a sixpence and insisted on paying for another half-pint all round.

'Let's 'ave a game of shove-'apenny,' said Bundy.

'All right,' said Easton who was beginning to feel reckless. 'But drink up first, and let's 'ave another.'

He had only sevenpence left, just enough to pay for another pint for Crass and half a pint for everyone else.

The shove-'apenny table was a planed mahogany board with a number of parallel lines scored across it, the game being to place the coin at the end of the board, the rim slightly projecting over the edge, and strike it with the back of the hand to the particular spot required by the player.

'What's become of Alf to-night?' inquired Philpot of the landlord, whilst Easton and Bundy were playing. Alf was the barman.

''E's doing a bit of a job down in the cellar; some of the valves gone a bit wrong. But the missus is comin' down to lend me a hand presently. 'Ere she is now.'

The landlady—who at this moment entered through the door at the back of the bar—was a large woman with a highly coloured countenance and a tremendous bust, encased in a black dress with a shot silk blouse. She had several jewelled gold rings on the fingers of each fat white hand, and a long gold watch guard hung round her fat neck. She greeted Crass and Philpot with condescension, smiling affably upon them.

Meantime the game of shove-'apenny proceeded merrily, Semi-Drunk taking a great interest in it and tendering advice to both players impartially. Bundy was badly beaten; and then Easton suggested that it was time to think of going home. This proposal—slightly modified—met with general approval, the modification being suggested by Philpot, who insisted on standing one final round of drinks before they went.

While they were pouring this down, Crass took a penny from his waistcoat pocket and put it in the slot of the polyphone. The landlord put a fresh disc into it and it began to play "The Boys of the Old Bulldog Breed." The Semi-Drunk happened to know the words of the chorus of this song, and when he heard the music he started unsteadily to his feet and with many fierce looks and gestures began to roar at the top of his voice:—

> 'They may build their ships, my lads,
> And try to play the game,
> But they can't build the boys of the Bulldog breed,
> Wot made ole Hingland's'—

''Ere! stop that, will yer?' cried the Old Dear fiercely, 'I told you once before that I don't allow that sort of thing in my 'ouse!'

The Semi-Drunk stopped in confusion. 'I didn't mean no 'arm,' he said unsteadily, appealing to the company.

'I don't want no chin from you!' said the Old Dear with a ferocious scowl. 'If you want to make that row you can go somewheres else, and the sooner you goes the better. You've been 'ere long enough.'

This was true. The man had been there long enough to spend every penny in his pocket. He had no money left now, a fact that the observant and experienced landlord had divined some time ago. He therefore wished to get rid of the fellow before he became helplessly drunk. The Semi-Drunk listened with indignation and wrath to the landlord's insulting words.

'I shall go when the bloody 'ell I like!' he shouted. 'I shan't ask you nor nobody else! Who the bloody 'ell are you? You're nobody! See? Nobody! It's orf the likes of me that you gets your bloody livin'! I shall stop 'ere as long as I bloody well like, and if you don't like it you can go to 'ell!'

'Oh! yer will, will yer?' said the Old Dear. 'We'll soon see about that,' and opening the door at the back of the bar he roared out:

'Alf!'

'Yes, sir,' replied a voice evidently from the basement.

'Just come up 'ere.'

'All right,' replied the voice, and footsteps were heard ascending some stairs.

'You'll see some fun in a minute,' gleefully remarked Crass to Easton.

The polyphone continued to play 'The Boys of the Bulldog Breed.'

Philpot crossed over to the Semi-Drunk. 'Look 'ere, old man,' he whispered, 'take my tip and go 'ome quietly. You'll only git the worst of it, you know.'

'Not me, mate,' replied the other, shaking his head doggedly. ''Ere I am, and 'ere I'm goin' to bloody well stop.'

'No you aint,' replied Philpot coaxingly. 'Look 'ere: I'll tell you wot we'll do. You 'ave just one more 'arf pint along of me, and then we'll both go 'ome together. I'll see you safe 'ome.'

'See me safe 'ome! Wotcher mean?' indignantly demanded the other. 'Do you think I'm *drunk*?'

'No: certainly not,' replied Philpot, hastily, 'you're all right, as right as I am myself. But you know wot I mean, let's go 'ome. You don't want to stop 'ere all night, do you?'

By this time Alf had arrived at the door at the back of the bar. He was a burly young man about twenty-two or twenty-three years of age.

'Put it outside,' growled the landlord indicating the culprit.

The barman instantly vaulted over the counter, and having opened wide the door leading into the street, he turned to the half-drunken man and jerking his thumb in the direction of the door said:

'Are yer goin'?'

'I'm goin' to 'ave 'arf a pint along of this genelman first—'

'Yes, it's all right,' said Philpot to the landlord. 'Let's 'ave two 'arf pints, and say no more about it.'

'You mind your own business,' shouted the landlord, turning savagely on him. ''E'll get no more 'ere! I don't want no drunken men in my 'ouse. Who asked *you* to interfere?'

'Now, then!' exclaimed the barman to the cause of the trouble. 'Outside!'

'Not me!' said the Semi-Drunk, firmly, 'not before I've 'ad my 'arf—'

But before he could conclude, the barman had clutched him by the collar, dragged him violently to the door and shot him into the middle of the road, where he fell in a heap almost under the wheels of a brewer's dray which happened to be passing. This accomplished, Alf shut the door, and retired behind the counter again.

'Serve 'im bloody well right,' said Crass.

'I couldn't 'elp laughin' when I seen 'im go flyin' through the bloody door,' said Bundy.

'You oughter 'ave more sense than to go interferin' like that,' said Crass to Philpot. 'It was nothing to do with you.'

Philpot made no reply. He was standing with his back to the others, peeping out into the street over the top of the window casing. Then he opened the door and went out into the street. Crass and the others—through the window—watched him assist the Semi-Drunk to his feet and rub some of the dirt off his clothes, and presently, after some argument they saw the two go away together, arm in arm.

Crass and the others laughed, and returned to their half finished drinks.

'Why, old Joe aint drunk 'ardly 'arf of '*is*!' cried Easton, seeing Philpot's porter on the counter. 'Fancy going away like that!'

'More fool 'im,' growled Crass, 'There was no need for it, the man's all right.'

The Besotted Wretch gulped his beer down as quickly as he could, with his eyes fixed greedily on Philpot's glass. He had just finished his own and was about to suggest that it was a pity to waste the porter, when Philpot unexpectedly reappeared.

'Hullo! what 'ave you done with 'im?' inquired Crass.

'I think 'e'll be all right,' replied Philpot. 'He wouldn't let me go no further with 'im; said if I didn't go away, 'e'd go for me! But I believe 'e'll be all right, I think the fall sobered 'im a bit.'

'Oh, 'e's all right,' said Crass, offhandedly. 'There's nothing the matter with '*im*.'

Philpot now drank his porter, and bidding good-night to the Old Dear, the landlady and the Besotted Wretch, they all set out for home.

As they went along the dark and lonely thoroughfare that led over the hill to Windley, they heard from time to time the weird roaring of the wild animals in the menagerie that was encamped in the adjacent field. Just as they reached a very gloomy and deserted part, they suddenly observed a dark object in the middle of the road some distance in front of them. It seemed to be a large animal of some kind, and was coming slowly and stealthily towards them.

They stopped, peering in a half frightened way through the darkness. The animal continued to approach. Bundy stooped down to the ground, groping about in search of a stone, and—with the exception of Crass, who was too frightened to move—the others followed his example. They found several large stones and stood waiting for the creature—whatever it was—to come a little nearer so as to get a fair shot at it. They were about to let fly when it fell over on its side and moaned as if in pain. Observing this the four men advanced cautiously towards it. Bundy struck a match, and held it over the prostrate figure. It was the Semi-Drunk.

After parting from Philpot the poor wretch had managed to walk all right for some distance. As Philpot had remarked, the fall had to some extent sobered him; but he had not gone very far before the drink he had taken began to affect him again and he had fallen down. Finding it impossible to get up, he began crawling along on his hands and knees, unconscious of the fact that he was travelling in the wrong direction. Even this mode of progression failed him at last, and he would probably have been run over if they had not found him. They raised him up, and Philpot, exhorting him to 'pull himself together,' enquired where he lived. The man had sense enough left to be able to tell them his address, which was fortunately at Windley.

Bundy and Philpot took him home, and Crass and Easton walked on together, as they both lived in the same street.

Crass felt very full and satisfied with himself. He had had six and a half pints of beer, and had listened to two selections on the polyphone at a total cost of one penny.

As soon as Easton parted from Crass, and he heard the latter's door close, he stopped and leant up against a lamp post feeling dizzy and ill. All the inanimate objects around him seemed to be in motion, the lights of the lamps appeared to be floating about and the pavement rose and fell, like a troubled sea. After a time he went on again and walked unsteadily up the narrow path to his door, the gate clanging loudly after him.

The baby was asleep in the cradle. Slyme had gone up to his own room, and Ruth was sitting sewing by the fireside. The table was still set for two persons, for she had not yet taken her tea.

Easton lurched in noisily. ''Ello, old girl!' he cried, throwing his dinner basket carelessly on the floor with an affectation of joviality, and resting his hands on the table to support himself; 'I've come at last, you see.'

Letting her hands fall into her lap, Ruth sat looking at him. She had never seen him like this before. His face was ghastly pale, the eyes bloodshot and red-rimmed, the lips tremulous and moist and the ends of his fair moustache hung untidily round his mouth in damp clusters. Perceiving that she did not speak or smile, Easton concluded that she was angry and became grave himself.

'I've come at last, you see, my dear; better late than never.'

He found it very difficult to speak plainly, for his lips trembled and refused to form the words.

'I don't know so much about that,' said Ruth, inclined to cry and trying not to let him see the pity she could not help feeling for him. 'A nice state you're in. You ought to be ashamed of yourself.'

Easton shook his head and laughed foolishly. 'Don't be angry, Ruth; it's no good, you know.'

He walked clumsily towards her, still leaning on the table to steady himself.

'Don't be angry,' he mumbled, as he stooped over her, putting his arm round her neck and his face close to hers. 'It's no good being angry, you know, dear.'

She shrank away, shuddering with involuntary disgust as he pressed his wet lips and filthy moustache upon her mouth. His fetid breath, foul with the smell of tobacco and beer, filled her with loathing. He kissed her repeatedly, and when at last he released her she hastily wiped her face with her handkerchief and shivered.

Easton said he did not want any tea, and went upstairs to bed almost immediately. Ruth did not want any tea either, although she had been very hungry before he came home. She sat up very late sewing, and when at length she went upstairs she found him lying on his back, partly undressed, on the outside of the bedclothes, with his mouth wide open, breathing stertorously.

CHAPTER XV

The Great Money Trick

During the next four weeks the usual reign of terror continued at 'The Cave'; the men slaved like so many convicts under the vigilant surveillance of Crass and Rushton, not to mention Misery, who had lately adopted the plan of crawling up one of the ladders and entering the house by an upper window. Even if he never caught any one, he accomplished the useful purpose of making the men afraid to stop working for an instant. The consequence was the job at 'The Cave' rapidly neared completion, and though the hands cursed and grumbled at their mates for 'tearing into it' they each tore into it themselves, for already there were dozens of men 'walking about' and little chance of obtaining employment elsewhere.

Sweater paid frequent visits to 'The Cave' while Owen was painting the drawing room, being interested in the progress of the work. On these occasions Crass always managed to be present and did most of the talking, an arrangement which suited Owen very well, for he was always ill at ease when conversing with a man like Sweater, who spoke in an offensively patronising way, and expected common people to kow-tow to and 'Sir' him at every second word. Crass, however, seemed to enjoy doing that kind of thing, and though he did not exactly grovel on the floor when Sweater spoke to him, he contrived to convey the impression that he was willing to do so if desired.

Outside the house Bundy and his mates had dug deep trenches in the damp ground for the new drains. It was a miserable job. Owing to the fact that there had been a spell of bad weather the ground was sodden with rain and there was mud everywhere, the men's clothing and boots were caked with it. But the worst thing about the job was the smell. For years the old drain-pipes had been defective and leaky. The ground a few feet below the surface was saturated with fetid moisture. The clothing of the men who were working in the trenches became saturated with this fearful stench, and for that matter, so did the men themselves. They said they could smell and taste it, even when they were away from the work, at home, and when they were at meals. Although they smoked their pipes all the time they were at work—Misery having ungraciously given them permission—several times Bundy and one or other of his mates were attacked with fits of nausea and vomiting.

But, as they began to realise that the finish of the job was in sight, a kind of panic seized upon all the hands, especially those who had been taken on last and who would therefore be the first to be 'stood still'. Easton, however, felt pretty confident that Crass would do his best to get him kept on till the end of the job, for they had become quite chummy lately, usually spending a few evenings together at the 'Cricketers' every week.

'There'll be a bloody slaughter 'ere soon,' remarked Harlow to Philpot, one day as they were painting the bannisters of the staircase. 'I reckon next week will about finish the inside.'

'And the outside ain't goin' to take very long, you know,' replied Philpot.

'They ain't got no other work in, have they?'

'Not that I knows of,' replied Philpot gloomily; 'and I don't think anyone else has either.'

'You know that little place they call the "Kiosk" down on the Grand Parade, near the bandstand?' asked Harlow, after a pause. 'I heard last night that Grinder, the fruit merchant, is going to open it again. If so, it will be a job for someone because it will 'ave to be done up.'

'Well, I hope it will,' said Philpot. 'It will be a job for some poor bleeder.'

'I wonder if they've started on the venetian blinds for this 'ouse.'

'I don't know,' said Philpot, and they relapsed into silence.

'I wonder what time it is,' said Philpot, at length. 'I don't know 'ow you feel, but I begin to want my dinner.'

'That's just what I was thinking: it can't be very far off it now. It's nearly 'arf an hour since Bert went down to make the tea. It seems a 'ell of a long morning to me.'

'So it does to me,' said Philpot. 'Slip upstairs and ask Slyme what time it is.'

Harlow laid his brush across the top of his paint pot and went upstairs. He was wearing a pair of cloth slippers, and walked softly, not wishing Crass to hear him leaving his work, so it happened that without any intention of spying, he reached the door of the room in which Slyme was working without being heard, and entering suddenly, surprised the latter, who was standing near the fireplace, in the act of breaking a whole roll of wall paper across his knee as one might break a stick. On the floor beside him was what had been another roll, now broken into two pieces. When Harlow came in, Slyme started, and his face became crimson with confusion. He hastily gathered the broken rolls together and stooping down, thrust the pieces up the flue of the grate and closed the register.

'Wot's the bloody game?' enquired Harlow, curiously.

Slyme laughed with an affectation of carelessness, but his hands trembled and his face was now very pale.

'We must get our own back somehow you know, Fred,' he said.

Harlow did not reply. He did not understand. After puzzling over it for a few minutes he gave it up.

'What's the time?' he asked.

'Fifteen minutes to twelve,' said Slyme, and added, as Harlow was going away: 'don't mention anything about that there paper to Crass or any of the others.'

'I shan't say nothing,' replied Harlow.

Gradually, as he pondered over it, Harlow began to comprehend the meaning of the destruction of the two rolls of paper. Slyme was doing the paperhanging piecework—so much for each roll hung. Four of the rooms upstairs had been done with the same pattern, and Hunter had evidently sent more paper than was necessary. By getting rid of these two rolls Slyme would be able to make it appear that he had hung two rolls more than was really the case. He had broken them in order to be able to take them away from the house without detection, and had hidden them up the chimney until an opportunity of so doing presented itself. Harlow had just arrived at this solution of the problem when, hearing the lower flight of stairs creaking, he peeped over and observed Misery crawling up, with the object of discovering someone who had stopped work before the proper time. Passing the two workmen without speaking, he ascended to the next floor and entered the room where Slyme was working.

'You'd better not do this room yet,' said Hunter, 'there's to be a new grate and mantelpiece put in.'

He crossed over to the fireplace and stood looking at it thoughtfully for a few minutes.

'It's not a bad little grate, you know, is it?' he remarked. 'We'll be able to use it somewhere or other.'

'Yes, it's all right,' said Slyme, whose heart was beating like a steam hammer.

'Do for a front room in a cottage,' continued Misery, stooping down to examine it more closely. 'There's nothing broke that I can see.'

He put his hand against the register and vainly tried to push it open.

'H'm, there's something wrong 'ere,' he remarked, pushing harder.

'Most likely a brick or some plaster fallen down,' gasped Slyme, coming to Misery's assistance, 'shall *I* try to open it?'

'Don't trouble,' replied Nimrod, rising to his feet. 'It's most likely what you say. I'll see that the new grate is sent up after dinner. Bundy can fix it this afternoon and then you can go on papering as soon as you like.'

With this, Misery went out of the room, downstairs and away from the house, and Slyme wiped the sweat from his forehead. Then he knelt down and opening the register he took out the broken rolls of paper and hid them up the chimney of the next room. While he was doing this the sound of Crass's whistle shrilled through the house.

'Thank Gord!' exclaimed Philpot, fervently, as he laid his brushes on the top of his pot and joined in the general rush to the kitchen, the luxurious banqueting hall of the workers.

The floor was unswept and littered with dirt, scraps of paper, bits of plaster, pieces of lead pipe and dried mud; and in the midst stood the steaming bucket of stewed tea and the collection of cracked cups, jam jars and condensed-milk tins. On the upturned pails, planks and dresser drawers sat the men in their shabby ragged clothing, eating their coarse food, cracking their coarser jokes, contented so long as they had plenty of work, something to eat, someone else's cast off clothing to wear, convinced that the good things of life were not for the likes of them, or for their children either.

'Wot's become of the Professor?' asked the man who sat on an upturned pail in the corner, referring to Owen, who had not yet come down from his work.

'P'r'aps 'e's preparing 'is sermon,' remarked Harlow with a laugh.

'We ain't 'ad no lectures from 'im lately, since 'e's been on that room,' observed Easton, ''ave we?'

'Dam good job too!' exclaimed Sawkins. 'It gives me the pip to 'ear 'im, the same old thing over and over again.'

'Poor ole Frank,' remarked Harlow, ''e does upset 'isself about things, don't 'e?'

'More fool 'im!' said Bundy, 'I'll take bloody good care I don't go worryin' myself to death like 'e's doin' about such dam rot as that.'

'I do believe that's wot makes 'im look so bad as 'e does,' observed Harlow; 'several times this morning I couldn't help noticing the way 'e kept on coughing.'

'I thought 'e seemed to be a bit better lately,' Philpot observed, 'more cheerful and happier like, and more inclined for a bit of fun.'

''E's a funny sort of chap, ain't 'e?' said Bundy. 'One day quite jolly, singing and cracking jokes and tellin' yarns, and the next you can't hardly get a word out of 'im.'

'Bloody rot, I call it,' chimed in the man on the pail. 'Wot the 'ell's the use of the likes of us troublin' our 'ed's about politics?'

'Oh, I don't see *that*,' replied Harlow. 'We've got votes and we're really the people what control the affairs of the country, so I reckon we ought to take *some* interest in it; but at the same time I can't see no sense in this 'ere Socialist wangle that Owen's always talkin' about.'

'Nor nobody else neither,' said Crass, with a jeering laugh.

'Even if all the bloody money in the world *was* divided out equal,' said the man on the pail, profoundly, 'it wouldn't do no good! In six months' time it would be all back in the same 'ands again.'

'Of course,' said everybody.

'But 'e 'ad a cuff the other day about money bein' no good at all,' observed Easton. 'Don't you remember 'e said as money was the principal cause of poverty?'

'So it is the principal cause of poverty,' said Owen, who entered at that moment.

'Hooray!' shouted Philpot, leading off a cheer which the others took up. 'The Professor 'as arrived and will now proceed to say a few remarks.'

A roar of merriment greeted this sally.

'Let's 'ave our dinner first, for Christ's sake,' appealed Harlow, with mock despair.

As Owen, having filled his cup with tea, sat down in his usual place, Philpot rose solemnly to his feet, and looking round upon the company said:

'Genelmen, with your kind permission, as soon as the Professor 'as finished 'is dinner 'e will deliver 'is well known lecture, entitled: "Money the Principal Cause of being 'ard up," proving as money ain't no good to nobody. At the hend of the lecture a collection will be took up to provide the lecturer with a little encouragement.' Philpot resumed his seat amid cheers.

As soon as they had finished eating, some of the men began to make remarks about the lecture, but Owen only laughed and went on reading the piece of newspaper that his dinner had been wrapped in. Usually most of the men went out for a walk after dinner but as it happened to be raining that day they were determined, if possible, to make Owen fulfil the engagement made in his name by Philpot.

'Let's 'oot 'im,' said Harlow, and the suggestion was at once acted upon; howls, groans, and catcalls filled the air, mingled with cries of 'Fraud!', 'Impostor!', 'Give us our money back!', 'Let's wreck the 'all!' and so on.

'Come on 'ere,' cried Philpot, putting his hand on Owen's shoulder. 'Prove that money is the cause of poverty.'

'It's one thing to say it and another to prove it,' sneered Crass, who was anxious for an opportunity to produce the long deferred 'Obscurer' cutting.

'Money *is* the real cause of poverty,' said Owen.

'Prove it,' repeated Crass.

'Money is the cause of poverty because it is the device by which those who are too lazy to work are enabled to rob the workers of the fruits of their labour.'

'Prove it,' said Crass.

Owen slowly folded up the piece of newspaper he had been reading and put it into his pocket.

'All right,' he replied, 'I'll show you how the Great Money Trick is worked.'

Owen opened his dinner basket and took from it two slices of bread, but as these were not sufficient, he requested anyone who had some bread left to give it to him. They gave him several pieces which he placed in a heap on a clean piece of paper, and having borrowed the pocket knives they used to cut and eat their dinners with from Easton, Harlow and Philpot, he addressed them as follows:

'These pieces of bread represent the raw materials which exist naturally in and on the earth for the use of mankind; they were not made by any human being, but were created by the Great Spirit for the benefit and sustenance of all, as were the air and the light of the sun.'

'You're about as fair speakin' a man as I've met for some time,' said Harlow, winking at the others.

'Yes, mate,' said Philpot, 'anyone would agree to that much: it's as clear as mud.'

'Now,' continued Owen, 'I am a capitalist; or rather, I represent the landlord and capitalist class. That is to say, all these raw materials belong to me. It does not matter for our present argument how I obtained possession of them, or whether I have any real right to them; the only thing that matters now is the admitted fact that all the raw materials which are necessary for the production of the necessaries of life are now the property of the Landlord and Capitalist Class. I am that class: all these raw materials belong to me.'

'Good enough,' agreed Philpot.

'Now you three represent the Working Class: you have nothing. And for my part, although I have all these raw materials, they are of no use to me; what I need is the things that can be made out of these raw materials by Work. But as I am too lazy to work myself, I have invented the Money Trick to make you work *for* me. But first I must explain that I possess something else besides the raw materials. These three knives represent all the machinery of production: the factories, tools, railways, and so forth, without which the necessaries of life cannot be produced in abundance. And these three coins'—taking three halfpennies from his pocket—'represent my Money Capital.'

'But before we go any further,' said Owen, interrupting himself, 'it is most important that you remember that I am not supposed to be merely "a" capitalist, I represent the whole Capitalist Class; you are not supposed to be just three workers, you represent the whole Working Class.'

'All right, all right,' said Crass, impatiently, 'we all understands that. Git on with it.'

Owen now proceeded to cut up one of the slices of bread into a number of little square blocks.

'These represent the things which are produced by labour, aided by machinery, from the raw materials. We will suppose that three of these blocks represent a week's work. We will suppose that a week's work is worth one pound, and we will suppose that each of these ha'pennies is a sovereign. We'd be able to do the trick better if we had real sovereigns, but I forgot to bring any with me.'

'I'd lend you some,' said Philpot, regretfully, 'but I left me purse on our grand pianner.'

As by a strange coincidence nobody happened to have any gold with them, it was decided to make shift with the half-pence.

'Now this is the way the trick works—'

'Before you goes on with it,' interrupted Philpot, apprehensively, 'don't you think we'd better 'ave someone to keep watch at the gate in case a slop comes along? We don't want to get runned in, you know.'

'I don't think there's any need for that,' replied Owen; 'there's only one slop who'd interfere with us for playing this game, and that's Police Constable Socialism.'

'Never mind about Socialism,' said Crass, irritably, 'get along with the bloody trick.'

Owen now addressed himself to the working classes as represented by Philpot, Harlow and Easton.

'You say that you are all in need of employment, and as I am the kind hearted capitalist class I am going to invest all my money in various industries so as to give you plenty of work. I shall pay each of you one pound per week; you must each produce three of these square blocks to represent a week's work. For doing this work you will each receive your wages; the money will be your own to do as you like with, and the things you produce will of course be mine, to do as I like with. You will each take one of these machines and as soon as you have done a week's work you shall have your money.'

The Working Classes accordingly set to work, and the Capitalist Class sat down and watched them. As soon as they had finished, they passed the nine little blocks of bread to Owen, who placed them on a piece of paper by his side and paid the workers their wages.

'These blocks represent the necessaries of life. You can't live without some of these things, but as they belong to me, you will have to buy them from me. My price for these blocks is one pound each.'

As the working classes were in need of the necessaries of life and as they could not eat, drink or wear the useless money, they were compelled to agree to the kind Capitalist's terms. They each bought back and at once consumed one third of the produce of their labour. The capitalist class also devoured two of the square blocks, and so the net result of the week's work was that the kind capitalist had consumed two pounds' worth of the things produced by the labour of others, and reckoning the squares at their market value of one pound each, he had more than doubled his capital, for he still possessed the three pounds in money and in addition four pounds' worth of goods. As for the working classes, Philpot, Harlow and Easton, having each consumed the pound's worth of necessaries they had bought with their wages, they were again in precisely the same condition as when they started work—they had nothing.

This process was repeated several times: for each week's work the producers were paid their wages. They kept on working and spending all their earnings. The kind-hearted Capitalist consumed twice as much as anyone of them and his pile of wealth continually increased. In a little while—reckoning the little squares at their market value of one pound each—he was worth about one hundred pounds, and the working classes were still in the same condition as when they began, and were still tearing into their work as if their lives depended upon it—which they did.

After a while the rest of the crowd began to laugh, and their merriment increased when the kind-hearted Capitalist, just after having sold a pound's worth of necessaries to each of his workers, suddenly took their tools—the Machinery of Production—the knives—away from them, and informed them that as owing to Over Production all his store-houses were glutted with the necessaries of life he had decided to close down the works.

'Well, and wot the bloody 'ell are we to do now?' demanded Philpot.

'That's not my business,' replied the kind-hearted Capitalist. 'I've paid you your wages, and provided you with Plenty of Work for a long time past. I have no more work for you to do at present. Come round again in a few months' time and I'll see what I can do for you.'

'But what about the necessaries of life?' demanded Harlow. 'We must have something to eat.'

'Of course you must,' replied the Capitalist, affably, 'and I shall be very pleased to sell you some.'

'But we ain't got no bloody money!'

'Well, you can't expect me to give you my goods for nothing! You didn't work for me for nothing you know. I paid you for your work and you should have saved something: you should have been thrifty like me. Look how I have got on by being thrifty!'

The unemployed looked blankly at each other, but the crowd only laughed; and then the three unemployed began to abuse the kind-hearted Capitalist, demanding that he should give them some of the necessaries of life that he had piled up in his warehouses, or to be allowed to work and produce some more for their own needs; and they even threatened to take some of the things by force if he did not comply with their demands. But the kind-hearted Capitalist told them not to be insolent, and spoke to them about honesty, and said if they were not careful he would have their faces battered in for them by the police, or if necessary he would call out the military and have them shot down like dogs.

'Of course,' continued the kind-hearted Capitalist, 'if it were not for foreign competition I should be able to sell these things that you have made, and then I should be able to give you plenty of work again. But until I have sold them to somebody or other, or until I have used them myself, you will have to remain idle.'

'Well, this takes the bloody biskit, don't it?' said Harlow.

'The only thing as I can see for it,' said Philpot, mournfully, 'is to 'ave a unemployed procession.'

'That's the idear,' said Harlow, and the three began to march about the room in Indian file, singing:—

'We've got no work to do-oo-oo!
We've got no work to do-oo-oo!
Just because we've been workin a dam sight too hard,
Now we've got no work to do.'

As they marched round, the crowd jeered at them and made offensive remarks.

Crass said that anyone could see that they were a lot of lazy, drunken loafers who had never done a fair day's work in their lives and never intended to.

'We shan't never get nothing like this, you know,' said Philpot. 'Let's try the religious dodge.'

'All right,' agreed Harlow, 'what shall we give 'em?'

'I know!' cried Philpot after a moment's deliberation. '"Let my lower lights be burning"; that always makes 'em part up.'

The three unemployed accordingly resumed their march round the room singing mournfully and imitating the usual whine of street-singers:—

'Trim your fee-bil lamp me brith-er-in,
Some poor sail-er tempest torst,
Strugglin' 'ard to save the 'arb-er,
Hin the dark-niss may be lorst.
So let my lower lights be burning,
Send er gleam acrost the wave,
Some poor shipwrecked, struggling seaman,
You may rescue, you may save.'

'Kind frens,' said Philpot, removing his cap and addressing the crowd, 'we're hall honest British workin' men, but we've been hout of work for the last twenty years on account of foreign competition and over-production. We don't come hout 'ere because we're too lazy to work, it's because we can't get a job. If it wasn't for foreign competition the kind-'earted Hinglish capitalists would be able to sell their goods and give us plenty of work, and if they could, I assure you that we should hall be perfectly willing and contented to go on workin' our guts out for the benefit of our masters for the rest of our lives. We're quite willin' to work: that's hall we arst for—plenty of work—but as we can't get it we're forced to come out 'ere and arst you spare a few coppers towards a crust of bread and a night's lodgin'.'

As Philpot held out his cap for subscriptions some of them attempted to expectorate into it, but the more charitable put in pieces of cinder or the dirt from the floor, and the kind-hearted Capitalist was so affected by the sight of their misery that he gave them one of the sovereigns he had in his pocket, but as this was no use to them they immediately returned it to him in exchange for one of the small squares of the necessities of life, which they divided and greedily devoured. And when they had finished eating they gathered round the philanthropist and sang "For he's a jolly good fellow," and afterwards Harlow suggested that they should ask him if he would allow them to elect him to Parliament.

CHAPTER XVI

The Reign of Terror

The following morning—Saturday—the men went about their work in gloomy silence; there were but few attempts at conversation and no jests or singing. The terror of the impending slaughter pervaded the house. Even those who were confident of being spared and kept on till the job was finished, shared the general depression, not only out of sympathy for the doomed but because they knew that a similar fate was in store for them a little later on.

They all waited anxiously for Nimrod to come, but hour after hour dragged slowly by and he did not arrive. At half-past eleven some of those who had made up their minds that they were to be 'stood still,' began to hope that the slaughter was to be deferred for a few days. After all, there was plenty of work still to be done; even if all hands were kept on, the job could scarcely be finished in another week. Anyhow, it would not be very long now before they would know one way or the other. If he did not come before twelve it was all right: all the hands were paid by the hour and were therefore entitled to an hour's notice.

Easton and Harlow were working together on the staircase, finishing the doors and other woodwork with white enamel. They had not been allowed to spend the time necessary to prepare this work in a proper manner; it had not been rubbed down smooth or properly filled up, nor had a sufficient number of coats of paint been put on to make it solid white. The consequence was the glossy enamel made the work look rather rough and shady.

'It ain't 'arf all right, ain't it?' remarked Harlow, sarcastically, indicating the door he had just finished.

Easton laughed: 'I can't understand how people pass such work,' he said.

'Old Sweater did make some remark about it the other day,' replied Harlow, 'and I heard Misery tell 'im it was impossible to make a perfect job of such old doors.'

'I believe that man's the biggest liar Gord ever made,' said Easton; an opinion in which Harlow entirely concurred.

'I wonder what the time is?' said the latter after a pause.

'I don't know exactly,' replied Easton, 'but it can't be far off twelve.'

''E don't seem to be comin' does 'e?' Harlow continued.

'No: and I shouldn't be surprised if 'e didn't turn up at all, now. P'rap's 'e don't mean to stop nobody to-day after all.'

They spoke in hushed tones and glanced cautiously about them, fearful of being heard or observed.

'This is a bloody life, ain't it?' Harlow said, bitterly. 'We works our guts out like a lot of slaves for the benefit of other people, and then as soon as they've done with you, you're chucked aside like a dirty rag.'

'Yes: and I begin to think that a great deal of what Owen says is true. But for my part I can't see 'ow it's ever goin' to be altered, can you?'

'Blowed if I know, mate. But whether it can be altered or not, there's one thing very certain; it won't be done in *our* time.'

Neither of them seemed to think that if the 'alteration' they spoke of were to be accomplished at all they themselves would have to help to bring it about.

'I wonder what they're doin' about the venetian blinds?' said Easton, 'is there anyone doin' 'em yet?'

'I don't know; ain't 'eard nothing about 'em since the boy took 'em to the shop.'

There was quite a mystery about these blinds. About a month ago they were taken to the paint shop down at the 'yard' to be re-painted and re-harnessed, and since then nothing had been heard of them by the men working at the 'Cave.'

'P'raps a couple of us will be sent there to do 'em next week,' remarked Harlow.

'P'rap's so. Most likely they'll 'ave to be done in a bloody 'urry at the last minute.'

Presently Harlow—who was very anxious to know what time it was—went downstairs to ask Slyme. It was twenty minutes to twelve.

From the window of the room where Slyme was papering, one could see into the front garden. Harlow paused a moment to watch Bundy and the labourers who were still working in the trenches at the drains, and as he looked out he saw Hunter approaching the house. Harlow drew back hastily and returned to his work, and as he went he passed the word to the other men, warning them of the approach of Misery.

Hunter entered in his usual manner, and after crawling quietly about the house for about ten minutes he went into the drawing-room.

'I see you're putting the finishing touches on at last,' he said.

'Yes,' replied Owen. 'I've only got this bit of outlining to do, now.'

'Ah, well, it looks very nice, of course,' said Misery, in a voice of mourning, 'but we've lost money over it. It's taken you a week longer to do than we allowed for; you said three weeks and it's taken you a month; and we only allowed for fifteen books of gold, but you've been and used twenty-three.'

'You can hardly blame me for that, you know,' answered Owen. 'I could have got it done in the three weeks, but Mr Rushton told me not to hurry for the sake of a day or two, because he wanted a good job. He said he would rather lose a little over it than spoil it; and as for the extra gold, that was also his order.'

'Well, I suppose it can't be helped,' whined Misery. 'Anyhow, I'm very glad it's done, because this kind of work don't pay. We'll 'ave you back on the brush on Monday morning; we want to get the outside done next week if it keeps fine.'

The 'brush' alluded to by Nimrod was the large 'pound' brush used in ordinary painting.

Misery now began wandering about the house, in and out of the rooms; sometimes standing for several minutes silently watching the hands as they worked. As he watched them the men became nervous and awkward, each one dreading that he might be one of those who were to be paid off at one o'clock.

At about five minutes to twelve Hunter went down to the paint shop—the scullery—where Crass was mixing some colour, and getting ready some 'empties' to be taken to the yard.

'I suppose the swine's gone to ask Crass which of us is the least use,' whispered Harlow to Easton.

'I wouldn't be surprised if it was you and me, for two,' replied the latter in the same tone; 'you can't trust Crass, you know, for all 'e seems so friendly to our faces. You never know what 'e ses behind our backs.'

'You may be sure it won't be Sawkins or any of the other lightweights, because Nimrod won't want to pay us sixpence ha'penny for painting guttering and rainpipes when *they* can do it near enough for fourpence ha'penny and fivepence. They won't be able to do the sashes, though, will they?'

'I don't know so much about that,' replied Easton; 'anything seems to be good enough for Hunter.'

'Look out! 'ere 'e comes!' said Harlow, and they both relapsed into silence and busied themselves with their work. Misery stood watching them for some time without speaking, and then went out of the house. They crept cautiously to the window of a room that overlooked the garden and peeping furtively out they saw him standing on the brink of one of the trenches, moodily watching Bundy and his mates as they toiled at the drains. Then, to their surprise and relief, he turned and went out of the gate! They just caught sight of one of the wheels of his bicycle as he rode away.

The slaughter was evidently to be put off until next week! It seemed too good to be true.

'P'raps 'e's left a message for some of us with Crass?' suggested Easton. 'I don't think it's likely, but it's just possible.'

'Well, I'm goin' down to ask 'im,' said Harlow, desperately. 'We may as well know the worst at once.'

He returned in a few minutes with the information that Hunter had decided not to stop anyone that day because he wanted to get the outside finished during the next week, if possible.

The hands received this intelligence with mixed feelings, because although it left them safe for the present, it meant that nearly everybody would certainly be stopped next Saturday, if not before; whereas if a few had been sacked to-day it would have made it all the better for the rest. Still, this aspect of the business did not greatly interfere with the relief they all felt at knowing that the immediate danger was over; and the fact that it was Saturday—pay day—also served to revive their drooping spirits. They all felt pretty certain that Misery would return no more that day, and presently Harlow began to sing the old favourite, 'Work! for the night is coming!', the refrain of which was soon taken up by nearly everyone in the house:—

'Work! for the night is coming,
Work in the morning hours,
Work! for the night is coming!
Work 'mid springing flowers!

Work while the dew is sparkling,
Work in the noonday sun!
Work, for the night is coming,
When man's work is done!'

When this hymn was finished, someone else, imitating the whine of a street singer, started 'Oh where is my wandering boy to-night?', and then Harlow—who by some strange chance had a penny—took it out of his pocket and dropped it on the floor, the ringing of the coin being greeted with shouts of 'Thank you, kind lady' from several of the singers. This little action of Harlow's was the means of bringing a most extraordinary circumstance to light. Although it was Saturday morning, several of the others had pennies or halfpence, and at the conclusion of each verse they all followed Harlow's example and the house resounded with the ringing of falling coins, cries of 'Thank you, kind lady', 'Thank you, sir,' and 'Gord bless you,' mingled with shouts of laughter.

'My wandering boy' was followed by a choice selection of choruses of well-known music hall songs, the whole being tastefully varied and interspersed with howls, shrieks, curses, and catcalls.

In the midst of the uproar Crass came upstairs.

''Ere!' he shouted, 'for Christ's sake make less row! Suppose Nimrod was to come back!'

'Oh, 'e ain't comin' any more to-day,' said Harlow, recklessly.

'Besides, what if 'e does come?' cried Easton. ''Oo cares for *im*?'

'Well, we never know; and for that matter Rushton or Sweater might come at any minit.'

With this, Crass went muttering back to the scullery, and the men relapsed into their usual silence.

At ten minutes to one they all ceased work, put away their colours and locked up the house. There were a number of 'empties' to be taken away and left at the yard on their way to the office; these Crass divided amongst the others—carrying nothing himself—and then they all set out for the office to get their money, cracking jokes as they went along. Harlow and Easton enlivened the journey by coughing significantly whenever they met a young woman, and audibly making some complimentary remark about her personal appearance. If the girl smiled, each of them eagerly claimed to have 'seen her first,' but if she appeared offended or 'stuck up,' they suggested that she was cross-cut or that she had been eating vinegar with a fork. Now and then they kissed their hands affectionately to servant girls whom they saw looking out of windows. Some of these girls laughed, others looked indignant, but whichever way they took it was equally amusing to Crass and the rest, who were like a crowd of boys just let out of school.

It will be remembered that there was a back door to Rushton's office; in this door was a small sliding panel or trap-door with a little shelf at the bottom. The men stood in the road and on the pavement outside the closed door, their money being passed out to them through the sliding panel. As there was no shelter, when it rained they occasionally got wet through while waiting to be paid. With some firms it is customary to call out the names of the men and pay them in order of seniority or ability, but there was no such system here; the man who got to the aperture first was paid first, and so on. The result was that there was always a sort of miniature 'Battle of Life,' the men pushing and struggling against each other as if their lives depended upon their being paid by a certain time.

After receiving their wages Crass, Easton, Bundy, Philpot, Harlow and a few others adjourned to the 'Cricketers' for a drink. Owen went away alone, and Slyme also went on by himself. There was no use waiting for Easton to come out of the public house because there was no knowing how long he would be; he might stay half an hour or two hours. On his way Slyme called at the post office to bank some of his wages.

This transaction finished, he resumed his homeward way, stopping only to purchase some sweets at a confectioner's. He spent a whole sixpence at once in this shop on a glass jar of sweets for the baby.

Ruth was not surprised when she saw him come in alone; it was the usual thing since Easton had become so friendly with Crass. She made no reference to his absence, but Slyme noticed with secret chagrin that she was annoyed and disappointed. She was just finishing scrubbing the kitchen floor and little Freddie was sitting up in a baby's high chair that had a little shelf or table fixed in front of it. To keep him amused while she did her work Ruth had given him a piece of bread and raspberry jam which the child had rubbed all over his face and into his scalp, and he now looked as if he had been in a fight or a railway accident.

Freddie hailed the arrival of Slyme with enthusiasm, being so overcome with emotion that he began to shed tears, and was only pacified when the man gave him the jar of sweets and took him out of the chair.

Slyme's presence in the house had not proved so irksome as Easton and Ruth had expected. Indeed, at first, he made a point of retiring to his own room after tea every evening, until they invited him to stay downstairs in the kitchen. Nearly every Wednesday and Saturday he went to a meeting, or an open-air preaching, when the weather permitted, for he was one of a little zealous band of people connected with the Shining Light Chapel who carried on the 'open-air' work all the year round. After awhile the Eastons not only became reconciled to his presence in the house but were even glad of it. Ruth especially would often have been very lonely if he had not been there, for it had lately become Easton's custom to spend a few evenings every week with Crass at the 'Cricketers.'

When at home Slyme passed his time playing a mandoline or making fretwork photo frames. Ruth had the baby's photograph taken a few weeks after Slyme came, and the frame he made for it was now one of the ornaments of the sitting-room. The instinctive, unreasoning aversion she had at first felt for him had in a measure passed away. He did her so many little services that she found it impossible to altogether dislike him. At first, she used to address him as 'Mr,' but after a time she fell naturally into Easton's practice of calling him by his Christian name.

As for the baby, *he* made no secret of his affection for the lodger, who nursed and played with him for hours at a stretch.

'I'll serve your dinner now, Alf,' said Ruth, when she had finished scrubbing the floor, 'but I'll wait for mine for a little while. Will may come.'

'I'm in no hurry,' replied Slyme, 'I'll go and have a wash; he may be here by then.'

As he spoke, Slyme—who had been sitting by the fire nursing the baby—put the child back into the high chair, giving him one of the sticks of sweets out of the jar to keep him quiet, and went upstairs to his own room. He came down again in about a quarter of an hour, and Ruth proceeded to serve his dinner, for Easton was still absent.

'If I was you I wouldn't wait for Will,' said Slyme. 'He may not come for another hour or two. It's after two o'clock now, and I'm sure you must be hungry.'

'I suppose I may as well have my dinner,' replied Ruth hesitatingly; 'he'll most likely get some bread and cheese at the "Cricketers," same as he did last Saturday.'

'Almost sure to,' responded Slyme.

The baby had had his face washed while Slyme was upstairs. Directly he saw his mother eating he threw away the sugarstick and began to cry, holding out his arms to her. She had to take him on her lap whilst she ate her dinner, and feed him with pieces from her plate.

Slyme talked all the time, principally about the child. He was very fond of children, he said, and always got on well with them, but he had really never known such an intelligent child for his age as Freddie. His fellow-workmen would have been astonished had they been present to hear him talking about the shape of the baby's head. They would have been astonished at the amount of knowledge he appeared to possess of the science of Phrenology. Ruth, at anyrate, thought he was very clever.

After a time the child began to grow fretful and refused to eat; when his mother gave him a fresh piece of sugar-stick out of the jar he threw it peevishly on the floor and began to whimper, rubbing his face against his mother's bosom and pulling at her dress with his hands. When Slyme first came Ruth had made a practice of withdrawing from the room if he happened to be present when she wanted to nurse the child, but lately she had been less sensitive. She was sitting with her back to the window and she partly covered the baby's face with a light shawl that she wore. By the time they finished dinner the child had dozed off to sleep. Slyme got up from his chair and stood with his back to the fire, looking down at them. Presently he spoke, referring, of course to the baby:

'He's very like you, isn't he?'

'Yes,' replied Ruth, 'everyone says he takes after me.'

Slyme moved a little closer, bending down to look at the slumbering infant.

'You know, at first I thought he was a girl,' he continued after a pause. 'He seems almost too pretty for a boy, doesn't he?'

Ruth smiled. 'People always take him for a girl at first,' she said. 'Yesterday I took him with me to the Monopole Stores to buy some things, and the manager would hardly believe it wasn't a girl.'

The man reached out his hand and stroked the baby's face.

Although Slyme's behaviour had hitherto always been very correct, yet there was occasionally an indefinable something in his manner when they were alone that made Ruth feel conscious and embarrassed. Now, as she glanced up at him and saw the expression on his face she crimsoned with confusion and hastily lowered her eyes without replying to his last remark. He did not speak again either, and they remained for several minutes in silence, as if spellbound, Ruth oppressed with instinctive dread, and Slyme scarcely less agitated, his face flushed and his heart beating wildly. He trembled as he stood over her, hesitating and afraid.

And then the silence was suddenly broken by the creaking and clanging of the front gate, heralding the tardy coming of Easton. Slyme went out into the scullery and taking down the blacking brushes from the shelf began cleaning his boots.

It was plain from Easton's appearance and manner that he had been drinking, but Ruth did not reproach him in any way; on the contrary she seemed almost feverishly anxious to attend to his comfort.

When Slyme finished cleaning his boots he went upstairs to his room, receiving a careless greeting from Easton as he passed through the kitchen. He felt nervous and apprehensive that Ruth might say something to Easton, and was not quite able to reassure himself with the reflection that after all, there was nothing to tell. As for Ruth, she had to postpone the execution of her hastily formed resolution to tell her husband of Slyme's strange behaviour, for Easton fell asleep in his chair before he had finished his dinner, and she had some difficulty in waking him sufficiently to persuade him to go upstairs to bed, where he remained until tea-time. Probably he would not have come down even then if it had not been for the fact that he had made an appointment to meet Crass at the 'Cricketers.'

Whilst Easton was asleep, Slyme had been downstairs in the kitchen, making a fretwork frame. He played with Freddie while Ruth prepared the tea, and he appeared to her to be so unconscious of having done anything unusual that she began to think that she must have been mistaken in imagining that he had intended anything wrong.

After tea Slyme put on his best clothes to go to his usual 'open air' meeting. As a rule Easton and Ruth went out marketing together every Saturday night, but this evening he could not wait for her because he had promised to meet Crass at seven o'clock; so he arranged to see her down town at eight.

CHAPTER XVII

The 'Open Air'

Ever since Owen had been engaged in the decoration of the drawing room, he had forgotten he was ill; he had forgotten that when 'The Cave' was finished he would have to stand off with the rest of the hands; in fact he had forgotten that, like them, he was on the brink of destitution and that a few weeks out of work or illness meant starvation.

As he walked homewards after being paid, a feeling of unutterable depression came over him and he began to think of his future. Even supposing he did not lose his employment, what was there to live for? He had been working with hand and brain all the week. These few coins he held were the result, and he laughed bitterly as he thought of all he must do with the money, and all he must leave undone.

That evening Frankie accompanied him to do the shopping as Nora was not well, and first of all the boy, remembering his pet, went to the butcher's to buy a pennyworth of cat's meat, while Owen went to the grocer's, arranging to meet Frankie at the corner of the street.

Owen was at the appointed place first and after waiting some time and seeing no sign of the boy decided to go towards the butcher's to meet him. When he came in sight of the shop he saw the boy standing outside in earnest conversation with the butcher, a jolly looking, stoutly built man, with a very red face. Owen perceived at once that the child was trying to explain something, because Frankie had a habit of holding his head sideways and supplementing his speech by spreading out his fingers and making quaint gestures with his hands whenever he found it difficult to make himself understood. The boy was doing this now, waving one hand about with the fingers and thumb extended wide, and with the other flourishing a paper parcel which evidently contained the pieces of meat. Presently the man laughed heartily and after shaking hands with the boy went into the shop to attend to a customer, while Frankie rejoined his father.

'That butcher's a very decent sort of chap, you know, Dad,' he said; 'he wouldn't take the penny for the meat.'

'Is that what you were talking to him about?'

'No; we were talking about Socialism. You see, this is the second time he wouldn't take the money, and the first time he did it I thought he must be a Socialist, but I didn't ask him then. But when he did it again this time I asked him if he was. So he said, No. He said he wasn't quite mad yet. So I said: "If you think that Socialists are all mad, you're very much mistaken, because I'm a Socialist myself, and I'm quite sure *I'm* not mad." So he said he knew I was all right, but he didn't understand anything about Socialism himself—only that it meant sharing out all the money so that everyone could have the same. So then I told him that's not Socialism at all! And when I explained it to him properly and advised him to be one, he said he'd think about it. So I said if he'd only do *that* he'd be *sure* to change over to our side. And then he laughed and promised to let me know next time he sees me, and I promised to lend him some papers. You won't mind, will you, Dad?'

'Of course not; when we get home we'll have a look through what we've got and you can take him some of them.'

As he walked through the crowded streets holding Frankie by the hand, the terror of the future once more possessed Owen's mind, and he felt that the frail little figure trotting by his side would never be fit to be a soldier in this ferocious Battle of Life, and that to allow him to grow up and suffer in his turn would be an act of callous criminal cruelty. He thought of Nora, always brave, always uncomplaining, though her life was one of incessant physical suffering. As for himself he was tired and sick of it all. He had worked like a slave all his life, and there was nothing to show for it—there never would be anything to show for it. Although it was December the evening was mild and clear, the full moon deluged the town with a silvery light, and the sky was cloudless. Looking into the unfathomable space above, Owen wondered what manner of Being or Power it was that had thus ordered the destiny of his creatures, and longed for something to believe in—for some hope for the future—for some compensation for misery and suffering.

'Dad,' said Frankie, suddenly, 'let's go over and hear what that man's saying.' He pointed across the way to where, a little distance back from the main road, a group of people were standing round a large lantern fixed on the top of a pole. A bright light was burning inside this lantern, and on the panes of white obscured glass which formed the sides, was written in bold plain letters the text:

'Be not deceived: God is not mocked!'

The man whose voice had attracted Frankie's attention was reading a verse of a hymn:—

'I heard the voice of Jesus say,
"Behold, I freely give
The living water, thirsty one,
Stoop down, and drink, and live":
I came to Jesus, and I drank

Of that life-giving stream;
My thirst was quenched,
My soul revived,
And now I live in Him.'

As Owen and Frankie drew near, the boy tugged at his father's hand and whispered: 'Dad! that man is the teacher at the Sunday School where I went that day with Charley and Elsie.'

Owen looked quickly and saw that it was Hunter.

As soon as the reading ceased, the little company of evangelists began to sing, accompanied by the strains of a small but peculiarly sweet-toned organ. A few persons in the crowd joined in, the words being familiar to them. During the singing their faces were a study, they looked as solemn and miserable as a gang of condemned criminals waiting to be led forth to execution. The greater number of the people standing around appeared to be listening more out of idle curiosity than anything else, and two well dressed young men, evidently strangers and visitors to the town, amused themselves by making audible remarks about the texts on the lantern. There was also a shabbily dressed, semi-drunken man in a battered bowler hat who stood on the inner edge of the crowd, almost in the ring itself, with folded arms and an expression of scorn on his thin, pale face. He had a large high-bridge nose, and bore a striking resemblance to the first Duke of Wellington. As the singing proceeded, the scornful expression faded from the visage of the Semi-Drunk, and he not only joined in, but unfolded his arms and began waving them about as if he were conducting the music.

By the time the singing was over a considerable crowd had gathered, and then Hunter stepped into the middle of the ring. He had evidently been offended by the unseemly conduct of the two well-dressed young men, for after a preliminary glance round upon the crowd, he fixed his gaze upon the pair, and immediately launched out upon a long tirade against what he called 'Infidelity.' Then, having heartily denounced all those who, as he put it, 'refused' to believe, he proceeded to ridicule those half-and-half believers who, while professing to believe the Bible, rejected the doctrine of Hell, and finally proved the existence of a place of eternal torture by a long succession of texts. As he proceeded the contemptuous laughter of the two unbelievers made him very excited. He shouted and raved, literally foaming at the mouth and glaring in a frenzied manner around, upon the faces of the crowd,

'There *is* a hell!' he shouted. 'And understand this clearly: "The wicked *shall* be turned into hell"; "He that believeth not shall be damned!"'

'Well, then, *you'll* stand a very good chance of being damned also,' exclaimed one of the two young men.

''Ow do you make it out?' demanded Hunter, wiping the froth from his lips and the perspiration from his forehead with his handkerchief.

'Why, because you don't believe the Bible yourselves.'

Nimrod and the other evangelists laughed, and looked pityingly at the young man.

'Ah, my dear brother,' said Misery, 'that's your delusion. I thank God I do believe it, every word!'

'Amen,' fervently ejaculated Slyme and several of the other disciples.

'Oh no you don't,' replied the other, 'and I can prove you don't.'

'Prove it then,' said Nimrod.

'Read out the seventeenth and eighteenth verses of the sixteenth chapter of Mark,' said the disturber of the meeting. The crowd began to close in on the centre, the better to hear the dispute. Misery, standing close to the lantern, found the verse mentioned and read aloud as follows:

'And these signs shall follow them that believe. In my name shall they cast out devils; they shall speak with new tongues; they shall take up serpents; and if they drink any deadly thing it shall not hurt them; they shall lay hands on the sick, and they shall recover.'

'Well, *you* can't heal the sick, neither can you speak new languages or cast out devils; but perhaps you can drink deadly things without suffering harm.' The speaker here suddenly drew from his waistcoat pocket a small glass bottle and held it out towards Misery, who shrank from it with horror, as he continued: 'I have here a most deadly poison. There is in this bottle sufficient strychnine to kill a dozen unbelievers. Drink it! If it doesn't harm you we'll know that you really are a believer and that what you believe is the truth!'

''Ear, 'ear!' said the Semi-Drunk, who had listened to the progress of the argument with great interest, ''Ear, 'ear! that's fair enough. Git it acrost yer chest.'

Some of the people in the crowd began to laugh, and voices were heard from several quarters calling upon Misery to drink the strychnine.

'Now, if you'll allow me, I'll explain to you what that there verse means,' said Hunter. 'If you read it carefully—*with* the context—'

'I don't want you to tell me what it means,' interrupted the other. 'I am able to read for myself. Whatever you may say, or pretend to think it means, I know what it *says*.'

'Hear, hear!' shouted several voices and angry cries of 'Why don't you drink the poison?' began to be heard from the outskirts of the crowd.

'Are you going to drink it or not?' demanded the man with the bottle.

'No! I'm not such a fool!' retorted Misery, fiercely, and a loud shout of laughter broke from the crowd.

'Pr'aps some of the other "believers" would like to,' said the young man scornfully, looking round upon the disciples. As no one seemed desirous of availing himself of this offer, the man returned the bottle regretfully to his pocket.

'I suppose,' said Misery, regarding the owner of the strychnine with a sneer, 'I suppose you're one of them there hired critics wot's goin' about the country doin' the devil's work?'

'Wot I wants to know is this 'ere,' said the Semi-Drunk, suddenly advancing into the middle of the ring and speaking in a loud voice: 'Where did Cain get 'is wife from?'

'Don't answer 'im, Brother 'Unter,' said Mr Didlum, one of the disciples. This was rather an unnecessary piece of advice, because Misery was not in a position to do so.

An individual in a long black garment—the 'minister'—now whispered something to Miss Didlum, who was seated at the organ, whereupon she began to play, and the 'believers' began to sing: 'Oh that will be, Glory for me,' as loud as they could so as to drown the voices of the disturbers of the meeting.

After this hymn the 'minister' invited a shabbily dressed 'brother'—a working man member of the P.S.A.—to say 'a few words,' and the latter accordingly stepped into the centre of the ring and held forth as follows:

'My dear frens, I thank Gord to-night that I can stand 'ere to-night, hout in the hopen hair and tell hall you dear people to-night of hall wot's been done for *me*. Ho my dear frens hi ham so glad to-night as I can stand 'ere to-night and say as hall my sins is hunder the blood to-night and wot 'E's done for me 'E can do for you to-night, if you'll honly do as I done and just acknowledge yourself a lost sinner——'

'Yes! that's the honly way!' shouted Nimrod.

'Amen,' cried all the other believers.

'—If you'll honly come to 'im to-night hin the same way as I done you'll see that wot 'E's done for me 'E can do for you. Ho, my dear frens, don't go on puttin of it orf from day to day like a door turnin' on its 'inges, don't go putting of it orf to some more convenient time because you may never 'ave another chance. 'Im that bein' orfen reproved 'ardeneth 'is neck shall be suddently cut orf and that without remedy! Ho come to 'im to-night for 'is name's sake and to 'im we'll give hall the glory. Amen.'

'Amen,' said the believers, fervently, and then the man who was dressed in the long garment entreated all those who were not yet true believers—and doers—of the Word to join earnestly and *meaningly* in the singing of the closing hymn, which he was about to read out to them.

The Semi-Drunk obligingly conducted as before, and the crowd faded away with the last notes of the music.

CHAPTER XVIII

RUTH

ONE evening, Crass and Slyme met by appointment at the corner of the street, and proceeded on their way down town. It was about half past six o'clock; the shops and streets were brilliantly lighted, and as they went along they saw numerous groups of men talking together in a listless way. Most of them were artizans and labourers out of employment and evidently in no great hurry to go home. Some of them had neither tea nor fire to go to, and stayed away from home as long as possible so as not to be compelled to look upon the misery of those who were waiting for them there. Others hung about hoping against all probability that they might even yet—although it was so late—hear of some job about to be started somewhere or other.

As they passed one of these groups they recognised and nodded to Newman and old Jack Linden, and the former left the others and came up and walked along with them.

'Anything fresh in, Bob?' he asked.

'No; we ain't got 'ardly anything,' replied Crass. 'I reckon we shall finish up at "The Cave" next week, and then I suppose we shall all be stood orf. We've got several plumbers on, and I believe there's a little gasfitting work in, but next to nothing in our line.'

'I suppose you don't know of any other firm what's got anything?'

'No; I don't, mate. Between you and me I don't think any of 'em has; they're all in about the same fix.'

'I've not done anything since I left, you know,' said Newman, 'and we've just about got as far as we can get, at home.'

Slyme and Crass said nothing in reply to this. They wished that Newman would take himself off, because they did not want him to know where they were going.

However, Newman continued to accompany them, and an awkward silence succeeded.

He seemed to wish to say something more, and they both guessed what it was. So they walked along as rapidly as possible in order not to give him any encouragement. At last Newman blurted out:

'I suppose—you don't happen—either of you—to have a tanner you could lend me? I'll let you have it back—when I get a job.'

'I ain't, mate,' replied Crass. 'I'm sorry; if I 'ad one on me you should 'ave it, with pleasure.'

Slyme also expressed his regret that he had no money with him, and at the corner of the next street Newman—ashamed of having asked—wished them good night, and went away.

Slyme and Crass hurried along and presently arrived at Rushton and Company's shop. The windows were lit up with electric light, displaying an assortment of wallpapers, gas and electric light fittings, glass shades, globes, tins of enamel, paint and varnish. There were also several framed showcards—'Estimates Free,' 'First Class Work Only at Moderate Charges', 'Only First Class Workmen Employed,' and others of the same type. On one side wall of the window was a large, shield shaped board, covered with black velvet, on which a number of brass fittings for coffins were arranged. The shield was on an oak mount with the inscription:—'Funerals conducted on modern principles.'

Slyme waited outside while Crass went in. Mr Budd, the shopman, was down at the far end near the glazed partition which separated Mr Rushton's office from the front shop. As Crass entered, Budd—a pale-faced, unhealthy looking, undersized youth about twenty years of age—looked round and, with a grimace, motioned him to walk softly. Crass paused, wondering what the other meant, but the shopman beckoned him to advance, grinning and winking and jerking his thumb over his shoulder in the direction of the office. Crass hesitated, fearing that possibly the miserable Budd had gone—or been driven—out of his mind; but as the latter continued to beckon and grin and point towards the office, he screwed up his courage and followed him behind one of the show-cases, and found that by peeping through a crack in the woodwork of the partition indicated by Budd, he could see Mr Rushton in the act of kissing and embracing Miss Wade, the young lady clerk. Crass watched them for some time and then whispered to Budd to call Slyme, and when the latter came they all three took turns at peeping through the crack in the partition.

When they had looked their fill they came out from behind the showcase, almost bursting with suppressed merriment. Budd reached down a key from where it was hanging on the wall and gave it to Crass and the two resumed their interrupted journey. But before they had proceeded a dozen yards from the shop, they were accosted by a short, elderly man, with grey hair and a beard. This man looked about sixty-five years of age, and was very shabbily dressed. The elbows of his coat were worn threadbare, the ends of his sleeves and the legs of his trousers were frayed and ragged and his boots were patched, broken, and down at heel. This man's name was Latham; he was a venetian blind maker and repairer. With his son, he was supposed to be 'in business' on his own account, but as most of their work was done 'for the trade,' that is, for such firms as Rushton and Company, they would be more correctly described as men who did piecework at home. He had been 'in business'—as he called it—for about forty years, working, working, always working; and ever since his son became old enough to labour, he had helped his father in the philanthropic task of manufacturing profits for the sweaters who employed them. They had been so busy working for the benefit of others, that they had overlooked the fact that they were only earning a bare living for themselves; and now, after forty years' hard labour, the old man was clothed in rags and on the verge of destitution.

'Is Rushton there?' he asked.

'Yes, I think so,' replied Crass, attempting to pass on; but the old man detained him.

'He promised to let us know about them blinds for "The Cave." We gave 'im a price for 'em about a month ago. In fact we gave 'im two prices, because he said the first was too high. Five and six a set I asked 'im, take 'em right through the 'ole 'ouse one with another, big and little. Two coats of paint, and new tapes and cords. That wasn't too much, was it?'

'No,' said Crass, walking on, 'that was cheap enough!'

'*He* said it was too much,' continued Latham; 'said as 'e could get 'em done cheaper! But I say as no one can't do it and make a living.'

As he walked along, talking, between Crass and Slyme, the old man became very excited.

'But we 'adn't nothing to do to speak of, so my son told 'im we'd do 'em for five bob a set, and 'e said 'e'd let us know, but we ain't 'eard nothing from 'im yet, so I thought I'd try and see 'im to-night.'

'Well, you'll find 'im in there now,' said Slyme, with a peculiar look, and walking faster. 'Good night.'

'I won't take 'em on for no less!' cried the old man as he turned back. 'I've got my livin' to get, and my son's got 'is wife and little 'uns to keep. We can't work for nothing!'

'Certainly not,' said Crass, glad to get away at last. 'Good night, and good luck to you.'

As soon as they were out of hearing they both burst out laughing at the old man's vehemence.

'Seemed quite upset about it,' said Slyme; and they laughed again.

They now left the main road and pursued their way through a number of badly lighted, mean looking streets, and finally turning down a kind of alley, arrived at their destination. On one side of this street was a row of small houses; facing these were a number of buildings of a miscellaneous description—sheds and stables; and beyond these a plot of waste ground on which could be seen, looming weirdly through the dusk, a number of empty carts and waggons with their shafts resting on the ground or reared up into the air. Threading their way carefully through the mud pools of water and rubbish which covered the ground, they arrived at a large gate fastened with a padlock. Applying the key, Crass swung back the gate and they found themselves in a yard filled with building materials and plant: ladders, huge trestles, planks and beams of wood, hand-carts and wheelbarrows, heaps of sand and mortar and innumerable other things that assumed strange fantastic shapes in the semi-darkness. And over all rose a gloomy, indistinct and shapeless mass, the buildings and sheds that comprised Rushton and Company's workshops.

Crass struck a match, and Slyme, stooping down, drew a key from a crevice in the wall near one of the doors, which he unlocked, and they entered. Crass struck another match and lit the gas at a jointed bracket fixed to the wall. This was the paint shop. At one end was a fireplace without a grate but with an iron bar fixed across the blackened chimney for the purpose of suspending pails or pots over the fire, which was usually made of wood on the hearthstone. All round the walls of the shop—which had once been whitewashed but were now covered with smears of paint of every colour where the men had 'rubbed out' their brushes—were rows of shelves, filled with kegs of paint. In front of the window was a long bench covered with an untidy litter of dirty paint pots including several earthenware mixing vessels or mortars, the sides of these being thickly coated with dried paint. Scattered about the stone floor were a number of dirty pails, either empty or containing stale whitewash; and standing on a sort of low platform or shelf at one end of the shop were four large round tanks fitted with taps and labelled 'Boiled Oil', 'Turps', 'Linseed Oil' and 'Turps Substitute.' The lower parts of the walls were discoloured with moisture. The atmosphere was cold and damp and foul with the sickening odours of the poisonous materials.

It was in this place that Bert—the apprentice—spent most of his time cleaning out pots and pails, during slack periods when there were no jobs going on outside.

In the middle of the shop, under a two armed gas pendant, was another table or bench, also thickly coated with old dried paint, and by the side of this were two large stands on which some of the lathes of the venetian blinds belonging to 'The Cave,' which Crass and Slyme were painting—piecework—in their spare time, were hanging up to dry. The remainder of the lathes were leaning against the walls or piled in stacks on the table.

Crass shivered with cold as he lit the two gas jets. 'Make a bit of a fire, Alf,' he said, 'while I gets the colour ready.'

Slyme went outside and presently returned with his arms full of old wood, which he smashed up and threw into the fireplace; then he took an empty paint pot and filled it with turpentine from the big tank and emptied it over the wood. Amongst the pots on the mixing bench he found one full of old paint, and he threw this over the wood also, and in a few minutes he had made a roaring fire.

Meantime, Crass had prepared the paint and brushes and had taken down the lathes from the drying frames. The two men now proceeded with the painting of the blinds, working rapidly, each lathe being hung on the wires of the drying frame after being painted. They talked freely as they worked, having no fear of being overheard by Rushton or Nimrod. This job was piecework, so it didn't matter whether they talked or not. They waxed hilarious over Old Latham's discomfiture and wondered what he would say if he could see them now. Then the conversation drifted to the subject of the private characters of the other men who were employed by Rushton and Company, and an impartial listener would have been forced to come to the conclusion that Crass and Slyme were the only two decent fellows on the firm. There was something wrong or shady about everybody else. There was that Sawkins. *He* was no class whatever. It was a well-known fact that he used to go round to Misery's house nearly every night to tell him every little thing that had happened on the job during the day! As for Payne, the foreman carpenter, the man was a perfect fool: he'd find out the difference if ever he got the sack from Rushton's and went to work for some other firm! He didn't understand his trade, and he couldn't make a coffin properly to save his life! Then there was that rotter Owen; there was a bright specimen for yer! An atheist! Didn't believe in no God or devil nor nothing else. A pretty state of things there would be if these Socialists could have their own way: for one thing, nobody would be allowed to work overtime!

Crass and Slyme worked and talked in this manner till ten o'clock, and then they extinguished the fire by throwing some water on it, put out the gas and locked up the shop and the yard, dropping the key of the latter into the letter box at Rushton's office on their way home.

When Saturday arrived the men working at 'The Cave' were again surprised that nobody was sacked, and they were divided in opinion as to the reason, some thinking that Nimrod was determined to keep them all on till the job was finished, so as to get it done as quickly as possible, and others boldly asserting the truth of a rumour that had been going about for several days that the firm had another big job in. Mr Sweater had bought another house; Rushton had to do it up, and they were all to be kept on to start this other work as soon as 'The Cave' was finished. Crass knew no more than anyone else and he maintained a discreet silence, but the fact that he did not contradict the rumour served to strengthen it. The only foundation that existed for this report was that Rushton and Misery had been seen looking over the garden gate of a large empty house near 'The Cave.' But although it had such an insignificant beginning the rumour had grown and increased in detail and importance day by day. That very morning at breakfast time the man on the pail had announced that he had heard on the very best authority that Mr Sweater had sold all his interest in the great business which bore his name and was about to retire into private life, and that he intended to buy up all the house property in the neighbourhood of 'The Cave.' Another individual—one of the new hands—said that he had heard someone else, in a public house, say that Rushton was about to marry one of Sweater's daughters, and that Sweater intended to give the couple a house to live in, as a wedding present; but the fact that Rushton was already married and the father of four children rather knocked the bottom out of this story, so it was regretfully dismissed. Whatever the reason, the fact remained that nobody had been discharged, and when pay time arrived they set out for the office in high spirits.

That evening, the weather being fine, Slyme changed his clothes and departed to his Saturday night 'open air meeting'; but Easton, although he had now made a habit of spending all his spare time at the 'Cricketers,' promised to wait for Ruth and go with her to do the marketing. The baby was left at home alone, asleep in the cradle.

By the time they had made all their purchases they had a fairly heavy load, Easton carrying the meat and the string bag containing the potatoes and other vegetables, and Ruth hugging the groceries. On their way home they had to pass the 'Cricketers,' and just before they reached that part of their journey they met Mr and Mrs Crass, also out marketing, who insisted on Easton and Ruth going in to have a drink with them. Ruth did not want to go but she allowed herself to be persuaded, for she could see that Easton was beginning to get angry with her for refusing. Crass had on a new overcoat and a new hat, with dark grey trousers and yellow boots, and a 'stand up' collar with a bright blue tie. His wife—a fat, vulgar-looking, well-preserved woman about forty—was arrayed in a dark red costume, with hat to match. Both Easton and Ruth—whose best clothes had been pawned to raise the money to pay the poor rate—felt very mean and shabby beside them.

When they arrived in the bar, Crass paid for the first round of drinks. A pint of Old Six for himself; the same for Easton; half a pint for Mrs Easton and threepenny worth of gin for Mrs Crass.

The Besotted Wretch was there, just finishing a game of hooks and rings with the Semi-Drunk—who had propitiated the Old Dear by calling round, the day after he was thrown out, to apologise for his conduct, and had since become a regular customer. Philpot was absent. He had been there that afternoon, so the Old Dear said, but he had gone home about five o'clock, but he was almost sure to look in again in the course of the evening.

Although the house was not nearly so full as it would have been in better times, there was a large number of customers, for the 'Cricketers' was one of the most popular houses in the town. Many of the seats in the public bar were occupied by women, some young and accompanied by their husbands, some old and evidently sodden with drink.

In one corner of the public bar, drinking beer or gin with a number of young fellows, were three young girls who worked at a steam laundry in the neighbourhood. Besides these there were two large, fat, gipsy-looking women, evidently hawkers, for on the floor beside them were two baskets containing bundles of chrysanthemums, and two plainly and shabbily dressed women about thirty-five years of age, who were always to be found here on Saturday nights, drinking with any man who was willing to pay for them. The behaviour of these two women was quiet and their manners unobtrusive. They seemed to realise that they were there only on sufferance, and their demeanour was shamefaced and humble.

The majority of the guests were standing. The floor was sprinkled with sawdust which served to soak up the beer that slopped out of the glasses of those whose hands were too unsteady to hold them upright. The air was foul with the smell of beer, spirits and tobacco smoke, and the uproar was deafening, for nearly everyone was talking at the same time, their voices clashing discordantly with the strains of the polyphone, which was playing 'The Garden of Your Heart.' In one corner a group of men was convulsed with laughter at the details of a dirty story related by one of their number. Several impatient customers were banging the bottoms of their empty glasses or pewters on the counter and shouting their orders for more beer. Oaths, curses and obscene expressions resounded on every hand, coming almost as frequently from the women as the men. And over all resounded the rattle of money, the ringing of the cash register, the clinking and rattling of the glasses and pewter pots as they were being washed, and the gurgling of the beer as it gushed into the drinking vessels from the taps of the beer engine, whose handles were almost incessantly manipulated by the barman, the Old Dear and the glittering landlady, whose silken blouse, bejewelled hair, ears, neck and fingers, scintillated gloriously in the blaze of the gaslight.

The scene was so novel and strange to Ruth that she felt dazed and bewildered. Before her marriage she had been a total abstainer, but since then had occasionally taken a glass of beer with Easton for company's sake with their Sunday dinner at home. But it was generally Easton who went out and bought it, and she had never before been in a public house to drink. So confused and ill at ease did she feel that she scarcely heard or understood Mrs Crass, who talked incessantly, principally about their other neighbours in North Street, and also promised Ruth to introduce her presently—if he came in, as he was almost certain to do—to Mr Partaker, one of her two lodgers, a most superior young man, who had been with them now for over three years and would not leave on any account. In fact, he had been their lodger in their old house and when they moved he came with them to North Street, although it was farther away from his place of business.

Meantime, Crass and Easton—the latter having deposited the string bag on the seat at Ruth's side—arranged to play a match of Hooks and Rings with the Semi-Drunk and the Besotted Wretch, the losers to pay for drinks for all the party including the two women. Crass and the Semi-Drunk tossed up for sides. Crass won and picked the Besotted Wretch, and the game began. It was a one-sided affair from the first, for Easton and the Semi-Drunk were no match for the other two. The end of it was that Easton and his partner had to pay for the drinks. The four men had a pint each of four ale and Mrs Crass had another three-pennyworth of gin. Ruth protested that she did not want any more to drink, but the others ridiculed this, and both the Besotted Wretch and the Semi-Drunk seemed to regard her unwillingness as a personal insult, so she allowed them to get her another halfpint of beer, which she was compelled to drink, because she was conscious that the others were watching her to see that she did so.

The Semi-Drunk now suggested a return match. He wished to have his revenge. He was a little out of practice, he said, and was only just getting his hand in as they were finishing the other game. Crass and his partner readily assented, and in spite of Ruth's whispered entreaty that they should return home without further delay, Easton insisted on joining the game.

Although they played more carefully than before, and notwithstanding the fact that the Besotted Wretch was very drunk, Easton and his partner were again beaten and once more had to pay for the drinks. The men had a pint each as before. Mrs Crass—upon whom the liquor so far seemed to have no effect—had another three-pennyworth of gin, and Ruth consented to take another glass of beer on condition that Easton would come away directly their drinks were finished. Easton agreed to do so, but instead of keeping his word he began to play a four handed game of shove-ha'penny with the other three, the sides and stakes being arranged as before.

The liquor was by this time beginning to have some effect upon Ruth; she felt dizzy and confused. Whenever it was necessary to reply to Mrs Grass's talk she found some difficulty in articulating the words and she knew she was not answering very intelligently. Even when Mrs Crass introduced her to the interesting Mr Partaker, who arrived about this time, she was scarcely able to collect herself sufficiently to decline that fascinating gentleman's invitation to have another drink with himself and Mrs Crass. After a time a kind of terror took possession of her, and she resolved that if Easton would not come when he had finished the game he was playing she would go home without him.

Meantime the game of shove-ha'penny proceeded merrily, the majority of the male guests crowding round the board, applauding or censuring the players as occasion demanded. The Semi-Drunk was in high glee for Crass was not much of a hand at this game, and the Besotted Wretch, although playing well, was not able to make up for his partner's want of skill. As the game drew near its end and it became more and more certain that his opponents would be defeated, the joy of the Semi-Drunk was unbounded, and he challenged them to make it double or quits, a generous offer which they wisely declined; and shortly afterwards, seeing that their position was hopeless, they capitulated and prepared to pay the penalty of the vanquished.

Crass ordered the drinks and the Besotted Wretch paid half the damage—a pint of four ale for each of the men and the same as before for the ladies. The Old Dear executed the order, but by mistake, being very busy, he served two 'three's' of gin instead of one. Ruth did not want any more at all, but she was afraid to say so, and she did not like to make any fuss about it being the wrong drink, especially as they all assured her that the spirits would do her more good than beer. She did not want either; she wanted to get away, and would have liked to empty the stuff out of the glass on to the floor, but she was afraid that Mrs Crass or one of the others might see her doing so and that it might lead to trouble. Besides, it seemed easier to drink this small quantity of spirits and water than a glass of beer, the very thought of which now made her feel ill. She drank the stuff, which Easton handed to her, at a single draught, and, handing back the empty glass with a shudder, stood up resolutely.

'Are you coming home now? You promised you would,' she said.

'All right; presently,' replied Easton. 'There's plenty of time; it's not nine yet.'

'That doesn't matter; it's quite late enough. You know we've left the child at home alone in the house. You promised you'd come as soon as you'd finished that other game.'

'All right, all right,' answered Easton, impatiently. 'Just wait a minute; I want to see this, and then I'll come.'

'This' was a most interesting problem propounded by Crass, who had arranged eleven matches side by side on the shove-ha'penny board. The problem was to take none away and yet leave only nine. Nearly all the men in the bar were crowding round the shove-ha'penny board, some with knitted brows and drunken gravity trying to solve the puzzle, and others waiting curiously for the result. Easton crossed over to see how it was done, and as none of the crowd were able to do the trick, Crass showed that it could be accomplished by simply arranging the eleven matches so as to form the word NINE. Everybody said it was very good indeed, very clever and interesting. Both the Semi-Drunk and the Besotted Wretch were reminded by this trick of several others equally good, and they proceeded to do them; and then the men had another pint each all round as a reviver after the mental strain of the last few minutes.

Easton did not know any tricks himself, but he was an interested spectator until Ruth came over and touched his arm.

'Aren't you coming?'

'Wait a minute, can't you?' he cried, roughly. 'What's your hurry?'

'I don't want to stay here any longer,' said Ruth, hysterically; 'you said you'd come as soon as you saw that trick. If you don't come I shall go home by myself. I don't want to stay in this place any longer.'

'Well, go by yourself if you want to!' shouted Easton fiercely, pushing her away from him. 'I shall stop 'ere as long as I please, and if you don't like it you can do the other thing.'

Ruth staggered and nearly fell from the force of the push he gave her, and the man turned again to the table to watch the Semi-Drunk, who was arranging six matches so as to form the numeral XII, saying he could prove that this was equal to a thousand.

Ruth waited a few minutes longer, and then, as Easton took no further notice of her, she took up the string bag and the other parcels, and without staying to say good-night to Mrs Crass, who was earnestly conversing with the interesting Partaker, opened the door with some difficulty and went out into the street. The cold night air seemed refreshing and sweet after the foul atmosphere of the public-house. But after a little while she began to feel faint and dizzy and was conscious also that she walking unsteadily, and she fancied that people stared at her strangely as they passed. The parcels felt very heavy and awkward to carry, and the string bag seemed as if it were filled with lead.

Although under ordinary circumstances it was only about ten minutes' walk home, she resolved to go by one of the trams which passed by the end of North Street. With this intention she put down her bag on the pavement at the stopping place, and waited, resting her hand on the iron pillar at the corner of the street, where a little crowd of people were standing, evidently with the same object as herself.

Two trams passed without stopping, for they were already full of passengers, a common circumstance on Saturday nights. The next one stopped, and several persons alighted, and then ensued a fierce struggle amongst the waiting crowd for the vacant seats. Men and women pushed, pulled and almost fought, shoving their fists and elbows into each other's sides and breasts and faces. Ruth was quickly thrust aside and nearly knocked down, and the tram, having taken aboard as many passengers as it had accomodation for, passed on. She waited for the next one, and the same scene was enacted with the same result for her, and then, reflecting that if she had not stayed for these trams she might have been home by now, she determined to resume her walk. The parcels felt heavier than ever, and she had not proceeded very far before she was compelled to put the bag down again upon the pavement outside an empty house.

Leaning against the railings, she felt very tired and ill. Everything around her, the street, the houses, the traffic, seemed vague and shadowy and unreal. Several people looked curiously at her as they passed, but by this time she was scarcely conscious of their scrutiny.

Slyme's 'open air' that night, conducted by the Shining Light Mission, had been a most successful meeting, the disciples—including Hunter, Rushton, Sweater, Didlum, and Mrs Starvem—Ruth's former mistress—had assembled in great force so as to be able to deal more effectively with any infidels or hired critics or drunken scoffers who might disturb the proceedings. When the meeting was over, Slyme set off to his lodging at a good pace, for the evening had turned cold and he was anxious to get home to the fire. He had not gone very far when he saw a small crowd of people on the pavement on the other side of the road, outside an unoccupied house, and in spite of his hurry he crossed over to see what was the matter, There were about twenty people standing there, and in the centre, close to the railings he could hear the voices of three or four women.

'What's up?' he enquired of a man on the edge of the crowd.

'Oh, nothing much,' returned the other; 'some young woman; she's either ill, come over faint, or something—or else she's had a drop too much.'

'Quite a respectable looking young party, too,' said another man.

Several young fellows in the crowd were amusing themselves by making suggestive jokes, and causing some laughter by their expressions of mock sympathy.

'Doesn't anyone know who she is?' said the second man who had spoken in reply to Slyme's enquiry.

'No,' said a woman who was standing a little nearer the middle of the crowd, 'and she won't say where she lives.'

'She'll be all right now she's had that glass of soda,' said another man, elbowing his way out of the crowd. As this individual came out, Slyme managed to work himself a little further into the group of people and he uttered an involuntary cry of astonishment as he caught sight of Ruth, very pale, and looking very ill, as she stood clasping one of the railings with her left hand, and holding the packages of groceries in the other. She had by this time recovered sufficiently to feel overwhelmed with shame and confusion before the crowd of strangers who hemmed her in on every side and some of whom she could hear laughing and joking about her. It was therefore with a sensation of intense relief and gratitude that she saw Slyme's familiar face and heard his friendly voice as he forced his way through to her side.

'I can walk home all right now,' she stammered in reply to his anxious questioning, 'if you wouldn't mind carrying some of these things for me.'

He insisted on taking the bag and all the parcels, and the crowd, having jumped to the conclusion that he was the young woman's husband, began to dwindle away, one of the jokers remarking 'It's all over!' in a loud voice, as he took himself off.

It was only about seven minutes' walk home from there, and as the streets along which they had to pass were not very brilliantly lighted, Ruth was able to lean on Slyme's arm most of the way. When they arrived home, after she had removed her hat, he made her sit down in the arm chair. The fire was burning brightly, and the kettle was singing on the hob, for she had banked up the fire with cinders and small coal before she went out.

The baby still lay asleep in the cradle, but his slumbers had evidently not been of the most restful kind, for he had kicked the bed clothes off him and was lying all uncovered.

Ruth obeyed passively when Slyme told her to sit down, and lying back languidly in the armchair she watched him, through half-closed eyes and with a slight flush on her face, as he deftly covered the sleeping child with the bed clothes and settled him more comfortably in the cot.

Slyme now turned his attention to the fire and as he placed the kettle upon it, he remarked: 'As soon as the water boils I'll make you some strong tea.'

During their walk home she had acquainted Slyme with the cause of the misfortune which had befallen her, and as she reclined in the armchair, drowsily watching him, she wondered what would have happened to her if he had not passed by when he did.

'Are you feeling better?' he asked, looking down at her.

'Yes. I feel quite well now; but I'm afraid I've given you a lot of trouble.'

'No, you haven't. Nothing I can do for *you* is a trouble to me. But don't you think you'd better take your jacket off? Here, let me help you.'

While he was helping with the jacket, Slyme suddenly took her in his arms and kissed her repeatedly.

There came a cry from the cradle, and at the sound a shudder went through Ruth's limp and unresisting form. She wrenched herself free from his passionate embrace, and struck at him so furiously that he recoiled before her and retired upstairs trembling and disconcerted.

The following week the Eastons' room was once again to let.

CHAPTER XIX

The Oblong

During the following week the work at 'The Cave' progressed rapidly towards completion, although the hours of daylight were now so few that the men worked only from 8 a.m. till 4 p.m., and had their breakfast before they came. This made forty hours a week, so that those who were paid sevenpence an hour earned £1 3s. 4d, those who got sixpence-halfpenny drew £1 1s. 8d, those whose wages were fivepence an hour were paid the princely sum of 16s. 8d. for their week's hard labour, and those whose rate was fourpence halfpenny 'picked up' 15s.

And yet there are people who say that Drink is the cause of poverty.

By Tuesday night all the inside work was finished with the exception of the kitchen and scullery. The painting of the kitchen had been delayed owing to the non-arrival of the new cooking range, and the scullery was still used as the paint shop. The outside work was also progressing rapidly, for though, according to the specification, all the outside woodwork was supposed to have three coats, and the guttering, rain pipes and other ironwork, two coats, Crass and Hunter had arranged to make two coats do for most of the windows and woodwork, and all the ironwork had one coat only. The windows were painted in two colours, the sashes dark green and the frames white. All the rest—gables, doors, railings, guttering, etc.—was dark green; and all the dark green paint was made with boiled linseed oil and varnish, no turpentine being allowed.

'This is some bloody fine stuff to 'ave to use, ain't it?' remarked Harlow to Philpot on Wednesday morning. 'It's more like a lot of treacle than anything else.'

'Yes; and it won't arf blister next summer when it gets a bit of sun on it,' replied Philpot with a grin.

'I suppose they're afraid that if they was to put a little turps in it wouldn't bear out, and they'd 'ave to give it another coat.'

'You can bet yer life that's the reason,' said Philpot; 'but all the same I mean to pinch a drop to put in mine as soon as Crass is gorn.'

'Gorn where?'

'Why, didn't you know? There's another funeral on to-day.'

'I reckon Crass and Slyme must be making a small fortune out of all these 'ere funerals,' said Harlow; 'this makes the fourth in the last fortnight. What is it they gets for 'em?'

'A shillin' for takin' 'ome the corfin and liftin' in the corpse, and four bob for the funeral five bob altogether.'

'That's a bit of all right, ain't it?' said Harlow. 'A couple of them in a week besides your week's wages. Five bob for two or three hours' work!'

'Yes, the money's all right, mate, but they're welcome to it for my part. I don't want to go messin' about with no corpses,' replied Philpot, with a shudder.

'Who is this last party what's dead?' asked Harlow. after a pause.

'It's a parson what used to belong to the Shinin' Light Chapel. He'd been abroad for 'is 'olerdays. It seems 'e was ill before 'e went away, but the change did 'im a lot of good; in fact, 'e was quite recovered, and 'e was coming back again. But while 'e was standin' on the platform waitin' for the train, a porter runned into 'im with a barrer load o' luggage, and 'e blowed up.'

'Blowed up?'

'Yes,' repeated Philpot solemnly. 'Blowed up! Busted! Exploded! All into pieces. But they swep 'em all up and put it in a corfin and it's to be planted this afternoon.'

Harlow maintained an awestruck silence, and Philpot continued:

'I had a drink the other night with a butcher bloke what used to serve this parson with meat, and we was talkin' about what a strange sort of death it was, but 'e said 'e wasn't at all surprised to 'ear of it; the only thing as 'e wondered at was that the man didn't blow up long ago, considerin 'the amount of grub as 'e used to make away with. He ses the quantities of stuff as 'e's took there and seen other tradesmen take was something chronic. Tons of it!'

'What was the parson's name?' asked Harlow.

'Belcher. You must 'ave noticed 'im about the town. A very fat chap,' replied Philpot. 'I'm sorry you wasn't 'ere on Saturday to see the corfin plate. Frank called me in to see the wordin' when 'e'd finished it. It had on: "Jonydab Belcher. Born January 1st 1849. Ascended, December 8th 19__"'

'Oh, I know the bloke now!' cried Harlow. 'I remember my youngsters bringin' 'ome a subscription list what they'd got up at the Sunday School to send 'im away for a 'olerday because 'e was ill, and I gave 'em a penny each to put on their cards because I didn't want 'em to feel mean before the other young 'uns. It seems to be gettin' colder, don't it?'

'It's enough to freeze the ears orf a brass monkey!' remarked Easton as he descended from a ladder close by, and placing his pot of paint on the ground began to try to warm his hands by rubbing and beating them together. He was trembling, and his teeth were chattering with cold.

'I could just do with a nice pint o' beer, now,' he said as he stamped his feet on the ground.

'That's just what I was thinkin',' said Philpot wistfully, 'and what's more, I mean to 'ave one, too, at dinner time. I shall nip down to the "Cricketers." Even if I don't get back till a few minutes after one, it won't matter, because Crass and Nimrod will be gorn to the funeral.'

'Will you bring me a pint back with you, in a bottle?' asked Easton.

'Yes, certainly,' said Philpot.

Harlow said nothing. He also would have liked a pint of beer, but, as was usual with him, he had not the necessary cash.

Having restored the circulation to a certain extent, they now resumed their work, and only just in time, for a few minutes afterwards they observed Misery peeping at them round the corner of the house and they wondered how long he had been there and whether he had overheard their conversation.

At twelve o'clock Crass and Slyme cleared off in a great hurry, and a little while afterwards Philpot took off his apron and put on his coat to go to 'The Cricketers.' When the others found out where he was going, several of them asked him to bring back a drink for them, and then someone suggested that all those who wanted some beer should give twopence each. This was done: one shilling and fourpence was collected and given to Philpot, who was to bring back a gallon of beer in a jar. He promised to get back as soon as ever he could, and some of the shareholders decided not to drink any tea with their dinners, but to wait for the beer, although they knew that it would be nearly time to resume work before he could get back. It would be a quarter to one at the very earliest.

The minutes dragged slowly by, and after a while the only man on the job who had a watch began to lose his temper and refused to answer any more enquiries concerning the time. So presently Bert was sent up to the top of the house to look at a church clock which was visible therefrom, and when he came down he reported that it was ten minutes to one.

Symptoms of anxiety now began to manifest themselves amongst the shareholders, several of whom went down to the main road to see if Philpot was yet in sight, but each returned with the same report—they could see nothing of him.

No one was formally 'in charge' of the job during Grass's absence, but they all returned to their work promptly at one because they feared that Sawkins or some other sneak might report any irregularity to Crass or Misery.

At a quarter past one Philpot was still missing and the uneasiness of the shareholders began to develop into a panic. Some of them plainly expressed the opinion that he had gone on the razzle with the money. As the time wore on this became the general opinion. At two o'clock, all hope of his return having been abandoned, two or three of the shareholders went and drank some of the cold tea.

Their fears were only too well founded, for they saw no mere of Philpot till the next morning, when he arrived looking very sheepish and repentant and promised to refund all the money on Saturday. He also made a long rambling statement from which it appeared that on his way to the 'Cricketers' he met a couple of chaps whom he knew who were out of work, and he invited them to come and have a drink. When they got to the pub they found there the Semi-Drunk and the Besotted Wretch. One drink led to another, and then they started arguing, and he had forgotten all about the gallon of beer until he woke up this morning.

Whilst Philpot was making this explanation they were putting on their aprons and blouses and Crass was serving out the lots of colour. Slyme took no part in the conversation, but got ready as quickly as possible and went outside to make a start. The reason for this haste soon became apparent to some of the others, for they noticed that he had selected and commenced painting a large window that was so situated as to be sheltered from the keen wind that was blowing.

The basement of the house was slightly below the level of the ground and there was a sort of a trench or area about three feet deep in front of the basement windows. The banks of this trench were covered with rose trees and evergreens, and the bottom was a mass of slimy, evil smelling, rain-sodden earth. To second coat these windows Philpot and Harlow had to stand in all this filth, which soaked through their worn and broken boot soles. As they worked, the thorns of the rose trees caught and tore their clothing and scratched the flesh of their half-frozen hands.

Owen and Easton were working on ladders at the windows immediately above Philpot and Harlow; Sawkins, on another ladder, was painting one of the gables, and the other men were busy at different parts of the outside of the house; and the boy Bert was painting the iron railings of the front fence. The weather was bitterly cold and a dreary expanse of grey cloud covered the wintry sky.

As the men worked they stood almost motionless, their right arms being the only part of their bodies that was exercised. The window painting required great care and deliberation, otherwise the glass would be 'messed up,' or the white paint of the frames would 'run into' the dark green of the sashes, for both colours were wet at the same time, each man having two pots of paint and two sets of brushes. The wind was not blowing in sudden gusts, but swept by in a strong persistent current that penetrated their clothing and left them trembling and numb with cold. It blew from the right, and this added to their discomfort, because the uplifted right arm left that side of the body fully exposed. They were able to keep their left hands in their trousers pockets and the left arm close to the side most of the time, which made a lot of difference.

Another reason why it is worse for the wind to strike from the right is that the buttons on a man's coat are always on the right side and consequently the wind getsunderneath. Philpot realised this all the more because some of the buttons of his coat and waistcoat were missing.

As they worked on, trembling with cold, and with their teeth chattering, their faces and hands turned that pale violet colour generally seen on the lips of a corpse. Their eyes became full of water and the lids were red and inflamed. Philpot's and Harlow's boots were soon wet through, and their feet were sore and intensely painful with cold.

Their hands, of course, suffered the most, becoming so numbed that they were unable to feel the brushes they held; in fact, presently, as Philpot was taking a dip of colour, the brush fell into the pot, and then, finding that he was unable to move his fingers, he put his hand into his trousers pocket to thaw, and began to walk about, stamping his feet upon the ground. His example was quickly followed by Owen, Easton, and Harlow, and they all went round the corner to the sheltered side of the house where Slyme was working, and began walking up and down, rubbing their hands, stamping their feet, and swinging their arms to warm themselves.

'If I thought Nimrod wasn't comin', I'd put my overcoat on and work in it,' remarked Philpot, 'but you never knows when to expect the blighter, and if 'e saw me in it, it would mean the bloody push.'

'It wouldn't interfere with our workin' if we did wear 'em,' said Easton, 'in fact, we'd be able to work all the quicker if we wasn't so cold.'

'Even if Misery didn't come, I suppose Crass would 'ave something to say if we put 'em on,' continued Philpot.

'Well, yer couldn't blame 'im if 'e did say something, could yer?' said Slyme, offensively. 'Crass would get into a row 'imself if 'Unter came and saw us workin' in overcoats. It would look ridiclus.'

Slyme suffered less from the cold than any of them, not only because he had secured the most sheltered window, but also because he was better clothed than most of the rest.

'What's Crass supposed to be doin' inside?' asked Easton, as he tramped up and down, with his shoulders hunched up and his hands thrust deep into the pockets of his trousers.

'Blowed if I know,' replied Philpot; 'messin' about touchin up or makin' colour. He never does 'is share of a job like this; 'e knows 'ow to work things all right for 'isself.'

'What if 'e does? We'd do the same if we was in 'is place, and so would anybody else,' said Slyme, and added sarcastically: 'or p'raps you'd give all the soft jobs to other people and do all the rough yerself!'

Slyme knew that although they were speaking of Crass they were also alluding to himself, and as he replied to Philpot he looked slyly at Owen, who had so far taken no part in the conversation.

'It's not a question of what *we* would do,' chimed in Harlow, 'it's a question of what's fair. If it's not fair for Crass to pick all the soft jobs for 'imself and leave all the rough for the other chaps, it wouldn't make it any more right for us to do the same if we 'ad the chance.'

'No one can be blamed for doing the best he can for himself under existing circumstances,' said Owen, in reply to Slyme's questioning look. 'That is the principle of the present system—every man for himself and the devil take the rest. For my own part I don't pretend to practise unselfishness. I don't pretend to guide my actions by the rules laid down in the Sermon on the Mount. But it's certainly surprising to hear you, who profess to be a follower of Christ, advocating selfishness; or rather, it *would be surprising* except that the name of "Christian" has ceased to signify one who follows Christ, and has come to mean only liar and hypocrite.'

Slyme made no answer. Possibly the fact that he was a true believer enabled him to bear this insult with meekness and humility.

'I wonder what time it is?' interposed Philpot.

Slyme looked at his watch. It was nearly ten o'clock.

'Jesus Christ! is that all?' growled Easton as they returned to work. 'Two hours more!'

The wind blew colder and colder. The sky, which at first had shown small patches of blue through rifts in the masses of clouds, had now become uniformly grey. There was every indication of an impending fall of snow.

The men perceived this with conflicting feelings. If it did begin to snow they would not be able to continue this work, and therefore they found themselves involuntarily wishing that it *would* snow, or rain, or hail, or anything that would stop the work. But on the other hand, if the weather prevented them getting on with the outside, some of them would have to 'stand off', because the inside was practically finished. None of them wished to lose any 'time' if they could help it, because there were only ten days more before Christmas.

Twelve o'clock came at last, and almost before Grass's whistle had ceased to sound the men were all assembled in the kitchen before a roaring fire. Sweater had sent in two tons of coal, and had given orders that large fires were to be lit each day in nearly every room to make the house habitable by Christmas.

'I wonder if it's true as the firm's got another job to do for old Sweater?' remarked Harlow, as he was toasting a bloater on the end of a pointed stick.

'True? No!' said the man on the pail scornfully. 'It's all bogey. You know that empty 'ouse as they said Sweater 'ad bought—the one that Rushton and Nimrod was seen lookin'at?'

'Yes,' replied Harlow. The other men listened with evident interest.

'Well, they wasn't pricing it up at all! The landlord of that 'ouse is abroad, and there was some plants in the garden as Rushton thought 'e'd like, and 'e was tellin' Misery which ones 'e wanted. And afterwards old Pontius Pilate came up with Ned Dawson and a truck. They made two or three journeys and took bloody near everything in the garden as was worth takin'. What didn't go to Rushton's place went to 'Unter's.'

The disappointment of their hopes for another job was almost forgotten in their interest in this story.

'Who told you about it?' said Harlow.

'Ned Dawson 'imself. It's right enough what I say. Ask 'im.'

Ned Dawson, usually called 'Bundy's mate', had been doing odd jobs at the yard, and had only come back to 'The Cave' that morning, and on being appealed to he corroborated Dick Wantley's statement.

'They'll be gettin' theirselves into trouble if they ain't careful,' remarked Easton.

'Oh no, they won't; Rushton's too artful for that. It seems the agent is a pal of 'is, and they worked it between 'em.'

'Wot a bloody cheek, though!' exclaimed Harlow.

'Oh, that's nothing to some o' the things I've knowed 'em do before now,' said the man on the pail. 'Why, don't you remember, back in the summer, that carved hoak hall table as Rushton pinched out of that 'ouse on Grand Parade?'

'Yes, that was a bit of all right, too, wasn't it?' cried Philpot, and several of the others laughed.

'You know, that big 'ouse we did up last summer—No 596,' Wantley continued, for the benefit of those not 'in the know'. 'Well, it 'ad bin empty for a long time, and we found this 'ere table in a cupboard under the stairs. A bloody fine table it was, too. One of them bracket tables what you fix to the wall, without no legs. It 'ad a 'arf round marble top to it, and underneath was a carved hoak figger, a mermaid, with 'er arms up over 'er 'ead 'oldin' up the table top—something splendid! Must 'ave been worth at least five quid. Well, just as we pulled this 'ere table out, who should come in but Rushton, and when 'e seen it 'e tells Crass to cover it over with a sack and not to let nobody see it. And then 'e clears orf to the shop and sends the boy down with the truck and 'as it took up to 'is own 'ouse; and it's there now, fixed in the front 'all. I was sent up there a couple of months ago to paint and varnish the lobby doors, and I seen it meself. There's a pitcher called "The Day of Judgmint" 'angin' on the wall just over it—thunder and lightnin' and earthquakes and corpses gettin' up out o' their graves—something bloody 'orrible; and underneath the picture is a card with a tex out of the Bible: "Christ is the 'ead of this 'ouse; the unknown guest at every meal, the silent listener to every conversation." I was workin' there for three or four days and I got to know it orf by 'eart.'

'Well, that takes the biskit, don't it?' said Philpot.

'Yes; but the best of it was,' the man on the pail proceeded; 'the best of it was, when ole Misery 'eard about the table, 'e was so bloody wild because 'e didn't get it 'imself that 'e went upstairs and pinched one of the venetian blinds, and 'ad it took up to 'is own 'ouse by the boy, and a few days arterwards one of the carpenters 'ad to go and fix it up in 'is bedroom.'

'And wasn't it never found out?' enquired Easton.

'Well, there was a bit of talk about it. The agent wanted to know where it was, but Pontius Pilate swore black and white as there 'adn't been no blind in that room, and the end of it was that the firm got the order to supply a new one.'

A number of similar stories were related by several others concerning the doings of their different employers, but after a time the conversation reverted to the subject that was uppermost in their thoughts—the impending slaughter, and the improbability of being able to obtain another job, considering the large number of men who were already out of employment.

'I can't make it out, myself,' remarked Easton; 'things seems to get worse every year. There don't seem to be 'arf the work about that there used to be, and even what there is is messed up anyhow, as if the people who 'as it done can't afford to pay for it.'

'You should ask Owen to explain it for yer,' said Crass, with a jeering laugh. ''E knows all about wot's the cause of poverty, but 'e won't tell nobody.'

Crass had never yet had an opportunity of producing the 'Obscurer' cutting, and he made this remark in the hope of turning the conversation into a convenient channel. But Owen did not respond, and went on reading his newspaper.

'We ain't 'ad no lectures at all lately, 'ave we?' said Harlow, in an injured tone, 'I think it's about time Owen explained what the real cause of poverty is. I'm beginning to get anxious about it.'

The others laughed.

When Philpot had finished eating his dinner he went out of the kitchen and presently returned with a small pair of steps, which he opened and placed in a corner of the room, with the back of the steps facing the audience.

'There you are, me son!' he exclaimed to Owen. 'There's a pulpit for yer.'

'Yes! Come on 'ere!' cried Crass, feeling in his waistcoat pocket for the cutting. 'Tell us wot's the real cause of poverty.'

''Ear, 'ear!' shouted the man on the pail. 'Git up into the bloody pulpit and give us a sermon.'

As Owen made no response to these invitations the crowd began to hoot and groan.

'Come on, man,' whispered Philpot, winking his goggle eye persuasively at Owen; 'come on, just for a bit of fun, to pass the time away.'

Owen accordingly ascended the steps, much to the secret delight of Crass, and was immediately greeted with a round of enthusiastic applause.

Philpot having been unanimously elected Chairman, Owen commenced:

'Mr Chairman and Gentlemen, in some of my previous lectures I have endeavoured to convince you that money is in itself of no value and of no real use whatever. In this I am afraid I have been rather unsuccessful.'

'Not a bit of it, mate,' cried Crass, sarcastically; 'we all agrees with it.'

''Ear, 'ear!' shouted Easton. 'If a bloke was to come in 'ere now and orfer to give me a quid I'd refuse it!'

'So would I,' said Philpot.

'Well, whether you agree or not, the fact remains. A man might possess so much money that, in England, he would be comparatively rich, and yet if he went to some country where the cost of living is very high he would find himself in a condition of poverty. Or he might be in a place where the necessaries of life could not be bought for money at all. Therefore it follows that to be rich consists not necessarily in having much money, but in being able to enjoy an abundance of the things that are made by work; and that poverty consists not merely in being without money, but in being short of the necessaries and comforts of life—or in other words in being short of the Benefits of Civilisation, those things that are all, without exception, produced by work. Whether you agree or not with anything else that I say, you will all admit that that is our condition at the present time. We do not enjoy a full share of the benefits of civilisation—we are all in a state of more or less abject poverty.'

'And the reason why we're short of the things that's made by work,' interrupted Crass, mimicking Owen's manner, 'is that we ain't got the bloody money to buy 'em.'

'Yes,' said the man on the pail, 'and as I said before, if all the money in the country was shared out equal to-day, according to Owen's ideas, in six months' time it would be all back again in the same 'ands as it is now, and what are you goin' to do then?'

'Share again, of course.'

This answer came derisively from several places at the same instant, and then they all began speaking at once, vicing with each other in ridiculing the foolishness of 'them there Socialists,' whom they called 'The Sharers Out.'

'I never said anything about "sharing out all the money,"' said Owen, during a lull in the storm, 'and I don't know of any Socialist who advocates it. Give me your authority for saying that Socialists believe in sharing out all the money equally!'

'Come to think of it,' remarked Crass, as he drew the 'Obscurer' cutting from his waistcoat pocket, 'I've got a little thing 'ere that I've been goin' to read to yer. It's out of the "Obscurer." I'd forgotten all about it.'

Remarking that the print was too small for his own eyes, he passed the slip of paper to Harlow, who read aloud as follows:

'PROVE YOUR PRINCIPLES; OR, LOOK AT BOTH SIDES.

'I wish I could open your eyes to the true misery of our condition: injustice, tyranny, and oppression!' said a discontented hack to a weary looking cob, as they stood side by side in unhired cabs.

'I'd rather have them opened to something pleasant, thank you,' replied the cob.

'I am sorry for you. If you could enter into the noble aspirations—' the hack began.

'Talk plain. What would you have?' said the cob, interrupting him.

'What would I have? Why, equality, and share and share alike all over the world,' said the hack.

'You *mean* that?' said the cob.

'Of course I do. What right have those sleek, pampered hunters and racers to their warm stables and high feed, their grooms and jockeys? It is really heart-sickening to think of it,' replied the hack.

'I don't know but you may be right,' said the cob; 'and to show I'm in earnest, as no doubt you are, let me have half the good beans you have in your bag, and you shall have half the musty oats and chaff I have in mine. There's nothing like proving one's principles.'—*Original Parables by Mrs Prosser*.'

'There you are!' cried several voices.

'What does THAT mean?' cried Crass, triumphantly. 'Why don't you go and share your wages with the chaps what's out of work?'

'What does it mean?' replied Owen, contemptuously. 'It means that if the Editor of the "Obscurer" put that in his paper as an argument against Socialism, either he is of feeble intellect himself or else he thinks that the majority of his readers are. That isn't, an argument against Socialism; it's an argument against the hypocrites who pretend to be Christians, the people who profess to "love their neighbours as themselves," who pretend to believe in "Universal Brotherhood" and who assert they do not love the world or the things of the world. As for why *I* don't do it—why should I? I don't pretend to be a Christian. But you're all "Christians"—why don't *you* do it?'

'We're not talkin' about religion,' exclaimed Crass, impatiently.

'Then what *are* you talking about? I never said anything about "sharing out" or "bearing one another's burdens." I don't profess to "give to everyone who asks of me" or to "give my cloak to the man who takes away my coat." I have read that Christ taught that his followers must do all these things, but as I do not pretend to be one of his followers I don't do them. But you believe in Christianity: why don't you do the things that He said?'

As nobody seemed to know the answer to this question, the lecturer proceeded:

'In this matter the difference between so-called "Christians" and Socialists is this: Christ taught the Fatherhood of God and the Brotherhood of men. Those who to-day pretend to be Christ's followers hypocritically profess to carry out those teachings *now*. But they don't. They have arranged "the Battle of Life" system instead!

'The Socialist—very much against his will—finds himself in the midst of this horrible battle, and he appeals to the other combatants to cease from fighting and to establish a system of Brotherly Love and Mutual Helpfulness, but he does not hypocritically pretend to practise brotherly love towards those who will not agree to his appeal and who compel him to fight with them for his very life. He knows that in this battle he must either fight or go under. Therefore, in self defence, he fights; but all the time he continues his appeal for the cessation of the slaughter. He pleads for the changing of the system. He advocates Co-operation instead of Competition. But how can he co-operate with people who insist on competing with him? No individual can practise cooperation by himself! Socialism can only be practised by the Community—that is the meaning of the word. At present, the other members of the Community—the "Christians"—deride and oppose the Socialist's appeal.

'No Socialist suggests "sharing out" money or anything else in the manner you say. And another thing: if you only had a little more sense you might be able to perceive that this stock "argument" of yours is really an argument against the present system, inasmuch as it proves that Money is in itself of no use whatever. Suppose all the money *was* shared out equally, and suppose there was enough of it for everyone to have ten thousand pounds; and suppose they then all thought they were rich and none of them would work. What would they live on? Their money? Could they eat it or drink it or wear it? It wouldn't take them very long to find out that this wonderful money, which under the present system is the most powerful thing in existence, is really of no more use than so much dirt. They would speedily perish, not from lack of money, but from lack of wealth—that is, from lack of the things that are made by work. And also it is quite true that if all the money were distributed equally amongst all the people to-morrow, it would all be up in heaps again in a very short time. But that only proves that while the present Money System remains it will be impossible to do away with poverty, for heaps in some places mean little or nothing in other places. Therefore while the money system lasts we are bound to have poverty and all the evils it brings in its train.'

'Oh, of course everybody's an idjit except you,' sneered Crass, who was beginning to feel rather fogged.

'I rise to a pint of order,' said Easton.

'And I rise to order a pint,' cried Philpot.

'Order what the bloody 'ell you like,' remarked Harlow, 'so long as I haven't got to pay for it.'

'Mine's a pint of porter,' observed the man on the pail.

'The pint is,' proceeded Easton, 'when does the lecturer intend to explain to us what is the real cause of poverty?'

''Ear, 'ear!' cried Harlow. 'That's what *I* want to know, too.'

'And what *I* should like to know is, who is supposed to be givin' this 'ere lecture?' enquired the man on the pail.

'Why, Owen, of course,' replied Harlow.

'Well, why don't you try to keep quiet for a few minutes and let 'im get on with it?'

'The next blighter wot interrupts,' cried Philpot, rolling up his shirt sleeves and glaring threateningly round upon the meeting, 'goes out through the bloody winder!'

At this everybody pretended to be very frightened, and edged away as far as possible from Philpot, except the man on the pail, who perhaps felt safer than the others because he was, as usual, surrounded by a moat.

'Poverty,' resumed the lecturer, 'consists of a shortage of the necessaries of life which are produced from the Raw Materials by the Workers, aided by Machinery.

'Now there is plenty of Raw Material, plenty of Labour, plenty of Machinery—and yet nearly everybody is going short of nearly everything.

'It is the Money System which is the cause of this shortage, which makes the worker starve in the midst of the means of abundance, and binds him in helpless idleness with a fetter of gold.

'Let us examine the details of this imbecile Money System.'

Owen took a piece of charred wood from the grate and drew a quadrangular figure on the wall.

This represents the whole of the adult population of the country.

'To discover the cause of shortage of the things that can be made by work, we must find how the people spend their time. This oblong represents the whole of the adult population of the country. All these people help to consume the things made by work, but though the majority are workers, only a comparatively small number actually produce the benefits of civilization, or the necessaries of life.'

The lecturer turned to the drawing on the wall to make some addition to it, then paused irresolutely and let his arm drop to his side.

He knew how unwilling his hearers were to think about such subjects as the cause of poverty. He knew they would ridicule what he said and refuse to try to understand his meaning if it was at all obscure. They would not worry their heads about such an unimportant matter; it would be different if it were a smutty story, or a game of hooks and rings or shove halfpenny, or some question concerning football, cricket or horseracing. The problem of the Cause of Poverty was only something that concerned their own and their children's welfare. Such an uninteresting subject must be put before them so plainly that they would be *compelled* to understand it at a glance, and this seemed almost impossible.

Observing his hesitation, some of the men began to snigger.

''E seems to 'ave got 'imself into a bit of a fog,' remarked Crass to Slyme, in a loud whisper; and both laughed.

The sound roused Owen, and he continued:

'This figure represents the adult population of this country. We will now divide them into separate classes. Those who help to produce, those who do nothing, those who do harm, and those who are engaged in unnecessary work.'

'And,' sneered Crass, 'those who are engaged in unnecessary talk.'

'First we will separate those who not only do nothing, but do not even pretend to be of any use, people who would consider themselves disgraced if they by any chance did any useful work. This class includes Tramps, Beggars, the Aristocracy, Society People, Great Landowners, and those people possessed of hereditary wealth generally.'

As he spoke he drew a vertical line across one end of the oblong.

1	
Tramps, Beggars, 'Society People,' The 'Aristocracy,' Great Landowners, All those possessed of hereditary Wealth.	

'These people do absolutely nothing except devour or enjoy the things produced by the labour of others.

'Our next division represents those who do work of a kind—"mental" work if you like to call it so—work that benefits themselves and harms other people. Employers—or rather Exploiters—of Labour, Thieves, Swindlers, Pickpockets, profit-seeking Shareholders, Burglars, Bishops, Financiers, Capitalists, and those persons humourously called "Ministers" of religion. If you remember that the word "minister" means "servant", you will be able to see the joke. None of these people produce anything themselves, but by means of cunning and scheming they contrive between them to obtain possession of a very large portion of the things produced by the labour of others.

1	2	
Tramps, Beggars, 'Society People, 'The 'Aristocracy,' Great Landowners, All those possessed of hereditary Wealth.	Exploiters of Labour, Thieves, Swindlers, Pickpockets, Burglars,Bishops, Financiers, Capitalists, Shareholders, 'Ministers' of Religion.	

'Number three stands for those who work for wages or salaries, doing *unnecessary* work: that is, producing or doing things which, though useful and necessary to the Imbecile System, cannot be described as the necessaries of life or the benefits of civilisation. This is the largest section of all. It comprises Commercial Travellers, Canvassers, Insurance Agents, Commission Agents, the greater number of Shop Assistants, the majority of Clerks, Workmen employed in the construction and adornment of business premises, People occupied with what they call "Business", which means being very busy without producing anything. Then there is a vast army of people engaged in designing, composing, painting or printing advertisements, things which are for the most part of no utility whatever, the object of most advertisements being merely to persuade people to buy from one firm rather than another.'

During the delivery of this part of the lecture the audience began to manifest symptoms of impatience and dissent. Perceiving this, Owen, speaking very rapidly, continued:

1	2	3	
Tramps, Beggars, 'Society People,' The 'Aristocracy,' Great Landowners, All those possessed of hereditary Wealth.	Exploiters of Labour, Thieves, Swindlers, Pickpockets, Burglars, Bishops, Financiers, Capitalists, Shareholders, 'Ministers' of Religion.	All those engaged in unnecessary work.	

'If you go down town you will see half a dozen drapers' shops within a stone's throw of each other, all selling the same things. You can't possibly think that all those shops are really necessary? You know that one of them would serve the purpose for which they are all intended. If you will admit that five out of the six shops are really unnecessary, you must also admit that the men who built them, and the assistants engaged in them, and the men who design and write and print their advertisements, are all doing unnecessary work, wasting their time and labour, which might be employed in helping to produce those things we are short of at present. You must admit that none of these people are engaged in producing either the necessaries of life or the benefits of civilisation. They handle them, and haggle over them, and display them, and make profit out of them, but these people themselves produce nothing that is necessary to life or happiness, and the things that some of them *do* produce are only necessary to the present imbecile system.'

'What the 'ell sort of a bloody system do you think we ought to 'ave, then?' interrupted the man on the pail.

'Yes. You're very good at finding fault,' sneered Slyme, 'but why don't you tell us 'ow it's all going to be put right?'

'Well, that's not what we're talking about now, is it?' replied Owen. 'At present we're only trying to find out how it is that there is not sufficient produced for everyone to have enough of the things that are made by work. Although most of the people in number three work very hard they produce Nothing.'

'This is a lot of bloody rot!' exclaimed Crass, impatiently.

'Even if there is more shops than what's actually necessary,' cried Harlow, 'it all helps people to get a livin'! If half of 'em was shut up it would just mean that all them what works there would be out of a job. Live and let live, I say: all these things makes work.'

''Ear 'ear!' shouted the man behind the moat.

'Yes, I know it makes "work",' replied Owen, 'but we can't live on mere "work", you know. To live in comfort we need a sufficiency of the things that can be made by work. A man might work very hard and yet be wasting his time if he were not producing something necessary or useful.

'Why are there so many shops and stores and emporiums? Do you imagine they exist for the purpose of giving those who build them, or work in them, a chance to earn a living? Nothing of the sort. They are carried on, and exorbitant prices are charged for the goods, to enable the proprietors to amass fortunes, and to pay extortionate rents to the landlords. That is why the wages and salaries of nearly all those who do the work created by these businesses are cut down to the lowest possible point.

'We knows all about that,' said Crass, 'but you can't get away from it that all these things makes Work; and that's what we wants—Plenty of Work.'

Cries of ''Ear, 'ear' and expressions of dissent from the views expressed by the lecturer resounded through the room, nearly everyone speaking at the same time. After a while, when the row had in some measure subsided, Owen resumed:

'Nature has not provided ready made all the things necessary for the life and happiness of mankind. In order to obtain those things we have to Work. The only rational labour is that which is directed to the creation of those things. Any kind of work which does not help us to attain this object is a ridiculous, idiotic, criminal, imbecile waste of time.

'That is what the great army of people represented by division number three are doing at present; they are all very busy, working very hard, but to all useful intents and purposes they are doing Nothing.

'The next division stands for those who are engaged in really useful work: the production of the benefits of civilisation, the refinements and comf orts of life.'

'Hooray,' cried Philpot, winking his goggle eyes at the meeting, 'this is where *we* come in!'

1	2	3	4	
Tramps, Beggars, 'Society Thieves, People,' The 'Aris- tocracy,'Great Landowners, All those possessed of hereditary Wealth.	Exploiters of Labour, Swindlers, Pickpockets, Burglars, Bishops, Financiers, Capitalists, Shareholders, 'Ministers' of Religion.	All those engaged in unnecessary work.	All those engaged in necessary work— the production benefits of the of civilisation.	UNEMPLOYED.

'As most of the people in number four are out of work at least one quarter of their time, we must reduce the size of this division by one fourth—so. The grey represents the unemployed.'

The lecturer now drew a small square upon the wall below the other drawing. This square he filled in solid black.

1	2	3	4	
Tramps, Beggars, 'Society Thieves, People,' The 'Aris- tocracy,'Great Landowners, All those possessed of hereditary Wealth.	Exploiters of Labour, Swindlers, Pickpockets, Burglars, Bishops, Financiers, Capitalists, Shareholders, 'Ministers' of Religion.	All those engaged in unnecessary work.	All those engaged in necessary work— the production benefits of the of civilisation.	UNEMPLOYED.

This represents the total of the thing sproduced by thepeople in division 4.

1	2	3	4	
Tramps, Beggars, 'Society Thieves, People,' The 'Aris-tocracy,'Great Landowners, All those possessed of hereditary Wealth.	Exploiters of Labour, Swindlers, Pickpockets, Burglars, Bishops, Financiers, Capitalists, Shareholders, 'Ministers' of Religion.	All those engaged in unnecessary work.	All those engaged in necessary work— the production benefits of the of civilisation.	UNEMPLOYED.

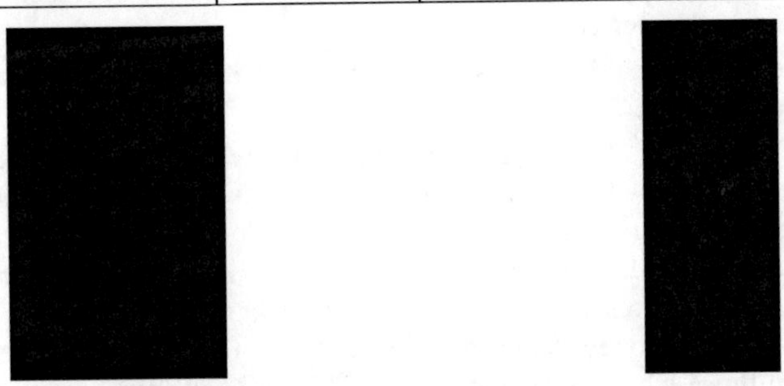

How the things produced by the people in division 4 are 'shared out' amongst the different classes of the population.

'This represents the total amount of the benefits of civilisation and necessaries of life produced by the people in number four. We now proceed to "share out" the things in the same way as they are actually divided amongst the different classes of the population under the present imbecile system.

'As the people in divisions one and two are universally considered to be the most worthy and deserving, we give them two thirds of the whole.

'The remainder we give to be 'shared out' amongst the people represented by divisions three and four.

'Now, you musn't run away with the idea that the people in three and four take their share quietly and divide the things equally between them. Some get more than their fair share, some get very little, some none at all. It is in these two divisions that "the battle of life," rages most fiercely.

'And all these people in numbers three and four are so fully occupied in this dreadful struggle to secure a little that but few of them pause to enquire why there are not more of the things they are fighting for, or why it is necessary to fight like this at all! The best of everything is reserved exclusively for the enjoyment of the people in divisions one and two, while the workers subsist on block ornaments, margarine, adulterated tea, mysterious beer, and are content, only grumbling when they are unable to obtain even such fare as this.'

Owen paused, and a gloomy silence followed, but suddenly Crass brightened up. He had detected a serious flaw in the lecturer's argument.

'You say the people in one and two gets all the best of everything, but what about the Tramps and Beggars? You've got them in division one!'

'Yes; I know. You see, that's the proper place for them. They belong to the loafer class. They are no better mentally or morally than any of the other loafers in that division, neither are they of any more use. Of course, when we consider them in relation to the amount they consume of the things produced by others they are not so harmful as the other loafers, because they consume comparatively little. But all the same they are in their right place in that division. All those people in division one don't get the same share. The section represents not individuals but the Loafer Class.'

'But I thought you said you was goin' to prove that money was the cause of poverty,' said Easton.

'So it is,' said Owen. 'Can't you see that it's money that's caused all these people to lose sight of the true purpose of labour—the production of the things we need? They are suffering from the delusion that it doesn't matter what kind of work they do, or whether they merely do nothing, so long as they get *money* for doing it. Under the present extraordinary system that's the only object they have in view—to get money. Their ideas are so topsy-turvey that they regard with contempt those who are engaged in useful work! With the exception of criminals and the poorer sort of loafers, the working classes are considered to be the lowest and least worthy in the community. Those who manage to get money for doing unproductive work are considered more worthy of respect on that account. Those who do nothing themselves but get money out of the labour of others are regarded as being more worthy still! But the ones who are esteemed most of all and honoured above all the rest are those who obtain money for doing absolutely nothing!'

'But I can't see as that proves that money is the cause of poverty,' said Easton.

'Look here,' said Owen; 'the people in division four produce everything, don't they?'

'Yes, we knows all about that,' interrupted Harlow; 'but they get's paid for it, don't they? They gets their wages.'

'Yes, and what does their wages consist of?' said Owen.

'Why, money of course,' replied Harlow, impatiently.

'And what do they do with their money when they get it? Do they eat it, or drink it, or wear it?'

At this apparently absurd question several of those who had hitherto been attentive listeners laughed derisively; it was really very difficult to listen patiently to such nonsense.

'Of course they don't,' answered Harlow, scornfully, 'they buy the things they want with it.'

'Do you think that most of them manage to save a part of their wages—put it away, in the bank.'

'Well, I can speak for meself,' replied Harlow, amid laughter; 'it takes me all my bloody time to pay my rent and other expenses and to keep my little lot in shoe leather; and it's dam little I spend on beer, p'raps a tanner or a bob a week at the most.'

'A single man can save money if he likes,' said Slyme.

'I'm not speaking of single men,' replied Owen, 'I'm referring to those who live natural lives.'

'What about all the money what's in the Post Office Savings Bank, and Building and Friendly Societies?' said Crass.

'A very large part of that belongs to people who are in business, or who have some other source of income than their own wages. There are some exceptionally fortunate workers who happen to have good situations and higher wages than the ordinary run of workmen. Then there are some who are so placed—by letting lodgings for instance—that they are able to live rent free; others whose wives go out to work; and others again who have exceptional jobs and work a lot of overtime. But these are all exceptional cases.'

'I say as no married workin' man can save any money at all,' shouted Harlow, 'not unless 'e goes without some of even the few things we *are* able to get—and makes 'is wife and kids go without as well.'

''Ear, 'ear!' said everybody except Crass and Slyme, who were both thrifty working men, each of whom had some money saved in one or other of the institutions mentioned.

'Then that means,' said Owen, 'that the wages received by the people in division four is not equivalent to the work they do.'

'Wotcher mean, quiverlent?' cried Crass. 'Why the 'ell don't yer talk plain English without draggin' in a lot of long words wot nobody can't understand?'

'I mean this,' replied Owen, speaking very slowly. ' Everything is produced by the people in number four. In return for their work they are given Money, and the things they have made become the property of the people who do nothing. Then, as the money is of no use, the workers go to shops and give it away in exchange for some of the things they themselves have made. They spend—or give back—*all* their wages; but as the money they got as wages is not equal in value to the things they produced, they find that they are only able to buy back a *very small part*. So you see that these little disks of metal, this Money, is a device for enabling those who do not work to rob the workers of the greater part of the fruits of their toil.'

The silence that ensued was broken by Crass.

'It sounds very pretty,' he sneered, 'but I can't make no 'ead or tail of it, meself.'

'Look here!' cried Owen. 'The Producing Class—these people in number four, are supposed to be paid for their work. Their wages are supposed to be equal in value to their work. But it's not so. If it were, by spending all their wages, the Producing Class would be able to buy *all* they have produced.

'But even if we include the whole of the working classes,' continued Owen, 'that is, the people in number three as well as those in number four, we find that their combined wages are insufficient to buy the things made by the producers. The total value of the wealth produced in this country during the last year was 1,800,000,000, and the total amount paid in wages during the same period was only 600,000,000. In other words, by means of the Money Trick, the workers were robbed of two-thirds of the value of their labour. All the people in numbers three and four are working and suffering and starving and fighting in order that the rich people in numbers one and two may live in luxury and do nothing. These are the wretches who cause poverty: they not only devour or waste or hoard the things made by the workers, but as soon as their own wants are supplied they compel the workers to cease working and prevent them producing the things they need. Most of these people,' cried Owen, his usually pale face flushing red and his eyes shining with sudden anger, 'most of these people do not deserve to be called human beings at all. They're devils! They know that whilst they are indulging in pleasures of every kind, all around them men and women and little children are existing in want or dying of hunger.'

The silence which followed was at length broken by Harlow.

'You say the workers is entitled to all they produce, but you forget there's the raw materials to pay for. They don't make *them*, you know.'

'Of course the workers don't *create* the raw materials,' replied Owen. 'But I am not aware that the capitalists or the landlords do so either. The raw materials exist in abundance in and on the earth, but they are of no use until labour has been applied to them."

'But then, you see, the earth belongs to the landlords!' cried Crass, unguardedly.

'I know that; and of course you think it's right that the whole country should belong to a few peope—'

'I must call the lecturer to horder,' interrupted Philpot. 'The land question is not before the meeting at present.'

'You talk about the producers being robbed of most of the value of what they produce,' said Harlow, 'but you must remember that it ain't all produced by hand labour. What about the things what's made by machinery?'

'The machines themselves were made by the workers,' returned Owen, 'but of course they do not belong to the workers, who have been robbed of them by means of the Money Trick.'

'But who invented all the machinery?' cried Crass.

'Certainly not the wealthy loafer class, or the landlords, or the employers,' replied Owen. 'Most inventors have lived and died unknown and often in actual want. The workers produce *Everything*. Look around you: Factories, Machinery, Houses, Railways, Tramways, Canals, Furniture, Clothing, Food, the very roads you walk on, are all made by the working class, whose wages only buy back a very small part of the things they produce. Therefore what remains in the possession of their masters represents the difference between the value of their work and their wages paid for doing it. This systematic robbery has been going on for generations. The value of the accumulated loot is enormous, and all of the wealth at present in the possession of the rich is the property of the Working Class, stolen from them by means of the Money Trick.'

Owen got down from his pulpit, and his listeners stared uncomfortably at each other. They were compelled to do a little thinking on their own account, and it was an unusual and painful process.

For some moments an oppressive silence prevailed. Several men had risen from their seats and were attentively studying the diagrams on the wall, and nearly all the others were trying to think of something to say in defence of those who robbed them of the fruits of their toil.

'I don't see no bloody sense in always runnin' down the rich,' said Harlow, at last. 'There's always been rich and poor in the world, and there always will be.'

'Of course,' said Slyme, 'it says in the Bible that the poor shall always be with us.'

'What the bloody 'ell kind of system do you think we ought to 'ave?' demanded Crass, 'If hevery thing's wrong, 'ow's it goin' to be haltered?'

At this everybody brightened up again and exchanged looks of satisfaction and relief. Of course! It wasn't necessary to think about these things at all! Nothing could ever be altered: it had always been more or less the same, and it always would be.

'It seems to me that you all *hope* it is impossible to alter it,' said Owen. 'Without trying to find out whether it could be done, you persuade yourselves that it is impossible, and then, instead of being sorry, you're glad!'

Some of them laughed in a silly, half ashamed way.

'How do *you* reckon it could be altered?' said Harlow.

'The way to alter it is, first, to enlighten thep eople as to the real cause of their sufferings, and theN—'

'Well,' interrupted Crass, with a self-satisfied chuckle, 'it'll take a bloody better man than you to henlighten *me*!'

'I don't want to be henlightened into Darkness!' said Slyme, piously.

'But what sort of a system do you propose, then,' repeated Harlow, 'after you've got 'em all enlightened? If you don't believe in sharing out all the money equal, how *are*you goin' to alter it?'

'I don't know 'ow 'e's goin' to alter it,' sneered Crass, looking at his watch and standing up, 'but I do know what the time is—two minits past one!'

'The next lecture,' said Philpot, addressing the meeting as they all prepared to return to work, 'the next lecture will be postponded till to-morrower at the usual time, when it will be my painful dooty to call upon Mr Owen to give 'is well known and most hobnoxious address entitled "Work, and how to avoid it." Hall them as wants to be henlightened kindly attend.'

'Or hall them as don't get the sack to-night,' remarked Easton, grimly.

CHAPTER XX

The Slaughter

The lecture announced by Philpot was not delivered. The men had had a surfeit of what they called politics; besides they had something even more disagreeable to think about—the impending slaughter.

About three o'clock in the afternoon Misery arrived and informed all the hands with the exception of Crass, Owen, Slyme and Sawkins that they would have to stand off that night. He told them that the firm had several jobs in view, work they had tendered for and hoped to get, and said they could look round after Christmas and he might, possibly, be able to start some of them again. They would be paid at the office to-morrow—Saturday—at one o'clock as usual, but if any of them wished they could have their money that night. The men thanked him, and most of them said they would come for their wages at the usual pay time and would call round, as he suggested, after the holidays to see if there was anything to do.

In all fifteen men, including Philpot, Harlow, Easton and Ned Dawson, were to 'stand off.' They took their dismissal stolidly, without any remark, some of them even with an affectation of indifference, but there were few attempts at conversation afterwards. The little work that remained to be done was done in silence, every man oppressed by the same terror—the dread of the impending privation and unhappiness which they and their families would have to suffer during the next few months.

Bundy and his mate Dawson were working in the kitchen fixing the new range in place of the old one which they had taken out. They had been engaged on this job all day, and their hands and faces and clothes were covered with soot, which they had also contrived to smear and dab all over the surfaces of the doors and other woodwork in the room, much to the indignation of Crass and Slyme, who had to wash it all off before they could put on the final coat of paint.

'You can't help makin' a little mess on a job of this kind, you know,' remarked Bundy, as he was giving the finishing touches to the work, making good the broken parts of the wall with cement, whilst his mate was clearing away the débris.

'Yes, but there's no need to claw 'old of the bloody doors every time you goes in and out,' snarled Crass; 'and you could 'ave put yer tools on the floor instead of makin' a bench of the dresser.'

'You can 'ave the bloody place all to yerself in about five minutes,' replied Bundy, as he assisted to lift a sack of cement weighing about two hundredweight on to Dawson's back. 'We're finished now.'

When they had cleared away all the dirt and fragments of bricks and mortar, while Crass and Slyme proceeded with the painting, Bundy and Dawson loaded up their hand-cart with the old range and the bags of unused cement and plaster, which they took back to the yard. Meantime, Misery was wandering about the house and grounds like an evil spirit seeking rest and finding none. He stood for some time gloomily watching the four gardeners, who were busily at work laying strips of turf, mowing the lawn, rolling the gravel paths and trimming the trees and bushes. The boy Bert, Philpot, Harlow, Easton and Sawkins were loading a hand-cart with ladders and empty paint pots to return to the yard. Just as they were setting out Misery stopped them, remarking that the cart was not half loaded. He said it would take a month to get all the stuff away if they went on like that; so by his direction they placed another long ladder on top of the pile and once more started on their way. But before they had gone two dozen yards one of the wheels of the cart collapsed and the load was scattered over the roadway. Bert was at the same side of the cart as the wheel that broke and he was thrown violently to the ground, where he lay half stunned, in the midst of the ladders and planks. When they got him out they were astonished to find that, thanks to the special Providence that watches over all small boys, he was almost unhurt—just a little dazed, that was all; and by the time Sawkins returned with another cart, he was able to help to gather up the fallen paint pots and to accompany the men with the load to the yard. At the corner of the road they paused to take a last look at the 'job.'

'There it stands!' said Harlow, tragically extending his arm towards the house. 'There it stands! A job that if they'd only have let us do it properly couldn't 'ave been done with the number of 'ands we've 'ad in less than four months! And there it is, finished, messed up, slobbered over and scamped, in nine weeks!'

'Yes, and now *we* can all go to 'ell.' said Philpot, gloomily.

At the yard they found Bundy and his mate, Ned Dawson, who helped them to hang up the ladders in their usual places. Philpot was glad to get out of assisting to do this for he had contracted a rather severe attack of rheumatism when working outside at the 'Cave.' Whilst the others were putting the ladders away he assisted Bert to carry the paint pots and buckets into the paint shop, where he filled a small medicine bottle he had brought with him for the purpose with turpentine from the tank. He wanted this stuff to rub into his shoulders and legs, and as he secreted the bottle in the inner pocket of his coat, he muttered: 'This is where we gets some of our own back.'

They took the key of the yard to the office, and as they separated to go home Bundy suggested that the best thing they could do would be to sew their bloody mouths up for a few months because there was not much probability of their getting another job until about March.

The next morning while Crass and Slyme were finishing inside Owen wrote the two gates, on the front entrance, 'The Cave,' and on the back, 'Tradesmen's Entrance,' in gilded letters. In the meantime Sawkins and Bert made several journeys to the yard with the hand-cart.

Crass, working in the kitchen with Slyme, was very silent and thoughtful. Ever since the job was started, every time Mr Sweater had visited the house to see what progress was being made Crass had been grovelling to him in the hope of receiving a tip when the work was finished. He had been very careful to act upon any suggestions that Sweater had made, and had taken a lot of trouble to get just the right tints of certain colours, making up a number of different shades and combinations, and doing parts of the skirtings or mouldings of rooms in order that Mr Sweater might see exactly what it would look like when finished. He made a great pretence of deferring to Sweater's opinion, and assured him that he did not care how much trouble he took as long as he was pleased. As the work neared completion Crass began to speculate upon the probable amount of the donation he would receive as the reward of nine weeks of cringing, fawning, abject servility. He thought it quite possible that he might get a quid! It would not be too much, considering all the trouble he had taken. At any rate he felt certain that he was sure to get ten bob: a gentleman like Mr Sweater would never have the cheek to offer less. The more he thought about it the more improbable it appeared that the amount would be less than a quid, and he made up his mind that whatever he got he would take good care that none of the other men knew anything about it. *He* was the one who had had all the worry of the job, and he was the only one entitled to anything there was to be had. Besides, by the time a quid was divided up amongst a dozen, or even two or three, it would not be worth having.

At about eleven o'clock Mr Sweater arrived and began to walk over the house, followed by Crass, who carried a pot of paint and a small brush and made believe to be 'touching up' and finishing off parts of the work. As Sweater went from one room to another Crass repeatedly placed himself in the way in the hope of being spoken to, but Sweater took no notice of him whatever. Once or twice Grass's heart began to beat quickly as he furtively watched the great man and saw him thrust his thumb and finger into his waistcoat pocket; but on each occasion Sweater withdrew his hand with nothing in it. After a while, observing that the gentleman was about to depart without having spoken, Crass determined to break the ice himself.

'It's a little better weather we're 'avin' now, sir.'

'Yes.' replied Sweater.

'I was beginnin' to be afraid as I shouldn't be hable to git heverything finished in time for you to move in before Christmas, sir,' Crass continued; 'but it's hall done now, sir.'

Sweater made no reply.

'I've kep the fires agoin' in hall the rooms, has you told me, sir.' resumed Crass, after a pause. 'I think you'll find as the place is nice and dry, sir; the honly places as is a bit damp is the kitching and scullery and the other rooms in the basement, sir, but of course that's nearly halways the case sir, when the rooms is partly hunder ground, sir. But of course it don't matter so much about the basement, sir,' he continued, 'because it's honly the servants what 'as to use it, sir, and even down there it'll be hall right hin the summer, sir.'

One would scarcely have guessed from the contemptuous way in which Crass spoke of 'servants' that his own daughter was 'in service.'

'Oh, yes; there's no doubt about that,' replied Sweater as he moved towards the front door; 'there's no doubt it will be dry enough in the summer. Good morning.'

'Good morning to *you*, sir,' said Crass, following him. 'I 'opes as you're pleased with all the work, sir; everything satisfactory, sir.'

'Oh, yes, I think it looks very nice; very nice indeed; I'm very pleased with it,' said Sweater affably. 'Good morning.'

'Good morning, sir,' replied the foreman with a sickly smile, as Sweater departed.

Crass sat down dejectedly on the bottom step of the stairs, overwhelmed by the ruin of his expectations. There was just a chance yet, as he would have to come to the house on Monday and Tuesday to fix the venetian blinds. But it was a forlorn hope as Sweater rarely visited the job early in the week, and if he had meant to give anything he would have done so that day. Still, pulling himself together, Crass determined to hope for the best and returned to the kitchen. He had not mentioned his expectations of a tip to his mates, but they eyed him keenly as he entered, fully determined to get their share.

'What did 'e give yer?' demanded Sawkins going straight to the point.

'Give me?' replied Crass. 'Nothink!'

Slyme laughed in a sneering, incredulous way, but Sawkins was inclined to be abusive. He averred that he had been watching Crass and Sweater and had seen the latter put his thumb and finger into his waistcoat pocket as he walked into the dining-room followed by Crass. It took the latter a long time to convince them of the truth of his own account, but he succeeded at last, and they all three agreed that Old Sweater was a sanguinary rotter, and lamented over the decay of the good old fashioned customs.

By half-past twelve everything was squared up, and having loaded up the cart they set out together for the yard. It was an unusually fine day for the time of year, and as they passed along the Grand Parade, which faced due south, they felt quite warm. The Parade was crowded with richly dressed people, whose countenances in many instances bore unmistakable signs of gluttony and excess. Mingling with and part of this crowd were a number of well-fed looking individuals dressed in long garments of black cloth of the finest texture and broad brimmed soft felt hats. Most of these persons had gold rings on their soft white fingers and glove-like kid or calfskin boots on their feet. They were the 'followers' and 'servants' of the lowly Carpenter of Nazareth—the Man of Sorrows, who had not where to lay His head.

None of these black garbed 'disciples' were associating with the groups of unemployed carpenters, bricklayers, plasterers and painters who stood here and there in the carriage way, dressed in mean and shabby clothing and with faces pale with privation. Many of these latter were known to Crass and his mates with the cart, and nodded to them as they passed or came over and walked a little distance by their side, enquiring whether there was any news of another job at Rushton's.

When they were about half way down the Parade, just near the Fountain, they encountered a number of men on whose arms were white bands with the word 'Collector' in black letters. They carried collecting boxes and accosted the people in the street, begging for money for the unemployed. These men were skirmishers for the main body, which could be seen some distance behind.

As the procession drew near, Sawkins steered the cart into the kerb and halted as they went past. There were about three hundred men altogether, marching four abreast. They carried three large white banners with black letters: 'Thanks to our Subscribers,' 'In aid of Genuine Unemployed,' 'The Children must be Fed.' Although there were a number of artizans in the procession, the majority of the men belonged to what is called the unskilled labourer class. The skilled artizan does not as a rule take part in such a procession except as a last resource. There was also a sprinkling of the unfortunate outcasts of society, tramps and destitute loafers.

Haggard and pale, shabbily or raggedly dressed, their boots broken and down at heel, they slouched past. Some of them stared about with a dazed or half wild expression, but most of them walked with downcast eyes or staring blankly straight in front of them. They appeared utterly broken-spirited, hopeless and ashamed.

'Anyone can see what *they* are,' sneered Crass; 'there isn't fifty genuine tradesmen in the whole crowd, and most of 'em wouldn't work if they 'ad the offer of it.'

'That's just what I was thinkin',' agreed Sawkins with a laugh.

'There will be plenty of time to say that when they have been offered work and have refused to do it,' said Owen.

'This sort of thing does the town a lot of 'arm,' remarked Slyme; 'it oughtn't to be allowed; the police ought to stop it. It's enough to drive all the gentry out of the place!'

'Bloody disgraceful, I call it,' said Crass, 'marchin along the Grand Parade on a beautiful day like this, just at the very time when most of the gentry is out enjoyin' the fresh hair.'

'I suppose you think they ought to stay at home and starve quietly,' said Owen. 'I don't see why these men should care what harm they do to the town. The town doesn't seem to care much what becomes of *them*.'

'Do you believe in this sort of thing, then?' asked Slyme.

'No; certainly not. I don't believe in begging as a favour for what they are entitled to demand as a right from the thieves who have robbed them and who are now enjoying the fruits of their labour. From the look of shame on their faces you might think that *they* were the criminals instead of being the victims.'

'Well you must admit that most of them is very inferior men,' said Crass, with a self satisfied air. 'There's very few good mechanics among them.'

'What about it if they are? What difference does that make?' replied Owen. 'They're human beings, and they have as much right to live as anyone else. What is called unskilled labour is just as necessary and useful as yours or mine. I am no more capable of doing the "unskilled" labour that most of these men do, than they would be capable of doing my work.'

'Well, if they was skilled tradesmen they might find it easier to get a job,' said Crass.

Owen laughed offensively.

'Do you mean to say you think that if all these men could be transformed into skilled carpenters, plasterers, bricklayers and painters, that it would be easier for all those other chaps whom we passed a little while ago to get work? Is it possible that you or any other sane man can believe anything so silly as that?'

Crass did not reply.

'If there is not enough work to employ all the mechanics whom we see standing idle about the streets, how would it help these labourers in this procession if they could all become skilled workmen?'

Still Crass did not answer, and neither Slyme nor Sawkins came to his assistance.

'If that could be done,' continued Owen, 'it would simply make things worse for those who are already skilled mechanics. There would be a greater number of skilled workers, keener competition for skilled workmen's jobs, a larger number of mechanics out of employment, and consequently improved opportunities for employers to reduce wages. That is probably the reason why the Liberal party, which consists for the most part of exploiters of labour, procured the great Jim Scalds to tell us that improved technical education is the remedy for unemployment and poverty.'

'I suppose you think Jim Scalds is a bloody fool, the same as everybody else what don't see things *your* way?' said Sawkins.

'I should think he was a fool if I thought he believed what he says. But I don't think he believes it. He says it because he thinks the majority of the working classes are such fools that they will believe him. If he didn't think that most of us are fools he wouldn't tell us such a yarn as that.'

'And I suppose you think as 'is opinion ain't far wrong,' snarled Crass.

'We shall be better able to judge of that after the next General Election,' replied Owen. 'If the working classes again elect a majority of Liberal or Tory landlords and employers to rule over them it will prove that Jim Scalds's estimate of their intelligence is about right.'

'Well, anyhow' persisted Slyme, 'I don't think it's a right thing that they should be allowed to go marchin' about like that, driving visitors out of the town.'

'What do you think they ought to do, then?' demanded Owen.

'Let the blighters go to the bloody workhouse!' shouted Crass.

'But before they could be received there they would have to be absolutely homeless and destitute, and then the rate-payers would have to keep them. It costs about twelve shillings a week for each inmate, so it seems to me that it would be more sensible and economical for the community to employ them on some productive work.'

They had by this time arrived at the yard. The steps and ladders were put away in their places, and the dirty paint pots and pails were placed in the paint shop on the bench and on the floor. With what had previously been brought back there were a great many of these things, all needing to be cleaned out, so Bert at any rate stood in no danger of being out of employment for some time to come.

When they were paid at the office, Owen on opening his envelope found it contained as usual a time sheet for the next week, which meant that he was not 'stood off', although he did not know what work there would be to do. Crass and Slyme were both to go to 'The Cave' to fix the Venetian blinds, and Sawkins also was to come to work as usual.

CHAPTER XXI

CHRISTMAS EVE

FOR the rest of the week Owen continued to work down at the yard with Sawkins, Crass and Slyme, painting some of the ladders, steps and other plant belonging to the firm.

Every day some of the men who had been 'stood off' called at the yard to ask if any other 'jobs' had 'come in'. From these callers they heard all the news. Old Jack Linden had not succeeded in getting anything to do at the trade since he was discharged from Rushton's, and it was reported that he was trying to earn a little money by hawking bloaters from house to house. As for Philpot, *he* said that he had been round to nearly all the firms in the town and none of them had any work to speak of.

Newman, the man who was sacked for taking too much pains with his work, had been arrested and sentenced to a month's imprisonment because he had not been able to pay his poor rates, and the Board of Guardians were allowing his wife three shillings a week to maintain herself and the three children. She had told Philpot that the landlord was threatening to turn them into the street, and would have seized their furniture and sold it if it had been worth the expense of the sale.

'I feel ashamed of meself,' Philpot added, in confidence to Owen, 'when I think of all the money I chuck away on beer. If it wasn't for that I shouldn't be in such a hole meself now, and I might be able to lend 'em a 'elpin' 'and.'

'It ain't so much that I likes the beer, you know,' he continued, 'it's the company. When you ain't got no 'ome, in a manner o' speakin', like me, the pub's about the only place where you can get a little enjoyment. But you ain't very welcome there unless you spends your money.'

'Is the three shillings all they have to live on?'

'I think she goes out charin' when she can get it,' replied Philpot. 'But I don't see as she can do a great deal o' that with three young 'uns to look after; and from what I hear of it she's only just got over a illness and ain't fit to do much.'

'My God!' said Owen.

'I'll tell you what,' said Philpot. 'I've been thinking we might get up a bit of a subscription for 'em. There's several chaps in work what knows Newman, and if they was each to give a trifle we could get enough to pay for a Christmas dinner, anyway. I've brought a sheet of foolscap with me, and I was goin' to ask you to write out the heading for me.'

As there was no pen available at the workshop Philpot waited till four o'clock and then accompanied Owen home, where the heading of the list was written. Owen put his name down for a shilling and Philpot put his for a similar amount.

Philpot stayed to tea and accepted an invitation to spend Christmas Day with them, and to come to Frankie's party on the Monday after.

The next morning Philpot brought the list to the yard and Crass and Slyme put their names down for a shilling each, and Sawkins for threepence, it being arranged that the money was to be paid on pay-day—Christmas Eve. In the meantime Philpot was to see as many as he could of those who were in work at other firms and get as many subscriptions as possible.

At paytime on Christmas Eve Philpot turned up with the list and Owen and the others paid him the amounts they had put their names down for. From other men he had succeeded in obtaining nine and sixpence, mostly in sixpences and threepences. Some of this money he had already received, but for the most part he had made appointments with the subscribers to call at their homes that evening.

It was decided that Owen should accompany him and also go with him to hand over the money to Mrs Newman.

It took them nearly three hours to get in all the money, for the places they had to go to were in different localities, and in one or two cases they had to wait because their man had not yet come home, and sometimes it was not possible to get away without wasting a little time in talk. In three instances those who had put down their names for threepence increased the amount to sixpence, and one who had promised sixpence gave a shilling. There were two items of threepence each which they did not get at all, the individuals who had put their names down having gone 'on the drunk.' Another cause of delay was that they met or called on several other men who had not yet been asked for a subscription, and there were several others, including some members of the Painters' Society, whom Owen had spoken to during the week, who had promised him to give a subscription. In the end they succeeded in increasing the total amount to nineteen and ninepence, and they then put three halfpence each to make it up to a pound.

The Newmans lived in a small house the rent of which was six shillings per week and taxes. It stood at the end of a dark and narrow passage between two shops, surrounded by the high walls of the back parts of larger buildings, chiefly business premises and offices. It was like living in a kind of well, for the air could not circulate and the rays of the sun never reached it. In the summer the atmosphere was close and foul with the various odours which came from the back yards of the adjoining buildings, and in the winter it was dark and damp and gloomy, a culture ground for bacteria and microbes.

The front door opened into the living room, or rather kitchen, which was dimly lighted by a small paraffin lamp on the table, where were also some tea cups and saucers, each of a different pattern, and the remains of a loaf of bread. The wall-paper was old and discoloured. A few almanacs and unframed prints were fixed to the walls, and on the mantelshelf were some cracked and worthless vases and ornaments. At one time they had possessed a clock and an overmantel and some framed pictures, but they had all been sold to obtain money to buy food. Furniture, pictures, bedclothes, carpet and oilcloth, piece by piece, nearly everything that had once constituted the home, had been either pawned or sold to buy food or to pay rent during the times when Newman was out of work. Now there was nothing left but these few old broken chairs and the deal table which no one would buy; and upstairs, the wretched bedsteads and mattresses whereon they slept at night, covering themselves with worn-out remnants of blankets and the clothes they wore during the day.

In answer to Philpot's knock the door was opened by a little girl about seven years old. She recognised Philpot at once, and called out his name to her mother, who came to the door closely followed by two other children, a little, fragile looking girl about three, and a boy about five years of age, who held on to her skirt and peered curiously at the visitors. Mrs Newman was about thirty, and her appearance confirmed the statement of Philpot that she had only just recovered from an illness: she was very white and thin and dejected looking. When Philpot explained the object of their visit and handed her the money, the poor woman burst into tears, and the two smaller children, thinking that this piece of paper betokened fresh calamity, began to cry also. They remembered that all their troubles had been preceded by the visits of men who brought pieces of paper, and it was rather difficult to reassure them.

That evening after Frankie was asleep, Owen and Nora went out to do their Christmas marketing. They had not much money to spend, for Owen had brought home only seventeen shillings.

There was a great deal to be done with this seventeen shillings. First of all there was the rent—seven shillings. That left ten. Then there was the week's bread bill—one and threepence. They had a pint of milk every day, chiefly for the boy's sake; that came to one and two. Then there was one and eight for a hundred-weight of coal that had been bought on credit. Fortunately there were no groceries to buy, for the things they had obtained with their Christmas club money would be more than sufficient for the ensuing week.

Frankie's stockings were all broken and beyond mending, so it was positively necessary to buy him another pair for fivepence three farthings. These stockings were not much good; a pair at double the price would have been much cheaper, for they would have lasted three or four times longer; but they were out of the question. It was just the same with the coal: if they had been able to afford it they could have bought a ton of the same class of coal for twenty six shillings, but buying it as they did, by the hundred-weight, they had to pay at the rate of thirty three shillings and fourpence a ton. It was just the same with nearly everything else. This is how the working classes are robbed. Although their incomes are the lowest, they are compelled to buy the most expensive articles: that is, the lowest priced articles. Everybody knows that good clothes, boots or furniture are really the cheapest in the end although they cost more money at first; but the working classes can seldom afford to buy good things: they have to buy cheap rubbish which is dear at any price.

Six weeks previously Owen had bought a pair of second-hand boots for three shillings and they were now literally falling to pieces. Nora's shoes were in much the same condition, but, as she said, it did not matter so much about hers because there was no need for her to go out in wet weather.

In addition to the articles already mentioned they had to spend fourpence for half a gallon of paraffin oil, and to put sixpence into the slot of the gas-stove. This reduced the money to five and sevenpence farthing and of this it was necessary to spend a shilling on potatoes and other vegetables.

They both needed some new underclothing, for what they had was so old and worn as to be almost useless; but they had now only four shillings and sevenpence farthing left, and every penny of that was needed. They wanted to buy something special for Frankie for Christmas, and it would also be necessary to get a toy for each of the children who were coming to the party on the following Monday. Fortunately there was no meat to buy, for Nora had been paying into the Christmas Club at the butcher's as well as at the grocer's.

They stopped to look at the display of toys at Sweater's Emporium. For several days past Frankie had been talking of the wonders contained in these windows, so they wished if possible to buy him something here. They recognised many of the things from the description the boy had given of them, but nearly everything was so dear that for a long time they looked in vain for something it would be possible to buy.

'That's the engine he talks so much about,' said Nora, indicating a model railway locomotive; 'that one marked five shillings.'

'It might just as well be marked five pounds as far as we're concerned,' replied Owen.

As they were speaking, one of the salesmen appeared at the back of the window and reaching forward removed the engine. It was probably the last one of the kind and had evidently just been sold. Owen and Nora experienced a certain amount of consolation in knowing that even if they had had the money they would not have been able to buy it.

After lengthy consideration they decided on a clock-work engine at a shilling; but the other toys they resolved to buy at a cheaper shop. Nora went into the Emporium to get the engine and whilst Owen was waiting for her Mr and Mrs Rushton came out. He did not appear to see Owen, who observed that the shape of one of several parcels they carried suggested that it contained the engine that had been taken from the window a little while before.

When Nora returned with her purchase they went in search of a cheaper place and after a time they found what they wanted. For sixpence they bought a cardboard box that had come all the way from Japan and contained a whole family of dolls—father, mother and four children of different sizes; and they bought a box of paints for threepence, a sixpenny tea service, a threepenny drawing slate, and a sixpenny rag doll.

On their way home they called at a greengrocer's where, a few weeks before, Owen had ordered and paid for a small Christmas tree. As they were turning the corner ot the street where they lived they met Crass, half drunk, with a fine fat goose slung over his shoulder by its neck. He greeted Owen jovially and held up the bird for their inspection.

'Not a bad tannersworth, eh?' he hiccoughed. 'This makes two we've got. I won this and a box of cigars—fifty—for a tanner; and the other one I got out of the club at our Church Mission 'All: threepence a week for twenty-eight weeks; that makes seven bob. But,' he added confidentially, 'you couldn't buy 'em for that price in a shop, you know. They costs the committee a good bit more nor that wholesale; but we've got some rich gents on our committee and they makes up the difference.' And with a nod and a cunning leer he lurched off.

Frankie was sleeping soundly when they reached home, and after they had had some supper, although it was after eleven o'clock, Owen fixed the tree in a large flower pot that had served a similar purpose before, and Nora brought out from the place where it had been stored away since last Christmas a cardboard box containing a lot of glittering tinsel ornaments—globes of silvered or gilded or painted glass, birds, butterflies and stars. Some of these things had done duty three Christmases ago, but although they were in a few instances slightly tarnished most of them were as good as new. In addition to these and the toys they had bought that evening they had a box of bon-bons and a box of small coloured wax candles, both of which had formed part of the things they got from the grocer's with the Christmas Club money; and there were also a lot of little coloured paper bags of sweets, and a number of sugar and chocolate toys and animals which had been bought two or three at a time for several weeks past and put away for this occasion. There was something suitable for each child who was coming, with the exception of Bert White. They had intended to include a sixpenny pocket knife for him in their purchases that evening, but as they had not been able to afford this Owen decided to give him an old set of steel graining combs which he knew the lad had often longed to possess. The tin case containing these tools was accordingly wrapped in some red tissue paper and hung on the tree with the other things.

They moved about as quietly as possible so as not to disturb those who were sleeping in the rooms beneath, because long before they were finished the people in the other parts of the house had all retired to rest, and silence had fallen on the deserted streets outside. As they were putting the final touches to their work the profound stillness of the night was suddenly broken by the voices of a band of carol singers.

The sound overwhelmed them with memories of other and happier times, and Nora stretched out her hands impulsively to Owen, who drew her close to his side.

They had been married just over eight years, and although during all that time they had never been really free from anxiety for the future, yet on no previous Christmas had they been quite so poor as now. During the last few years periods of unemployment had gradually become more frequent and protracted, and the attempt he had made in the early part of the year to get work elsewhere had only resulted in plunging them into even greater poverty than before. But all the same there was much to be thankful for: poor though they were, they were far better off than many thousands of others; they still had food and shelter, and they had each other and the boy.

Before they went to bed Owen carried the tree into Frankie's bedroom and placed it so that he would be able to see it in all its glittering glory as soon as he awoke on Christmas morning.

CHAPTER XXII

The 'Pandoramer'

Bert White had not only accepted the invitation to the Christmas party but had promised to bring his home-made 'Pandoramer' with him, to entertain the other guests. It was, as he explained, 'a show, like what they have at the Hippodrome'; and he supplied his own orchestra in the shape of a mouth organ.

Although the party was not to begin till six o'clock, Bert turned up at half past four, bringing the 'Pandoramer' under his arm.

At about half past five the other guests began to arrive. Elsie and Charley Linden came first, the girl in a pretty blue frock trimmed with white lace, and Charley resplendent in a new suit, which, like his sister's dress, had been made out of somebody's cast off clothes that had been given to their mother by a visiting lady. It had taken Mrs Linden many hours of hard work to contrive these garments; in fact, more time than the things were worth, for although they looked all right, especially Elsie's, the stuff was so old that it would not wear very long; but as this was the only way in which she could get clothes for the children, she spent hours and hours making things which she knew would fall to pieces almost as soon as they were made.

Then followed Nellie, Rosie and Tommy Newman, who presented a much less prosperous appearance as their mother was not so skilful in contriving new clothes out of old. Nellie was wearing a grown up woman's blouse, and by way of ulster she had on an old-fashioned jacket of thick cloth with large pearl buttons. This was also a grown up person's garment. It was shaped to fit the figure of a tall woman with wide shoulders and a small waist. Consequently it did not fit Nellie to perfection, the waist reaching below the poor child's hips.

Tommy was arrayed in the patched remains of what had once been a good suit of clothes. They had been purchased at a second-hand shop last summer, and had been his 'best' for several months, but they were now much too small for him.

Little Rosie, who was only just over three years old, was better off than either of the other two, for she had a red cloth dress that fitted her perfectly; indeed, as the district visitor who gave it to her mother had remarked, it looked as if it had been made for her.

'It's not much to look at,' observed Nellie, referring to her big jacket, 'but all the same we was very glad of it when the rain came on.'

The coat was so big that by withdrawing her arms from the sleeves and using it as a cloak or shawl she had managed to make it cover all three of them.

Tommy's boots were so broken that the wet had got in and saturated his stockings, so Nora made him take them off and wear some old ones of Frankie's whilst his own were drying at the fire.

Philpot arrived with two large paper bags full of oranges and nuts, and after tea he started a fine game, pretending to be a dreadful wild animal which he called a 'Pandroculus.' He wore a funny mask out of one of the crackers, and, crawling about on all fours, rolled his goggle eyes and growled out that he must have a little boy or girl for his supper. He looked so terrible that although they knew it was only a joke they were almost afraid of him and ran away laughing and screaming to shelter themselves behind Nora or Owen. But all the same, whenever Philpot left off playing, they entreated him to 'be it again,' and so he had to keep on being a 'Pandroculus' until exhaustion compelled him to return to his natural form.

After this they all sat round the table and had a game of cards. 'Snap' they called it, but nobody paid much attention to the rules: the principal idea seemed to be to make as much noise as possible. After a while Philpot suggested a change to 'Beggar my neighbour,' and won quite a lot of cards before they found out that he had hidden all the jacks in the pocket of his coat, and mobbed him for a cheat. He might have been seriously injured if it had not been for Bert, who created a diversion by standing on a chair and announcing that he was about to introduce to their notice 'Bert White's World Famed Pandoramer as exhibited before all the nobility and crowned heads of Europe, England, Ireland and Scotland, including North America and Wales.'

Loud cheers greeted the conclusion of Bert's speech. The box was placed on the table, which was then moved to the end of the room, and the chairs were ranged in two rows in front.

The 'Pandoramer' consisted of a stage front made of painted cardboard and fixed on the front of a wooden box about three feet long by two feet six inches high, and about one foot deep. The 'show' consisted of a lot of pictures cut out of illustrated weekly papers and pasted together, end to end, so as to form a long strip or ribbon. Bert had painted all the pictures with water colours.

Just behind the wings of the stage front, at each end of the box, was an upright roller, on which the long strip of pictures was rolled. The upper ends of the rollers came through the top of the box and had handles attached to them. When these handles were turned the pictures passed across the stage, unrolling from one roller and rolling on to the other, and were illuminated by the light of three candles placed behind.

The idea of constructing this machine had been suggested to Bert by a panorama entertainment he had been to see some time before.

'The style of the decorations,' he remarked, alluding to the painted stage-front and inspired by memories of the drawing-room of 'The Cave', 'is Moorish.'

He lit the candles at the back and, having borrowed a tea-tray from Nora, desired the audience to take their seats. When they all had done so, he requested Owen to put out the lamp and the candles on the Christmas tree, and then he made another speech, imitating the manner of the lecturer at the panorama entertainment before mentioned:

'Ladies and Gentlemen: with your kind permission I am about to hinterduce to your notice some pitchers of events in different parts of the world. As each pitcher appears on the stage I will give a short explanation of the subject; and afterwards the band will play a suitable collection of appropriated music, consisting of hymns and all the latest and most popular songs of the day, and the audience is kindly requested to join in the chorus'.

'Our first scene,' continued Bert, as he turned the handles and brought the picture into view, 'represents the docks at Southampton. The magnificent steamer which you see lying alongside the shore is the ship which is waiting to take us to foreign parts. As we have already paid our fare, we will now go on board and set sail.'

As an accompaniment to the picture Bert played the tune of 'Good-bye, Dolly, I must leave you,' and by the time the audience had finished singing the chorus he had rolled on another scene, which depicted a dreadful storm at sea, with a large ship evidently on the point of foundering. The waves were running mountains high and the inky clouds were riven by forked lightning. To increase the terrifying effect Bert rattled the tea-tray and played 'The Bay of Biscay', and the children sung the chorus whilst he rolled the next picture into view. This scene showed the streets of a large city; mounted police with drawn swords were dispersing a crowd; several men had been ridden down and were being trampled under the hoofs of the horses, and a number of others were bleeding profusely from wounds on the head and face.

'After a rather stormy passage we arrives safely at the beautiful city of Berlin, in Germany, just in time to see a procession of unemployed workmen being charged by the military police. This picture is hintitled "Tariff Reform means Work for All."'

As an appropriate musical selection Bert played the tune of a well known song, and the children sang the words:

'To be there! to be there!
Oh, I knew what it was to be there!
And when they tore me clothes,
Blacked me eyes and broke me nose,
Then I knew what it was to be there!'

During the singing Bert turned the handles backwards and again brought on the picture of the storm at sea.

'As we don't want to get knocked on the 'ed, we clears out of Berlin as soon as we can, whiles we're safe, and once more embarks on our gallint ship, and after a few more turns of the 'andle we finds ourselves back once more in

Merry Hingland, where we see the inside of a blacksmith's shop with a lot of half-starved women making iron chains. They work seventy hours a week for seven shillings. Our next scene is hintitled "The Hook and Eye Carders." 'Ere we see the inside of a room in Slumtown, with a mother and three children and the old grandmother sewin' hooks and eyes on cards to be sold in drapers' shops. It ses underneath the pitcher that 384 hooks and 384 eyes has to be joined together and sewed on cards for one penny.'

While this picture was being rolled away the band played and the children sang with great enthusiasm:

'Rule Britannia, Britannia rules the waves!
Britons, never, never, never shall be slaves!'

'Our next picture is called "An Englishman's Home." 'Ere we see the inside of another room in Slumtown, with the father and mother and four children sitting down to dinner—bread and drippin' and tea. It ses underneath the pitcher that there's thirteen millions of people in England always on the verge of starvation. These people that you see in the pitcher might be able to get a better dinner than this if it wasn't that most of the money wot the bloke earns 'as to go to pay the rent. Again we turns the 'andle and presently we comes to another very beautiful scene, "Early Morning in Trafalgar Square." 'Ere we see a lot of Englishmen who have been sleepin' out all night because they ain't got no 'omes to go to.'

As a suitable selection for this picture Bert played the tune of a Music Hall song, the words of which were familiar to all the youngsters, who sang at the top of their voices:

'I live in Trafalgar Square,
With four lions to guard me,
Pictures and statues all over the place,
Lord Nelson staring me straight in the face.
Of course it's rather draughty,
But still I'm sure you'll agree,
If it's good enough for Lord Nelson,
It's quite good enough for me.'

'Next we 'ave a view of the dining hall at the Topside Hotel in London, where we see the tables set for a millionaire's banquet. The forks and spoons is made of solid gold and the plates is made of silver. The flowers that you see on the tables and 'angin' down from the ceilin' and on the walls is worth £2000, and it cost the bloke wot give the supper over £30,000 for this one beano. A few more turns of the 'andle shows us another glorious banquet—the King of Rhineland being entertained by the people of England. Next we finds ourselves looking on at the Lord Mayor's supper at the Mansion House. All the fat men that you see sittin' at the tables is Liberal and Tory members of Parlimint. After this we 'ave a very beautiful pitcher hintitled "Four-footed Haristocrats." 'Ere you see Lady Slumrent's pet dogs sittin' up on chairs at their dinner table with white linen napkins tied round their necks, eatin' orf silver plates like human people and bein' waited on by real live waiters in hevening dress. Lady Slumrent is very fond of her pretty pets and she does not allow them to be fed on anything but the very best food; they gets chicken, rump steak, mutton chops, rice pudding, jelly and custard.'

'I wished *I* was a pet dog, don't you?' remarked Tommy Newman to Charlie Linden.

'Not arf!' replied Charley.

'Here we see another unemployed procession,' continued Bert as he rolled another picture into sight; 'two thousand able-bodied men who are not allowed to work. Next we see the hinterior of a Hindustrial 'Ome—blind children and cripples working for their living. Our next scene is called "Cheap Labour." 'Ere we see a lot of small boys about twelve and thirteen years old bein' served out with their Labour Stifficats, which gives 'em the right to go to work and earn money to help their unemployed fathers to pay the Slumrent.

'Once more we turns the 'andle and brings on one of our finest scenes. This lovely pitcher is hintitled "The Hangel of Charity," and shows us the beautiful Lady Slumrent seated at the table in a cosy corner of 'er charmin' boodore, writin' out a little cheque for the relief of the poor of Slumtown.

'Our next scene is called "The Rival Candidates; or, A Scene during the General Election." On the left you will observe, standin' up in a motor car, a swell bloke with a eye-glass stuck in one eye, and a overcoat with a big fur collar and cuffs, addressing the crowd: this is the Honourable Augustus Slumrent, the Conservative candidate. On the other side of the road we see another motor car and another swell bloke with a round pane of glass in one eye and a overcoat with a big fur collar and cuffs, standin' up in the car and addressin' the crowd: this is Mr Mandriver, the Liberal candidate. The crowds of shabby lookin' chaps standin' round the motor cars wavin' their 'ats and cheerin' is workin' men. Both the candidates is tellin' 'em the same old story, and each of 'em is askin' the workin' men to elect 'im to Parlimint, and promisin' to do something or hother to make things better for the lower horders.'

As an appropriate selection to go with this picture Bert played the tune of a popular song, the words being well known to the children, who sang enthusiastically, clapping their hands and stamping their feet on the floor in time with the music:

'We've both been there before,
Many a time, many a time!
We've both been there before
Many a time!
Where many a gallon of beer has gone,
To colour his nose and mine,
We've both been there before,
Many a time, many a time!'

At the conclusion of the singing Bert turned another picture into view.

''Ere we 'ave another election scene. At each side we see the two candidates the same as in the last pitcher. In the middle of the road we see a man lying on the ground, covered with blood, with a lot of Liberal and Tory working men kickin' 'im, jumpin' on 'im, and stampin' on 'is face with their 'obnailed boots. The bloke on the ground is a Socialist, and the reason why they're kickin' 'is face in is because 'e said that the only difference between Slumrent and Mandriver was that they was both alike.'

Whilst the audience were admiring this picture Bert played another well known tune, and the children sang the words:

'Two lovely black eyes,
Oh what a surprise!
Only for telling a man he was wrong,
Two lovely black eyes!'

Bert continued to turn the handles of the rollers and a long succession of pictures passed across the stage to the delight of the children, who cheered and sang as occasion demanded. But the most enthusiastic outburst of all greeted the appearance of the final picture, which was a portrait of the King Directly the children saw it, without waiting for the band, they gave three cheers and began to sing the chorus of the National Anthem.

A round of applause for Bert concluded the Pandoramer performance. The lamp and the candles of the Christmas tree were re-lit, for although all the toys had been taken off the tree still made a fine show with the shining glass ornaments, and then they had some more games, including blind man's buff and a tug of war in which Philpot was defeated with great slaughter. When they were tired of these, each child 'said a piece' or sang a song, learnt specially for the occasion. The only one who had not come prepared in this respect was little Rosie, and even she—so as to be the same as the others—insisted on reciting the only piece she knew. Kneeling on the hearthrug, she put her hands together, palm to palm, and shutting her eyes very tightly she repeated the verse she always said every night before going to bed:

'Gentle Jesus, meek and mild,
Look on me, a little child,
Pity my simplicity,
Suffer me to come to Thee.'

Then she stood up and kissed everyone in turn, and Philpot crossed over and began looking out of the window, and coughed and blew his nose, because a nut that he had been eating had gone down the wrong way.

Most of them were by this time quite tired out, so after some supper the party broke up. Although they were nearly all very sleepy none of them were very willing to go; but they were consoled by the thought of another entertainment to which they were going later on in the week—the Band of Hope Tea and Prize Distribution of the Shining Light Chapel.

Bert undertook to see Elsie and Charley safely home, and Philpot volunteered to accompany Nellie and Tommy Newman, and to carry Rosie, who was so tired that she fell asleep on his shoulder before they left the house.

As they were going down the stairs Frankie held a hurried consultation with his mother, with the result that he was able to shout after them an invitation to come again next Christmas.

CHAPTER XXIII

The Brigands

The town of Mugsborough was governed by a set of individuals called the Municipal Council. Most of these 'representatives of the people' were well-to-do or retired tradesmen, for in the opinion of the inhabitants of Mugsborough the fact that a man had succeeded in accumulating money in business was a clear demonstration of his fitness to be intrusted with the business of the town.

The Municipal Council did just what they pleased. No one ever interfered with them. They never consulted the ratepayers in any way. Even at election times they did not trouble to hold meetings: each one of them issued a kind of manifesto setting forth his many noble qualities and calling for votes from the people, who never failed to respond, and who elected the same old crew of highly respectable brigands time after time.

The chief of the band was Mr Adam Sweater, managing director and principal shareholder of the large drapery business from which he had amassed a considerable fortune. Then there was Mr Rushton, 'the working man's Candidate'; Mr Amos Grinder, who had practically monopolised the greengrocery trade of the town; Mr Jeremiah Didlum, house-furnisher and 'Hire System' trader, who also did a big business in second hand stuffs; and various other prosperous tradesmen chosen by the inhabitants of Mugsborough to watch over their interests. There was only one member of the Council who did not belong to the band of brigands. This was Councillor Weakling, a retired physician, whose feeble protests against measures he disapproved of always ended in collapse.

For many years the brigands had looked with envious eyes on the huge profits of the Gas Company, and, bent on capturing the spoils, they formed themselves into anassociation called 'The Mugsborough Electric Light Supply and Installation Co., Ltd.,' and vowed a solemn vow to drive the Gas 'Bandits' out of the town. With this end in view they bought a piece of town land from the municipality, that is to say, *themselves*, for half its value, and built the Electric Light Company works thereon. The Municipal Council then passed a measure that the duty on all coal brought into the borough should be raised from two to three shillings a ton, by which manœuvre they piously hoped to drive a final nail in the Gas Company Bandits' coffin.

That was two years ago, and since that time the Electric Light Works had been built and the war against the gasworks carried on vigorously. After several encounters in which they lost a few customers and a portion of the public lighting, the Gasworks Bandits retreated out of the town and entrenched themselves in a strong position beyond the borough boundary, where they erected a number of gasometers from which they were enabled to pour gas into the town at long range without having to pay the coal dues.

This masterly stratagem created something like a panic in the ranks of The Mugsborough Electric Light Supply, Ltd. At the end of two years they found themselves exhausted with the protracted campaign, their movements hampered by a lot of worn out plant and antiquated machinery, and harassed on every side by the lower charges of the Gas Company. They were reluctantly constrained to admit that the attempt to undermine the Gasworks was a melancholy failure, and that the Mugsborough Electric Light and Installation Company was a veritable white elephant. They began to ask themselves what they should do with it; and some of them even urged unconditional surrender, or an appeal to the arbitration of the bankruptcy court.

In the midst of all the confusion and demoralisation, however, there was one man who did not lose his presence of mind, who in this dark hour of disaster remained calm and immovable, and, like a vast mountain of flesh, reared his head above the storm, and perceived a way to turn this apparently hopeless defeat into a glorious victory.

That man was Adam Sweater, the Chief of the Band, and it was to Sweater's office that three harassed directors of the Mugsborough Electric Light Supply and Installation Company Ltd., Messrs Rushton, Didlum and Grinder, met their chief in order to discuss their unfortunate commercial venture.

'For my part,' Grinder was saying, 'I think the best thing as we can do is to chuck up the sponge at once. The Company is practically bankrupt now, and the longer we waits the worser it'll be.'

'That's my opinion,' said Didlum dejectedly. 'If we could supply the electric light at the same price as gas, or a little cheaper, we might have some chance; but we can't do it. The fact is that the machinery we've got is no dam good; it's too small and it's wore out, consequently the light we supply is inferior to gas and costs more.'

'Yes, I think we're fairly beaten this time,' said Rushton. 'Why, even if the Gas Company hadn't moved their works beyond the borough boundary still we shouldn't 'ave been hable to compete with 'em.'

'Of course not,' said Grinder. 'The truth of the matter is just wot Didlum says. Our machinery is too small, it's worn hout, and good for nothing but to be throwed on the scrap-heap, so there's only one thing left to do and that is, go into liquidation.'

'I don't see it,' remarked Sweater.

'Well, what *do* you propose, then?' demanded Grinder. 'Reconstruct the company? Ask the shareholders for more money? Pull down the works and build fresh and buy some new machinery and then most likely not make a do of it after all? Not for me, old chap! I've 'ad enough. You won't catch me chuckin' good money after bad like that.'

'Nor me neither,' said Rushton.

'Dead orf!' remarked Didlum, very decidedly.

Sweater laughed. 'I'm not such a fool as to suggest anything of that sort,' he said. 'You seem to forget that I am one of the largest shareholders myself. No. What I propose is that we sell out.'

'Sell out!' replied Grinder, with a contemptuous laugh in which the others joined. 'Who's going to buy the shares of a concern that's practically bankrupt and never paid a dividend?'

'I've tried to sell my little lot several times already,' said Didlum, with a sickly smile, 'but nobody won't buy 'em.'

'Who's to buy?' repeated Sweater, replying to Grinder, 'The Municipality of course! The ratepayers! Why shouldn't Mugsborough go in for Socialism as well as other towns?'

Rushton, Didlum and Grinder fairly gasped for breath: the audacity of the chiefs proposal nearly paralyzed them.

'I'm afraid we should never git away with it,' ejaculated Didlum, as soon as he could speak; 'when the people tumbled to it, there'd be no hend of a row.'

'*People! Row!*' replied Sweater, scornfully. 'The majority of the people will never know anything about it! Listen to me—'

'Are you quite sure as we can't be over-'eard?' interrupted Rushton, glancing nervously at the door and round the office.

'It's all right,' answered Sweater, who nevertheless lowered his voice almost to a whisper; and the others drew their chairs closer and bent forward to listen.

'You know we still have a little money in hand. Well, what I propose is this. At the Annual Meeting, which, as you know, comes off next week, we'll arrange for the secretary to read a highly satisfactory report, and we'll declare a dividend of 15 per cent—we can arrange it somehow between us. Of course we'll have to cook the accounts a little, but I'll see that it's done properly. The other shareholders are not going to ask any awkward questions, and we all understand each other.'

Sweater paused, and regarded the other three brigands intently. 'Do you follow me?' he asked.

'Yes, yes,' said Didlum eagerly; 'go on with it.' And Rushton and Grinder nodded assent.

'Afterwards,' resumed Sweater, 'I'll arrange for a good report of the meeting to appear in the "Weekly Ananias." I'll instruct the Editor to write it himself, and tell him just what to say. I'll also get him to write a leader saying that electricity is sure to supersede gas for lighting purposes in the very near future, referring to the huge profits made by the Gas Company, and remarking how much better it would have been if the town had bought the gasworks years ago so that those profits might have been used to reduce the rates the same as has been done in other towns. Finally the article will declare that it's a great pity that the Electric Light Supply should be in the hands of a private company, and suggest that an effort be made to acquire it for the town. In the meantime we can all go about—in a very quiet and judicious way, of course—bragging of what a good thing we've got, and saying we don't mean to sell. We shall say that we've overcome all the initial expenses and difficulties connected with the installation of the works, that we are only just beginning to reap our reward, and so on.'

'Then,' continued the Chief, 'we can arrange for it to be proposed in the Council that the Town should purchase the Electric Light Works.'

'But not by one of us four, you know,' said Grinder, with a cunning leer.

'Certainly not. Several members who are not shareholders can do most of the talking. As directors of the company we must pretend to be against selling, and stick out for our own price; and when we do finally consent we must make out that we are sacrificing our private interests for the good of the town. We'll get a committee appointed, we'll have an expert engineer down from London—I know a man that will suit our purpose admirably—we'll pay him a trifle and he'll say whatever we tell him to, and we'll rush the whole business through before you can say "Jack Robinson" and before the ratepayers have time to realise what's being done. Not that we need worry ourselves much about *them*; most of them take no interest in public affairs. But even if there is something said it won't matter much to us once we've got the money. It'll be a nine days' wonder and then we'll hear no more of it.'

As the Chief ceased speaking the other brigands also remained silent, speechless with admiration of his cleverness.

'Well, what do you think of it?' he asked.

'Think of it!' cried Grinder, enthusiastically, 'I reckon it'll be one of the smartest things we've ever done.'

'Smart ain't the word!' exclaimed Rushton.

'The great thing is,' continued Sweater, 'to get the business properly worked up in the newspapers. I'll see that "The Ananias" and "The Chloroform" are all right, and you must take care that "The Obscurer" backs me up, Grinder.'

'Trust me for that,' said Grinder grimly. The three local papers were run by limited companies, Sweater holding nearly all the shares of 'The Ananias' and 'The Weekly Chloroform,' while Grinder held the same position with regard to 'The Obscurer.'

'I wonder 'ow Dr Weakling will take it,' said Rushton.

'That's what I was thinkin' about,' remarked Didlum. 'Couldn't we arrange to 'ave somebody took bad, in a fit or something, just outside the Town 'All, and call 'im out to attend to the party and keep 'im busy till our business is done?'

'Who could we get to 'ave a fit?' said Grinder thoughtfully. 'It would 'ave to be someone as we could trust.'

''Ow about Rushton? You wouldn't mind, would yer?' suggested Didlum.

'I should strongly object!' returned Rushton haughtily, apparently regarding the suggestion as an insult.

'Well, well,' said Sweater, 'we needn't worry about Weakling; we can soon put a stopper on *him*. But now, as we're all agreed, I want to tell you a bit of good news. The Gas Company may have beaten us, but it hasn't been much of a picnic for them. We hit them pretty hard over the coal dues. I happen to know they are getting a bit sick of the fight because they don't know exactly how hard we're hit. Anyhow, to make a long story short: I've had a talk with the managing director and one or two others and they are willing for us to go in with them. So we can put the money for the Electric Light Works into the gas shares.'

This was indeed glad tidings, and after deciding the coal dues must now be abolished in order to relieve the poor, they concluded the proceedings with a whisky and soda all round, in spite of the fact that Didlum was a teetotaller.

CHAPTER XXIV

The Veteran

Old Jack Linden had tried hard to get work—work of any kind—but nobody wanted him; and to make things worse his eyesight, which had been failing for a long time, became very bad. Once he was given a job by a big provision firm to carry an advertisement board about the streets, its previous bearer, an old soldier, having been sacked the day before for getting drunk on duty. The advertisement was not an ordinary pair of sandwich boards, but a sort of box without any bottom or lid: a wooden frame, four sides covered with canvas, on which were pasted printed bills advertising margarine.

Old Linden had to get inside this thing and carry it about the streets. It swayed about a good deal as he walked along, especially when the wind caught it, but there were two handles inside to steady it by. The pay was eighteen pence a day, and he was obliged to travel a certain route, up and down the busiest streets.

At first the frame did not feel very heavy, but the weight seemed to increase as the time went on, and the straps hurt his shoulders. He felt very much ashamed, also, whenever he encountered any of his old mates, some of whom laughed at him.

What with the frame requiring so much attention to keep it steady, and his sight being so bad, the old man several times narrowly escaped being run over. Another thing that added to his embarrassment was the jeering of the other sandwich men, the loafers outside the public houses, and the boys, who shouted 'old Jack-in-the-box!' after him. Sometimes the boys threw refuse at the frame, and once a decayed orange thrown by one of them knocked his hat off.

By the time evening fell he was scarcely able to stand for weariness. His shoulders, legs and feet ached terribly, and as he was taking the thing back to the shop he was accosted by a ragged, dirty-looking, beer-sodden old man whose face was inflamed with drink and fury. This was the old soldier who had been discharged the previous day. He cursed and swore, and accused Linden of 'taking the bread out of his mouth'; and, shaking his fist fiercely at him, shouted that he had a good mind to knock his face through his head and out at the back of his neck. He might possibly have tried to put this threat into practice but for the timely appearance of a policeman, when he calmed down at once and took himself off.

Jack did not go back the next day; he felt that he would rather starve than have any more of the advertisement frame, and from this time forth he seemed to abandon all hope of earning money: wherever he went it was the same, no one wanted him. So he just wandered about the streets aimlessly, now and then meeting an old workmate who asked him to have a drink; but this was not often, for nearly all of them were out of work and penniless.

During most of this time Mary Linden, his daughter-in-law, however, had 'plenty of work,' making blouses and pinafores for Sweater and Company. At first they had employed her exclusively on the cheapest kind of blouses, those paid for at the rate of two shillings a dozen, but latterly, as she did the work very neatly, they kept her busy on the better qualities, which did not pay her so well, because, although she was paid more per dozen, there was a great deal more work in them than in the cheaper kinds. Once she had a very special one to make, for which she was paid six shillings; but it took her four and a half days, working early and late, to do it. The lady who bought this blouse was told that it came from Paris and paid three guineas for it. But of course young Mrs Linden knew nothing of that, and even if she had known, it would have made no difference.

Most of the money she earned went to pay the rent, and sometimes there were only two or three shillings left to buy food for all of them, sometimes not even so much, because although she had Plenty of Work she was not always able to do it. There were times when the strain of working the machine was unendurable; her shoulders ached, her arms became cramped, and her eyes became so painful it was impossible to go on.

When they owed four weeks' rent and the threats of the agent, who acted for Mr Sweater, their landlord, terrified them with the thought of being sold up and turned out of the house, she decided to sell the round mahogany table and other things out of the sitting-room. Nearly all the furniture that was left in the house now belonged to her, and had formed her home before her husband died at the war.

Mr Didlum, the furniture dealer, called to see the various articles, and looked at them with open contempt. Five shillings was the very most he could think of giving for the table, and even then he doubted whether he would ever get his money back. Eventually he gave her thirty shillings for the table, the overmantel, the easy-chair, three other chairs and the two best pictures, one a large steel engraving of 'The Good Samaritan,' and the other 'Christ Blessing Little Children.'

He paid the money at once. Half-an-hour afterwards the van came to take the things away, and when they were gone Mary Linden sank down on the hearthrug in the wrecked room and sobbed as if her heart would break.

This was the first of several similar transactions. Slowly, piece by piece, in order to buy food and to pay the rent, the furniture was sold. Every time Didlum came he affected to be doing them a very great favour by buying the things at all. He did not want them; business was so bad it might be years before he could sell them again; and so on. Once or twice he asked Mary if she did not want to sell the clock—the one that her late husband had made for his mother; but Mary shrank from the thought of selling this, until at last there was nothing else left that Didlum would buy, and one week, when she was too ill to do her needlework, it had to go. Didlum gave them ten shillings for it.

Mary had expected the old woman to be heartbroken at parting with this clock, but she was surprised to see her almost indifferent. The truth was that lately both the old people seemed stunned and incapable of taking an intelligent interest in what was happening around them.

From time to time nearly all their other possessions, things of inferior value that Didlum would not look at, were sold at small second-hand shops in back streets or pledged at the pawnbroker's. The feather pillows, sheets and blankets, bits of carpet or oilcloth, and as much of their clothing as was saleable or pawnable.

They felt the loss of the bedclothes more than anything else, for although all the clothes they wore during the day and all the old clothes and dresses in the house and even an old coloured table-cloth were put on the beds at night, they did not compensate for the blankets, and they were often unable to sleep on account of the intense cold.

A lady district visitor who called occasionally sometimes gave an order for a hundredweight of coal or a shilling's worth of groceries, or a ticket for a quart of soup which Elsie fetched in the evening from the Soup Kitchen. But this was not very often, because, as the lady said, there were so many cases similar to theirs that it was impossible to do more than a very little for any one of them.

Sometimes Mary became so weak and exhausted through overwork, worry and lack of proper food that she broke down altogether for the time being. Then she used to lie down on the bed in her room and cry.

On these occasions Elsie and Charley did the housework when they came home from school, made tea and toast for her, and brought it to her bedside.

The children rather enjoyed these times; the quiet and leisure were so different from other days when their mother was so busy she had no time to speak to them. They would sit on the side of the bed, the old grandmother in her chair opposite, and talk together about the future. Elsie said she was going to be a teacher and earn a lot of money to bring home to her mother to buy things with. Charley was thinking of opening a grocer's shop and having a horse and cart. When you have a grocer's shop, he said, there is always plenty to eat, for even if you have no money, you can take as much as you like out of your shop, good stuff too, tins of salmon, jam, sardines, eggs, cakes, biscuits and all those sorts of things. When delivering the groceries with the horse and cart, he went on, he would give rides to all the boys he knew; and in the summer-time, after the work was done and the shop shut up, Mother and Elsie and Granny could also come for long rides into the country.

The old grandmother, who had latterly become quite childish, would sit and listen to all this talk with a superior air. Sometimes she argued with the children about their plans, and ridiculed them. She used to say with a chuckle that she had heard people talk like that before, lots of times, but it never came to nothing in the end.

One week about the middle of February, when they were in very sore straits indeed, old Jack applied to the secretary of the Organised Benevolence Society for assistance. It was about eleven o'clock in the morning when he turned the corner of the street where the office was situated and he saw a crowd of about thirty men waiting for the doors to be opened in order to apply for soup tickets. Some of them were of the tramp or the drunken loafer class; some were old broken down workmen like himself; and others were labourers wearing corduroy or moleskin trousers with straps round their legs under their knees.

Linden waited at a distance until all these were gone before he went in. The secretary received him sympathetically and gave him a big form to fill up, but as Linden's eyes were so bad and his hand so unsteady the secretary very obligingly wrote in the answers himself, and informed him that he would enquire into the case and lay the application before the committee at the next meeting, which was to be held on the following Thursday.

Linden explained to him that they were actually starving. He had been out of work for sixteen weeks, and during all that time they had lived for the most part on the earnings of his daughter-in-law. There was no food in the house and the children were crying for something to eat. All last week they had been going to school hungry, for they had had nothing but dry bread and tea every day; but this week, as far as he could see, they would not get even that. After some further talk the secretary gave him two soup tickets and an order for a loaf of bread, and repeated his promise to enquire into the case and bring it before the committee.

As Jack was returning home he passed by the Soup Kitchen, where he saw the same lot of men who had been to the office of the Organised Benevolence Society for the soup tickets. They were waiting in a long line to be admitted; the premises being so small, the proprietor served them in batches of ten at a time.

On Wednesday the secretary called at the house, and on Friday Jack received a letter from him to the effect that the case had been duly considered by the committee who had come to the conclusion that as it was a 'chronic' case they were unable to deal with it, and advised him to apply to the Board of Guardians. This was what Linden had hitherto shrunk from doing, but the situation was desperate, and feeling utterly crushed and degraded, he swallowed all that remained of his pride and went like a beaten dog to see the relieving officer. He was taken before the Board, with the result that his case was not considered suitable for out-relief; and after some preliminaries it was finally arranged that

Linden and his wife were to go into the workhouse, and Mary was to be allowed three shillings a week to help her to support herself and the two children.

Mary accompanied the old people to the gates of their future dwelling place, and on her return home found a letter addressed to J. Linden. It was from the house agent, and contained a notice to leave the house before the end of the ensuing week. Nothing was said about the five weeks' rent that was due. Perhaps Mr Sweater thought that as he had already received nearly six hundred pounds in rent from Linden he could afford to be generous about the amount that was still owing, or he thought there was no possibility of getting the money. However that may have been, there was no reference to it in the letter; it was simply a notice to clear out, addressed to Linden, but meant for Mary.

She was faint with fatigue and hunger, for she had had nothing but a cup of tea and a slice of bread that day, her usual fare for many weeks past. The children were at school, and the house, now almost destitute of furniture and without carpets or oilcloth on the floors, was deserted and cold and silent as a tomb. On the kitchen table were a few cracked cups and saucers, a broken knife, some lead tea spoons, a part of a loaf, a small basin containing some dripping, and a brown earthenware teapot with a broken spout. Near the table were two broken kitchen chairs. The bareness of the walls was relieved only by a coloured almanac and some paper pictures which the children had tacked upon them, and there by the side of the fire-place was the empty wicker chair where the old woman used to sit. There was no fire in the grate, and the cold hearth was untidy with an accumulation of ashes, for during the trouble of these last few days Mary had not had time or heart to do any housework. The floor was unswept and littered with scraps of paper and dust. In one corner was a heap of twigs and small branches of trees that Charley had found somewhere and brought home for the fire.

The same disorder prevailed all through the house. All the doors were open, and from where she stood in the kitchen she could see the bed she shared with Elsie, with its wretched heap of coverings. The sitting room contained nothing but a collection of odds and ends of rubbish which belonged to Charley, his 'things' as he called them: bits of wood, string and rope; one wheel of a perambulator, a top, an iron hoop, and other treasures. Through the other door she could see the dilapidated bedstead that had been used by the old people, the flock protruding through the ragged covering of the mattress.

As she stood there with the letter in her hand, faint and weary in the midst of all this desolation, it seemed to her as if the whole world were falling to pieces and crumbling away all around her. She sank down on a chair by the table and her head fell limply forward on her arms.

CHAPTER XXV

The New Tenants

The week before old Linden went into the workhouse Owen earned nothing, and to make matters worse the grocer suddenly refused to let them have any more credit. Owen went to see him, and the man said he was very sorry but he could not let them have anything more without the money; he did not mind waiting a few weeks for what was already owing, but he could not let the amount get any higher; his books were full of bad debts already. In conclusion he said that he hoped Owen would not follow the example of many others and take his ready money elsewhere. People came and got credit from him when they were hard up, and afterwards spent their ready money at the Monopole Company's Stores on the other side of the street because their goods were a trifle cheaper, and it was not fair. Owen admitted that it was not fair, but reminded him that they always bought their things at his shop. The grocer, however, was inexorable; he repeated several times that his books were full of bad debts and his own creditors were pressing him. During their conversation the shopkeeper's eyes wandered continually to the big store on the other side of the street; the huge gilded letters of the name 'Monopole Stores' seemed to have an irresistible attraction for him. Once he interrupted himself in the middle of a sentence to point out to Owen a little girl who was just coming out of the stores with a small parcel in her hand.

'Her father owes me nearly thirty shillings,' he said, 'but they spend their ready money there.'

The front of the grocer's shop badly needed repainting, and the name on the fascia, 'A. Smallman,' was so faded as to be almost undecipherable. It had been Owen's intention to offer to do this work, the cost to go against his account, but the man appeared to be so harassed that he refrained from making the suggestion.

They still had credit at the baker's, but they did not take much bread: when one has had scarcely anything else but bread to eat for nearly a month it is difficult to eat at all. That same day, when he returned home after his interview with the grocer, they had a loaf of beautiful fresh bread, but none of them could eat it, although they were hungry: it seemed to stick in their throats, and they could not swallow it even with the help of a drink of tea. But they drank the tea, which was the one thing that enabled them to go on living.

The next week Owen earned eight shillings altogether; a few hours he put in assisting Crass to wash off and whiten a ceiling and paint a room, and there was one coffin plate. He wrote the latter at home, and while he was doing it he heard Frankie, who was out in the scullery with Nora, say to her:

'Mother, how many more days do you think we'll have to have only dry bread and tea?'

Owen's heart seemed to stop as he heard the child's question and listened for Nora's answer; but the question was not to be answered at all just then, for at that moment they heard someone running up the stairs, and presently the door was unceremoniously thrown open and Charley Linden rushed into the house, out of breath, hatless, and crying piteously. His clothes were old and ragged; they had been patched at the knees and elbows, but the patches were tearing away from the rotting fabric underneath. He had on a pair of black stockings full of holes through which the skin was showing. The soles of his boots were worn through at one side right to the uppers, and as he walked the sides of his bare heels came into contact with the floor. The front part of the sole of one boot was separated from the upper, and his bare toes, red with cold and covered with mud, protruded through the gap.

All that they could make out between his heartrending sobs was that his grandfather and grandmother had gone to the workhouse that afternoon, and he thought his mother was dead or dying; he could not make her open her eyes or speak to him.

When Nora hurried back with him to the house she found that Mary had recovered from her faint and was lying down on the bed. Nora lit the fire and gave the children their tea. There was still some coal and food left of what had been bought with the three shillings obtained from the Board of Guardians. Afterwards she tidied the house, and talked things over.

Mary said that she did not know exactly what she would have to do in the future. If she could get a room somewhere for two or three shillings a week her allowance from the Guardians would pay the rent, and she would be able to earn enough for herself and the children to live on.

This was the substance of the story that Nora told Owen when she returned home. He had finished writing the coffin-plate and as it was now nearly dry he put on his coat and took it down to the carpenter's shop at the yard.

On his way back he met Easton, who had been hanging about in the vain hope of seeing Hunter and finding out if there was any chance of a job. As they walked along together Easton confided to Owen that he had earned scarcely anything since he had been stood off at Rushton's, and what he had earned had gone, as usual, to pay the rent. Slyme had left them some time ago. Ruth did not seem able to get on with him; she had been in a funny sort of temper altogether; but since he had gone she had had a little work at a boarding house on The Grand Parade. But things had been going from bad to worse. They had not been able to keep up the payments for the furniture they had hired so the things had been seized and carted off. They had even stripped the oilcloth from the floor. Easton remarked he was sorry he had not tacked the bloody stuff down in such a manner that they would not have been able to lift it up without destroying it. He had been to see Didlum, who said he didn't want to be hard on them, that he would keep the things together for three months and if Easton had paid up arrears by that time he could have them back again; but there was in Easton's opinion very little chance of that.

Owen listened with contempt and anger. Here was a man who grumbled at the present state of things; yet took no trouble to think for himself and try to alter them, and who, at the first chance, would vote for the perpetuation of the system which produced his misery.

'Have you heard that old Jack Linden and his wife went to the workhouse to-day?' he said.

'No,' replied Easton, indifferently. 'It's only what I expected.'

Owen then suggested it would not be a bad plan for Easton to let his front room, now that it was empty, to Mrs Linden, who would be sure to pay her rent, which would help Easton to pay his. Easton agreed and said he would mention it to Ruth; and a few minutes later they parted.

The next morning Nora found Ruth talking to Mary Linden and they all went round to look at the room.

The appearance of the Easton's house from outside was unaltered. The white lace curtains still draped the front window, and in the centre of the bay was what appeared to be a small round table covered with a red cloth, upon which stood a geranium standing in a saucer with a frill of coloured tissue paper round the pot. These things and the curtains, which fell close together, made it impossible for anyone to see that the room was, otherwise, absolutely bare. The 'table' consisted of an empty wooden box, with the lid of the scullery copper placed upside down upon it for a top, and covered with an old piece of red cloth. The purpose of this stratagem was to prevent people thinking that they were hard up, although they knew that nearly all their neighbours were in more or less similar straits.

It was not a very large room, considering that it would have to serve all purposes for herself and the two children, but Mrs Linden knew it was not likely that she would be able to get one as good elsewhere for the same price. So she agreed to take it from the following Monday at two shillings a week.

As the distance was so short they were able to carry most of the smaller things to their new home, and in the evening, when it was dark, Owen and Easton brought the remainder on a truck they borrowed for the purpose from Hunter.

Though trade was quiet in the ordinary way, during the months of January and February Rushton and Company had several 'boxing up' jobs to do, and as Crass not only polished the coffins, but assisted to take 'the box' home, helped to 'lift in' the corpse, and acted as bearer in the funeral, he frequently made as much as 6s. 9d. on each occasion, and sometimes a little more. But one of these funeral jobs led to a desperate encounter between Crass and Sawkins. The corpse was that of a well-to-do woman who had died of cancer, and although the disease is not supposed to be infectious, Sawkins was instructed to take all the bedding away to be destroyed at the Town Refuse Destructor. There was a feather bed, a bolster and two pillows, in such good condition that Sawkins secretly determined to sell them to a second-hand dealer instead. As he was wheeling the things away on a truck he met Hunter, who told him to leave the truck at the yard for the present as he wanted him on another job. Meanwhile Crass saw the things in the yard and hearing that they were to be destroyed determined to keep them for himself; and when Sawkins came later to take the bedding to the destructor, Crass told him he need not trouble to do so, as there was nothing wrong with the things and *he* was going to have the lot. This did not suit Sawkins at all. He had been ordered to take them to the destructor, he said, and he was going to do it; and in fact he began dragging the truck out of the yard when Crass rushed after him, seized the bundle of bedding and carried it into the paint shop. Sawkins pursued him, and the place resounded with their curses, while they indulged in a frenzied tug of war over their booty, reeling and struggling all over the place. Finally Sawkins wrenched the bundle away and flung it on the truck, while Crass hurriedly put on his coat and announced his intention of going to ask Mr Rushton if he might have the things. Hearing this, Sawkins became so infuriated that he lifted the bundle off the cart, and throwing it upon the muddy ground, right into a pool of dirty water, trampled it underfoot; then, taking his clasp knife, he began savagely hacking the ticking so that the feathers all came tumbling out. In a few minutes he had damaged the things beyond all hope of repair, while Crass stood by, white and trembling, watching the proceedings but lacking the courage to interfere.

'Now go to the office and ask Rushton for 'em, if you like!' shouted Sawkins. 'You can 'ave 'em now, if you want em!'

Crass made no answer and after a moment's hesitation, went back to his work, and Sawkins piled the things on the cart once more and took them away to the destructor. He would not be able to sell them now, but at any rate he had stopped that dirty swine Crass from getting them.

When Crass went back to the paint shop he found one of the pillows, which had fallen out of the bundle during the struggle. He took it home with him that evening and slept upon it. It was a fine pillow, much fuller and softer and more cosy than the one he had been accustomed to.

A few days afterwards, when he was re-papering the room where the woman died, they gave him some other things that had belonged to her to have destroyed, and amongst them was a kind of wrap of grey knitted wool. Crass kept this for himself, thinking it was just the thing to wrap round his neck when going to work on a cold morning; and he used it for that purpose during the rest of the winter.

CHAPTER XXVI

The Brigand's Cave

All through the severe weather the wise, practical, philanthropic, fat persons whom the people of Mugsborough had elected to manage their affairs, or whom they permitted to manage them without being elected, grappled, or pretended to grapple, with the 'problem' of unemployment and poverty. They continued to hold meetings, rummage and jumble sales, entertainments and special services. They continued to distribute the rotten cast-off clothing and boots and the nourishment tickets. They were all so sorry for the poor, especially for the 'dear little children!' They did all sorts of things to help the children. In fact there was nothing that they would not do for them except levy a halfpenny rate. It would never do to do that. It might pauperise the parents and destroy parental responsibility. They evidently thought that it would be better to destroy the health or even the lives of the 'dear little children' than to pauperise the parents or undermine parental responsibility. These people seemed to think that the children were the property of their parents. They had not sense enough to see that the children are not the property of their parents at all but the property of the community. When they attain to manhood and womanhood they will be, if mentally or physically inefficient, a burden on the community; if they become criminals they will prey upon the community; and if they are healthy, educated and brought up in good surroundings, they will become useful citizens, able to render valuable service, not merely to their parents, but to the community. Therefore the children are the property of the community, and it is the business and to the interest of the community to see that their constitutions are not undermined by starvation. The secretary of the local Trades' Council, a body formed of delegates from all the different trades unions in the town, wrote a letter to the 'Obscurer' setting forth this view. He pointed out that a halfpenny rate in that town would produce a sum of £800, which would be more than sufficient to provide food for all the hungry school children. In the next issue of the paper several other letters appeared from leading citizens, including, of course, Sweater, Rushton, Didlum and Grinder, ridiculing the proposal of the Trades' Council, who were insultingly alluded to as 'pothouse politicians,' 'beer-sodden agitators,' and so forth. Their right to be regarded as representatives of the working men was denied, and Grinder, who, having made enquiries amongst the working men, was acquainted with the facts, stated that there was scarcely one of the local branches of the trades unions which had more than a dozen members; and as Grinder's statement was true, the secretary was unable to contradict it. The majority of the working men were also very indignant when they heard about the secretary's letter: they said the rates were quite high enough as it was, and they sneered at him for presuming to write to the papers at all.

'Who the bloody 'ell was e'?' they said. ''E was not a gentleman! 'E was only a workin' man the same as themselves—a common carpenter! What the 'ell did 'e know about it? Nothing. 'E was just trying to make 'isself out to be Somebody, that was all. The idea of one of the likes of them writing to the papers!'

One afternoon when Crass, Harlow, Philpot and Easton were talking together in the street, they presently caught sight of Owen across the way. They had been discussing the secretary's letter and the halfpenny rate, and as Owen was one of the members of the Trades' Council Crass suggested that they should go and tackle him about it.

'How much is your house assessed at?' asked Owen, after listening for about a quarter of an hour to Grass's objections.

'Fourteen pound,' replied Crass.

'That means that you would have to pay sevenpence per year if we had a halfpenny rate. Wouldn't it be worth sevenpence a year to you to know that there were no starving children in the town?'

'Why should I 'ave to 'elp to keep the children of a man who's too lazy to work, or spends all 'is money on drink?' shouted Crass. ''Ow are yer goin' to make out about the likes o' them?'

'If his children are starving we should feed them first and punish him afterwards.'

'The rates is quite high enough as it is,' grumbled Harlow, who had four children himself.

'That's quite true, but you must remember that the rates the working classes at present pay are spent mostly for the benefit of other people. Good roads are maintained for people who ride in motor cars and carriages; the Park and the Town Band for those who have leisure to enjoy them; the police force to protect the property of those who have something to lose; and so on. But if we pay this rate we shall get something for our money.'

'We gets the benefit of the good roads when we 'as to push a 'andcart with a load o' paint and ladders,' said Easton.

'Of course,' said Crass; 'and besides, the workin' class gets the benefit of all the other things too, because it all makes work.'

'Well, for my part,' said Philpot, 'I wouldn't mind payin' my share towards a 'apenny rate, although I ain't got no kids o' me own.'

Sir Graball D'Encloseland, the member of Parliament for the borough, was one of the bitterest opponents of the halfpenny rate, but as he thought it was probable that there would soon be another General Election and he wanted the children's fathers to vote for him again he was willing to do something for them in another way. He had a little ten year old daughter whose birthday came in that month, so the kind-hearted baronet made arrangements to give a Tea to all the school children in the town in honour of the occasion. The tea was served in the schoolrooms, and each child was presented with a gilt-edged card on which was a printed portrait of the little hostess, with 'From your loving little friend, Honoria D'Encloseland' in gold letters. During the evening the little girl, accompanied by Sir Graball and Lady D'Encloseland, motored round to all the schools where the tea was being consumed; the baronet said a few words, and Honoria made a pretty little speech, specially learnt for the occasion, at each place, and was loudly cheered and greatly admired by everyone. The enthusiasm was not confined to the boys and girls, for while the speech-making was going on inside a crowd of 'grown-up children' were gathered round outside the entrance, worshipping the motor car; and when the little party came out the crowd worshipped them also, going into ecstacies of admiration of their benevolence and their beautiful clothes.

For several weeks everybody in the town was in raptures over this tea, or rather everybody except a miserable little minority of socialists, who said it was bribery, an electioneering dodge, and did no real good, and who continued to clamour for a half-penny rate.

Another method of dealing with the Problem of Poverty was the 'Distress Committee.' This body, or corpse, for there was not much vitality in it, was supposed to exist for the purpose of providing employment for 'deserving cases.' One might be excused for thinking that any man, no matter what his past may have been, who is willing to work for his living, is a 'deserving case', but this was evidently not the opinion of the persons who devised the regulations for the working of this committee. Every applicant for work was immediately given a long job, the filling up of a 'Record Paper' three pages of which were covered with insulting, inquisitive, irrelevant questions concerning the private affairs and past life of the 'case' who wished to be permitted to work for his living, and which had to be answered to the satisfaction of Sir Graball D'Encloseland, Messrs Sweater, Rushton, Didlum, Grinder and the other members of the committee, before the case stood any chance of getting employment.

However notwithstanding the offensive nature of the questions on the application form, during the five months that this committee was in session, no fewer than 1237 broken spirited and humbled 'lion's whelps' filled up the forms and answered the questions as meekly as if they had been sheep. The funds of the committee consisted of £500 obtained from the Imperial Exchequer, and about £250 in charitable donations. This money was used to pay wages for certain work—some of which would have had to be done even if the committee had never existed—and if each of the 1237 applicants had had an equal share of the work their grand total of earnings would have come to about twelve shillings each. This was what the 'practical' persons, the 'business men,' called 'dealing with the problem of unemployment'—twelve shillings to keep a wife and family *for five months*!

It is true that some of the members of the committee would have been very glad if they could have put the means of earning a living within the reach of every man who was willing to work; but they simply did not know what to do, or how to do it. They could not be ignorant of the reality of the evil they were 'dealing with'; appalling evidences of it faced them on every side; and as after all these committee men were human beings and not devils, they would have been glad to mitigate it if they could have done so without hurting themselves.

One evening during the time that distress was most acute a meeting was held in the drawing-room at 'The Cave' by certain of the 'Shining Lights' to arrange the details of a Rummage Sale to be held in aid of the unemployed. It was an informal affair, and while they were waiting for the other luminaries, the early arrivals, Messrs Rushton, Didlum and Grinder, Mr Oyley Sweater, the Borough Surveyor, Mr Wireman, the electrical engineer who had been engaged as an 'expert' to examine and report upon the Electric Light works, and two or three other gentlemen, all members of the Brigand's Band, took advantage of the opportunity to discuss a number of things they were mutually interested in which were to be dealt with at the next meeting of the Town Council. First, there was the affair of the untenanted Kiosk on the Grand Parade. This building belonged to the Corporation, and Mr Grinder, as Managing Director of The Cosy Corner Refreshment Company, was thinking of opening a high-class refreshment lounge, provided the Corporation would make certain alterations and let the place at a reasonable rent.

Another item which was to be discussed at the Council Meeting was Mr Sweater's generous offer to the Corporation respecting the new drain connecting 'The Cave' with the town main.

The report of Mr Wireman, the electrical expert, was also to be dealt with, and after that a resolution in favour of the purchase of the Mugsborough Electric Light and Installation Company Ltd. by the town was to be proposed.

In addition to these matters several other items, including a proposal by Mr Didlum for an important reform in the matter of conducting the meetings of the Council, formed subjects for animated conversation between the brigands and their host.

The drawing-room of 'The Cave' was now elaborately furnished. A large mirror in a richly gilt frame, reached from the carved marble mantelpiece to the cornice. A magnificent clock in an alabaster case stood in the centre of the mantelpiece and was flanked by two exquisitely painted and gilded vases of Dresden ware. The windows were draped with costly hangings and the floor was covered with a luxurious carpet and expensive rugs; and sumptuously upholstered couches and easy-chairs added to the comfort of the apartment, which was warmed by the immense fire of coal and oak logs blazing and crackling in the grate.

This was Mr Grinder's first visit at the house, and he expressed his admiration of the manner in which the ceiling and the walls were decorated, remarking that he had always liked this 'ere Japanese style.

'Hardly wot you'd call Japanese, though, is it?' observed Didlum, looking round with the air of a connoisseur. 'I should be inclined to say it was rather more of the—er—Chinese or Egyptian.'

'Moorish,' explained Mr Sweater with a smile. 'I got the idear at the Paris Exhibition. It's simler to the decorations in the Alambra, the palace of the Sultan of Morocco. That clock there is in the same style.'

The case of the clock referred to, which stood on a table in a corner of the room, was of fretwork, in the form of an Indian Mosque, with a pointed dome and pinnacles. This was the case that Mary Linden had sold to Didlum, who had had it stained a dark colour, polished and further improved it by substituting a clock of more suitable design than the one it originally held. Mr Sweater noticing it in Didlum's window had purchased it seeing that the design was similar in character to the painted decorations on the ceiling and walls of his drawing-room.

'I went to the Paris Exhibition meself,' said Grinder, when everyone had admired the exquisite workmanship of the clock-case. 'I remember 'avin a look at the moon through that big telescope. I was never so surprised in me life; you can see it quite plain, and it's round, not flat like a plate, but round like a football.'

'Of course it is,' said Rushton, rather scornfully. 'But what gets over me, is this: according to science, the earth turns round on its axle at the rate of about twenty miles a minit. Well, what about when a lark goes up in the sky and stays there about a quarter of an hour? Why, if it was true that the earth was turnin' round at that rate all the time, when the bird came down it would find itself 'undreds of miles away from the place where it went up from! But that doesn't 'appen at all; the bird always comes down in the same spot.'

'Yes, and the same thing applies to balloons and flyin' machines,' said Grinder. 'If it was true that the world is spinnin' round on its axle so quick as that, if a man started out from Calais to fly to Dover, by the time he got to England he'd find 'imself in North America, or p'raps further off still.'

'Talking about science,' said Grinder, breaking the puzzled silence which followed; 'talking about science reminds me of a conversation I 'ad with Dr Weakling the other day. You know, he believes we're hall descended from monkeys.'

Everyone laughed, the thing was so absurd. The idea of placing intellectual beings on a level with animals!

'But just wait and 'ear 'ow nicely I flattened 'im out,' continued Grinder. 'After we'd been arguin' a long time about Everlution or some sich name, and a lot more tommy rot I couldn't make no 'ead or tail of—and to tell you the truth I don't believe 'e understood 'arf of it 'imself—I ses to 'im: "Well," I ses, "if it's true that we're hall descended from monkeys," I ses, "I think your family must 'ave left orf where mine begun."'

In the midst of the laughter that greeted the conclusion of Grinder's story, the other members of the committee arrived, and put an end to the interesting discussion, and the business for which the meeting had been called, the arrangements for the forthcoming Rummage Sale, was proceeded with.

CHAPTER XXVII

THE BRIGANDS AT WORK

AT the next meeting of the Town Council Mr Wireman's report concerning the Electric Light Works was duly read. The expert's opinion was so favourable—and it was endorsed by the Borough Engineer, Mr Oyley Sweater—that a resolution was unanimously carried in favour of acquiring the Works for the town, and a secret committee was appointed to arrange the preliminaries. Alderman Sweater then suggested that a suitable honorarium be voted to Mr Wireman for his services. This was greeted with a murmur of approval from most of the members, and Mr Didlum rose with the intention of proposing a resolution to that effect when he was interrupted by Alderman Grinder, who said he couldn't see no sense in giving the man a thing like that; why not give him a sum of money?

Several members said 'hear, hear,' to this, but some of the others laughed.

'I can't see nothing to laugh at,' cried Grinder, angrily. 'For my part, I wouldn't give you tuppence for all the honorariums in the country. I move that we pay him a sum of money.'

'I'll second that,' said another member of the band—one of those who had cried 'hear, hear'.

Alderman Sweater said that there seemed to be a little misunderstanding, and explained that an honorarium *was* a sum of money.

'Oh, well, in that case I'll withdraw my resolution,' said Grinder. 'I thought you wanted to give 'im a 'luminated address or something like that.'

Didlum now moved that a letter of thanks and a fee of fifty guineas be voted to Mr Wireman, and this was also unanimously agreed to. Dr Weakling said that it seemed rather a lot, but he did not go so far as to vote against it.

The next business was the proposal that the Corporation should take over the drain connecting Mr Sweater's house with the town main. Mr Sweater, being a public spirited man, proposed to present this connecting drain, which ran through a private road, to the Corporation, to be theirs and their successors' for ever, on condition that they would pay him the cost of construction—£55—and agree to keep it in proper repair. After a brief discussion it was decided to take over the drain on the terms offered, and then Councillor Didlum proposed a vote of thanks to Alderman Sweater for his generosity in the matter. This was promptly seconded by Councillor Rushton, and would have been carried *nem. con.* but for the disgraceful conduct of Dr Weakling, who had the bad taste to suggest that the amount was about double what the drain could possibly have cost to construct, that it was of no use to the Corporation at all, and that they would merely acquire the liability to keep it in repair.

However, no one took the trouble to reply to Weakling, and the Band proceeded to the consideration of the next business, which was Mr Grinder's offer on behalf of the Cosy Corner Refreshment Company to take the Kiosk on the Grand Parade. Mr Grinder submitted a plan of certain alterations that he would require the Corporation to make at the Kiosk, and, provided the Council agreed to do this work, he was will-to take a lease of the place for five years at £20 per year.

Councillor Didlum proposed that the offer of the Cosy Corner Refreshment Company Ltd. be accepted, and the required alterations proceeded with at once. The Kiosk had brought in no rent for nearly two years, but apart from that consideration, if they accepted this offer they would be able to set some of the unemployed to work. (Applause).

Councillor Rushton seconded.

Dr Weakling pointed out that, as the proposed alterations would cost about £175 according to the estimate of the borough engineer, and the rent being only £20 a year, it would mean that the council would be £75 out of pocket at the end of the five years, to say nothing of the expense of keeping the place in repair during all that time. (Disturbance). He moved as an amendment that the alterations be made, and that they then invite tenders, and let the place to the highest bidder. (Great uproar).

Councillor Rushton said he was disgusted with the attitude taken up by that man Weakling. (Applause). Perhaps it was hardly right to call him a man (hear, hear). In the matter of these alterations they had had the use of Councillor Grinder's brains; it was he who first thought of making these improvements in the Kiosk, and therefore he, or rather the company he represented, had a moral right to the tenancy. (Loud cheers).

Dr Weakling said that he thought it was understood that when a man was elected to that council it was because he was supposed to be willing to use his brains for the benefit of his constituents. (Sardonic laughter).

The Mayor asked if there was any seconder to Weakling's amendment, and as there was not, the original proposition was put and carried.

Councillor Rushton suggested that a large shelter with seating accommodation for about two hundred persons should be erected on the Grand Parade near the Kiosk. The shelter would serve as a protection against rain, or the rays of the sun in summer; it would add materially to the comfort of visitors, and would be a notable addition to the attractions of the town.

Councillor Didlum said it was a very good idear, and proposed that the surveyor be instructed to get out the plans.

Dr Weakling opposed the motion (laughter): it seemed to him that the object was to benefit, not the town, but Mr Grinder (disturbance). If this shelter were erected it would increase the value of the Kiosk as a refreshment bar by a hundred per cent. If Mr Grinder wanted a shelter for his customers he should pay for it himself (uproar). He (Dr Weakling) was sorry to have to say it, but he could not help thinking that this was a put-up job. (Loud cries of 'withdraw,' 'apologize,' 'turn 'im out,' and terrific uproar).

Weakling did not apologize or withdraw, but he said no more. Didlum's proposition was carried, and the 'Band' went on to the next item on the agenda, which was a proposal by Councillor Didlum to increase the salary of Mr Oyley Sweater, the Borough Engineer, from fifteen pounds to seventeen pounds per week.

Councillor Didlum said that when they had a good man they ought to appreciate him (applause). Compared with other officials, the Borough Engineer was not fairly paid (hear, hear). The magistrate's clerk received seventeen pounds a week, and the Town Clerk, seventeen pounds per week. He did not wish it to be understood that these gentlemen were hoverpaid—far from it (hear, hear). It was not that they got too much, but that the Engineer got too little. How could they expect a man like that to hexist on a paltry fifteen pounds a week? Why, it was nothing more or less than sweating! (hear, hear). He had much pleasure in moving that the Borough Engineer's salary be increased to seventeen pounds a week, and that his hannual 'oliday be extended from a fortnight to one calendar month with hard la—he begged pardon—with full pay. (Loud cheers.)

Councillor Rushton said that he did not propose to make a long speech—it was not necessary. He would content himself with formally seconding Councillor Didlum's excellent proposition. (Applause.)

Councillor Weakling, whose rising was greeted with derisive laughter, said he must oppose the resolution. He wished it to be understood that he was not actuated by any feeling of personal animosity towards the Borough Engineer, but at the same time he considered it his duty to say that in his opinion that official would be dear at half the price they were now paying him. (Disturbance). He did not appear to understand his business; nearly all the work that was done cost in the end about double what the Borough Engineer estimated it could be done for. (Liar). He considered him to be a grossly incompetent person (uproar), and was of opinion that if they were to advertise they could get dozens of better men who would be glad to do the work for five pounds a week. He moved that Mr Oyley Sweater be asked to resign, and that they advertise for a man at five pounds a week (great uproar).

Councillor Grinder rose to a point of order. He appealed to the Chairman to squash the amendment. (Applause).

Councillor Didlum remarked that he supposed Councillor Grinder meant 'quash': in that case he would support the suggestion.

Councillor Grinder said it was about time they put a stopper on that feller Weakling. He (Grinder) did not care whether they called it squashing or quashing; it was all the same so long as they nipped him in the bud. (Cheers). The man was a disgrace to the Council, always hinterfering and 'indering the business.

The Mayor, Alderman Sweater, said that he did not think it consistent with the dignity of that Council to waste any more time over this scurrilous amendment. (Applause) He was proud to say that it had not even been seconded, and therefore he would put Mr Didlum's resolution—a proposition which he had no hesitation in saying reflected the highest credit upon that gentleman and upon all those who supported it. (Vociferous cheers.)

All those who were in favour signified their approval in the customary manner, and as Weakling was the only one who opposed, the resolution was carried, and the meeting proceeded to the next business.

Councillor Rushton said that several influential ratepayers and employers of labour had complained to him about the 'igh wages of the Corporation workmen, some of whom were paid sevenpence-'apenny an hour. Sevenpence an hour was the maximum wage paid to skilled workmen by private employers in that town, and he failed to see why the Corporation should pay more. (Hear, hear.) It had a very bad effect on the minds of the men in the employment of private firms, tending to make them dissatisfied with their wages. The same state of affairs prevailed with regard to the unskilled labourers in the Council's employment. Private employers could get that class of labour for fourpence-'apenny or fivepence an hour, and yet the Corporation paid fivepence-'apenny and even sixpence for the same class of work. (Shame.) It wasn't fair to the ratepayers. (Hear, hear.) Considering that the men in the employment of the Corporation had almost constant work, if there was to be a difference at all, they should get not more but less than those who worked for private firms. (Cheers.) He moved that the wages of the Corporation workmen be reduced in all cases to the same level as those paid by private firms.

Councillor Grinder seconded. He said it amounted to a positive scandal. Why, in the summer time some of these men drew as much as 35s. in a single week! (Shame.) And it was quite common for unskilled labourers, fellers who did nothing but the very roughest work sich as carrying sacks of cement, digging up the roads to get at the drains, and sich like easy jobs, to walk off with 25s. a week! (Sensation.) He had often noticed some of these men swaggering about the town on Sundays, dressed like millionaires and cigared up! They seemed quite a different class of men from those who worked for private firms; and to look at the way some of their children was dressed you'd think their fathers was Cabinet Minstrels! No wonder the ratepayers complained of the high rates. Another grievance was that all the Corporation workmen were allowed two days' holiday every year in addition to the Bank Holidays, and were paid for them! (Cries of 'shame,' 'scandalous,' 'disgraceful,' etc.). No private contractor paid his men for Bank Holidays, and why should the Corporation do so? He had much pleasure in seconding Councillor Rush ton's resolution.

Councillor Weakling opposed the motion. He thought that thirty-five shillings a week was little enough for a man to keep a wife and family on (rot), even if all the men got it regularly, which they did not. Members should consider what was the average amount per week throughout the whole year, not merely the busy time; and if they did that they would find that even the skilled men did not average more than twenty-five shillings a week, and in many cases not so much. If this subject had not been introduced by Councillor Rushton, he (Dr Weakling) had intended to propose that the wages of the Corporation workmen should be increased to the standard recognised by the Trades' Unions. (Loud laughter). It had been proved that the notoriously short lives of the working people, whose average span of life was about twenty years less than that of the well-to-do classes, their increasingly inferior physique, and the high rate of mortality amongst their children, were caused by the wretched renumeration they received for hard and tiring work, the excessive number of hours they have to work when employed, the bad quality of their food, the badly constructed and insanitary homes which their poverty compels them to occupy, and the anxiety, worry, and depression of mind they suffer when out of employment. (Cries of 'rot' 'bosh', and loud laughter). Councillor Didlum said 'Rot.' It was a very good word to describe the disease that was sapping the foundations of society and destroying the health and happiness and the very lives of so many of their fellow-countrymen and women. (Renewed merriment and shouts of 'Go and buy a red tie.') He appealed to the members to reject the resolution. He was very glad to say that he believed it was true that the workmen in the employ of the Corporation were a little better off than those in the employ of private contractors, and if it were so, it was as it should be. They had need to be better off than the poverty-stricken, half-starved wretches who worked for private firms.

Councillor Didlum said that it was very hevident that Dr Weakling had obtained his seat on that Council by false pretences. If he had told the ratepayers as he was a Socialist they would never have elected him. (Hear hear). Practically every Christian minister in the country would agree with him (Didlum) when he said that the poverty of the working classes was not caused by the 'wretched renumeration they receive as wages,' but by Drink (loud applause), and he was sure enough of one thing, that the testimony of the clergy of all denominations was more to be relied upon than the opinion of a man like Dr Weakling. (Hear, hear).

Dr Weakling said that if some of the clergy referred to or some of the members of that Council had to exist and toil amid the same sordid surroundings, overcrowding and ignorance as prevailed among the working classes, they would probably seek to secure some share of pleasure and forgetfulness in drink themselves. (Great uproar and shouts of 'order', 'withdraw', 'apologise.')

Councillor Grinder said that even if it was true that the haverage lives of the working classes was twenty years shorter than those of the better classes, he could not see what it had got to do with Dr Weakling. (Hear, hear). So long as the working class was contented to die twenty years before their time he failed to see what it had got to do with other people. They was not runnin' short of workers, was they? There was still plenty of 'em left. (Laughter). So long as the workin' class was satisfied to die orf, let 'em die orf! It was a free country. (Applause). The workin' class 'adn't arst Dr Weakling to stick up for them, had they? If they wasn't satisfied they would stick up for theirselves! The working men didn't want the likes of Dr Weakling to stick up for them, and they would let 'im know it when the next election came round. If he (Grinder) was a worldly man he would not mind betting that the workin' men of Dr Weakling's ward would give him 'the dirty kick out' next November. (Applause).

Councillor Weakling, who knew that this was probably true, made no further protest. Rushton's proposition was carried, and then the clerk announced that the next item was the resolution Mr Didlum had given notice of at the last meeting, and the Mayor accordingly called upon that gentleman.

Councillor Didlum, who was received with loud cheers, said that unfortunately a certain member of that Council seemed to think he had a right to oppose nearly everything that was brought forward.

The majority of the members of the band glared malignantly at Weakling.

He hoped that for once the hindividual he referred to would have the decency to restrain hisself, because the resolution he (Didlum) was about to have the honour of proposing was one that he believed as no right-minded man, no matter what his politics or religious opinions, could possibly object to; and he trusted that for the credit of the Council it would be entered on the records as an unopposed motion. The resolution was as follows: 'That from this date all the meetings of this Council shall be opened with prayer and closed with the singing of the Doxology' (Loud applause).

Councillor Rushton seconded the resolution, which was also supported by Mr Grinder, who said that at a time like the present, when there was sich a lot of infiddles about who said that we all came from monkeys, the council would be showing a good example to the working classes by adopting the resolution.

Councillor Weakling said nothing, so the new rule was carried *nem. con.* and as there was no more business to be done it was put into operation for the first time there and then, Mr Sweater conducting the singing with a roll of paper—the plan of the drain of 'The Cave'—and each member singing a different tune.

Weakling withdrew during the singing, and afterwards, before the Band dispersed, it was agreed that a certain number of them were to meet the following evening to arrange the details of the proposed raid on the finances of the town in connection with the sale of the Electric Light Works.

CHAPTER XXVIII

The Beano Meeting

Towards the end of March the outlook began to improve. By the middle of April Rushton and Company were working eleven and a half hours a day. In May, as the jobs increased and the days grew longer, they were allowed to put in overtime; and as the summer months came round, once more the crowd of ragged trousered philanthropists began to toil and sweat at their noble and unselfish task of making money for Mr Rushton. Papering, painting, whitewashing, distempering, digging up drains, repairing roofs, their zeal and enthusiasm was unbounded. Their operations extended all over the town. At all hours of the day they were to be seen going to or returning from jobs, carrying planks and ladders, paint and whitewash, chimney pots and drainpipes, a crowd of tattered Imperialists, in broken boots, paint-splashed caps, their clothing saturated with sweat and plastered with mortar. The daily spectacle of the workmen, tramping wearily home along the pavement of the Grand Parade, caused some annoyance to the better classes, and a letter appeared in 'The Obscurer' suggesting that it would be better if they walked on the road. When they heard of this letter most of the men adopted the suggestion and left the pavement for their betters.

On the jobs themselves, meanwhile, the same old conditions prevailed, the same frenzied hurry, the same scamping the work, slobbering it over, cheating the customers; the same curses behind the foreman's back, the same grovelling in his presence, the same strident bellowing from Misery: 'Get it *Done*! For Gord's sake get it *Done*! 'Aven't you finished yet? We're losing money over this! If you chaps can't tear into it we'll 'ave a *Alteration*!' and the result was that the philanthropists often tore into it to such an extent that they worked themselves out of a job, for business fluctuated, and occasionally everybody was 'stood off' for a few days. Still, on the whole, there was 'plenty of work'. Nearly all Rushton's old hands were back again, and several new ones, including the Semi-Drunk, several cheap 'light-weight' men, and a few improvers, also cheap, because they were paid at a reduced rate.

It was about the beginning of June that Crass, after due consultation with several of the others, including Philpot, Harlow, Bundy, Slyme, Easton and the Semi-Drunk, decided to call a meeting of the hands for the purpose of considering the advisability of holding the usual beano later on in the summer.

The meeting was held in the carpenters' shop down at the yard one evening at six o'clock, which allowed time for those interested to attend after leaving work.

The hands sat on the benches or carpenters' stools, or reclined upon heaps of shavings. On a pair of trestles in the centre of the work-shop stood a large oak coffin which Crass had just finished polishing.

When all those who were expected to turn up had arrived, Payne, the foreman carpenter, was voted to the chair, and then a solemn silence ensued, which was broken at last by the chairman, who, in a lengthy speech, explained the object of the meeting. He took the trouble to explain this several times, going over the same ground and repeating the same words over and over again, whilst the audience waited in a deathlike and miserable silence for him to stop. Payne, however, did not appear to have any intention of stopping, for, like a man in a trance, he continued to repeat what he had said before, evidently under the impression, that he had to make a separate explanation to each individual member of the audience. At last the crowd could stand it no longer, and began to shout 'hear, hear,' and to bang bits of wood and hammers on the floor and the benches, and then, after a final repetition of the statement, that the object of the meeting was to consider the advisability of holding an outing or beanfeast, the chairman collapsed on to a carpenter's stool and wiped the sweat from his forehead.

Crass then reminded the meeting that the last year's beano had been an unqualified success, and for his part he would be very sorry if they did not have one this year. Last year they had four brakes, and they went to Tubberton Village. It was true that there was nothing much to see at Tubberton, but there was one thing they could rely on getting there that they could not be sure of getting for the same money anywhere else, and that was a good feed. (Applause). Just for the sake of getting on with the business, he would propose that they decide to go to Tubberton, and that a committee be appointed to make arrangements about the dinner with the landlord of the 'Queen Elizabeth's Head' at that place.

Philpot seconded the motion, and Payne was about to call for a show of hands, when Harlow rose to a point of order. It appeared to him that they were getting on a bit too fast. The proper way to this business was first to take the feeling of the meeting as to whether they wished to have a beano at all, and then, if the meeting was in favour of it, they could decide where they were to go, and whether they would have a whole day or only half a day.

The Semi-Drunk said that he didn't care a 'something' where they went; he was willing to abide by the majority. (Applause.) It was a matter of indifference to him whether they had a day, or half a day, or two days; he was agreeable to anything.

Easton suggested that a special saloon carriage might be engaged, and they could go and visit Madame Tussaud's Waxworks. He had never been to that place and had often wished to see it. But Philpot objected that if they went there, Madame Tussaud might be unwilling to let them out again.

Bundy endorsed the remarks that had fallen from Crass with reference to Tubberton. He did not care where they went, they would never get such a good spread for the money as they did last year at the 'Queen Elizabeth.' (Cheers.)

The chairman said that he remembered the last beano very well. They had half a day—left off work on Saturday at twelve instead of one, so there was only one hour's wages lost; went home, had a wash and changed their clothes, and got up to the 'Cricketers' where the brakes was waiting at one. Then they had two hours' drive to Tubberton, stopping on the way for drinks at the 'Blue Lion,' the 'Warrior's Head,' the 'Bird in Hand,' the 'Dewdrop Inn' and 'The World Turned Upside Down.' (Applause). They arrived at the 'Queen Elizabeth' at three thirty, and the dinner was ready; and it was one of the finest blow-outs he had ever had. (Hear, hear). There was soup, vegetables, roast beef, roast mutton, lamb and mint sauce, plum duff, yorkshire, and a lot more. The landlord of the 'Queen Elizabeth' kept as good a drop of beer as anyone could wish to drink, and as for the teetotallers, they could have tea, coffee or ginger beer.

Having thus made another start Payne found it very difficult to leave off, and was proceeding to relate further details of the last beano when Harlow again rose up from his heap of shavings and said he wished to call the chairman to order. (Hear, hear). What the hell was the use of all this discussion before they had even decided to have a beano at all? Was the meeting in favour of a beano or not? That was the question.

A prolonged and awkward silence followed. Everybody was very uncomfortable, looking stolidly on the ground or staring straight in front of them.

At last Easton broke the silence by suggesting that it would not be a bad plan if someone was to make a motion that a beano be held. This was greeted with a general murmur of 'hear, hear,' followed by another awkward pause, and then the chairman asked Easton if he would move a resolution to that effect. After some hesitation Easton agreed, and formally moved: 'That this meeting is in favour of a Beano.'

The Semi-Drunk said that, in order to get on with the business he would second the resolution. But meantime several arguments had broken out between the advocates of different places, and several men began to relate anecdotes of previous beanos. Nearly everyone was speaking at once, and it was some time before the chairman was able to put the resolution. Finding it impossible to make his voice heard above the uproar, he began to hammer on the bench with a wooden mallet and to shout requests for order; but this only served to increase the din.

Whilst the chairman was trying to get the attention of the meeting in order to put the question, Bundy had become involved in an argument with several of the new hands who claimed to know of an even better place than the 'Queen Elizabeth'—a pub called 'The New Found Out,' at Mirkfield, a few miles further on than Tubberton; and another individual joined in the dispute, alleging that a house called 'The Three Loggerheads,' at Slushton-cum-Drydicth, was the finest place for a beano within a hundred miles of Mugsborough. He went there last year with Pushem and Driver's crowd, and they had roast beef, goose, jam tarts, mince pies, sardines, blancmange, calves' feet jelly, and one pint for each man was included in the cost of the dinner. In the middle of the discussion, ever, they noticed that most of the others were holding up their hands, so to show there was no ill feeling, they held up theirs also, and then the chairman declared the motion was carried unanimously.

Bundy said he would like to ask the chairman to read out the resolution which had just been passed, as he had not caught the words.

The chairman replied that there was no written resolution. The motion was just to express the feeling of this meeting as to whether there was to be an outing or not.

Bundy said he was only asking a civil question, a point of information: all he wanted to know was, what was the terms of the resolution? Was they in favour of the beano or not?

The chairman responded that the meeting was unanimously in favour. (Applause.)

Harlow said that the next thing to be done was to decide upon the date. Crass suggested the last Saturday in August. That would give them plenty of time to pay in.

Sawkins asked whether it was proposed to have a day or only half a day. He himself was in favour of the whole day. It would only mean losing a morning's work. It was hardly worth going at all if they only had half the day.

The Semi-Drunk remarked that he had just thought of a very good place to go if they decided to have a change. Three years ago he was working for Dauber and Botchit and they went to 'The First In and the Last Out' at Bashford. It was a very small place, but there was a field where you could have a game of cricket or football, and the dinner was AI at Lloyd's. There was also a skittle alley attached to the pub and no charge was made for the use of it. There was a bit of a river there, and one of the chaps got so drunk that he went orf his onion and jumped into the water, and when they got him out the village policeman locked him up, and the next day he was took before the beak and fined two pounds or a month's hard labour for trying to commit suicide.

Easton pointed out that there was another way to look at it. Supposing they decided to have the beano he supposed it would come to about six shillings a head. If they had it at the end of August and started paying in now, say a tanner a week, they would have plenty of time to make up the amount; but supposing the work fell off and some of them got the push?

Crass said that in that case a man could either have his money back or he could leave it and continue his payments even if he were working for some other firm; the fact that he was off from Rushton's would not prevent him from going to the beano.

Harlow proposed that they decide to go to the 'Queen Elizabeth' the same as last year, and that they have half a day.

Philpot said that in order to get on with the business he would second the resolution.

Bundy suggested as an amendment that it should be a whole day, starting from the 'Cricketers' at nine in the morning, and Sawkins said that in order to get on with the business he would second the amendment.

One of the new hands said he wished to move another amendment. He proposed to strike out the 'Queen Elizabeth' and substitute the 'Three Loggerheads.'

The chairman after a pause enquired if there were any seconder to this, and the Semi-Drunk said that although he did not care much where they went, still, to get on with the business he would second the amendment, although for his own part he would prefer to go to the 'First In and Last Out' at Bashford.

The new hand offered to withdraw his suggestion re the 'Three Loggerheads' in favour of the Semi-Drunk's proposition, but the latter said it didn't matter, it could go as it was.

As it was getting rather late several men went home, and cries of 'Put the question' began to be heard on all sides. The chairman accordingly was proceeding to put Harlow's proposition when the new hand interrupted him by pointing out that it was his duty as chairman to put the amendments first. This produced another long discussion, in the course of which a very tall thin man with a harsh metallic voice gave a long rambling lecture about the rules of order and the conduct of public meetings. He spoke very slowly and deliberately, using very long words and dealing with the subject in an exhaustive manner. A resolution was a resolution, and an amendment was an amendment; then there was what was called an amendment to an amendment; and so on.

This man kept on talking for about ten minutes, and might have continued for ten hours if he had not been rudely interrupted by Harlow, who said he wanted his tea, and he would also like to get a few hours' sleep before going to work in the morning. He was getting about sick of all this talk. (Hear, hear.) In order to get on with the business he would withdraw his resolution if the others would withdraw their amendments. If they would agree to do this, he would then propose another resolution which, if carried, would meet all the requirements of the case. (Applause.)

The man with the metallic voice observed that it was not necessary to ask the consent of those who had moved amendments; if the original proposition was withdrawn all the amendments fell to the ground.

'Last year,' observed Crass, 'when we was goin' out of the room after we'd finished our dinner at the "Queen Elizabeth" the landlord pointed to the table and said: "There's enough left over for you all to 'ave another lot."' (Cheers.)

Harlow said that he would move that it be held on the last Saturday in August; that it be for half a day, starting at one o'clock so that they could work up till twelve, which would mean that they would only lose one hour's pay; that they go to the same place as last year—the "Queen Elizabeth" (Hear, hear); and that the same committee that acted last year, Crass and Bundy, be appointed to make all the arrangements and collect the subscriptions. (Applause.)

The tall man observed that this was what was called a compound resolution, and was proceeding to explain further, when the chairman exclaimed that it did not matter a dam what it was called—would anyone second it? The Semi-Drunk said that he would, in order to get on with the business.

Bundy moved, and Sawkins seconded, as an amendment, that it should be a whole day.

The new hand moved to substitute the 'Loggerheads' for the 'Queen Elizabeth.'

Easton proposed to substitute Madame Tussaud's Waxworks for the 'Queen Elizabeth.' He said he moved this just to test the feeling of the meeting.

Harlow pointed out that it would cost at least a pound a head to defray the expenses of such a trip. It would not be possible for any of them to save the necessary amount during the next three months. (Hear, hear.)

Philpot repeated his warning as to the danger of visiting Madame Tussaud's. He was certain that if she once got them she would never let them go. He had no desire to pass the rest of his life as an image in a museum.

Easton said that he would withdraw his amendment.

Acting under the directions of the man with the metallic voice, the chairman now proceeded to put the amendment to the vote. Bundy's proposal that it should be a whole day was defeated, only himself, Sawkins, and the Semi-Drunk being in favour. The motion to substitute the 'Loggerheads' for the 'Queen Elizabeth' was also defeated, and the compound resolution proposed by Harlow was then carried *nem. con.*

Philpot now proposed a hearty vote of thanks to the chairman for the very able manner in which he had conducted the meeting. When this had been unanimously agreed to the Semi-Drunk moved a similar tribute of gratitude to Crass for his services to the cause, and the meeting dispersed.

The Semi-Drunk's engagement at Rushton's was not of very long duration, the job of cleaning and decorating 'Macaroni's Royal Café' on the Grand Parade being the cause of his downfall. The place was disgustingly dirty, but in no part was the filth of such an unspeakable description as in the kitchen and scullery, which the Semi-Drunk and another man called Bill Bates were ordered to clean out and prepare for painting and distempering.

At the start the job made them feel so ill that they went out and had a pint each before continuing operations.

After a little more work they felt that it was imperatively necessary to have another drink, and this time they had two pints each. Bill paid for the first two and then the Semi-Drunk refused to return to work unless Bill would consent to have another pint with him before going back. When they had drunk the two pints they decided, in order to save themselves the trouble and risk of leaving the job, to take a couple of quarts back with them in two bottles.

On their returning they found the coddy in the kitchen, looking for them. He began to talk and grumble, but the Semi-Drunk told him he could either have a drink out of one of the bottles or a punch in the bloody nose, whichever he liked! Or if he did not fancy either he could go to hell!

As the coddy was a sensible man he took the beer and advised them to pull themselves together and try to get some work done before Misery came, which they promised to do.

Shortly afterwards Misery came and began shouting at them because he said it looked as if they had been asleep all the morning! Here it was nearly ten o'clock, and so far as he could see they had done Nothing!

When he was gone they drank the rest of the beer and then felt more inclined to laugh than work. What did they care for Hunter or Rushton either? To hell with both of 'em! They left off scraping and scrubbing, and began throwing buckets of water over the dresser and the walls, laughing uproariously all the time.

'We'll show the blighters how to wash down paintwork!' shouted the Semi-Drunk, as he stood in the middle of the room and hurled a pailful of water over the door of the cupboard. 'Bring us another bucket of water, Bill.'

Bill was out in the scullery filling his pail under the tap, and laughing so much that he could scarcely stand. As soon as it was full he passed it to the Semi-Drunk, who threw it bodily, pail and all, on to the bench in front of the window, smashing one of the panes of glass. The water poured off the table and all over the floor.

Bill brought the next pailful in and threw it at the kitchen door, splitting one of the panels from top to bottom; and then they threw about half a dozen more pailfuls over the dresser.

'We'll show the blighters 'ow to clean paintwork,' they shouted, as they hurled the buckets at the walls and doors.

By this time the floor was deluged with water, which mingled with the filth and formed a sea of mud.

They left the two taps running in the scullery, and as the waste pipe of the sink was choked up with dirt the sink filled up and overflowed like a miniature Niagara.

The water ran out under the doors into the back yard and along the passage out to the front door. But Bill Bates and the Semi-Drunk remained in the kitchen, smashing the pails at the walls and the doors of the dresser, and cursing and laughing hysterically.

They had just filled the two buckets and were bringing them into the kitchen when they heard Hunter's voice in the passage bellowing enquiries as to where all that water was coming from. Then they heard him advancing towards them and stood waiting, and directly he put his head in at the door they let fly at him with both pails at once. Unfortunately they were too drunk and excited to aim straight. One pail struck the middle of the door and the other the wall at the side of it.

Misery hastily shut the door and ran upstairs, and presently the coddy came down and called out to them from the passage.

They went out to see what he wanted, and he told them that Misery had gone to the office to get their wages ready; they were to make out their time sheets and go for their money at once. Misery had said that if they were not there in ten minutes he would have the pair of them locked up.

The Semi-Drunk said that nothing would suit them better than to have all their pieces at once, they had spent all their money and wanted another drink. Bill Bates concurred, so they borrowed a piece of black lead pencil from the coddy and made out their time sheets, took off their aprons, put them into their tool bags, and went to the office for their money, which Misery passed out to them through the trap door.

The news of this exploit spread all over the town during that day and evening, and although it was in July, the next morning at six o'clock there were half a dozen men waiting at the yard to ask Misery if there was 'any chance of a job.'

Bill Bates and the Semi-Drunk had had their spree and had got the sack for it, and most of their mates said it served them right for there was very little real sympathy between the men, and there were few who would not seize the opportunity of 'telling each other off' to the coddy or foreman with a view to currying favour in high places.

But to hear them talking in the pub of a Saturday afternoon just after pay time one would think them the best friends and mates and the most independent spirits in the world, fellows whom it would be very dangerous to trifle with and who would stick up for each other through thick and thin. All sorts of stories were related of the wonderful things they had done and said; of jobs they had 'chucked up,' and masters they had 'told off'; of pails of whitewash thrown over offending employers. But strange to say, for some reason or other it seldom happened that a third party ever witnessed any of these incidents. It seemed as if a chivalrous desire to spare the feelings of their victims had always prevented them from doing or saying anything to them in the presence of witnesses.

When he had drunk a few pints, Crass was a very good hand at these stories. He told one in the bar of the 'Cricketers' on the Saturday afternoon of the same week that Bill Bates and the Semi-Drunk got the sack.

'Last Thursday night about five o'clock,' said Crass, ''Unter comes inter the paint shop an' ses to me: "I wants a pail o' wash made up to-night, Crass," e' ses, "ready for fust thing in the mornin'," 'e ses. "Oh," I ses, lookin' 'im straight in the bloody eye. "Oh, yer do, do yer?"—just like that. "Yes," 'e says. "Well, you can bloody well make it yerself", I ses, "'cos I ain't agoin' to," I ses, just like that. "Wot the 'ell do yer mean," I ses, "by comin' 'ere at this time o' the night with a order like that?" I ses. You'd a larfed,' continued Crass, as he wiped his mouth with the back of his hand after taking another drink out of his glass, and looking round to note the effect of the story; 'you'd a larfed if you'd bin there. 'E was fairly flabbergasted! An' then 'e started apoligising and said as 'e 'ad'nt meant no offence; but I told 'im bloody straight not to come no more of it. "You bring the horder at a reasonable time," I ses—just like that—"and I'll attend to it," I ses, "but not otherwise," I ses.'

As he concluded this story Crass drained his glass and gazed round upon his admiring audience. Yes, undoubtedly that was the proper way to deal with such bounders as Nimrod: take up a strong attitude, an' let 'em see as you'll stand no nonsense!

'Yer don't blame me, do yer?' continued Crass. 'Why should we put up with a lot of old buck from the likes of 'im! We're not a lot of bloody Chinamen, are we?'

Far from blaming him, they all assured him that they would have acted in precisely the same way under similar circumstances.

'For my part, I'm a bloke like this,' said a tall man with a very loud voice, who as a matter of fact nearly fell down dead every time Rushton or Misery looked at him; 'I'm a bloke like this 'ere: I never stands no cheek from no gaffers! If a guv'nor ses two bloody words to me, I downs me tools an' I ses to 'im: "Wot! don't I suit yer, guv'nor? Ain't I done enuff for yer? Werry good! Gimmie me bleedin' 'a'pence."'

'Quite right too,' said everybody. That was the way to serve 'em. If only everyone would do the same as the tall man, who had just paid for another round of drinks, things would be a lot more comfortable than they was.

'Last summer I was workin' for ole Buncer,' said a little man with a cutaway coat several sizes too large for him. 'I was workin' for ole Buncer, over at Windley, an' you all knows as 'e don't arf lower it. Well, one day, wen I knowed 'e was on the drunk, I 'ad to first coat a room out, white; so thinks I to meself: "If I buck up I shall be able to get this lot done by about four o'clock, an' then I can clear orf 'ome." 'Cos I reckoned as 'e'd be about flattened out by that time, an' you know 'e ain't got no foreman. So I tears into it an' gets this 'ere room done about a quarter past four an' I'd jist got me things put away for the night wen 'oo should come fallin' up the bloody stairs but ole Buncer, drunk as a howl! An' no sooner 'e gits inter the room than 'e starts yappin' an' rampin'! "Is this 'ere hall you've done?" 'e shouts out. "Wothcher bin up to hall day?" 'e ses; an' 'e keeps on shoutin' an' swearin' till at last I couldn't stand it no longer, 'cos you can guess I wasn't in a very good temper with 'im comin' along jist then wen I thought I was goin' to get orf a bit early. So wen 'e kept on shoutin' I never made no answer to 'im but I ups with me fist an' I gives 'im a slosh in the dial an' stopped 'is clock! Then I chucked the pot o' wite paint hover 'im an' kicked 'im down the bloody stairs.'

'Serve 'im blooming well right, too,' said Crass, as he took a fresh glass of beer from one of the others, who had just 'stood' another round.

'What did the blighter say to that?' enquired the tall man.

'Not a bloody word!' replied the little man. ''E picked 'iself up and called a keb wot was passin' an' got inter it an' went 'ome, an' I never seen no more of 'im until about arf past eleven the next day, wen I was second coatin' the room, an' 'e comes up with a noo suit o' clothes on an' arsts me if I'd like to come hover to the pub an' 'ave a drink? So we goes hover an' 'e calls for a whisky an' soda for 'isself an' arsts me wot I'd 'ave, so I 'ad the same. An' wile we was gettin' it down us, 'e ses to me: "Ah, Garge," 'e ses, "you losed your temper with me yesterday," 'e ses.'

'There you are, you see!' said the tall man. 'There's an example for yer! If you 'adn't served 'im as you did you'd most likely have 'ad to put up with a lot more ole buck.'

They all agreed that the little man had done quite right. They all said that they didn't blame him in the least; they would all have done the same; in fact, this was the way they all conducted themselves whenever occasion demanded it.

Crass stood the final round of drinks, and as he evidently thought that circumstance deserved to be signalised in some special manner he proposed the following toast, which was drunk with enthusiasm:

'To hell with the man,
(May he never grow fat)
What carries two faces,
Under one 'at.'

CHAPTER XXIX

The Socialist Van

Rushton and Company did a lot of work that summer, not many big jobs but a lot of little ones, and the boy Bert was kept busy running from one to the other. He spent most of his time dragging a hand-cart with loads of paint, or planks and steps, and seldom went out to work with the men, for when he was not taking things out to the various places where the philanthropists were working, he was in the paint-shop at the yard, scraping out dirty paintpots or helping Crass to mix up colours. Although scarcely anyone seemed to notice it, the boy presented a truly pitiable spectacle. He was very pale and thin. Dragging the hand-cart did not help him to put on flesh, for the weather was very hot and the work made him sweat.

His home was right away on the other side of Windley. It took him more than three-quarters of an hour to walk to the shop, and as he had to be at work at six that meant that he must leave home at a few minutes past five every morning, so that he always got up about half past four.

About the middle of June Hunter met with an accident. He was tearing off to one of the jobs on his bicycle about five minutes to twelve, to see if he could catch anyone knocking off before the proper time, and while going down a rather steep hill his brakes failed to act, and to save himself from being smashed against the railings at the bottom of the hill, Misery threw himself off the machine, with the result that his head and face and hands were terribly cut and bruised. He was so badly knocked about that he had to remain at home for nearly three weeks, much to the delight of the men and the annoyance—not to say indignation—of Mr Rushton, who could not make out estimates without assistance. There were several jobs to be tendered for just at that time, so Rushton sent the specifications round to Hunter's house for him to figure out the prices, and while he was laid up he spent most of his time sitting up in bed, swathed in bandages, trying to calculate the probable cost of these jobs. Rushton did not come to see him, but he sent Bert nearly every day, either with some specifications, or some accounts, or something of that sort, or with a note inquiring when Hunter thought he would be able to return to work.

All sorts of rumours became prevalent amongst the men concerning Hunter's condition. He had 'broken his spiral column,' he had 'conjunction of the brain,' or he had injured his 'innards' and would probably never be able to 'do no more slave-drivin''. Crass, who had helped Mr Rushton to 'price up' several small jobs, began to think it might not be altogether a bad thing for himself if something were to happen to Hunter, and he began to put on side and to assume airs of authority, and became so bumptious and offensive in his position of deputy foreman that most of the men were almost glad when Nimrod did return. They said that if Crass ever got the job he would be a damn sight worse than Hunter, who when he first came back seemed to have improved in character. But the change was only of short duration and he was soon driving, spying and bullying as hard as ever, while one of the new rules he instituted, at Crass's private instigation, made him more unpopular, if possible, than before. When the men worked overtime it had been their custom to snatch a few minutes off at six o'clock for a mouthful of food. Misery knew they could not work from dinner till 7.30 without something to eat, but he instituted a new regulation that they were to stop work from 6 to 6.30, and lose half an hour's pay, so that instead of knocking off at 7.30 they were obliged to work till 8 o'clock without extra pay. The men cursed and grumbled, but put up with it like sheep, though there were one or two, who apparently had become contaminated with Socialistic theories, who said that they did not desire to work overtime at all, ten hours a day were quite enough for them, in fact they would rather do only eight. What they wanted, they said, was not more work, but more grub, more clothes, more leisure, more pleasure and better homes. They wanted to be able to go for country walks or bicycle rides, to go out fishing or to go to the seaside and bathe and lie on the beach. But there were not many so selfish as this. The majority desired nothing but to be allowed to work, and as for their children, why, 'what was good enough for them, oughter be good enough for the kids.'

One Sunday morning towards the end of July, a band of about twenty-five men and women on bicycles invaded the town. Two of them, who rode a few yards in front of the others, had affixed to their handle bars a slender upright standard from the top of one of which fluttered a small flag of crimson silk with 'International Brotherhood and Peace,' in gold letters. The other standard was similar in size and colour, but with a different legend: 'One for all and All for one.'

As they rode along they gave leaflets to the people in the streets, and whenever they came to a place where there were many people they dismounted and walked about, distributing leaflets. They made several long halts during their progress along the Grand Parade, where there was a considerable crowd, and then they rode over the hill to Windley, which they reached just before opening time. There were little crowds waiting outside the several public-houses, and a number of people passing through the streets on their way home from church and chapel. To all who would take them the strangers distributed leaflets, and they also went through the side streets putting them under the doors and in the letter boxes. When they had exhausted their stock they remounted and rode back the way they came.

Meantime the news of their arrival had spread, and as they returned through the town they were greeted with jeers and booing. Presently someone threw a stone, and as there happened to be plenty of stones just there, several others followed suit and began running after the retreating cyclists, throwing stones, hooting and cursing.

The leaflet which had given rise to all this fury read as follows:

WHAT IS SOCIALISM?

At present the workers with hand and brain produce continually food, clothing and all useful and beautiful things in great abundance,

BUT THEY LABOUR IN VAIN

for they are mostly poor and often in want. They find it a hard struggle to live.Their women and children suffer, and their old age is branded with pauperism.Socialism is a plan by which poverty will be abolished and all will be enabled to live in plenty and comfort, with leisure and opportunity for ampler life.If you wish to hear more of this plan, come to the field at the Cross Roads on the hill at Windley, on Tuesday evening next at 8 p.m., and

LOOK OUT FOR THE SOCIALIST VAN.

The cyclists rode away amid showers of stones without sustaining much damage. One had his hand cut and another, who happened to look round, was struck on the forehead, but these were the only casualities.

On the following Tuesday evening, long before the appointed time, a large crowd assembled at the cross roads on the hill at Windley, evidently prepared to give the Socialists a warm reception. There was only one policeman in uniform but several plain-clothes were amongst the crowd.

Crass, Dick Wantley, the Semi-Drunk, Sawkins, Bill Bates and several other frequenters of the 'Cricketers' were there, and also a sprinkling of tradespeople including the Old Dear and Mr Smallman, the grocer, and a few ladies and gentlemen, well-to-do visitors; but the bulk of the gathering consisted of working-men, labourers, mechanics and boys.

As it was quite evident that the crowd meant mischief—many of them had their pockets filled with stones, and were armed with sticks—several of the local Socialists, including Owen, were in favour of going to meet the van to endeavour to persuade those in charge from coming further, and with that object they went down the road in the direction from which the van was expected. They had not gone very far, however, before the people, divining their intention, began to follow them, and while they were hesitating what course to pursue, the Socialist Van, escorted by five or six men on bicycles, appeared round the corner at the bottom of the hill.

As soon as the crowd saw the van they gave an exultant cheer, or rather, yell, and began running down the hill, and in a few minutes it was surrounded by a howling mob. The van was drawn by two horses; there was a door and a small platform at the back and over this was a sign with white letters on a red ground: 'Socialism, the only hope of the Workers.'

The driver pulled up, and another man on the platform at the rear attempted to address the crowd, but his voice was inaudible in the din of howls, catcalls, hooting, and obscene curses. After about an hour of this, as the crowd began pushing against the van and trying to overturn it, the terrified horses became restive and uncontrollable, and the man on the box attempted to drive up the hill. This seemed still further to infuriate the horde of savages who surrounded the van. Numbers of them clutched the wheels and turned them the reverse way, screaming that it must go back to where it came from; and several of them accordingly seized the horses' heads and, amid cheers, turned them round.

The man on the platform was still trying to make himself heard, but without success. The strangers who had come with the van and the little group of local socialists, who had forced their way close to the platform in front of the would-be speaker, only increased the din by their shouts of appeal to the crowd to 'give the man a fair chance.' This little bodyguard closed round the van as it began to move slowly downhill, but it was completely out-numbered, and the mob, being dissatisfied with the rate at which the van was proceeding, began to shout: 'Run it away!', 'Take the brake off!'; and several savage rushes were made with the intention of putting these suggestions into execution.

Some of the defenders were hampered by their bicycles, but by tremendous efforts they succeeded in keeping the crowd off until the foot of the hill was reached, and then someone threw the first stone, which by a strange chance happened to strike one of the cyclists, whose head was already bandaged. It was the same man who had been hit on the Sunday. This stone was soon followed by others, and the man on the platform was the next to be struck. He got it right on the mouth, and as he put up his handkerchief to staunch the blood another stone struck him on the forehead just above the temple, and he dropped forward on his face onto the platform as if he had been shot. As the speed of the vehicle increased, a regular hail of stones fell upon the roof and against the sides of the van and whizzed past the retreating cyclists, while the crowd followed close behind, cheering, shrieking out volleys of obscene curses, and howling like wolves.

'We'll give the swines Socialism!' shouted Crass, who was literally foaming at the mouth.

'We'll teach 'em to come 'ere trying to undermine our bloody morality!' howled Dick Wantley, as he hurled a lump of granite at one of the cyclists.

After pursuing the van until it was out of range the mob bethought themselves of the local Socialists; but these were nowhere to be seen, having prudently withdrawn as soon as the van had got clear. The victory gained, the upholders of the present system returned to the piece of waste ground on the top of the hill, where a gentleman in a silk hat and frock coat stood up on a little hillock and made a speech. He said nothing about the Distress Committee or the Soup Kitchen or the children who went to school without proper clothes or food, and made no reference to what was to be done next winter when nearly everybody would be out of work. But he said a great deal about the

Glorious Empire and the Flag, and his remarks were received with rapturous applause; and at the conclusion of his address the crowd sang the National Anthem with great enthusiasm and dispersed, congratulating themselves that they had shown, to the best of their ability, what Mugsborough thought of Socialism.

CHAPTER XXX

The Beano

When the eventful day of the beano arrived, the hands were paid at twelve o'clock and rushed off home to have a wash and change.

The brakes were to start from the 'Cricketers' at one, but it was arranged for the convenience of those who lived at Windley that they were to be picked up at the Cross Roads at one-thirty.

There were four brakes altogether, three large ones for the men, and one small one for the accommodation of Mr Rushton and a few of his personal friends, Didlum, Grinder, Mr Toonarf, an architect, and Mr Lettum, a house and estate agent. One of the drivers was accompanied by a friend who carried a long coach horn. This gentleman was not paid to come, but being out of work, he thought that the men would be sure to stand him a few drinks and would probably make a collection for him in return for his services.

A brief halt was made at the Cross Roads to pick up several of the men, including Philpot, Harlow, Easton, Ned Dawson, Sawkins, Bill Bates and the Semi-Drunk. The two last named were now working for Smeariton and Leavit, but as they had been paying in from the first, they had elected to go to the beano rather than have their money back. The Semi-Drunk and one or two other habitual boozers were very shabby and down at heel, but the majority of the men were decently dressed. Some had taken their Sunday clothes out of pawn especially for the occasion. Crass, Slyme and one or two of the single men were in new 'secondhand' suits. Harlow's wife had cleaned up his old straw hat with oxalic acid, and Easton had carefully dyed the faded ribbon of his black bowler with ink.

The small brake with Rushton and his friends led the way, followed by the largest brake, with Misery in the front seat. Payne, the foreman carpenter, occupied the position of honour on the third brake, while Crass presided over the fourth, on the step of which was perched the man with the coach horn.

The mean streets of Windley were soon left far behind and the bean-feasters found themselves journeying along a sunlit, winding road bordered with hedges of hawthorn, holly and briar, past rich brown fields of standing corn, through lofty avenues of elms and oaks, over old mossy stone bridges, past thatched wayside cottages where the people waved their hands in friendly greeting, and the sunburnt children ran, cheering, behind the brakes, for the pennies the men threw to them.

From time to time the men made half-hearted attempts at singing, but it never came to much because most of them were very hungry. They had not had time for dinner and would not have taken any even if they had, for they wished to reserve their appetites for the banquet at the 'Queen Elizabeth' at half past three. However, they cheered up a little after the first halt at the 'Blue Lion', where most of them got down and had a drink. Two or three, including the Semi-Drunk, Ned Dawson, Bill Bates and Joe Philpot, had more than one and felt so much happier that shortly after they started off again sounds of melody were heard from their brake. But it was not very successful, and though after the second halt—about five miles further on—at the 'Warrior's Head' fitful bursts of singing arose from time to time from each of the brakes, there was no heart in it. It is not easy to be jolly on an empty stomach. Neither could they properly appreciate the scenes through which they were passing. They wanted their dinners, and that was the reason why this long ride, instead of being a pleasure, after a while became a weary journey which seemed as if it were never coming to an end.

The next stop was at the 'Bird in Hand', a wayside public house that stood all by itself in a lonely hollow. The landlord was a fat, jolly-looking man, and there were several customers in the bar, men who looked like farm labourers, but there were no other houses to be seen anywhere. This extraordinary circumstance exercised the minds of the travellers and formed the principal topic of conversation until they arrived at the 'Dewdrop Inn' about half-an-hour afterwards. The first brake, containing Rushton and his friends, passed on without stopping here. The occupants of the second brake, which was only a little way behind the first, were divided in opinion whether to stop or go on. Some shouted out to the driver to pull up, others ordered him to proceed, the rest were uncertain which course to pursue. Their indecision, however, was not shared by the coachman, who, knowing that if they stopped somebody would be sure to stand him a drink, drew rein at the inn, an example that was followed by both the other brakes as they drove up.

It was a very brief halt, not more than half the men getting down at all, and those who remained in the brakes grumbled so much at the delay that the others hastily drank their beer and the journey proceeded almost in silence. No attempts at singing, no noisy laughter; they scarcely spoke to each other, but sat gloomily gazing out over the surrounding country.

Instructions had been given to the drivers not to stop again till they reached the 'Queen Elizabeth,' and they therefore drove past the 'World turned Upside Down' without stopping, much to the chagrin of the landlord of that house, who stood at the door with a sickly smile on his face. Some of the men shouted out that they would give him a call on their way back, and with this he had to be content.

They reached the long desired 'Queen Elizabeth' at twenty minutes to four, and were immediately ushered into a large room where a round table and two long ones were set for dinner in a manner worthy of the reputation of the house.

The table-cloths and the serviettes, arranged fanwise in the drinking-glasses, were literally as white as snow. About a dozen knives, forks and spoons were laid for each person, and down the centre of the table glasses of delicious yellow custard and cut glass dishes of glistening red and golden jelly alternated with vases of sweet-smelling flowers.

Rushton, with Didlum and Grinder and his other friends, sat at the round table near the piano. Hunter took the head of the longer of the other two tables and Crass the foot, while on either side of Crass were Bundy and Slyme, who had acted with him as the committee who had arranged the beano. Payne, the foreman carpenter, occupied the head of the other table.

The dinner was all that could be desired.

There was soup, roast beef, boiled mutton, roast turkey, roast goose, ham, cabbage, peas, beans and potatoes, plum pudding, custard, jelly, fruit tarts, bread and cheese, and as much beer or lemonade as they liked to pay for, the drinks being an extra.

Everything was cooked to a turn, and although the diners were somewhat bewildered by the multitude of knives and forks, they all, with one or two exceptions, rose to the occasion and enjoyed themselves famously.

The turkeys, the roast beef and the boiled mutton, the peas and beans and the cabbage, disappeared with astonishing rapidity, which was not to be wondered at, for they were all very hungry from the long drive, and nearly everyone made a point of having at least one helping of everything and some of them went in for two lots of soup.

Crass frequently paused to mop the perspiration from his face and neck with his serviette, an example followed by many others. The beer was of the best, and all the time, amid the rattle of the crockery and the knives and forks, the proceedings were enlivened by many jests and flashes of wit which continuously kept the table in a roar.

'Chuck us over another dollop of that there "white stuff," Bob,' shouted the Semi-Drunk to Crass, indicating the blanc-mange.

Crass reached out his hand and took hold of the dish containing the 'white stuff,' but instead of passing it to the Semi-Drunk he proceeded to demolish it himself, gobbling it up quickly from the dish with a spoon.

'Why, you're eating it all yerself, yer swine,' cried the Semi-Drunk indignantly, as soon as he realised what was happening.

'That's all right, matey,' replied Crass, affably, as he deposited the empty dish on the table. 'It don't matter, there's plenty more where it come from. Tell the landlord to bring in another lot.'

Upon being applied to the landlord, who was assisted in the waiting by his daughter, two other young women and two young men, brought in several more lots and so the Semi-Drunk was appeased.

As for the plum pudding, it was unanimously voted a fair knock out, just like Christmas; but as Ned Dawson and Bill Bates had drunk all the brandy sauce before the pudding was served, the others all had to have their first helping without any. However, the landlord soon supplied the deficit, so that the incident passed off without unpleasantness.

As soon as dinner was over Crass rose to make his statement as secretary. Thirty-seven men had paid in five shillings each; that made nine pounds five shillings. The committee had decided that the three boys, the painter's boy, the carpenter's boy, and the front shop boy, should be allowed to come half-price; that made it nine pounds twelve and six. In addition to paying the ordinary five shilling subscription, Mr Rushton had given one pound ten towards the expenses (loud cheers), and several other gentlemen had also given something towards it:—

Mr Sweater, of 'The Cave,' one pound (applause).

Mr Grinder, ten shillings in addition to the five shilling subscription (applause).

Mr Lettum, ten shillings as well as the five shilling subscription (applause).

Mr Didlum, ten shillings in addition to the five shillings (cheers).

Mr Toonarf, ten shillings as well as the five shilling subscription.

They had also written to some of the manufacturers who supplied the firm with materials, and asked them to give something. Some of 'em had sent half-a-crown, some five shillings, some hadn't answered at all, and two of 'em had written back to say that as things is cut so fine nowadays they didn't get hardly no profit on their stuff, so they couldn't afford to give nothing. But out of all the firms they wrote to they managed to get thirty-two and sixpence altogether, making a grand total of seventeen pounds.

As for the expenses, the dinner was two and six a head, and there was forty-five of them there, so that came to five pounds twelve and six. Then there was the hire of the brakes, also two and six a head, five pounds twelve and six, which left a surplus of five pound fifteen to be shared out (applause). This came to three shillings each for the thirty-seven men, and one and fourpence for each of the boys. (Loud and prolonged cheers).

Crass, Slyme and Bundy now walked round the tables distributing the share out, which was very welcome to everybody, especially those who had spent nearly all their money during the journey from Mugsborough, and when the ceremony was completed, Philpot moved a hearty vote of thanks to the committee for the manner in which they had carried out their duties, which was accorded with acclamation. A collection was made for the waiters and the three waitresses, which amounted to eleven shillings, for which the host returned thanks on behalf of the recipients, who were all smiles.

Then Mr Rushton requested the landlord to serve drinks and cigars all round. Some had cigarettes and the teetotallers had lemonade or ginger beer. Those who did not smoke themselves took the cigar all the same and gave it to someone else who did. When all were supplied there suddenly arose loud cries of 'Order!' and it was seen that Hunter was upon his feet.

As soon as silence was obtained Misery said that he believed that everyone there present would agree with him when he said that they should not let that occasion pass without drinking the 'ealth of their esteemed and respected employer, Mr Rushton (hear, hear!). Some of them had worked for Mr Rushton hon and hoff for many years, and as far as *they* was concerned it was not necessary for him (Hunter) to say much in praise of Mr Rushton (hear, hear!). They knew Mr Rushton as well as he did himself, and to know him was to esteem him (cheers). As for the new hands, although they did not know Mr Rushton as well as the old hands did, he felt sure that they would agree as no one could wish for a better master (loud applause). He had much pleasure in asking them to drink Mr Rushton's 'ealth.

Everyone rose.

'Musical honours, chaps,' shouted Crass, waving his glass and leading off the singing, which was immediately joined in with great enthusiasm by most of the men, the Semi-Drunk conducting the music with a table knife:

'For he's a jolly good fellow,
For he's a jolly good fellow,
For he's a jolly good fell-ell-o
And so say all of us.
So 'ip, 'ip, 'ip 'ooray!
So 'ip, 'ip, 'ip 'ooray!

For 'e's a jolly good fellow,
For 'e's a jolly good fellow,
For 'e's a jolly good fel-ell-o
And so say all of us.'

'Now three cheers!' shouted Crass, leading off:

'Hip, hip, hip Hooray!
Hip, hip, hip Hooray!!
Hip, hip, hip Hooray!!!'

Everyone present drank Rushton's health, or at any rate went through the motions of doing so, but during the roar of cheering and singing that preceded it several of the men stood with expressions of contempt or uneasiness upon their faces, silently watching the enthusiasts or looking at the ceiling or on the floor.

'I will say this much,' remarked the Semi-Drunk as they all resumed their seats—he had had several drinks during dinner, besides those he had taken on the journey—'I will say this much, although I did have a little misunderstanding with Mr 'Unter when I was workin' at the Royal Caif, I must admit that this is the best firm that's ever worked under me.'

This statement caused a shout of laughter, which, however, died away as Mr Rushton rose to acknowledge the toast of his 'health. He said that he had now been in business for nearly sixteen years and this was, he believed, the eleventh houting he had had the pleasure of attending. During all that time the business had steadily progressed and had increased in volume from year to year, and he 'oped and believed that the progress made in the past would be continued in the future (hear, hear). Of course he realised that the success of the business depended very largely upon the men as well as upon himself. The masters could not do without the men, and the men could not live without the masters (hear, hear). It was a matter of division of labour; the men worked with their 'ands and the masters worked with their brains, and one was no use without the other. He 'oped the good feeling which had hitherto hexisted between himself and his workmen would always continue, and he thanked them for the way in which they had responded to the toast of his 'ealth.

Loud cheers greeted the conclusion of this speech, and then Crass stood up and said that he begged to propose the 'ealth of Mr 'Unter (hear, hear). He wasn't going to make a long speech as he wasn't much of a speaker (cries of, 'You're all right,' 'Go on,' etc.), but he felt sure as they would all hagree with him when he said that, next to Mr Rushton, there wasn't no one the men had more respect and liking for than Mr 'Unter (cheers). A few weeks ago when Mr 'Unter was laid up many of them began to be afraid as they was going to lose 'im. He was sure that all the 'ands was glad to 'ave this hoppertunity of congratulating him on his recovery (hear, hear), and of wishing him the best of 'ealth in the future and 'oping as he would be spared to come to a good many more beanos.

Loud applause greeted the conclusion of Grass's remarks, and once more the meeting burst into song:

'For he's a jolly good fellow,
For he's a jolly good fellow,
For he's a jolly good fellow,
And so say all of us.'
So 'ip, 'ip, 'ip ooray!
So 'ip, 'ip, 'ip ooray!'

When they had done cheering Nimrod rose. His voice trembled a little as he thanked them for their kindness, and said that he 'oped he deserved their good will. He could only say as he was sure as he always tried to be fair and considerate to heveryone (cheers). He would now request the landlord to replenish their glasses (hear, hear).

As soon as the drinks were served Nimrod again rose and said he wished to propose the 'ealths of their visitors who had so kindly contributed to their expenses—Mr Lettum, Mr Didlum, Mr Toonarf and Mr Grinder (cheers). They were very pleased and proud to see them there (hear, hear), and he was sure the men would agree with him when he said that Messrs Lettum, Didlum, Toonarf and Grinder were jolly good fellows.

To judge from the manner in which they sang the chorus and cheered, it was quite evident that most of the hands did agree. When they left off, Grinder rose to reply on behalf of those included in the toast. He said that it gave them much pleasure to be there and take part in such pleasant proceedings, and they were glad to think that they had been hable to 'elp to bring it about. It was very gratifying to see the good feeling that existed between Mr Rushton and his workmen, which was as it should be, because masters and men was really fellow workers—the masters did the brain work, the men the 'and work. They was both workers, and their interests was the same. He liked to see men doing their best for their master and knowing that their master was doing his best for them, that he was not only a master, but a friend. That was what he (Grinder) liked to see, master and men pulling together, doing their best, and realising that their interests was identical (cheers). If only all masters and men would do this they would find that heverything would go on hall right. There would be more work and less poverty. Let the men do their best for their masters and the masters do their best for their men and they would find that that was the true solution of the social problem, and not that there silly nonsense as was talked by people what went about with red flags (cheers and laughter). Most of those fellers were chaps who was too lazy to work for their livin' (hear, hear). They could take it from him that if hever the Socialists got the upper 'and there would just be a few of the hartful dodgers who would get all the cream, and there would be nothing left but 'ard work for the rest (hear, hear)! That's wot hall those hagitators was hafter: they wanted them (his hearers), to work and keep 'em in idleness (hear, hear). On behalf of Mr Didlum, Mr Toonarf, Mr Lettum and himself he thanked them for their good wishes, and hoped to be with them on a simler occasion in the future.

Loud cheers greeted the termination of this speech and when Grinder sat down many jeering glances were sent towards the corner of the table where Owen sat.

'What have you got to say to that?' they shouted. 'That's up against yer!'

'He ain't got nothing to say now.'

'Why don't you get up and make a speech?'

This last appeared a very good idea and there arose shouts of 'Owen!', 'Owen!', 'Come on 'ere; get up and make a speech,' 'Be a man!' and so on. Several of those who had been loudest in applauding Grinder joined in the demand that Owen should make a speech, because they were certain that the last speaker and the other gentlemen would be able to dispose of all his arguments. But Owen made no response except to laugh, so presently Crass tied a white handkerchief on a cane walking stick that belonged to Mr Didlum, and stuck it, amid roars of laughter, in the vase of flowers that stood on the end of the table where Owen was sitting.

When the noise had in some measure ceased, Grinder again rose. 'When I made those few remarks,' he said, 'I didn't know as there was any Socialists 'ere. I could tell from the look of you that most of you had more sense. At the same time I'm rather glad I said what I did, because it just shows you what sort of chaps these Socialists are. They're pretty hartful; they know when to talk and when to keep their mouths shut. What they like is to get 'old of a few ignorant workin' men in a workshop or a public-'ouse, and then they can talk by the mile—reg'ler shop lawyers, you know wot I mean—"I'm right and everybody else is wrong" (laughter). But when they finds theirselves in the company of edicated people wot knows a little more nor what they does theirselves, and who isn't likely to be misled by a lot of claptrap, why then, mum's the word. So next time you hears any of these shop lawyers' arguments, you'll know how much it's worth.'

Most of the men were delighted with this speech, which was received with much laughing and knocking on the tables. They remarked to each other that Grinder was a smart man; he'd got the Socialists weighed up just about right, to an ounce.

Then it was seen that Owen was on his feet facing Grinder, and a sudden silence fell.

'It may or may not be true, that Socialists always know when to speak and when to keep silent,' he said, 'but the present occasion hardly seemed a suitable one to discuss such subjects. We are here to-day as friends and want to forget our differences and enjoy ourselves for a few hours. But after what Mr Grinder has said I am quite ready to reply to him to the best of my ability.

'The fact that I am a Socialist and that I am here to-day as one of Mr Rushton's employees should be an answer to the charge that Socialists are too lazy to work for their living. And as to taking advantage of the ignorance and simplicity of working men and trying to mislead them with nonsensical claptrap, it would have been more to the point if Mr Grinder had taken some particular socialist doctrine and had proved it to be untrue or misleading, instead of adopting the method of making vague general charges that he cannot prove. Mr Grinder tells us that the employers work with their brains and the men with their hands. If it is true that no brains are required to do manual labour, why put idiots into imbecile asylums? Why not let them do some of the hand work for which no brains are required? As they are idiots they would probably be willing to work for even less than the ideal "living wage". If Mr Grinder had ever tried he would know that manual workers have to concentrate their minds and their attention on their work or they would not be able to do it at all. Neither can I agree with what he says about the masters being the "friends" of their workmen, because he knows as well as we do that no matter how good or benevolent an employer may be, no matter how much he might desire to give his men better conditions, it is impossible for him to do so, because he has to compete against other employers who would not adopt his methods. It is the bad employer, the sweating, slave-driving employer, who sets the pace for the others. If any employer to-day were to resolve to pay his workmen such wages as he would be able to live upon in comfort himself, and if he did not require them to do more work every day than he himself would like to perform, he would be bankrupt in a month.

'Mr Grinder tells us that the interests of masters and men are identical, but if an employer has a contract it is to his interest to get the work done quickly for the sake of his profits, but the sooner the job is done, so much the sooner will the men be out of employment. How can it be true then that their interests are identical?

'Again, let us suppose that an employer is, say, thirty years of age when he commences business, and that he carries it on for twenty years, and employs forty men more or less regularly during that period, and that their average age is also thirty years. At the end of the twenty years it usually happens that the employer has made enough money to enable him to live for the remainder of his life in ease and comfort. But what about the workmen? All through those twenty years they have earned but a bare living wage, and have had to endure such privations that those who are not already dead are broken in health.

'In the case of the employer there had been twenty years of steady progrees towards ease and leisure and independence. In the case of the majority of the men there were twenty years of deterioration, twenty years of steady, continuous sinking towards the scrap heap, the workhouse, and premature death. How can it be true to say that their interests were identical with those of their employer?

'Such talk as that is not likely to deceive any but children or fools. We are not children, but it is very evident that Mr Grinder thinks we are fools.

'At the same time it is quite true that the real interests of employers and workmen are the same, but not in the sense that Mr Grinder would have us believe. Under the existing system of society only very few people, no matter how wealthy they are, can be absolutely certain that they or their children will not eventually come to want, and even those who think they are secure themselves find their happiness diminished by the knowledge of the poverty and misery that surrounds them on every side.

'In that sense only is it true that the interests of masters and men are identical, for it is to the true interest of all, both 'rich and poor, to help to destroy a system that inflicts suffering upon the many and allows true happiness to none.'

Here Crass jumped up and interrupted, shouting out that they hadn't come there to listen to a lot of speechmaking, a remark that was greeted with unbounded applause by most of those present. Loud cries of 'Hear, hear!' resounded through the room, and the Semi-Drunk suggested that someone should sing a song.

The men who had clamoured for a speech from Owen said nothing, and Mr Grinder seemed very glad of the interruption.

The Semi-Drunk's suggestion that someone should sing a song was received with unqualified approbation by everybody. The landlord's daughter sat down at the piano, and the Semi-Drunk, taking his place at the side of the instrument and facing the audience, sang 'Down at the old Bull and Bush' with appropriate gestures, the chorus being rendered by the full strength of the company, including Misery, who by this time was slightly drunk with gin and ginger beer.

Crass next approached the piano and gave them 'Work Boys Work!', at the end of which three cheers were given for Tariff Reform and 'Plenty of Work.' Then Philpot was called upon to oblige, and received a great ovation when he stood up. Everybody liked Philpot, ''E never did no 'arm to nobody,' and was always ready to do a mate a good turn, and shouts of 'good old Joe!' were enthusiastically raised as he crossed over to the piano, and, in response to numerous requests for 'the old song,' gave them 'Won't you buy my pretty Flowers?'.

Dick Wantley, 'the man behind the moat,' sang 'Put me among the Girls' with many suggestive grimaces, after which Payne gave them 'I'm the Marquis of Camberwell Green.' He was ghastly pale and very nervous, but went through a lot of galvanic motions and gestures which were part of the business. During the song the audience maintained a frigid silence, which so disconcerted Payne that he stopped half-way and said he couldn't remember any more. But to atone for this failure he sang another called 'We all must die like the Fire in the Grate,' which annoyed the audience so much, that it was loudly suggested that if he couldn't do better than that the sooner *he* died the better.

This was followed by a Tory ballad with a chorus that all the men sang with great fervour:

'His clothes may be ragged, his 'and may be soiled,
But where's the disgrace if for bread he has toiled!
His 'art's in the right place, deny it who can
The back bone of England's the honest Working Man.'

After the concert the men strolled into the garden and some played skittles, some played quoits, some sat on the grass and watched the others, and some amused themselves drinking beer and playing shove ha'penny in the bar parlour. The time passed quickly enough and by half-past seven the brakes were loaded up again and a start made for the return journey.

They called at all the taverns on the road, and by the time they reached the 'Blue Lion' half of them were three sheets in the wind and five or six were very drunk, including the driver of Crass's brake and the man with the coach horn. The latter was so helpless that they had to let him lie down amongst their feet, where he fell fast asleep, while the others amused themselves by blowing weird sounds out of the horn.

There was an automatic penny-in-the-slot piano at the 'Blue Lion,' and as this was the last house on the road they made a rather long stay there, playing hooks and rings and shove ha'penny, drinking, singing, dancing and finally quarrelling.

Several of them seemed to fall foul of Newman. They made offensive remarks in his hearing, knocked his lemonade over, and a little later someone else collided violently with him just as he was in the act of drinking. Unfortunately most of the rowdy ones were his fellow-passengers in Crass's brake, and there was not much chance of getting a seat in either of the other carriages, which were overcrowded already.

Finally Dick Wantley shouted out that he was going to go for the dirty tyke who had offered to work underprice last winter. It was *his* fault they were all working for sixpence half-penny, and he was going to wipe the floor with him. Some of his friends eagerly offered to assist but others interposed, and for a time it looked as if there was going to be a free fight, the aggressors struggling hard to get at their inoffensive victim. Eventually, however, Newman found a seat in Misery's brake, squatting on the floor with his back to the horses, thankful enough to be out of reach of the drunken savages, who were now roaring out ribald songs and startling the countryside as they drove along with unearthly blasts on the coach horn.

Meantime, although none of them seemed to notice it, the brake was travelling at a furious rate, and swaying about from side to side. It should have been the last of the procession but things had got a bit mixed at the 'Blue Lion' and instead of bringing up the rear it had taken second place, just behind the small vehicle containing Rushton and his friends.

Crass several times reminded them that the other carriage was so near that Rushton must be able to hear every word that was said, and these repeated admonitions at length enraged the Semi-Drunk, who shouted out that they didn't care if he could hear. To hell with him!

'Damn Rushton, and you too!' cried Bill Bates, addressing Crass. 'You're only a dirty toe-rag! That's all you are! That's the only reason you gets put in charge of jobs, 'cos you're a good nigger driver! You're a bloody sight worse than Rushton or Misery either!'

'Knock 'im orf into the road,' suggested Bundy.

Everybody seemed to think this was a very good idea, but when the Semi-Drunk attempted to rise for the purpose of carrying it out he was thrown down by a sudden lurch of the carriage on top of the prostrate figure of the owner of the coach horn, and by the time he had got right end up he had forgotten all about the plan of getting rid of Crass.

Meanwhile Rushton and the other occupants of the little wagonette had been for some time shouting to them to moderate the pace of their horses, but as the driver of Crass's brake was too drunk to understand what they said, he took no notice, and they had no alternative but to increase their own speed to avoid being run down. The drunken driver now began to imagine that they were trying to race him, and became fired with the determination to pass them.

It was a very narrow road, but there was just about room to pass, and he had sufficient confidence in his own skill with the ribands to believe that he could do it.

The terrified gesticulations and the shouts of Rushton's party only served to infuriate him. He stood up on the foot board and lashed the horses till they almost flew over the ground, while the brake swayed and skidded appallingly.

In front, the horses of Rushton's conveyance were also galloping at top speed, the vehicle bounding and reeling from one side of the road to the other, whilst its occupants, with panic-stricken faces, sat clinging to their seats and to each other, looking back with terror at their pursuers, who were encouraging the drunken driver and urging on the horses with curses and yells.

However, notwithstanding his frantic efforts, the driver was unable to overtake the smaller vehicle, and when the hill to Windley was reached he reluctantly abandoned the race, while Rushton and his friends, without waiting to say goodnight, drove off towards Mugsborough as fast as they could.

Crass's brake halted at the summit for the arrival of the others, and then amid shouts of 'good night!' and 'don't forget six o'clock Monday morning' the bean-feasters dispersed and the great event of the year was over.

CHAPTER XXXI

The Great Oration

On the Monday morning after the beano a man named Jim Smith was painting an upper room in a house where several of Rushton's men were working. He was an odd looking individual with a big body and short legs, and the other men used to say there was something wrong with the way that 'Little Jim' was made. About ten minutes to eight, while he was waiting for the coddy to shout 'Yo ho,' the signal for breakfast time, he began to hum some of the tunes that had been sung at the beano, for having rubbed down and stopped all the woodwork and painted the window since six o'clock, he decided not to make a start on the door till after breakfast. He only earned 6½d. an hour, and as he said to himself, it was a good two hours' work and if he hadn't earned a bob he hadn't earned nothing. Anyhow he wasn't going to do no more before breakfast. The tune of 'For he's a jolly good fellow' kept running through his head, he thrust his hands deep down in his trousers pockets and began to polka round the room, singing softly:

'I won't do no more before breakfast!
I won't do no more before breakfast!
I won't do no more before breakfast!
So 'ip 'ip 'ip 'ooray!
So 'ip 'ip 'ip 'ooray! So 'ip 'ip 'ip 'ooray!
I won't do no more before breakfast!
....etc.'

'No, and you won't do but very little after breakfast, 'ere!' shouted Hunter, suddenly entering the room.

'I've bin a watchin' of you through the crack of the door for the larst 'arf hour and you've not done a dam stroke all the time. Make out yer time sheet and go to the office at nine o'clock and git yer money. We can't afford to pay you for playing the fool.'

Leaving the man dumbfounded and without waiting for a reply, Misery went downstairs, and after bellowing at the foreman for the lack of discipline on the job, he rode away, having come in so stealthily that none of the men knew of his arrival until they heard him shouting at Smith, who did not wait to have his breakfast but went off at once. When he had gone his mates agreed that it served him right; he ought to have had more sense. Most of them realised that this was the beginning of another slaughter; it would only be a matter of a week or two before all the jobs were finished up. They were working at a large house called 'The Refuge,' nicknamed 'The Hospital' by the men because as the other jobs were completed they were all sent on here, so that there were quite a crowd of them at work. All the inside was finished except the kitchen and scullery, and everyone was busy on the outside. Poor old Joe Philpot, whose rheumatism had been very bad lately, was doing a very rough job, painting the gables from a long ladder. But though there were plenty of younger men more suitable he did not like to complain for fear Crass or Misery should think he was not up to his work. At dinner time all the old hands assembled in the kitchen, including Crass, Easton, Harlow, Bundy and Dick Wantley, who still sat on a pail behind his usual moat. Philpot and Harlow were absent and everybody wondered what had become of them. Several times during the morning they had been seen whispering together and comparing scraps of paper, and various theories were put forward to account for their disappearance.

'Looks to me as if they'll stand a very good chance of gettin' drowned if they've gone very far,' remarked Easton, for the weather had been threatening all the morning and within the last few minutes the sky had become so dark that Crass lit the gas so that they could see the way to their mouths. The wind grew more boisterous every moment; the darkness increased; and presently a torrential downfall of rain beat fiercely against the windows, and poured down the glass. The men glanced gloomily at each other. No more work could be done outside that day, and there was nothing left to do inside. As they were all paid by the hour this meant the loss of half a day's pay.

'If it keeps on like this we won't be able to go home neither,' remarked Easton.

'Well, we're all right 'ere, ain't we?' said the man behind the moat. 'There's a nice fire and plenty of heasy-chairs. Wot the 'ell more do you want?'

'Yes,' remarked another philosopher, 'if we only had a shove ha'penny table or a ring board I reckon we should be able to enjoy ourselves all right.'

At this moment the two truants returned, looking very important. Philpot was armed with a hammer, and carrying a pair of steps, while Harlow bore a large piece of wall-paper which they proceeded to tack on the wall, much to the amusement of the others, who read the following announcement, written in charcoal:—

IMPERIAL BANKQUET HALL

'THE REFUGE'

On Thursday at 12.30 Prompt

PROFESSOR OWEN

Will Deliver a

ORATION

Entitled

The Great Secret, or How to Live
Without Work

The Rev. Joe Philpot

(Late absconding secretary of the Light
Refreshment Fund)

Will take the chair and anything else he can lay
his hands on.

At The End of The Lecture

A Meeting will be Arranged

And carried out according to The Marquis of
Queensberry's Rules.

A collection will be took up in aid of the cost
of printing.

When they had fixed the poster on the wall Philpot stood the steps in the corner of the room with the back part facing outwards to form a pulpit, and then, everything being ready for the lecturer, the two sat down in their accustomed places and began to eat their dinners, Harlow remarking that they would have to buck up or they would be too late for the meeting; and the rest of the crowd began to discuss the poster.

'Well, 'e's the finest speaker I ever 'eard,' said the man on the pail, with enthusiam. 'I wouldn't miss this 'ere lecture for anything. I got 'ere about two hours before the doors was opened so as to be sure to get a seat.'

'I've 'eard a 'ell of a lot about Socialism,' said Crass, with a sneer, 'but up to now I've never met nobody wot could tell you plainly exactly wot it is.'

'Yes, that's what I should like to know, too,' said Easton.

'Socialism means "what's yours is mine, and what's mine's me own,"' observed Bundy, and during the laughter that greeted this definition Slyme was heard to say that Socialism meant Materialism, Atheism and Free Love, and if it were ever to come about it would degrade men and women to the level of brute beasts. Harlow said Socialism was a very fine idea, but he was afraid it would never come off. Sawkins said that Socialism was a lot of bloody rot, and Crass expressed the opinion, which he had culled from the delectable columns of the 'Obscurer,' that it meant robbing the industrious for the benefit of the idle and thriftless.

Philpot had by this time finished his bread and cheese, and, crossing over to the corner of the room, ascended the pulpit, being immediately greeted with a tremendous outburst of hooting, howling and booing, which he smilingly acknowledged by removing his cap from his bald head, winking his goggle eyes, and bowing repeatedly. When the storm of shrieks, yells, groans and catcalls had in some degree subsided, he addressed the meeting as follows:

'Gentlemen, first of hall I beg to thank you for the magnificent reception you 'ave given me, and I shall try to deserve your good opinion by shutting my mouth as soon as possible.

'Putting hall jokes aside, I think we're hall agreed about one thing, and that is, that there's plenty of room for improvement in things in general (hear, hear). As our lecturer, Professor Owen, pointed hout in one of 'is lectures, and as most of you 'ave read in the newspapers, although trade was never so good as now there's more misery and poverty than there ever 'as been, and more of small shopkeepers goin' hup the spout. Now, some people tells us as Free Trade means plenty of cheap food. Well, we've got the one but not the other. Then there's hothers as tells us as this "Friscal Policy" is wot we want ('hear, hear,' from Crass and several others). And then there's another lot as ses that Socialism is the only 'ope for the poor. Well, we know pretty well all about Free Trade and the Friscal Policy, but most of us don't know exactly what Socialism means; and I say as its the dooty of hevery man to try and find hout which is the right thing to vote for, and then to do wot 'e can to 'elp to bring it about. And that's the reason we've gorn to the enormous expense of hengaging Professor Owen to come 'ere this afternoon and tell us exactly what Socialism is. So now I will call upon 'im to address you.'

Philpot was loudly applauded as he descended from the pulpit, and in response to clamourous demands Owen mounted the steps, beneath which the chairman sat on a carpenter's stool, with an upturned pail for a table, a plumber's hammer in his hand, and a chipped jam jar of tea by his side.

'Mr Chairman and Gentlemen,' said Owen, 'it is childish to imagine that any measures of Tariff Reform or Political Reform, or abolishing the House of Lords, or disestablishing the Church, or miserable Old Age Pensions, or a contemptible tax on land, can deal with the abject condition of millions of Englishmen, their wives and children. You may be deceived into thinking that such measures as those are great things. You may fight for them and vote for them but after you have got them you will find that they will make no appreciable improvement in your condition. You will still have to slave and drudge to gain a bare sufficiency of the necessaries of life. You will still have to eat the same kind of food and wear the same kind of clothes and boots as now. Your masters will still have you in their power to insult you and sweat you and drive you. Such measures are not remedies, but delusions to distract your attention from the only real solution, which is to be found only in the Public Ownership of the Machinery, and the National Organization of Industry for the production and distribution of the necessaries of life, not for the profit of a few, but for the benefit of all!

'That is the next great change, not merely desirable, but imperatively necessary and inevitable! That is Socialism!'

'Seems to me as if 'e's swallered a bloody dictionary,' remarked Dick Wantley.

'Horder, horder!' shouted the chairman, banging the pail with the plumber's hammer.

'Socialism,' continued Owen, 'is not a wild dream of Superhuman Unselfishness. No one will be asked to sacrifice himself for the benefit of others or to love his neighbours better than himself, as is the case under the present system, which demands that the majority shall be content to labour and live in wretchedness for the benefit of a few.

'Under existing circumstances the community is exposed to the danger of being invaded and robbed and massacred by some foreign power. Therefore the community has organized and owns and controls an Army and Navy to protect it from that danger. Under existing circumstances the community is menaced by another equally great danger: the people are mentally and physically degenerating from lack of proper food and clothing. Socialists say that the community should undertake and organize the business of producing and distributing all these things; that the State should be the only employer of labour and should own all the factories, mills, mines, farms, railways, and fishing fleets.

'Socialists say that the community should undertake the business of providing suitable dwellings for all its members, that the State should be the only landlord and that all the land and all the houses should belong to the whole people.

'The hundreds of thousands of pounds that are yearly wasted in well meant but useless charity accomplish no lasting good, because while charity deals with the symptoms it ignores the disease, which is the private ownership of the means of producing the necessaries of life, and the restriction of production by a few selfish individuals for their own profit. And for that disease there is no other remedy than the public ownership and cultivation of the land; the public ownership of the mines, railways, canals, ships, factories, and all other means of production; and the establishment of an Industrial Civil Service, a National Army of Industry, for the purpose of producing the necessaries, comforts and refinements of life in all the abundance which has been made possible by science and machinery for the use and benefit of *the whole of the people*.'

'Yes; and where's the money to come from for all this?' shouted Crass, fiercely.

'Hear, hear,' cried the man behind the moat.

'There's no money difficulty about it,' replied Owen. 'We can easily find all the money we shall need.'

'Of course,' said Slyme, 'there's all the money in the Post Office Savings Bank. The Socialists could steal that for a start. And as for the mines and land and factories, they can all be took from the owners by force.'

'There will be no need for force and no need to steal anything from anybody.'

'And there's another thing I objects to,' said Crass, 'and that's all this 'ere talk about hignorance. Wot about all the money wots spent every year for eddication!'

'You should rather say, What about all the money that's wasted every year on education! What can be more brutal or senseless than trying to "educate" a poor little hungry, ill-clad child? The majority of us forget in a year or two all that we learnt at school because the conditions of our lives are such as to destroy all inclination for culture or refinement. We must see that the children are properly clothed and fed and that they are not made to get up in the middle of the night to go to work for several hours before they go to school. We must make it illegal for any greedy, heartless profit-hunter to hire their labour for several hours in the evening after school, or all day until nearly midnight on Saturday. We must first see that our children are fed and clothed and cared for before we can expect a proper return for the money that we spend on education.'

'I don't mind admitting that this 'ere scheme of national ownership and industries is all right if it could only be done,' said Harlow, 'but at present all the land, railways and factories belongs to private capitalists; they can't be bought without money, and you say you ain't goin' to take 'em away by force, so I should like to know how the bloody 'ell you *are* goin' to get 'em!'

'We certainly don't propose to buy them with money, for the simple reason that there is not sufficient money in existence to pay for them. The people who own all these things now never really paid for them with money, they obtained possession of them by means of the "*money trick*" which I explained some time ago.'

'They obtained possession of them by usin' their brains,' said Crass.

'Exactly,' replied the lecturer. 'They tell us themselves that that is how they got them away from us; they call their profits the "wages of intelligence". Whilst we have been working they have been using their intelligence in order to obtain possession of the things we have created. The time has now arrived for us to use *our* intelligence in order to get back the things they have robbed us of.'

'Oh, then you *do* mean to rob them after all,' cried Slyme, triumphantly.

'When a thief is caught having in his possession the property of others it is not robbery to take the things away from him and to restore them to their rightful owners,' retorted Owen.

'I can't allow this 'ere disorder to go on no longer,' shouted Philpot, banging the table with the plumber's hammer as several men began talking at the same time. 'There will be plenty of tuneropperty for questions and opposition at the hend of the horation, when the pulpit will be throwed open to anyone as likes to debate the question. I now calls upon the professor to proceed with the horation, and anyone wot interrupts will get a lick under the ear 'ole with this'—waving the hammer—'and the body will be chucked out of the bloody winder.'

Loud cheers greeted this announcement, because as it was still raining heavily the audience thought they might as well pass the time in listening to Owen as in any other way.

'A large part of the land may be got back in the same way as it was taken from us. The ancestors of the present holders obtained possession of it by simply passing Acts of Enclosure; the nation should regain possession of those lands by passing *Acts of Resumption*. And with regard to the other land, the present holders should be allowed to retain possession of it during their lives and then it should revert to the State, to be used for the benefit of all. Britain should belong to the British people, not to a few selfish individuals. As for the railways, they have already been nationalised in some other countries, and what other countries can do we can do also. As for the method by which we can obtain possession of them, the difficulty is not to discover *a* method, but rather to decide which of many methods we shall adopt. One method would be to pass an act declaring that as it was contrary to the public interest that they should be owned by private individuals, the railways would henceforth be the property of the nation. All railway servants, managers and officials would continue in their employment, the only difference being that they would now be in the employ of the State. As to the shareholders—'

'They could all be knocked on the 'ead, I suppose,' interrupted Crass.

'Or go to the workhouse,' said Slyme.

'Or to 'ell,' suggested the man behind the moat.

'—the State would continue to pay to the shareholders the same dividends they had received on an average for, say, the previous three years. These payments would be continued to the present shareholders for life, or the payments might be limited to a stated number of years and the shares would be made non-transferable. As for the factories, shops, and other means of production and distribution, the State must adopt the same methods of doing business as the present owners. I mean that even as the big Trusts and Companies are crushing by competition the individual workers and small traders, so the State should crush the trusts by competition. It is surely justifiable for the State to do for the benefit of the whole people that which the capitalists are already doing for the profit of a few shareholders. The first step in this direction will be the establishment of Retail Stores for the purpose of supplying all national and municipal employees with the necessaries of life at the lowest possible prices. At first the Administration will purchase these things from the private manufacturers in such large quantities that it will be able to obtain them at the very cheapest rate, and as there will be no heavy rents to pay for showy shops and no advertising expenses, and as the object of the Administration will be not to make profit but to supply its workmen and officials with goods at the lowest price, they will be able to sell them much cheaper than the profit-making private stores.

'The National Service Retail Stores will be for the benefit of those in the public service only; and gold, silver or copper money will not be accepted in payment for the things sold. At first, all public servants will continue to be paid in metal money, but those who desire it will be paid all or part of their wages in paper money of the same nominal value, which will be accepted in payment for their purchases at the National Stores, and at the National Hotels, Restaurants and other places which will be established for the convenience of those in the State service. The money will resemble bank-notes.

'As the National Service Stores will sell practically everything that could be obtained elsewhere, and as twenty shillings in paper money will be able to purchase much more at the stores than twenty shillings of metal money would purchase anywhere else, it will not be long before nearly all public servants will prefer to be paid in paper money. As far as paying the salaries and wages of most of its officials and workmen is concerned, the Administration will not then have any need of metal money. But it will require metal money to pay the private manufacturers who supply the goods sold in the National Stores. But all these things are made by labour, so in order to avoid having to pay metal money for them the State will now commence to employ productive labour. All the public land suitable for the purpose will be put into cultivation and State factories will be established for manufacturing food, boots, clothing, furniture and all other necessaries and comforts of life. All those who are out of employment and willing to work will be given employment on these farms and in these factories. In order that the men employed shall not have to work unpleasantly hard, and that their hours of labour may be as short as possible—at first, say eight hours per day—and also to make sure that the greatest possible quantity of everything shall be produced, these factories and farms will be equipped with the most up-to-date and efficient labour-saving machinery.

'The quantities of goods we shall be able to produce will be so enormous that we shall be able to pay our workers very high wages—in paper money—and we shall be able to sell our produce so cheaply that all public servants will be able to enjoy abundance of everything.

'When the workers who are being exploited and sweated by the private capitalists realise the position they will come and ask to be allowed to work for the State, also for paper money. That will mean that the State Army of Production Workers will be continually increasing in numbers. More State factories will be built, more land will be put into cultivation. Men will be given employment making bricks, woodwork, paints, glass, wall-papers and all kinds of building materials; and others will be set to work building, on State land, beautiful houses, which will be let to those employed in the service of the State. The rent will be paid with paper money.

'State fishing fleets will be established, and the quantities of commodities of all kinds produced will be so great that the State employees and officials will not be able to use them all. With their paper money they will be able to buy enough and more than enough to satisfy all their needs abundantly, but there will still be a great and continuously increasing surplus stock in the possession of the State.

'The Socialist Administration will now acquire or build fleets of steam trading vessels, which will of course be manned and officered by State employees the same as the Royal Navy is now; these fleets of National trading vessels will carry the surplus stocks I have mentioned to foreign countries, and will there sell or exchange them for some of the products of those countries, things that we do not produce ourselves. These things will be brought to England

and sold at the National Service Stores, at the lowest possible price, for paper money, to those in the service of the State. This of course will only have the effect of introducing greater variety into the stocks, it will not diminish the surplus; and as there would be no sense in continuing to produce more of these things than necessary, it would then be the duty of the Administration to curtail or restrict the production of the necessaries of life. This could be done by reducing the hours of the workers without reducing their wages, so as to enable them to continue to purchase as much as before.

'Another way of preventing over-production of mere necessaries and comforts will be to employ a larger number of workers producing the refinements and pleasures of life, more artistic houses, furniture, pictures, musical instruments and so forth.

'In the centre of every district a large Institute or pleasure house could be erected, containing a magnificently appointed and decorated Theatre, Concert Hall, Lecture Hall, Gymnasium, Billiard Rooms, Reading Rooms, Refreshment Rooms, and so on. A detachment of the Industrial Army would be employed as actors, artists, musicians, singers and entertainers. In fact everyone that could be spared from the most important work of all, that of producing the necessaries of life, would be employed in creating pleasure, culture, and education. All these people, like the other branches of the public service, would be paid with paper money, and with it all of them would be able to purchase abundance of all those things which constitute civilisation.

'Meanwhile, as a result of all this, the private employers and capitalists, finding that no one would come and work for them to be driven and bullied and sweated for a miserable trifle of metal money, will protest against what they call the unfair competition of State industry, and some of them may threaten to leave the country and take their capital with them. As most of these persons are too lazy to work, and as we shall not need their money, we shall be very glad to see them go. But with regard to their real capital, their factories, farms, mines or machinery, that will be a different matter. To allow these things to remain idle and unproductive, would constitute an injury to the community. So a law will be passed, declaring that all land not cultivated by the owner, or any factory shut down for more than a specified time, will be taken possession of by the State and worked for the benefit of the community. Fair compensation will be paid in paper money to the former owners, who will be granted an income or pension of so much a year either for life or for a stated period according to circumstances and the ages of the persons concerned.

'As for the private traders, the wholesale and retail dealers in the things produced by labour, they will be forced by the State competition to close down their shops and warehouses, first, because they will not be able to replenish their stocks, and secondly because even if they were able to do so they would not be able to sell them. This will throw out of work a great host of people who are at present engaged in useless occupations, such as the managers and assistants in the shops of which there are now half-a-dozen of the same sort in a single street, and the thousands of men and women who are slaving away their lives producing advertisements. These people are in most cases working for such a miserable pittance of metal money that they are unable to procure sufficient of the necessaries of life to secure them from starvation.

'The masons, carpenters, painters, glaziers and all the others engaged in maintaining these unnecessary stores and shops will all be thrown out of employment, but all those who are willing to work will be welcomed by the State and will be at once employed in producing or distributing the necessaries and comforts of life. They will have to work fewer hours than before. They will not have to work so hard for there will be no need to drive or bully, because there will be plenty of people to do the work, and most of it will be done by machinery, and with their paper money they will be able to buy abundance of the things they help to produce. The shops and stores where these people were formerly employed will be acquired by the State, which will pay the former owners fair compensation in the same manner as to the factory owners. Some of the buildings will be utilised by the State as National Service Stores, others transformed into factories, and others will be pulled down to make room for dwellings or public buildings. It will be the duty of the Government to build a sufficient number of houses to accommodate the families of all those in its employment, and as a consequence of this and because of the general disorganisation and decay of what is now called "business," all other house property of all kinds will rapidly depreciate in value. The slums and the wretched dwellings now occupied by the working classes, the miserable, uncomfortable, jerry built "villas" occupied by the lower middle classes and by "business" people, will be left empty and valueless upon the hands of their rack-renting landlords, who will very soon voluntarily offer to hand them, and the ground they stand upon, to the State on those terms accorded to the other property owners, namely, in return for a pension. Some of these people will be content to live in idleness on the income allowed them for life as compensation by the State; others will devote themselves to art or science; and some others will offer their services to the commuuity as managers and superintendents; and the State will always be glad to employ all those who are willing to help in the great work of production and distribution.

'By this time the nation will be the sole employer of labour, and as no one will be able to procure the necessaries of life without paper money, and as the only way to obtain this will be by working, it will mean that every mentally and physically capable person in the community will be helping in the great work of production and distribution. We shall not need, as at present, to maintain a police force to protect the property of the idle rich from the starving wretches whom they have robbed. There will be no unemployed and no overlapping of labour, which will be organised and concentrated for the accomplishment of the only rational object, the creation of the things we require. For every one labour-saving machine in use to-day, we will, if necessary, employ a thousand machines, and consequently there will be produced such a stupendous, enormous, prodigious, overwhelming abundance of everything, that soon the community will be faced once more with the serious problem of over-production.

'To deal with this, it will be necessary to reduce the hours of our workers to four or five hours a day. All young people will be allowed to continue at the public schools and universities and will not be required to take any part in the work of the nation until they are twenty-one years of age. At the age of forty-five everyone will be allowed to retire from the State service on full pay. All these will be able to spend the rest of their days according to their own inclinations. Some will settle down quietly at home, and amuse themselves in the same ways as people of wealth and leisure do at the present day. Some will prefer to continue in the service of the State. Actors, artists, sculptors, musicians and others will go on working for their own pleasure and honour. Some will devote their leisure to science, art, or literature. Others will prefer to travel on the State steamships to different parts of the world to see for themselves all those things of which most of us have now but a dim and vague conception. Thus, for the first time in the history of humanity, the benefits and pleasures conferred upon mankind by science and civilisation will be enjoyed equally by all, upon the one condition, that they shall do their share of the work in order to make all these things possible.

'These are the principles upon which the Co-Operative Commonwealth of the future will be organised: the State in which no one will be distinguished or honoured above his fellows except for Virtue or Talent; where no man will find his profit in another's loss, and we shall no longer be masters and servants, but brothers, free men, and friends; where there will be no weary, broken men and women passing their joyless lives in toil and want, and no little children crying because they are hungry or cold.'

As Owen descended from the pulpit and walked back to his accustomed seat a loud shout of applause burst from a few men in the crowd, but the majority maintained a sullen silence. When order was restored Philpot rose and addressed the meeting:

'Is there any gentleman wot would like to ask the speaker a question?'

Crass and most of the others tried hard to think of something to say in defence of the existing state of affairs, or against the proposals put forward by the lecturer; but finding nothing, they maintained a sullen and gloomy silence. To judge by their unwillingness to alter the present system it might have been supposed that they were afraid of losing something, instead of having nothing to lose except their poverty. It was not until the Chairman had made several appeals for questions that Crass brightened up, a glad smile overspreading his greasy visage; at last he had thought of some insurmountable obstacle to the establishment of the Co-operative Commonwealth.

'Do you mean to say,' he said with a sneer, 'as the time will ever come when the gentry will mix up on equal terms with the likes of us?'

'Oh no,' replied the lecturer. 'When we get Socialism there won't be any people like us, we shall *all* be civilised.'

The man behind the moat seemed very much taken aback at this prospect, and when one or two of the others laughed, he remarked gloomily 'as he didn't see anything to laugh at.'

'Anybody else want to be flattened out?' inquired the Chairman. 'Or any Liberal or Tory Capitalist like to get up in the pulpit and oppose the speaker?' As no one offered, he said: 'It is now my painful dooty to call upon someone to move a resolution.'

'Well, Mr Chairman,' said Harlow, 'I may say as when I come on this firm I was a Liberal, but through listening to several lectures by Professor Owen I've come to the conclusion that it's a mug's game to vote for the Capitalists, whether they calls themselves Liberals or Tories. I couldn't quite make out, though, how Socialism was going to 'elp us but the lecture Professor Owen 'as given us this afternoon has been a bit of an eye-opener to me, and I should like to move as a resolution "That it is the opinion of this 'ere meeting that Socialism is the only Remedy for Unemployment and Poverty."'

'I'll second that resolution,' said Easton.

'And I'll lay a bob both ways,' remarked Bundy.

The resolution was then put, and though the great majority were against it, the Chairman declared it was carried unanimously.

By this time the violence of the storm had in a great measure abated, but as rain was still falling it was decided not to attempt to resume work that day.

'P'raps it's just as well it 'as rained,' remarked one man, 'or else some of us might 'ave got the sack to-night. As it is, there'll be hardly enough for all of us to do to-morrow and Saturday mornin', even if it is fine.'

This was true, and with sudden panic at their hearts they all realised that unless the firm had some other work there would be a great slaughter on Saturday.

'Now, look 'ere,' said Philpot, with a wink, assuming a patronising air. 'I wants you hall to make a speshall heffort and get 'ere very hearly in the mornin', say about four o'clock, and them wot doos the most work to-morrer, will get a prize on Saturday.'

'What'll it be, the sack?' inquired Harlow.

'Yes,' replied Philpot, 'and not honly will you get a prize, but if you hall keep on workin like we've bin doing lately till you're too hold and too wore hout to do any more, you'll be allowed to go to a nice workhouse for the rest of your lives, and each one of you will be given a title—"Pauper!"'

And they laughed! In spite of the fact that the majority of them had mothers or fathers who had already succeeded to the title—they laughed!

As they were going home Crass paused at the gate, and pointing up to the large gable at the end of the house, said to Philpot:

'You'll want the longest ladder, the sixty-five, for that, to-morrow.'

Philpot looked up at the gable. It was very high.

CHAPTER XXXII

The Sixty-five

The next morning after breakfast Philpot, Sawkins, Harlow and Easton went to the yard to get the long ladder. It was called 'the Sixty-five' because it had sixty-five rungs; it was a builder's scaffold ladder, and altogether too heavy and cumbrous for painter's work. However, as none of the others were long enough to reach the high gable at 'The Refuge,' they managed with a struggle to get it down from the hooks and put it on one of the handcarts, and soon passed through the streets of mean and dingy houses in the vicinity of the yard and began the ascent of the long hill.

There had been a lot of rain during the night and the sky was still overcast with dark grey clouds. The cart went heavily over the muddy road. Sawkins was at the helm, holding the end of the ladder and steering; the others walked a little further ahead, at the sides of the cart.

It was such an exhausting shove that half-way up the hill they stopped for a rest, keeping a good look-out for Rushton or Hunter, who might pass at any moment.

'This is a bit of all right, ain't it?' remarked Harlow as he took off his cap and wiped the sweat from his forehead with his handkerchief.

At first no one made any reply, for they were all out of breath and Philpot's lean fingers trembled violently as he wiped the perspiration from his face.

'Yes, mate,' he said despondently, after a while. 'It's one way of gettin' a livin', and there's plenty better.'

In addition to the fact that his rheumatism was exceptionally bad, he felt low-spirited this morning. The gloomy weather and the prospect of a long day of ladder work probably accounted for his unusual dejection.

They relapsed into silence. The depression that possessed Philpot deprived him of all his usual jocularity and filled him with melancholy thoughts. He had travelled up and down this hill a great many times before under similar circumstances, and he said to himself that if he had half a quid now for every time he had pushed a cart up this road he wouldn't need to do anyone out of a job all the rest of his life.

The shop where he had been apprenticed used to be just down at the bottom; the place had been pulled down years ago and the ground was now occupied by more pretentious buildings. Not quite so far down the road, on the other side, he could see the church where he was married just thirty years ago. Presently, when they reached the top of the hill, he would be able to look across the valley to the spire of the other church, the one in the graveyard, where wife and children, all those who were dear to him, had been laid to rest, one by one. He felt that he would not be sorry when the time came to join them there. Possibly in the next world, if there were such a place, they might all be together again.

He was suddenly aroused from these thoughts by an exclamation from Harlow:

'Look out! Here comes Rushton.'

They immediately resumed their journey. Rushton was coming up the hill in his dog-cart, with Grinder sitting by his side. They passed so closely that Philpot was splashed with mud from the wheels of the trap.

'Them's some of your chaps, ain't they?' remarked Grinder.

'Yes,' replied Rushton, 'We're doing a job up this way.'

'I should 'ave thought it would pay you better to use a 'orse for sich work as that,' said Grinder.

'We do use the horses whenever it's necessary, for very big loads,' answered Rushton, and added with a laugh: 'but the donkeys are quite strong enough for such a job as that.'

The 'donkeys' struggled on up the hill for about another hundred yards and then they were forced to halt again.

Whilst they were resting another two-legged donkey passed by pushing another cart, or rather, holding it back, for he was going slowly down the hill; another Heir of all the Ages, another Imperialist, a degraded, brutalised wretch, clad in filthy, stinking rags, his toes protruding from the rotten broken boots that were tied with bits of string upon his stockingless feet. The ramshackle cart was loaded with empty bottles and putrid rags, old coats and trousers, dresses, petticoats and underclothing, greasy, mildewed and malodorous. As he crept along, with his eyes on the ground, he uttered at intervals uncouth, inarticulate sounds.

'That's another way of gettin' a livin',' said Sawkins, with a laugh as the miserable creature slunk by. The others laughed, and Harlow was about to make some reply but at that moment a cyclist appeared coming down the hill from the direction of the job. It was Nimrod, so they resumed their journey once more, and presently Hunter shot past on his machine without taking any notice of them.

When they arrived at their destination they found that Rushton had not been there at all, but Nimrod had. Crass said that he had kicked up no end of a row because they had not called at the yard at six o'clock that morning for the ladder instead of after breakfast, and also because the big gable had not been started the first thing that morning.

They carried the ladder into the garden and laid it on the ground by the gable in a passage about six feet wide between the side of the house and the garden wall.

Next, it was necessary that two men should go up into the attic, the window of which was just under the point of the gable, and drop the end of a long rope down to the others who would tie it to the top of the ladder. Then two men would stand on the bottom rung so as to keep the 'foot' down, and three others would have to raise the ladder while the two men up in the attic hauled on the rope.

They called Bundy and his mate Ned Dawson to help, and it was arranged that Harlow and Crass should stand on the foot because they were the heaviest. Philpot, Bundy, and Easton were to 'raise,' and Dawson and Sawkins were to go up to the attic and haul on the rope.

'Where's the rope?' asked Crass.

The others looked blankly at him. None of them had thought of bringing one from the yard.

'Why, ain't there one 'ere?' said Philpot, feebly.

'One 'ere? Of course there ain't one 'ere!' snarled Crass. 'Do you mean to say as you ain't brought one, then?'

Philpot stammered out something about having thought there was one at the house already.

'Well, what the bloody hell are we to do now?' cried Crass angrily. ''Ere it's nearly ten o'clock and we 'aven't begun the gable yet, wot we oughter 'ave started on first thing this morning.'

'Well, the only thing as I can see for it.' he continued, 'is that the boy will 'ave to go down to the yard and get the long rope. It won't do for anyone else to go; there's been row enough already.'

Bert was called and given the necessary instructions, chief of which was to get back again as soon as ever he could. The boy ran off, and while they were waiting, Philpot returned to the small gable he had been painting before breakfast, which he had not quite finished. As he worked, a sudden and unaccountable terror took possession of him. He did not want to do that high gable—he felt too ill; and he almost resolved that he would ask Crass if he would mind letting him do something else. There were several younger men who would find the job mere child's play.

But then he remembered what the probable consequences would be, and tried to persuade himself that he would be able to get through it all right. It would not do to let Crass or Hunter mark him as being too old for ladder work.

Bert came back in about half an hour flushed and sweating with the weight of the rope and the speed he had made. He delivered it to Crass who passed the word for Philpot and the others to come and raise the ladder. He handed the rope to Ned Dawson, who took it up to the attic, accompanied by Sawkins. Arrived there, they lowered one end out of the window down to the others.

'If you ask me,' said Ned Dawson, who was critically examining the strands of the rope as he passed it out through the open window; 'if you ask me, I don't see as this 'ere rope is much good. Look 'ere'; he indicated a part which was very frayed and worn; 'and 'ere's another place just as bad.'

'Well, for Christ's sake don't say nothing about it now,' replied Sawkins; 'there's been enough talk and waste of time over this job already.'

Ned made no answer, and the end having by this time reached the ground, Bundy made it fast to the ladder, about six rungs from the top.

The ladder was lying on the ground, parallel to the side of the house. The task of raising it would have been much easier if they had been able to lay it at right angles to the house wall, but this was impossible because of the premises next door and the garden wall between the two houses. As it was, the men at the top would not be able to get a straight pull on the rope, and would have to stand back in the room without being able to see the ladder, while the rope would have to be drawn round the corner of the window, rasping against the edge of the stone sill and the brickwork.

Crass and Harlow now stood on the foot and the other three raised the top from the ground. As Easton was the tallest he took the middle position, underneath, grasping the rungs, Philpot being on his left and Bundy on his right, each holding one side of the ladder.

At a signal from Crass, Dawson and Sawkins began to haul on the rope, and the top of the ladder rose slowly in the air.

The fact that Philpot was not of much use at this work made it all the harder for the other two who were lifting, besides putting an extra strain on the rope. His lack of strength and the efforts of Easton and Bundy to make up for him caused the ladder to sway from side to side.

Meanwhile, upstairs, Dawson and Sawkins, although the ladder was as yet only a little more than halfway up, noticed, as they hauled and strained on the rope, that it had worn a groove for itself in the corner of the brickwork at the side of the window; and every now and then, although they pulled with all their strength, they were not able to draw in any part of the rope at all, and it seemed to them as if those others down below must have either let go their hold altogether or ceased lifting.

That was what actually happened. The three men found the weight so overpowering that once or twice they were compelled to relax their efforts for a few seconds, and at those times the rope had to carry the whole weight of the ladder; and the part of the rope that had to bear the greatest strain was the particular part that chanced to be at the angle of the brickwork at the side of the window. And presently it happened that one of the frayed and worn places that Dawson had remarked was just at the angle during one of those momentary pauses. On one end of the rope there hung the ponderous ladder, straining the frayed part against the corner of the brickwork and the sharp edge of the stone sill, at the other end were Dawson and Sawkins, pulling with all their strength, and next instant the rope snapped like a piece of thread. Sawkins and Dawson reeled backwards into the room, and the broken rope flew up into the air, writhing like the lash of a gigantic whip. For a moment the heavy ladder swayed from side to side. Easton, standing underneath, with his hands raised above his head grasping one of the rungs, struggled desperately to hold it up. At his right stood Bundy, also with arms upraised holding the side; and on the left, between the ladder and the wall, was Philpot.

For a brief space they strove fiercely to support the overpowering weight, but Philpot had no strength, and the ladder, swaying over to the left, crashed down, crushing him upon the ground and against the wall of the house. He fell face downwards, with the ladder across his shoulders. The side that had the iron bands twisted round it fell across the back of his neck, forcing his face against the bricks at the base of the wall. He uttered no cry and was quite still, with blood streaming from the cuts on his face, and trickling from his ears.

None of the others were hurt, for they had all had time to jump clear when the ladder fell. Their shouts soon brought all the other men running to the spot, and the ladder was quickly lifted off the motionless figure.

Easton rushed off for a neighbouring doctor, who came in a few minutes. He knelt down and carefully examined the crushed and motionless form, while the other men stood by in terrified silence.

The examination was a very brief one, and when the doctor rose from his knees, even before he spoke, they knew from his manner that their worst fears were realized.

Philpot was dead.

CHAPTER XXXIII

The Ghouls

When Hunter arrived at the house shortly afterwards he first began to shout and bully because the gable had not been begun; then, on hearing of the accident, he blamed the men for using the rope; and finally after Philpot's body had been removed to the mortuary, he had a long private talk with Crass. The result of his confidential investigations proved that Philpot had no relatives, that his life was insured for ten pounds and that the money was to be paid to the old woman with whom he lodged. Crass and Hunter came to the conclusion that it was probable that she would be very glad to be relieved of the trouble of attending to the business of the funeral, and that Crass, as a close friend of the dead man and a fellow-member of the Insurance Society, was the most suitable person to take charge of the business for her. Of course, they would not be able to do much until after the inquest, but they could get the coffin made; and as Hunter knew the mortuary keeper there would be no difficulty about getting in for a minute to measure the corpse.

This matter having been arranged, Hunter departed to order a new rope, and shortly afterwards Crass, having made sure that everyone would have plenty to do while he was gone, quietly slipped away to see Philpot's landlady.

The new rope was brought to the house about one o'clock, and this time the ladder was raised without any mishap. Harlow was put on to paint the gable, but his nerve was so shaken that he was allowed to have Sawkins to stand by and hold the ladder all the time. Everyone felt nervous that afternoon, and they all went about their work in an unusually careful manner.

While Bert was painting the gate of the side entrance he was accosted by a solemn looking man who asked him about the accident. The solemn stranger was very sympathetic and enquired what was the name of the man who had been killed, and whether he was married. Bert informed him that Philpot was a widower, and that he had no children.

'Ah, well, that's so much the better, isn't it?' said the stranger, shaking his head mournfully. 'It's a dreadful thing, you know, when there's children left unprovided for. You don't happen to know where he lived, do you?'

'Yes,' said Bert, mentioning the address and beginning to wonder what the solemn man wanted to know for, and why he appeared to be so sorry for Philpot, since it was quite evident that he was quite a stranger to him.

'Thanks very much,' said the man, pulling out his pocket book and making a note in it. 'Thanks very much, indeed. Good afternoon.' And he hurried off.

'Good afternoon, sir,' said Bert, and turned to resume his work. Crass came along the garden path just as the mysterious stranger was disappearing round the corner.

'What did *he* want?' said Crass, who had seen the man talking to Bert.

'I don't know exactly. He was asking about the accident, and whether Joe left any children, and where he lived. He must be a very decent sort of chap, I should think. He seems quite sorry about it.'

'Oh, he does, does he?' said Crass, with a peculiar expression. 'Don't you know who he is?'

'No,' replied the boy. 'But I thought p'raps he was a reporter of some paper.'

''E ain't no reporter. That's old Snatchum, the undertaker; 'e's smellin' round after a job; but 'e's out of it this time, smart as 'e thinks 'e is.'

The accident was a constant topic of conversation among the men. They said that it was all very well for Hunter to talk like that about the rope, but he had known for a long time that it was nearly worn out. Newman said that only about three weeks previously, when they were raising a ladder at another job, he had shown the rope to him, and Misery had replied that there was nothing wrong with it. Several others besides Newman claimed to have mentioned the matter to Hunter, and he had made the same sort of reply in each case. But when Owen suggested that they should attend the inquest and give evidence to that effect, they became suddenly silent, and Newman afterwards pointed out to Owen that by doing so he could not bring Philpot back again and would only do himself a lot of harm. He would never get another job at Rushton's, while many of the other employers would 'mark' him as well.

'So if *you* say anything about it,' concluded Newman, 'don't bring my name into it.'

Owen was bound to admit that all things considered it was right for Newman to mind his own business. He felt that it would not be fair to urge him or anyone else to do or say anything that would injure their own prospects.

Misery came to the house about eleven o'clock on Saturday and informed several of the hands that as work was very slack they would get their back day at pay time. He said the firm had tendered for one or two jobs, so they could call round about Wednesday and perhaps he then might be able to give some of them another start. Owen was not one of those who were 'stood off,' although he had expected to be on account of the speech he had made at the beano, and everyone said that he would have got the push sure enough if it had not been for the accident.

Before he went away, Nimrod instructed Owen and Crass to go to the yard at once to help Payne finish off the coffin.

As it was such a cheap job there was no time to polish it properly, so Crass proceeded to give it a couple of coats of spirit varnish, and while he was doing this Owen wrote the plate, which was made of very thin zinc lacquered over to make it look like brass:

JOSEPH PHILPOT

Died

September 1*st*, 19—

Aged 56 Years

....

The inquest was held on the following Monday morning, and as both Rushton and Hunter thought it possible that Owen might attempt to impute some blame to them, they had worked the oracle and had contrived to have several friends of their own put on the jury. There was, however, no need for their alarm, because Owen could not say that he had himself noticed, or called Hunter's attention to, the state of the rope; and he did not wish to mention the names of the others without their permission. Crass and the other men gave evidence that it was a pure accident. None of them had noticed that the rope was unsound. Hunter also swore that he did not know of it, none of the men had ever called his attention to it; if they had done so he would have procured a new one immediately.

Philpot's landlady and Mr Rushton were also called as witnesses, and the end was that the jury returned a verdict of accidental death, and added that they did not think any blame attached to anyone.

As the witnesses passed out of the room, Hunter followed Rushton with the hope of being honoured by a little conversation on the satisfactory issue of the case; but Rushton went off without taking any notice of him, so Hunter returned to the room where the court had been held, to get the coroner's certificate authorising the interment of the body. This document is usually handed to the friends of the deceased or to the undertaker acting for them. When Hunter got back to the room he found that during his absence the coroner had given it to Philpot's landlady, and when he hastened outside to ask her for it the woman was nowhere to be seen.

Crass and the other men were also gone. They had hurried off to return to work, and after a moment's hesitation Hunter decided that it did not matter much about the certificate. Crass had arranged the business with the landlady and he could get the paper from her later on. Having come to this conclusion he dismissed the subject from his mind.

That evening, after having been home to tea, Crass and Sawkins met by appointment at the carpenter's shop to take the coffin to the mortuary, where Misery had arranged to meet them at half-past eight o'clock. Hunter's plan was to have the funeral take place from the mortuary, which was only about a quarter of an hour's walk from the yard; so to-night they were just going to lift in the body and get the lid screwed down.

It was blowing hard and raining heavily when they set out, carrying the coffin, covered with a black cloth, on their shoulders. They also carried a small pair of trestles.

On their way they had to pass the 'Cricketers' and the place looked so inviting that they decided to stop and have a drink, just to keep the damp out, and as they could not very well take the coffin inside with them, they stood it up against the wall outside, Crass remarking with a laugh, there was not much danger of anyone pinching it. Just as they finished drinking the two half-pints there was a loud crash outside, and rushing out they found that the coffin had blown down and was lying bottom upwards across the pavement, while the black cloth that had been wrapped round it was out in the middle of the muddy road. Having recovered this, they shook off as much of the dirt as they could, and once more wrapping it round the coffin resumed their journey to the mortuary, where they found Hunter waiting for them engaged in earnest conversation with the keeper. The electric light was switched on, and they saw that the marble slab was empty.

'Snatchum came this afternoon with a handtruck and a corfin,' explained the keeper. 'I was out at the time, and the missis thought it was all right, so she let him have the key.'

Hunter and Crass looked blankly at each other.

'Well, this takes the biskit!' said the latter as soon as he could speak.

'I thought you said you had settled everything all right with the old woman?' said Hunter.

'So I did,' replied Crass; 'I seen 'er on Friday, and I told 'er to leave it all to me to attend to, and she said she would. I told 'er that Philpot said to me that if ever anything appened to 'im I was to take charge of everything for 'er, because I was 'is best friend. And I told 'er we'd do it as cheap as possible.'

'Well, it seems to me as you've bungled it somehow,' said Nimrod gloomily. 'I ought to have gone and seen 'er myself. I was afraid you'd make a mess of it,' he added in a wailing tone. 'It's always the same; everything that I don't attend to myself goes wrong.'

An uncomfortable silence followed. Crass thought that the principal piece of bungling in this affair was Hunter's failure to secure possession of the coroner's certificate after the inquest, but he was afraid to say so.

'I can see 'ow it's been worked,' said Crass at last; 'there's one of the members of the club who works for Snatchum, and 'e's took it on 'isself to give the order for the funeral; but 'e's got no right to do it.'

'Right or no right, 'e's done it,' replied Misery, 'so you'd better take the box back to the shop.'

Crass and Sawkins accordingly returned to the workshop, where they were presently joined by Nimrod.

'I've been thinking this business over as I came along,' he said, 'and I don't see being beat like this by Snatchum; so you two can just put the trestles and the box on a handcart and we'll take it over to Philpot's house.'

Nimrod walked on the pavement while the other two pushed the cart, and it was about half-past nine when they halted in a dark part of the street, a few yards away from the house and on the opposite side.

'I think the best thing we can do,' said Misery, 'is for me and Sawkins to wait 'ere while you go to the 'ouse and see 'ow the land lies. You've done all the business with 'er so far. It's no use takin' the box unless we know the corpse is there. For all we know Snatchum may 'ave taken it 'ome with 'im.'

'Yes; I think that'll be the best way,' agreed Crass, after a moment's thought.

Nimrod and Sawkins accordingly took shelter in the doorway of an empty house, leaving the handcart at the kerb, while Crass went across the street and knocked at Philpot's door. They saw it opened by an elderly woman holding a lighted candle in her hand; then Crass went inside and the door was shut. In about a quarter of an hour he re-appeared and leaving the door partly open behind him he came out and crossed over to where the others were waiting. As he drew near they could see that he carried a piece of paper in his hand.

'It's all right,' he said in a hoarse whisper, 'I've got the stifficut.'

Misery took the paper eagerly and scanned it by the light of a match that Crass struck. It was the certificate right enough, and with a sigh of relief Hunter put it into his notebook and stowed it safely away in the inner pocket of his coat, while Crass explained the result of his errand.

It appeared that the other member of the Society, accompanied by Snatchum, had called upon the old woman and had bluffed her into giving them the order for the funeral and had put her up to getting the certificate from the coroner.

'When they brought the body 'ome this afternoon,' Crass went on, 'Snatchum tried to get the stifficut orf 'er, but she'd been thinkin' things over and was a bit frightened 'cos she knowed she'd made arrangements with me, and she thought she'd better see me first; so she told 'im she'd give it to 'im on Thursday, the day as 'e was goin to 'ave the funeral.'

'He'll find he's a day too late,' said Misery, with a ghastly grin. 'We'll get the job done on Wednesday.'

'She didn't want to give it to me, at first,' Crass concluded, 'but I told 'er we'd see 'er right if old Snatchum tried to make 'er pay for the other corfin.'

'I don't think he's likely to make much fuss about it,' said Hunter. 'He won't want everybody to know he was so anxious for the job.'

Crass and Sawkins pushed the hand-cart over to the other side of the road, and carried the coffin into the house, Nimrod going first.

The old woman was waiting for them with the candle at the end of the passage.

'I shall be very glad when it's all over,' she said, as she led the way up the narrow stairs, closely followed by Hunter, who carried the trestles, Crass and Sawkins bringing up the rear with the coffin. 'I shall be very glad when it's all over, for I'm sick and tired of answerin' the door to undertakers. If there's been one 'ere since Friday there's been a dozen after the job, not to mention all the cards what's been put under the door, besides the ones what I've had give to me by different people.'

Arrived at the top landing the old woman opened a door and entered a small and wretchedly furnished room. Across the lower sash of the window hung a tattered piece of lace curtain. The low ceiling was cracked and discoloured. There was a rickety little wooden washstand, and along one side of the room a narrow bed was covered with a ragged grey quilt, on which lay a bundle containing the clothes that the dead man was wearing at the time of the accident. In the middle of this dreary room upon a pair of trestles stood a coffin covered with a white sheet, terrible in its silent pathetic solitude.

The old woman placed the candle on the mantelpiece, and withdrew, while the men laid the empty coffin on the floor by the side of the bed. Crass took two large screw drivers from the pocket of his overcoat and handed one to Hunter.

Sawkins held the candle while they unscrewed and took off the lid of the coffin they had brought with them.

'I think we shall be able to work better if we takes the other one orf the trussels and put it on the floor,' remarked Crass.

'Yes, I think so, too,' replied Hunter.

Crass took off the sheet and threw it on the bed, revealing the other coffin, which was very similar in appearance to the one they had brought. Hunter took hold of the head and Crass the foot and they lifted it off the trestles on to the floor.

''E's not very 'eavy, that's one good thing,' observed Hunter.

''E always was a very thin chap,' remarked Crass.

The screws that held down the lid had been covered over with large-headed brass nails and these had to be wrenched off, the screws themselves were old ones, rusty and of odd sizes, and were screwed in so firmly that by the time half of them were drawn the two men were streaming with perspiration. After a while Hunter took the candle from Sawkins and the latter had a try at the screws.

'Anyone would think the dam things had been in there for a 'undred years,' remarked Hunter, savagely, as he wiped the sweat from his face and neck with his handkerchief.

Kneeling on the lid of the coffin and panting and grunting with the exertion, the other two continued to struggle with their task. Suddenly Crass uttered an obscene curse: he had broken off one side of the head of the screw he was trying to turn; and about at the same instant a similar misfortune happened to Sawkins.

After this, Hunter again took a screwdriver himself, and when they had got all the screws out with the exception of the two broken ones, Crass took a hammer and chisel and proceeded to cut off what was left of the tops of these. But even after this was done the two screws still held the lid on the coffin, and so they had to hammer the end of the blade of the chisel underneath and lever up the lid so that they could get hold of it with their fingers. It split up one side as they tore it off, and exposed the dead man to view.

Although the marks of the cuts and bruises were still visible on old Joe's face, they were softened by the pallor of death, and his features wore a placid, peaceful expression. His hands were crossed upon his breast, and lying there in the snow white grave clothes, almost covered in by the white frill that bordered the sides of the coffin, he looked like one in a profound and tranquil sleep.

They laid the broken lid on the bed, and placed the two coffins side by side on the floor as close together as possible. Sawkins stood at one side holding the candle. Crass, at the foot, took hold of the body by the ankles, Hunter at the other end seized it by the shoulders with his huge claw-like hands, which resembled the talons of some obscene bird of prey, and they lifted it out and placed it in the other coffin.

Whilst Hunter, hovering ghoulishly over the corpse, arranged the grave cl

After a brief consultation they resolved that it would be safer to take the corpse on the handcart to the yard and keep it in the carpenter's shop until the funeral, which could take place from there. Crass and Sawkins accordingly lifted the coffin off the trestles, and, while Hunter held the light, proceeded to carry it downstairs, a task of considerable difficulty owing to the narrowness of the staircase and the landing. However, they succeeded at last and placing it on the handcart, covered it over with the black wrapper.

Hunter wished them 'good-night' at the corner of the street, saying he would make the arrangements for the funeral as soon as possible the next morning, and would come to the job and let them know what time they would have to be in attendance to act as bearers. He had gone a little distance when he stopped and turned back to them.

'It's not necessary for either of you to make a song about this business, you know,' he said.

The two men said that they quite understood that: he could depend on their keeping their mouths shut.

When Hunter had gone Crass drew out his watch. It was a quarter to eleven. A little way down the road the lights of a public house were gleaming through the mist.

'We shall be just in time to get a drink before closing time, if we buck up,' he said, and with this object they hurried on as fast as they could.

When they reached the tavern they left the cart standing by the kerb, and went inside, where Crass ordered two pints of four ale, which he permitted Sawkins to pay for.

'How are we going on about this job?' enquired the latter after they had each taken a long drink, for they were thirsty after their exertions; 'I reckon we ought to 'ave more than a bob for it, don't you? It's not like a ordinary "lift in."'

'Of course it ain't,' replied Crass. 'We ought to 'ave about, say'—reflecting—'say 'arf a dollar each at the very least.'

''Ow are we goin' on about chargin' it on our time sheets?' asked Sawkins, after a pause. 'If we just put a "lift in" they might only pay us a bob as usual.'

Crass smoked reflectively.

'I think the best way will be to put it like this,' he said at length: '"Philpot's funeral: one lift out and one lift in. Also taking corpse to carpenter's shop." 'Ow would that do?'

Sawkins said that would be a very good way to put it, and they finished their beer just as the landlord intimated that it was closing time. The cart was standing where they left it, the black cloth saturated with the rain, which dripped mournfully from its sable folds.

When they reached the plot of waste ground over which they had to pass in order to reach the gates of the yard, they had to proceed cautiously, for it was very dark and the lantern did not give much light. A number of carts and lorries were standing there, and the path wound through pools of water and heaps of refuse. After much difficulty and jolting, they reached the gate, which Crass unlocked with the key he had obtained from the office earlier in the evening. They then opened the door of the carpenter's shop and, after lighting the gas, brought in the coffin and placed it upon the trestles, and then locked the door behind them.

The next morning was a very busy one for Hunter, who had to see several new jobs started. They were all small affairs; most of them would only take two or three days from start to finish. Attending to this work occupied most of his morning, but all the same he managed to do the necessary business connected with the funeral, which he arranged to take place at two o'clock on Wednesday afternoon, from the mortuary, where the coffin had been removed during the day, Hunter concluding that it would not look well to let the funeral start from the workshop.

Although he had kept it as quiet as possible there was a small crowd of Philpot's old mates who happened to be out of work waiting outside the mortuary to see the funeral start, and amongst them were Bill Bates and the Semi-Drunk, who were both quite sober. Owen and Harlow were also there, having left off work early in order to go to the funeral. They were there too in a sense as the representatives of the other workmen, for Owen carried a large wreath which had been subscribed for voluntarily by Rushton's men.

Promptly at two o'clock the hearse and mourning coach drove up with Hunter, Crass, Slyme, Payne and Sawkins, the four bearers, all dressed in black with frock coats and silk hats. Although they were nominally attired in the same way, there was a remarkable dissimilarity in their appearance. Crass's coat was of smooth, intensely black cloth, having been recently dyed, and the crown of his hat was rather low, and curved outwards towards the top. Hunter's coat was a kind of rusty black serge, and his hat was very tall and straight, slightly narrower at the crown than at the brim. As for the others, each of them had a hat of a different fashion and date, and their clothes were rather rustier than Hunter's.

When the coffin was brought out and placed in the hearse, Hunter laid upon it the men's wreath, together with another he had brought himself, inscribed 'From Rushton and Company, with deep sympathy.'

Seeing that Harlow and Owen were the only occupants of the carriage, Bill Bates and the Semi-Drunk came up to the door and asked if there was any objection to their coming, and as neither Owen nor Harlow objected, they got in.

Meanwhile, Hunter had taken his position a few yards in front of the hearse, with the bearers two on each side. As the procession turned into the main road, they saw Snatchum standing at the corner looking very gloomy. Hunter kept his eyes fixed straight ahead, but Crass could not resist indulging in a jeering smile, which so enraged Snatchum, that he shouted out:

'It don't matter! I shan't lose much. I can use it for someone else!'

The distance to the cemetery was about three miles, so as soon as they got out of the busy streets of the town, Hunter got up on the hearse beside the driver, Crass sat on the other side, and two of the other bearers stood in the space behind the driver's seat, the fourth getting up beside the driver of the coach; and then they proceeded at a rapid pace.

About fifty yards from the cemetery gate, Hunter and the bearers resumed their former positions, and they passed up to the chapel at walking pace.

After a wait of about ten minutes the clergyman entered, and at once began to recite the usual office in a wholly unintelligible gabble.

If it had not been for the fact that each of his hearers had a copy of the words, for there was a little book in each pew, none of them would have been able to gather the sense of what the man was saying. His attitude and manner hardly suggested that he was addressing the Supreme Being. While he recited, intoned, or gabbled the words of the office, he was reading the certificate and some other paper the clerk had placed upon the desk, and when he had finished reading these, his gaze wandered abstractedly round the chapel resting for a long time with an expression of curiosity upon Bill Bates and the Semi-Drunk, who were doing their best to follow the service in their books. He next turned his attention to his fingers, holding his hand away from him nearly at arm's length and critically examining the nails.

From time to time as this miserable mockery proceeded the clerk in the rusty black cassock mechanically droned out a sonorous 'Ah-men,' and after the conclusion of the lesson the clergyman went out of the church, taking a short cut through the gravestones and monuments, while the bearers again shouldered the coffin and followed the clerk to the grave. When they arrived within a few yards of their destination they were rejoined by the clergyman, who was waiting for them at the corner of one of the paths. He put himself at the head of the procession with an open book in his hand, and as they walked slowly along, he resumed his reading or repetition of the words of the service.

He wore an old black cassock and a much soiled and slightly torn surplice. The unseemly appearance of this dirty garment was heightened by the fact that as he had not taken the trouble to adjust it properly, it hung all lop-sided, showing about six inches more of the black cassock at one side than the other.

He continued his unintelligible jargon while they were lowering the coffin into the grave, and those who happened to know the words of the office by heart were, with some difficulty, able to understand what he was saying:

'Forasmuch as it hath pleased Almighty God of His great mercy to take unto Himself the soul of our dear brother here departed, we therefore commit his body to the ground; earth to earth, ashes to ashes, dust to dust;——'

The earth fell from the clerk's hand and rattled on the lid of the coffin with a mournful sound, and when the clergyman had finished repeating the remainder of the service, he turned and walked away in the direction of the church. Hunter and the rest of the funeral party made their way back towards the gate of the cemetery, where the hearse and the carriage were waiting.

On their way they saw another funeral procession coming towards them. It was a very plain looking closed hearse with only one horse. There was no undertaker in front and no bearers walked by the sides.

It was a pauper's funeral.

Three men, evidently dressed in their Sunday clothes, followed the hearse. As they reached the church door, four old men who were dressed in ordinary everyday clothes, came forward and carried the coffin into the church, followed by the other three, who were evidently relatives of the deceased. The four old men were paupers, inmates of the workhouse, who were paid sixpence each for acting as bearers.

It happened that just as they were taking out the coffin from the hearse Hunter's party passed by, and paused for a moment to watch.

The roughly made coffin was of white deal, not painted or covered in any way, and devoid of any fittings or ornament with the exception of a square piece of zinc tacked on the lid, upon which was roughly painted in black letters:

J.	L.
AGED	67.

It was Jack Linden's funeral, and his bearers were all retired working men who had come into their 'titles,' one of them being old Latham, the venetian blind maker.

CHAPTER XXXIV

The Wise Men of the East

About the middle of October an event happened which threw the town into such a state of wild excitement, that the comparatively unimportant matters of unemployment and distress were almost forgotten.

Sir Graball D'Encloseland had been chosen for an even higher post in the service of his country, and his promotion made it necessary for him to resign his seat and seek re-election. The ragged trousered Tory workmen, as they loitered about the streets with empty stomachs, said to each other that it was a great honour for Mugsborough that their member should be promoted in this way. They boasted about it, and assumed as much swagger in their gait as their broken boots permitted. They stuck election cards bearing Sir Graball's photograph in their windows, and tied bits of blue and yellow ribbon, Sir Graball's colours, on their under-fed children.

The Liberals were furious. They said that an election had been sprung upon them; they had been taken a mean advantage of; they had no candidate ready. It wasn't fair either, because while they, the leading Liberals, had been treating the electors with contemptuous indifference, for months past Sir Graball D'Encloseland had been most active amongst his constituents, cunningly preparing for the contest. He had really been electioneering for the past six months. Last winter he had kicked off at quite a number of football matches, besides doing all sorts of things for the local teams. He had joined the Buffaloes and the Druids, been elected president of the Skull and Crossbones Boys Society, and, although he was not himself an abstainer, he was so friendly to Temperance that he had on several occasions taken the chair at teetotal meetings, to say nothing of the teas to the poor school children and things of that sort. In short, he had been quite an active politician in the Tory sense of the word for months past, and the poor Liberals had not smelt a rat until the election was sprung upon them.

A hurried meeting of the Liberal Three Hundred was held, and a deputation sent to London to find a candidate, but as there was only a week before polling day they were unsuccessful in their mission. Another meeting was held, presided over by Mr Adam Sweater, Rushton and Didlum also being present.

Profound dejection prevailed as the meeting listened to the delegates' report. The sombre silence that followed was broken at length by Mr Rushton, who suddenly started up and said that he began to think they had made a mistake in going outside the constituency at all to look for a man. Precious time had been wasted running about all over the country, begging and praying for a candidate, and overlooking the fact that they had in their midst a gentleman, a fellow townsman, who, he believed, would have a better chance of success than any stranger. Surely they would all agree, if they could only prevail upon him to stand, that Adam Sweater would be an ideal Liberal Candidate!

While Mr Rushton was speaking the drooping spirits of the Three Hundred were reviving, and at the name of Sweater they all began to clap their hands and stamp their feet. Loud shouts of enthusiastic approval burst forth, and cries of 'Good old Sweater' resounded through the room.

When Sweater rose to reply, the tumult died away as suddenly as it had commenced. He thanked them for the honour they were conferring upon him. There was no time to waste in words or idle compliments; rather than allow the enemy to have a walk over, he would accede to their request and contest the seat.

A roar of applause burst from the throats of the delighted Three Hundred.

Outside the hall in which the meeting was being held, a large crowd of poverty-stricken Liberal working men was waiting to hear the report of the deputation, and as soon as Sweater had consented to be nominated, Didlum rushed and opened the window overlooking the street and shouted the good news down to the crowd, which joined in the cheering. In response to their demands for a speech, Sweater came to the window and said a few words, reminding them of the shortness of the time at their disposal, and intreating them to work hard in order that the Grand Old Flag might be carried to victory.

At such times these people forgot all about unemployment and starvation in their enthusiasm about 'Grand Old Flags'. Their devotion to this flag was so great that the fact that they had carried it to victory so often in the past without obtaining any of the spoils did not seem to damp their ardour in the least. Being philanthropists, they were content, after winning the victory, to let their masters do the looting.

At the conclusion of Sweater's remarks the philanthropists gave three frantic cheers, and then someone in the crowd shouted: 'What's the colour?' After a hasty consultation with Rushton, who being a 'master' decorator was thought to be an authority on colours, green, grass-green was decided upon, and the information was shouted down to the crowd, who cheered again. Then a rush was made to Sweater's Emporium, and several yards of cheap green ribbon were bought and divided up into little pieces, which they tied into their button-holes, and thus appropriately decorated, they formed themselves into military order, four deep, and marched through all the principal streets, up and down the Grand Parade, round and round the Fountain, and finally over the hill to Windley, singing, to the tune of 'Tramp, tramp, tramp, the Boys are marching':

'Vote, Vote, Vote for Adam Sweater!
Hang old Closeland on a tree!
Adam Sweater is our man,
And we'll have him if we can,
Then we'll always have the biggest loaf for tea.'

The spectacle presented by these men, some of them with grey heads and beards, as they marked time or tramped along singing this childish twaddle, might have been amusing if it had been less pathetic.

By way of variety they sang several other things, including:

'We'll hang ole Closeland
On a sour apple tree.'

and:

'Rally, Rally, men of Windley,
For Sweater's sure to win.'

The town was soon deluged with mendacious literature, and smothered with huge posters:

'VOTE FOR ADAM SWEATER!
THE WORKING-MAN'S FRIEND!'

'VOTE FOR SWEATER AND TEMPERANCE REFORM.'

'VOTE FOR SWEATER—FREE TRADE AND CHEAP FOOD,'

or

'VOTE FOR D'ENCLOSELAND: TARIFF REFORM AND PLENTY OF WORK!'

This beautiful ideal—Plenty of Work—appealed strongly to the Tory workmen. All they desired for themselves and their children was 'Plenty of Work.' They marched about the streets singing their Marseillaise: 'Work, Boys, Work and be contented,' to the tune of 'Tramp, tramp, tramp the Boys are marching'; and at intervals as they tramped along they gave three cheers for Sir Graball, Tariff Reform, and Plenty of Work!

Both sides imported gangs of hired orators, who held forth every night at the corners of the principal streets and on the open spaces from portable platforms, motor cars and lorries. The Tories said that the Liberal Party in the House of Commons was composed principally of scoundrels and fools; the Liberals said the Tory Party were fools and scoundrels. A host of richly dressed canvassers descended upon Windley in carriages and motor cars, and begged for votes from the poverty-stricken working men who lived there.

One evening a Liberal demonstration was held at the cross roads on Windley hill. Notwithstanding the cold weather there was a great crowd of shabbily dressed people, many of whom had not had a really good meal for months. It was a clear night. The moon was at the full, and the scene was further illuminated by the fitful glare of several torches, stuck on the end of twelve-foot poles. The platform was a large lorry, and there were several speakers, including Adam Sweater himself and a real live Liberal Peer, Lord Ammenegg. This individual had made a considerable fortune in the grocery and provision line, and had been elevated to the peerage by the last Liberal Government on account of his services to the party.

Both Sweater and Ammenegg were to speak at two other meetings that night and were not expected at Windley until about eight-thirty, so to keep the ball rolling several other gentlemen, including Rushton, who presided, and Didlum and one of the five-pounds-a-week orators, addressed the meeting. Mingled with the crowd were about twenty rough-looking men, strangers to the town, who wore huge green rosettes and loudly applauded the speakers. They also distributed Sweater literature and cards with lists of the different meetings that were to be held during the election. These men were bullies hired by Sweater's agent. They came from the neighbourhood of Seven Dials, in London, and were paid ten shillings a day. One of their duties was to incite the crowd to bash anyone who disturbed the meetings or tried to put awkward questions to the speakers.

The hired orator was a tall slight man with dark hair, beard and moustache. He might have been called good-looking if it had not been for an ugly scar upon his forehead, which gave him a rather sinister appearance. He was an effective speaker. The audience punctuated his speech with cheers, and when he wound up with an earnest appeal to them, as working men, to vote for Adam Sweater, their enthusiasm knew no bounds.

'I've seen him somewhere before,' remarked Owen, who was standing in the crowd with Harlow and Easton.

'So have I,' said Harlow, with a puzzled expression, 'but I can't remember where.'

Easton also thought he had seen the man before, but their speculations were put an end to by the roar of cheering that heralded the arrival of the motor car containing Adam Sweater and his friend, Lord Ammenegg. Unfortunately those who had arranged the meeting had forgotten to provide a pair of steps, so Sweater found it a matter of considerable difficulty to mount the platform. However, while his friends were hoisting and pushing him up, the meeting beguiled the time by singing:

'Vote, vote, vote for Adam Sweater.'

When he was in the cart at last, and while he was recovering his wind, Rushton made a few remarks to the crowd. Sweater then advanced to the front, but in consequence of the cheering and singing he was unable to make himself heard for several minutes. When at length silence was restored, he made a very clever speech, specially written for him at a cost of ten guineas. A large part of it consisted of warnings against the dangers of Socialism. Sweater had carefully rehearsed this speech and he delivered it very effectively. Some of those Socialists, he said, were well-meaning but mistaken people, who did not realise the harm that would result if their extraordinary ideas were ever put into practice. He lowered his voice to a bloodcurdling stage whisper as he asked:

'What is this Socialism that we hear so much about, but which so few understand? What is it, and what does it mean?'

Then, raising his voice till it rang through the air and fell upon the ears of the assembled multitude like the clanging of a funeral bell, he continued:

'It is Madness! Chaos! Anarchy! It means Ruin! Black Ruin for the rich, and consequently, of course, Blacker Ruin still for the poor!'

As Sweater paused, a thrill of horror ran through the meeting. Men wearing broken boots and with patches upon the seats and knees, and ragged fringes round the bottoms of the legs, of their trousers, grew pale and glanced apprehensively at each other. If ever Socialism did come to pass they evidently thought it very probable, that they would have to go without any trousers or boots at all.

Toil-worn women, most of them dressed in other women's shabby cast-off clothing, weary, tired-looking mothers who fed their children for the most part on adulterated tea, tinned skimmed milk, bread and margarine, grew furious as they thought of the wicked Socialists who were trying to bring Ruin upon them.

The awful silence that had fallen on the panic-stricken crowd was presently broken by a ragged trousered philanthropist, who shouted out:

'We knows wot they are, sir. Most of 'em is chaps wot's got tired of workin' for their livin', so they wants us to keep 'em.'

Encouraged by numerous expressions of approval from the other philanthropists, the man continued:

'But we ain't such fools as they thinks, and so they'll find out next Monday. Most of 'em wants 'anging, and I wouldn't mind lendin' a 'and with the rope myself.'

Applause and laughter greeted these noble sentiments, and Sweater resumed his address, when another man, evidently a Socialist for he was accompanied by three or four others who like himself wore red ties, interrupted and said that he would like to ask him a question. No notice was taken of this request either by Mr Sweater or the chairman, but a few angry cries of 'Order!' came from the crowd. Sweater continued, but the man again interrupted, and the cries of the crowd became more threatening. Rushton started up and said that he could not allow the speaker to be interrupted, but if the gentleman would wait till the end of the meeting he would have an opportunity of asking his question then.

The man said he would wait as desired. Sweater resumed his oration, and presently the interrupter and his friends found themselves surrounded by the gang of hired bullies, who wore the big rosettes and who glared menacingly at them.

Sweater concluded his speech with an appeal to the crowd to deal a 'Slashing Blow at the Enemy' next Monday, and then, amid a storm of applause,

Lord Ammenegg stepped to the front. He said that he did not intend to inflict a long speech upon them that evening, and as it was nomination day to-morrow he would not be able to have the honour of addressing them again during the election; but even if he had wished to make a long speech, it would be very difficult after the brilliant and eloquent address they had just listened to from Mr Sweater, for it seemed to him (Ammenegg) that Adam Sweater had left nothing for anyone else to say. But he would like to tell them of a thought that had occurred to him that evening. They read in the Bible that the Wise Men came from the East. Windley, as they all knew, was the East end of the town. They were the men of the East, and he was sure that next Monday they would prove that they were the Wise Men of the East by voting for Adam Sweater and putting him at the top of the poll with a 'Thumping Majority.'

The Wise Men of the East greeted Ammenegg's remarks with prolonged cheers, and amid the tumult his Lordship and Sweater got into the motor car and cleared off without giving the man with the red tie, or anyone else who desired to ask questions, any opportunity of doing so. Rushton and the other leaders got into another motor car and followed, to take part in another meeting down town.

The crowd now resolved itself into military order, headed by the men with torches and a large white banner on which was written in hugh black letters: 'Our man is Adam Sweater.' They marched down the hill singing, and when they reached the Fountain on the Grand Parade they saw another crowd holding a meeting there. These were Tories, and they became so infuriated at the sound of the Liberal songs and by the sight of the banner that they abandoned their meeting and charged the processionists. Both sides fought like savages, but as the Liberals were outnumbered by about three to one they were driven off the field with great slaughter; most of the torch poles were taken from them, and the banner was torn to ribbons. Then the Tories went back to the Fountain carrying the captured torches, and singing to the tune of 'Has anyone seen a German Band':

'Has anyone seen a Lib'ral Flag,
Lib'ral Flag, Lib'ral Flag.'

While the Tories resumed their meeting at the Fountain, the Liberals rallied in one of the back streets. Messengers were sent in various directions for reinforcements, and about half an hour afterwards they emerged from their retreat and swooped down upon the Tory meeting. They overturned the platform, recaptured their torches, tore the enemy's banner to tatters and drove them from their position. Then the Liberals in their turn paraded the streets singing: 'Has anyone seen a Tory Flag.'

The following evening Owen and a few others of the same way of thinking, who had subscribed enough money between them to purchase a lot of Socialist leaflets, employed themselves distributing them to the crowds at the Liberal and Tory meetings, and whilst they were doing this they frequently became involved in arguments with the supporters of the capitalist system. In their attempts to persuade others to refrain from voting for either of the candidates, they were opposed even by some who professed to believe in Socialism, who said that as there was no Socialist candidate the thing to do was to vote for the better of the two. This was the view of Harlow and Easton, whom they met. Harlow had a green ribbon in his buttonhole, but Easton wore D'Encloseland's colours.

One man said that if he had his way all those who had votes should be compelled to record them, whether they liked it or not, or be disfranchised! Owen asked him if he believed in Tariff Reform. The man said no.

'Why not?' demanded Owen.

The other replied that he opposed Tariff Reform because he believed it would ruin the country. Owen inquired if he were a supporter of Socialism. The man said he was not; and when further questioned he said that he believed if it were ever adopted it would bring black ruin upon the country. He believed this because Mr Sweater had said so. When Owen asked him, supposing there were only two candidates, one a Socialist and the other a Tariff Reformer, how he would like to be compelled to vote for one of them, he was at a loss for an answer.

At considerable danger to themselves, Owen and the other Socialists continued to distribute their leaflets and to heckle the Liberal and Tory speakers. They asked the Tories to explain the prevalence of unemployment and poverty in protected countries like Germany and America; and at Sweater's meetings they requested to be informed what was the Liberal remedy for unemployment. From both parties the Socialists obtained the same kinds of answers: threats of violence and requests 'not to disturb the meeting.'

These Socialists held quite a lot of informal meetings of their own. Every now and then when they were giving their leaflets away some unwary supporter of the capitalist system would start an argument, and soon a crowd would gather round and listen.

Sometimes the Socialists succeeded in arguing their opponents to an absolute standstill, for the Liberals and Tories found it impossible to deny that machinery is the cause of the overcrowded state of the labour market; that the overcrowded labour market is the cause of unemployment; and that the fact of there being always an army of unemployed waiting to take other men's jobs away from them destroys the independence of those who are in employment, and keeps them in subjection to their masters. They found it impossible to deny that this machinery is being used, not for the benefit of all, but to make fortunes for a few. In short, they were unable to disprove that the monopoly of the land and machinery by comparatively few persons is the cause of the poverty of the majority. But when they were faced with unanswerable arguments they would begin to shout and bluster about some utterly unimportant side issue; and in the angry wrangle that ensued the original subject would be overlooked.

Usually after one of these arguments Owen would wander off by himself, with his head throbbing and a feeling of unutterable depression and misery at his heart, weighed down by a growing conviction of the hopelessness of everything, of the folly of expecting that his fellow workmen would ever be willing to try to understand for themselves the causes that produced their sufferings. They did not want to know, they did not want to understand; it seemed as if they feared rather than welcomed the prospect of deliverance, and scorned and hated their would-be deliverers.

One night about nine o'clock Owen was in a large Liberal crowd, listening to the same hired orator who had spoken a few evenings before on the hill, the man with the scar on his forehead. The crowd was applauding him loudly and Owen again fell to wondering where he had seen this man before, and presently he remembered that this was one of the Socialists who had come with the band of cyclists into the town that Sunday morning, at the beginning of the summer—the man who had come afterwards with the van, and who had been struck down by a stone while attempting to speak from the platform. Though the Socialist had been clean shaven, and this man wore beard and moustache, Owen was certain that it was he.

At the conclusion of his speech the hired orator got down and stood in the shade behind the platform, while someone else addressed the meeting, and Owen went round to where he was standing, intending to speak to him.

All around them, pandemonium reigned supreme. They were in the vicinity of the Fountain on the Grand Parade, where several roads met. There was a meeting going on at every corner, and a number of others in different parts of the roadway and on the pavement of the parade.

Every now and then some of these poor wretches—they were all paid speakers—were surrounded and savagely mauled and beaten by a hostile crowd. If they were Tariff Reformers the Liberals mobbed them; and *vice versa*. Lines of rowdies swaggered to and fro, arm in arm, singing 'Vote, Vote, Vote, for good ole Closeland,' or 'good ole Sweater,' according to their colours. Gangs of hooligans paraded up and down, armed with sticks, singing, howling, cursing and looking for somebody to hit.

The walls were covered with huge Liberal and Tory posters which showed in every line the contempt of those who published them for the intelligence of the working men to whom they were addressed.

When Owen got round to the back of the platform, he found the man with the scarred face standing alone, gloomily silent, in the shadow. Owen gave him one of the Socialist leaflets, which he took, and after glancing at it, put it in his coat pocket without making any remark.

'I hope you'll excuse me for asking, but were you not formerly a Socialist?' said Owen.

Even in the semi-darkness he saw the other man flush deeply and then become very pale, while the unsightly scar upon his forehead showed with ghastly distinctness.

'I am still a Socialist,' he replied. 'No man who has once been a Socialist can ever cease to be one.'

'You seem to have accomplished that impossibility, to judge by the work you are doing at present,' remarked Owen.

'No one who has once been a Socialist can ever cease to be one,' repeated the other. 'It is impossible for a man who has once acquired knowledge to relinquish it. A Socialist is one who understands the causes of the misery and degradation around us; who not only knows the remedy, but knows that that remedy must eventually be adopted; but it does not follow that everyone who has sense enough to acquire that amount of knowledge, must, in addition, be willing to sacrifice himself in order to help to bring that state of society into being. When I first acquired that knowledge,' he continued, bitterly, 'I was eager to tell the good news to others. I sacrificed my time, my money and my health, in order that I might teach others what I had learned myself. I did it willingly and happily, because I thought they would be glad to hear, and that they were worth the sacrifices I made for their sakes. Now I know better.'

'Even if you no longer believe in working for Socialism, there's no need to work *against* it,' said Owen. 'If you don't want to help to bring about a better state of affairs, there's no reason why you should help to perpetuate the present system.'

The other man laughed bitterly. 'Oh, yes there is, and a very good reason too.'

'I don't think you could show me a good reason,' said Owen.

The man with the scar laughed again, the same unpleasant, mirthless laugh, and thrusting his hand into his trouser pocket drew it out again full of silver coins, amongst which one or two gold pieces glittered.

'That is my reason. When I devoted my life and what abilities I possess to the service of my fellow workmen, when I sought to teach them how to break their chains, when I tried to show them how they might save their children from poverty and shameful servitude, I did not want them to give me money. I did it for love. And they paid me with hatred and injury. But since I have been helping their masters to rob them, they have treated me with respect.'

Owen made no reply and the other man, having returned the money to his pocket, indicated the crowd with a sweep of his hand.

'Look at them!' he continued with a contemptuous laugh. 'Look at them, the people you are trying to make idealists of! Look at them! Some of them howling and roaring like wild beasts, or laughing like idiots; others standing with dull and stupid faces devoid of any trace of intelligence or expression, listening to the speakers whose words convey no meaning to their stultified minds; and others with their eyes gleaming with savage hatred of their fellow men, watching eagerly for an opportunity to provoke a quarrel that they may gratify their brutal natures by striking someone—their eyes are hungry for the sight of blood! Can't you see that these people, whom you are trying to make understand your plan for the regeneration of the world, your doctrine of universal brotherhood and love, are for the most part, intellectually, on a level with

Hottentots? The only things they feel any real interest in are beer, football, betting and, of course, one other subject—their highest ambition is to be allowed to Work. And they desire nothing better for their children! These are the people who you hope to inspire with lofty ideals! You might just as well try to make a gold brooch out of a lump of dung! Try to reason with them, to uplift them, to teach them the way to higher things, devote your whole life and intelligence to the work of trying to get better conditions for them, and you will find that they themselves are the enemy you will have to fight against. They'll hate you, and, if they get the chance, they'll tear you to pieces. But if you're a sensible man you'll use whatever talents and intelligence you possess for your own benefit. Don't think about Socialism or any other "ism." Concentrate your mind on getting money, it doesn't matter how you get it. If you can't get it honestly, get it dishonestly; but get it! It is the only thing that counts. Do as I do—rob them, exploit them, and then they'll have some respect for you!'

'There's something in what you say,' replied Owen after a long pause, 'but it's not all. Circumstances make us what we are. And anyhow the children are worth fighting for.'

'You may think so now,' said the other, 'but you'll come to see it my way some day. As for the children, if their parents are satisfied to let them grow up to be half-starved drudges for other people, I don't see why you or I need trouble about it. If you like to listen to reason,' he continued after a pause, 'I can put you on to something that will be worth more to you than all your Socialism.'

'What do you mean?'

'Look here: you're a Socialist. Well, I'm a Socialist too: that is, I have sense enough to believe that Socialism is practical and inevitable and right. It will come when the majority of the people are sufficiently enlightened to demand it, but that enlightenment will never be brought about by reasoning or arguing with them, for these people are simply not intellectually capable of abstract reasoning; they can't grasp theories. You know what the late Lord Salisbury said about them when somebody proposed to give them some free libraries. He said: "They don't want libraries: give them a circus." You see these Liberals and Tories understand the sort of people they have to deal with; they know that although their bodies are the bodies of grown men, their minds are the minds of little children. That is why it has been possible to deceive and bluff and rob them for so long. But your party persists in regarding them as rational beings, and that's where you make a mistake; you're simply wasting your time.

'The only way in which it is possible to teach these people is by means of object lessons, and those are being placed before them in increasing numbers every day.

'The trustification of industry, the object lesson which demonstrates the possibility of collective ownership, will in time compel even these to understand, and by the time they have learnt that they will also have learned, by bitter experience and not from theoretical teaching, that they must either own the trusts or perish; and then, and not till then, they will achieve Socialism. But meanwhile we have this election. Do you think it will make any real difference, for good or evil, which of these two men is elected?'

'No,' replied Owen.

'Well, you can't keep them both out, you have no candidate of your own, why should you object to earning a few pounds by helping one of them to get in? There are plenty of voters who are doubtful what to do. As you and I know, there is every excuse for them being unable to make up their minds which of these two candidates is the worse. A word from your party would decide them. Since you have no candidate of your own you will be doing no harm to Socialism, and you will be doing yourself a bit of good. If you like to come along with me now, I'll introduce you to Sweater's agent, no one need know anything about it.'

He slipped his arm through Owen's but the latter released himself.

'Please yourself,' said the other with an affectation of indifference; 'you know your own business best. You may choose to be a Jesus Christ if you like, but for my part I'm finished. For the future I intend to look after myself. As for these people, they vote for what they want; they get what they vote for, and, by God, they deserve nothing better! They are being beaten with whips of their own choosing, and if I had my way they should be beaten with scorpions! For them, the present system means joyless drudgery, semi-starvation, rags and premature death. They vote for it all and uphold it. Well, let them have what they vote for, let them drudge, let them starve!'

The man with the scarred face ceased speaking, and for some moments Owen did not reply.

'I suppose there is some excuse for your feeling as you do, he said slowly at last, 'but it seems to me that you do not make enough allowance for the circumstances. From their infancy most of them have been taught to regard themselves and their own class with contempt, as inferior animals, and to regard those who possess wealth with veneration, as superior beings. The idea that they are really human creatures, naturally absolutely the same as their so-called betters, is an idea they have been taught to regard as preposterous. Your resentment should be directed against the deceivers, not the dupes.'

The other man laughed bitterly.

'Well, go and try to undeceive them,' he said, as he returned to the platform in response to a call from one of his associates; 'go and try to teach them that the Supreme Being made the earth and all its fulness for the use and benefit of all His children. Go and try to explain to them that they are poor in body and mind and social condition, not because of any natural inferiority, but because they have been robbed of their inheritance. Go and try to show them how to secure that inheritance for themselves and their children—and see how grateful they'll be to you.'

For the next hour Owen walked about the crowded streets in a dispirited fashion. His conversation with the renegade seemed to have taken all the heart out of him. He still had a number of the leaflets, but the task of distributing them had suddenly grown distasteful, and after a while he discontinued it. All his enthusiasm was gone. Like one awakened from a dream he saw the people who surrounded him in a different light. For the first time he properly appreciated the offensiveness of most of those to whom he offered the handbills: some, without even troubling to ascertain what they were about, rudely refused to accept them; some took them and after glancing at the printing threw them away, or rejected them with contempt or abuse.

Monday was polling day and the result was to be shown on an illuminated sign at the Town Hall at eleven o'clock at night. Long before that hour a vast crowd gathered in the adjacent streets, and, in spite of the rain, increased in numbers as the time went by. At a quarter to eleven the shower changed to a terrible downpour, but the people remained waiting to know which flag had been carried to victory. Eleven o'clock came and an intense silence fell upon the crowd, whose eyes were fixed eagerly upon the window where the sign was to be exhibited. To judge by the extraordinary interest manifested on all sides one might have thought the saturated multitude was waiting to hear of some great personal benefit, instead of being perfectly aware that this election would make no more difference to them than former ones had done. At a quarter past eleven the sign was illuminated but the figures were not yet shown. Next the names of the two candidates slid into sight. The figures were still missing but D'Encolseland's name was on top, and a hoarse roar of triumph came from the throats of his admirers. Then the two slides with the names were withdrawn, and the sign was again left blank. After a time the people grew unable to restrain their frantic impatience, and some of them began to groan and hoot.

After a few minutes the names again slid into view, this time with Sweater's name on top, and the figures appeared immediately afterwards.

SWEATER.........................4221
D'ENCLOSELAND.............4200

It was several seconds before the Liberals could believe their eyes: it was too good to be true. It is impossible to say what actually inspired the wild outburst of frenzied enthusiasm that followed, but, whatever the reason, they were all cheering and dancing and shaking hands with each other, and some of them were so overcome with joy and emotion that they were literally unable to speak.

A few minutes after the declaration Sweater appeared at the window and made a sort of a speech, but only fragments of it were audible to the yelling crowd who at intervals caught such phrases as 'Slashing Blow,' 'Sweep the country,' 'Grand old Liberal Flag,' and so on. Next D'Encloseland appeared, and he was seen to shake hands with Mr Sweater, whom he referred to as 'My friend'.

When the two 'friends' disappeared from the window, the part of the Liberal crowd that was not engaged in hand to hand fights with their enemies the Tories made a rush to the front entrance of the Town Hall where Sweater's carriage was waiting, and as soon as he had placed his plump rotundity inside they unharnessed the horses and, amid frantic cheers, dragged it through the mud and pouring rain all the way to 'The Cave'; but as most of them were accustomed to acting as beasts of burden the experience brought no novelty with it.

Then, having successfully carried the 'grand old flag to victory,' the electors, drenched, exhausted and covered with mud from head to foot, toiled back to their wretched homes.

CHAPTER XXXV

The Widow's Son

While painting the conservatory in Sweater's house in bitterly cold weather Owen caught such a severe chill that he was obliged to take his overcoat out of pawn. Although he had been luckier than most of his mates in getting odd jobs at Rushton's, he had never been able to save any money. All through the summer most of his wages had gone to pay off arrears of rent and other debts, and now that the winter was upon them and work was very scarce his Saturday pay amounted to half a sovereign, seven-and-six, five shillings, or even less.

One morning he did not get to the yard till ten o'clock and felt so ill that he would not have gone at all if they had not been in sore need of all the money he could earn. The least exertion brought on a violent fit of coughing, and it was only by an almost superhuman effort of will that he managed to get through his work. When he arrived at the yard he found Bert White cleaning out the dirty pots in the paint shop. The noise he made with the scraping knife prevented him hearing Owen's approach, and the latter stood watching him for some minutes without speaking. The stone floor of the paint shop was damp and slimy and the whole place as chilly as a tomb. The boy was trembling with cold, and he looked pitifully undersized and frail as he bent over his work with an old apron girt about him. Although it was so cold he had turned back the sleeves of his jacket to keep them clean, or to prevent them getting any dirtier, for like the rest of his attire they were thickly encrusted with dried paint of many colours.

He was wearing a man's coat and a pair of skimpy, boy's trousers, and his thin legs appearing under the big jacket gave him a grotesque appearance. There were smears of paint on his face, and his hands and finger nails were grimed with it. But most pitiful of all were his dreadful hob-nailed boots, the uppers of which were an eighth of an inch thick and very stiff. Across the front of the boot the leather had warped into ridges and valleys which chafed his chilblained feet and made them bleed. The soles were five-eigths of an inch thick, hard and inflexible, and almost as heavy as iron, and studded with hob nails.

As he watched the poor boy bending over his task Owen thought of Frankie, and with a feeling akin to terror wondered whether he would ever be in a similar plight.

When Bert saw Owen he left off working and wished him good morning, remarking that it was very cold.

'Why don't you light a fire? There's lots of wood lying about the yard,' said Owen.

'No,' replied Bert, shaking his head. 'That would never do! Misery wouldn't 'arf ramp if 'e caught me at it. I used to 'ave a fire 'ere last winter till Rushton found out, and 'e kicked up an orful row and told me to move meself and get some work done and then I wouldn't feel the cold.'

'Oh, he said that, did he?' said Owen, his pale face becoming suddenly suffused with blood. 'We'll see about that.'

He went out into the yard and crossing over to where, under a shed, there was a great heap of waste wood, stuff that had been taken out of places where Rushton and Company had made alterations, he gathered an armful of it and was returning to the paintshop when Sawkins, who was clearing the place up, accosted him.

'You musn't go burnin' any of that, you know! That's all got to be saved and took up to the bloke's house. Misery spoke about it only this mornin'.'

Owen did not answer. He carried the wood into the shop and after throwing it into the fireplace he poured some old paint over it, and applying a match produced a roaring fire. Then he brought in several more armfuls of wood and piled them in a corner of the shop. Bert took no part in these proceedings, and at first rather disapproved of them because he was afraid there would be trouble when Misery came, but when the fire was an accomplished fact he warmed his hands and shifted his work to the other side of the bench so as to get the benefit of the heat.

Owen waited for about half-an-hour to see if Hunter would return, but as he did not appear, he decided not to wait any longer. Before leaving he gave Bert some instructions:

'Keep up the fire with all the old paint that you can scrape off those things and any other old paint or rubbish that's here, and whenever it grows dull put more wood on. There's a lot of stuff here that's of no use except to be thrown away or burnt. Burn it all. If Hunter says anything, tell him that I lit the fire, and that I told you to keep it burning. If you want more wood, go out and take it.'

'All right,' replied Bert.

On his way out Owen spoke to Sawkins. His manner was so menacing, his face so pale, and there was such a strange glare in his eyes, that the latter thought of the talk there had often been about Owen being mad, and felt half afraid of him.

'I am going to the office to see Rushton. If Hunter comes here you say I told you to tell him that if I find the boy in that shop again without a fire I'll report it to the Society for the Prevention of Cruelty to Children. And as for you, if the boy comes out here to get more wood, don't you attempt to interefere with him.'

'I don't want to interefere with the bloody kid,' grunted Sawkins. 'It seems to me as if he's gorn orf 'is bloody crumpet,' he added, as he watched Owen walking rapidly down the street. 'I can't understand why people can't mind their own business. Anyone would think the boy belonged to '*im*.'

That was just how the matter presented itself to Owen. The idea that it was his own child who was to be treated in this way possessed and infuriated him as he strode savagely along. In the vicinity of the Grand Parade he passed, without seeing them, several groups of unemployed artizans whom he knew. Some of them were offended and remarked that he was getting stuck up, but others, observing how strange he looked, repeated the old prophecy that one of these days Owen would go out of his mind.

As he drew near to his destination large flakes of snow began to fall. He walked so rapidly and was in such a fury that by the time he reached the shop he was scarcely able to speak.

'Is—Hunter—or Rushton—here?' he demanded of the shopman.

'Hunter isn't, but the guvner is. What was it you wanted?'

'He'll soon—know—that,' panted Owen as he strode up to the office door, and without troubling to knock, flung it violently open and entered.

The atmosphere of this place was very different from that of the damp cellar where Bert was working. An asbestos gas fire threw out a genial warmth, and the air was fragrant with the cigar that Rushton was smoking, as he looked through his letters.

Owen stood panting and quivering in the middle of the office and pointed a trembling finger at his employer:

'I've—come here—to tell—you—that—if I find young—Bert White—working—down in that shop—without—a fire—I'll have you—prosecuted. The place is not good enough for a stable—if you owned a valuable dog—you wouldn't keep it there—. I give you fair warning—I know—enough—about you—to put you—where you deserve to be—if you don't treat him better—I'll have you punished—I'll show you up.'

Rushton continued to stare at him in mingled confusion, fear and perplexity. He did not yet comprehend exactly what it was all about. The fact that he was guiltily conscious of having done so many things which he might be shown up or prosecuted for if they were known helped to reduce him to a condition approaching terror.

'If the boy has been there without a fire I haven't known anything about it,' he stammered at last. 'Mr 'Uunter has charge of all those matters.'

'You—yourself—forbade him—to make a fire last winter—and anyhow—you know about it *now*—. You obtained money from his mother under the pretence—that you were going to teach him a trade—but for the last twelve months—you have been using him—as if he were—a beast of burden. I advise you to see to it—or I shall—find—means—to make you—sorry.'

With this Owen turned and went out, leaving the door open and Rushton in a state of mind compounded of fear, amazement and anger.

As he walked homewards through the snow storm, Owen began to realise that Rushton would not give him any more work after this, and as he reflected on all it would mean to those at home for a moment he doubted whether he had done right. But when he told Nora what had happened she said cheerfully that there were plenty of other firms in the town who would employ him, when they had the work. He had done without Rushton before and could do so again; for her part, whatever the consequences might be, she was glad that he had acted as he did.

'We'll get through somehow, I suppose,' said Owen, wearily. 'There's not much chance of getting a job anywhere else just now, but I shall try to get some work on my own account. I shall do some samples of show cards the same as I did last winter and try to get orders from some of the shops—they usually want something extra at this time. But I'm afraid it is rather too late: most of them already have all they want.'

'I shouldn't go out again to-day if I were you,' said Nora, noticing how ill he looked, 'You should stay at home and read, or write up those minutes.'

The minutes referred to were those of the last meeting of the local branch of the Painters' Society of which Owen was the secretary, and as the snow continued to fall, he occupied himself after dinner in the manner his wife suggested, until four o'clock, when Frankie returned from school bringing with him a large snowball, and crying out as a piece of good news that the snow was still falling heavily, and that he *believed* it was freezing!

They went to bed very early that night for it was necessary to economise the coal, and because, as the rooms were so near the roof, it was not possible to keep the place warm however much coal was used. The fire seemed, if anything, to make the place colder, for it caused the outer air to pour in through the joints of the ill fitting doors and windows.

Owen lay awake for the greater part of the night. The terror of the future made rest or sleep impossible. He got up very early the next morning, long before it was light, and after lighting the fire, set about preparing the samples he had mentioned to Nora, but found that it would not be possible to do much in this direction without buying more cardboard.

They breakfasted on bread and butter and tea. Frankie had his in bed, and it was decided to keep him away from school until after dinner because the weather was so very cold and his only pair of boots were so saturated from having been out in the snow the previous day.

'I shall make a few enquiries to see if there's any other work to be had before I buy the cardboard,' said Owen, 'although I'm afraid it's not much use.'

When he was preparing to go out, the front door bell rang, and as he was going down to answer it he saw Bert White coming upstairs. The boy was carrying a flat brown paper parcel under his arm.

'A corfin plate,' he explained as he arrived at the door. 'Wanted at once—Misery ses you can do it at 'ome, an' I've got to wait for it.'

Owen and his wife looked at each other with intense relief. So he was not to be dismissed after all. It was almost too good to be true.

'There's a piece of paper inside the parcel with the name of the party what's dead,' continued Bert, 'and here's a little bottle of brunswick black for you to do the inscription with.'

'Did he send any other message?'

'Yes: 'e told me to tell you there's a job to be started Monday morning—a couple of rooms to be done out somewhere. Got to be finished by Thursday. And there's another job 'e wants you to do this afternoon after dinner, so you've got to come to the yard at one o'clock. 'E told me to tell you 'e meant to leave a message for you yesterday morning but 'e forgot.'

'What did he say to you about the fire—anything?'

'Yes: they both of 'em came about an hour after you went away, Misery and the Bloke too, but they didn't kick up a row. I wasn't arf frightened I can tell you when I saw 'em both coming, but they was quite nice. The Bloke ses to me: "Ah, that's right, my boy," 'e ses, "keep up a good fire, I'm going to send you some coke," 'e ses. And then they 'ad a look round and 'e told Sawkins to put some new panes of glass where the winder was broken, and—you know that great big packing case what was under the truck shed?'

'Yes.'

'Well, 'e told Sawkins to saw it up and cover over the stone floor of the paint shop with it. It ain't 'arf all right there now. I've cleared out all the muck from under the benches and we've got two sacks of coke sent from the gas works, and the Bloke told me when that's all used up I've got to get a order orf Miss Wade at the office for another lot.'

At one o'clock Owen was at the yard, where he saw Misery, who instructed him to go to the front shop and paint some numbers on the racks where the wall papers were stored. Whilst he was doing this work Rushton came in and greeted him in a very friendly way.

'I'm very glad you let me know about the boy working in that paint shop,' he observed after a few preliminary remarks; 'I can assure you as I don't want the lad to be uncomfortable, but you know I can't attend to heverything myself. I'm much obliged to you for telling me about it. I think you did quite right; I should have done the same myself.'

Owen did not know what to reply, but Rushton walked off without waiting for one.

For many weeks past Hunter, who had been looking more worried and miserable than ever, was occupied every day in supervising what work was being done and in running about seeking for more. Nearly every night he remained at the office until a late hour, poring over specifications and making out estimates. The police had become so accustomed to seeing the light in the office that as a rule they took no notice of it, but one Thursday night—exactly one week after the scene between Owen and Rushton about the boy—the constable on the beat observed the light there much later than usual. At first he paid no particular attention to the fact, but when night merged into morning and the light still remained, his curiosity was aroused.

He knocked at the door, but no one came in answer, and no sound disturbed the deathlike stillness that reigned within. The door was locked, but he was not able to tell whether it had been closed from the inside or outside because it had a spring latch. The office window was low down, but it was not possible to see in because the back of the glass had been painted.

The constable thought that the most probable explanation of the mystery was that whoever had been there earlier in the evening had forgotten to turn out the light when they went away. It was not likely that thieves or anyone who had no business to be there would advertise their presence by lighting the gas.

He made a note of the incident in his pocket book and was about to resume his beat when he was joined by his inspector. The latter agreed that the conclusion arrived at by the constable was probably the right one, and they were about to pass on when the inspector noticed a speck of light shining through the lower part of the painted window, where a small piece of the paint, had either been scratched or had shelled off the glass. He knelt down and found that it was possible to get a view of the interior of the office, and as he peered through he gave a low exclamation. When he made way for his subordinate to look in his turn, the constable was with some difficulty able to distinguish the figure of a man lying prone upon the floor.

It was an easy task for the burly policeman to force open the office door. A single push of his shoulder wrenched it from its fastenings, and as it flew back the socket of the lock fell with a splash into a great pool of blood that had accumulated against the threshold, flowing from the place where Hunter was lying on his back, his arms extended and his head nearly severed from his body. On the floor, close to his right hand, was an open razor. An overturned chair lay on the floor by the side of the table where he usually worked, the table itself being littered with papers and drenched with blood.

During the next few days Crass resumed the role he had played when Hunter was ill during the summer, taking charge of the work and generally doing his best to fill the dead man's place, although—as he confided to certain of his cronies in the bar of the 'Cricketer's'—he had no intention of allowing Rushton to drive him to do the same as Hunter had done. One of his first jobs, on the morning after the discovery of the body, was to go with Mr Rushton to look over a house where some work was to be done for which an estimate had to be given. It was the estimate that Hunter had been trying to make out the previous evening in the office, for they found that the papers on his table were covered with figures and writing relating to this work. These papers justified the subsequent verdict of the coroner's jury that Hunter committed suicide in a fit of temporary insanity, for they were covered with a lot of meaningless scribbling, the words having no intelligible connection with each other. There was one sum he had evidently tried to do repeatedly but which came wrong in a different way every time. The fact that he had the razor in his possession seemed to point to his having premeditated the act, but this was accounted for at the inquest by the evidence of the last person who saw him alive, a hairdresser, who stated that Hunter had left the razor with him to be sharpened a few days previously and that he had called for it on the evening of the tragedy. He had ground the razor for Mr Hunter several times before.

Crass took charge of all the arrangements for the funeral. He bought a new second-hand pair of black trousers at a cast-off clothing shop in honour of the occasion, and discarded his own low-crowned silk hat—which was getting rather shabby—in favour of Hunter's tall one which he found in the office and annexed without hesitation or scruple. It was rather large for him, but he put some folded strips of paper inside the leather lining. Crass was a proud man as he walked in Hunter's place at the head of the procession, trying to look solemn, but with a half smile on his fat, pasty face, which was destitute of colour except one spot on his chin near his under lip, where there was a small patch of inflammation about the size of a threepenny piece. This spot had been there for a very long time. At first, as well as he could remember, it was only a small pimple, but it had grown larger, with something the appearance of scurvy. Crass attributed its persistency to the cold having 'got into it last winter,' but this was rather strange, because he generally took care of himself in cold weather, always wearing the warm wrap that had formerly belonged to the old lady who died of cancer. However, Crass did not worry much about this little sore place, he just put some zinc ointment on it occasionally and had no doubt that it would get well in time.

CHAPTER XXXVI

The End

ABOUT the middle of December there was a heavy fall of snow followed by a hard frost lasting several days. At ten o'clock one night a policeman found a man lying unconscious in the middle of a lonely road. At first he thought he was drunk, and after dragging him on to the footpath out of the way of passing vehicles he went for the stretcher. They took the man to the station and put him into a cell, already occupied by a man who had been caught in the act of stealing swede turnips from a barn. When the police surgeon came he pronounced the supposed drunken man to be dying from bronchitis and starvation ; and further said that there was nothing to indicate that the man was addicted to drink. At the inquest the coroner remarked that it was the third case of death from destitution that had occurred in the town within six weeks.

The evidence showed that the man was a plasterer, who had walked from London with the hope of finding work somewhere in the country. He had no mone}' in his possession when he was found by the policeman, all that his pockets contained being several pawn-tickets and a letter from his wife. The day before the inquest was held, the man who had been arrested for stealing the turnips had been taken before the magistrates. The poor wretch's defence was that he was starving, but Alderman Grinder, after telling him that starvation was no excuse for dishonesty, sentenced him to pay a fine of seven shillings and costs, or go to prison for seven days with hard labour. As the convict had neither money nor friends he went to jail, where he was, after all, better off than most of those who were still outside because they lacked either the courage or the opportunity to steal.

As time went on the long continued privation began to tell upon Owen and his family. Owen's cough grew worse, his eyes became deeply sunken and of remarkable brilliancy and his thin face was always either deathly pale or dyed with a crimson flush.

Frankie also began to show the effects of being obliged to go so often without his porridge and milk. He became very pale and thin and his long hair came out in handfuls when his mother combed or brushed it. This was a great trouble to the boy, who since hearing the story of Samson read out of the Bible at school had ceased from asking to have his curls cut short, lest he should lose his strength also. He used to test himself by going through a certain exercise he had invented with a flat iron, and he was always much relieved when he found that notwithstanding the loss of the porridge, he was still able to lift the iron the proper number of times. But after a while, as he found it became increasing^ difficult, he gave it up altogether, secretly resolving to wait until ' Dad ' had more work to do, so that he could have the porridge and milk again. He was sorry to have to discontinue the exercise, but he said nothing about it to his father or mother because he did not want to ' worry ' them.

Nora managed to get a 'charing' job at a boarding house where the servant was laid up. Owen did not want her to go, knowing how physically incapable she was of doing heavy work. On the second day in consequence of continually running up and down stairs with heavy cans of water she was in such intense pain that she was scarcely able to walk home, and for several days afterwards had to lie in bed through a recurrence of her old illness, which caused her to suffer untold agony whenever she tried to stand.

Alternately dejected and maddened by the knowledge of his own helplessness, Owen went about the town trying to find some other work, but with scant success. He did samples of show cards and window tickets and endeavoured to get orders by canvassing the shops in the town, but this was also a failure, for these people generally had a ticket writer to whom they gave their work, and when he did get a few trifling orders, they were scarcely worth doing at the price.

He used to feel like a criminal each time he entered a shop to ask for the work, because he realised that in effect, he was saying to them : ' Take your work away from the other man and employ me' He was so conscious of this that it gave him a shamefaced manner, which, coupled as it was with his shabby clothing, did not create a very favourable impression on the shopkeepers, who usually treated him with about as much courtesy as they would have extended to any other sort of beggar. Generally, after a day's canvassing, he returned home unsuccessful and faint with hunger and fatigue.

One night, when a bitterly cold east wind was blowing, after he had been out on one of these canvassing expeditions, his chest became so bad that he found it almost impossible to speak, because the effort to do so often brought on a violent fit of coughing. A firm of drapers, for whom he had done some show-cards, sent him an order for one which they wanted in a hurry and which must be delivered the next morning, so he stayed up by himself till nearly midnight to do it. As he worked he felt a strange sensation in his chest : it was not exactly a pain, and he would have found it difficult to describe it in words.

He did not attach much importance to the symptom, thinking it was caused by the cold he had taken, but he could not help feeling conscious of the strange sensation all the time.

Frankie had been put to bed that evening at the customary hour, but did not seem to be sleeping as well as usual. Owen could hear him twisting and turning about and uttering little cries in his sleep. He left his work several times to go into the boy's room and cover him with the bed-clothes, which his restless movements had disordered. As the time wore on, the child became more tranquil, and about eleven o'clock, when Owen went in to look at him, he found him in a deep sleep, lying on his side with his head thrown back on the pillow, breathing so softly through his slightly parted lips that the sound was almost imperceptible. The fair hair that clustered round his forehead was damp with perspiration, and he was so still and pale and silent that one might have thought he was sleeping the sleep that knows no awakening.

About an hour later, when he had finished writing the showcard, Owen went out into the scullery to wash his hands before going to bed ; and whilst he was drying them on the towel, the strange sensation he had been conscious of all the evening became more intense, and a few seconds afterwards he was terrified to find his mouth suddenly filled with blood.

For what seemed an eternity he fought for breath against the suffocating torrent, and when at length it stopped, he sank trembling into a chair by the side of the table, holding the towel to his mouth and scarcely daring to breathe, whilst a cold sweat streamed from every pore and gathered in large drops upon his forehead.

Through the deathlike silence of the night there came from time to time the chimes of the clock of a distant church, but he continued to sit there motionless, taking no heed of the passing hours, and possessed with an awful terror.

So this was the beginning of the end ! And afterwards, the other two would be left by themselves at the mercy of the world. In a few years' time the boy would be like Bert White, in the clutches of some psalm-singing devil like Hunter or Rushton, who would use him as if he were a beast of burden, to be worked, driven, and bullied. His boyhood would be passed in carrying loads, dragging carts, and running here and there, trying his best to satisfy the brutal tyrants whose only thought would be to get profit out of him for themselves. As the vision of the future rose before him Owen resolved that it should never be. He would not leave his wife and child alone and defenceless in the midst of the ' Christian ' wolves who were waiting to rend them as soon as he was gone. If he could not give them happiness, he could at least put them out of the reach of further suffering. If he could not sta}r and protect them, it would be kinder and more merciful to take them with him.

THE END